GARBAGE MAN

JOSEPH D'LACEY

For Iain 1968 - 2004

Introduction to *Garbage Man*, 2019 edition

It strikes me that books are, on the whole, the absolute antitheses of a cheap, plastic, supermarket carrier bag. Let me explain: a book is just about completely biodegradable (or virtual in the case of an ebook) whereas a Tesco carrier bag is likely to last for an unfortunately long length of time. Supermarket carrier bags used to be mass produced in their hundreds of thousands with minimal thought or consideration whereas by contrast a book, even a poorly-written pulpy mess of a novel, requires hour after hour of effort from the writer to perfect. Plastic is artificially resilient, the words on the page are deceptively fragile. Looking at the contrast another way, a supermarket carrier bag has a detrimental effect on the environment and will typically be discarded in a heartbeat, but a novel has the potential to enrich generation after generation of readers with themes, ideas, imagery and concepts which might continue to resonate long after the poor author has passed away and been reduced to mulch (or ash).

Having said all that, I'm now going to contradict myself. Books can also become landfill.

I've known Joseph for a number of years, and I remember being at an event with him a while back, I think it was in Edinburgh, where he talked about the lifespan of a book. As an author it's difficult to accept that, sometimes, that story you toiled for weeks, months and maybe years to write might not have the kind of longevity you'd hoped. Many of us have experienced it: our fabulous creation is set free into the wild, only to be greeted with a collective shrug of indifference from the book reading public at large. Or, if you're really lucky, you might find some initial success, but after your post-release bow wave has reduced to a millpond ripple, it's hard to keep your novel afloat and visible in an apparently endless sea of other releases.

Often, of course, the success of a book is a matter of timing, and no one – the author, their editor, their agent, their publisher, publicist or cover designer – will have any control over this. It's a case of releasing the right book at the right time, and much of it is down to chance. Some books are borne of a moment, many others have to wait for their moment to arrive.

Which brings me to Garbage Man. It's a decade-old novel which, I believe, might have finally found its time. I've read it a number of times, and its impact has never been greater than when I recently read it again in order to write this introduction.

We've all seen the reports and heard the outrage; the ire so rightly directed inwardly at ourselves for the way we, as a species, have polluted our planet and continue to do so. We've listened and maybe half-heartedly heeded the warnings about what might happen if we go on this way – the potential effects on the climate, the wildlife, the ecosystem and, ultimately, ourselves. Only yesterday I was reading an article about the deepest ever submarine dive where American Victor Vescovo descended around seven miles to the bottom of the Mariana Trench in the Pacific Ocean, only to find he'd been beaten to the sea bed by a plastic bag and some sweet wrappers. It's terrifying to think that our garbage is already exploring parts of the planet we've not yet reached ourselves!

I think Joseph saw all of this coming, and with Garbage Man he's firing a warning shot across the bows. Christ, the only way this novel could be made any more relevant would be if Joe could persuade David Attenborough to narrate the audiobook! All joking apart, the story you're about to read is an occasionally surreal and frequently terrifying cautionary tale. All the wrappers you discard, the meals you don't finish, the clothes you wear out and throw away, the cars you scrap, the supermarket plastic bags you use once then bin... they've all got to go somewhere... they all combine to make *something*.

But it couldn't happen here, could it?

By setting his story in the immediately familiar surroundings of the Meadowlands Estate in Shreve and populating it with a cast of ordinary people who could have been plucked from any street in any town, the impact of Joseph's grotesque and nightmarish tale is massively increased. I challenge you not to be disturbed by the succession of horrific images you're about to witness, which culminate in a denouement which is quite unlike anything I've read before.

Garbage Man is a wonderful horror novel which, despite the blood and guts and landfill chaos, has a serious and increasingly relevant environmental message at its filth-filled heart. I'm so pleased it's being relaunched (recycled?) at a time when the issues it addresses are so high on the global agenda.

Consume this book, then dispose of it carefully!

David Moody
May 2019

Foreword

Ten years ago, the story of Mason Brand's ill-fated encounter with a foetus of melded flesh and garbage took on its own life as a real, live novel. My wife was pregnant with our daughter, so it was a fertile time all round. Our daughter has since become very concerned about our environment. She's a keen recycler and composter and has joined an eco-club so that she can do more to help the planet.

Some of the statements taken from Mason Brand's journal are, word for word, messages that I received during my own vision quests in the hills of North Wales. Like Mason, I know that the Earth is a living, breathing, thinking entity; a cosmic being with all the attributes of a true mother.

She is kind. She is nurturing. She is a good listener.

As with any mother, she also has her limits.

I don't proselytise in my fiction – stories are for entertainment not propaganda. That said, a foreword is an appropriate place for an author to express personal feelings. *Garbage Man* is an ecologically inspired horror tale, exploring how humans deal with their 'leavings' – that's all it will ever be and I hope you'll enjoy it on that level. However, I do have a heartfelt connection with nature and the land and I'd like to use this opportunity to say just a few words about that.

When a build-up of toxins or pathogens sends an organism's system out of balance, that organism will do whatever it can to rid itself of the problem. Unfortunately, in the case of Earth, it is us humans that have become both toxic and pathogenic. Like any living thing, large or small, our planet intends to remain alive and healthy for as long as possible. The cataclysms that we see all around us now – storms, quakes, fires, landslides, eruptions, floods and tsunamis – may be a sign that the planet's immune response has kicked in and that a cleansing has begun.

Gloomy, I know. And, unlike Garbage Man, it's not fiction.

Living on Earth means to be in relationship with her. Everything we need comes from her and everything we do affects her. I don't believe that anyone who understands this interaction is deliberately destroying the planet. So, who is?

Well, let's see.

Who manufactures and advertises the bulk of what we consume? Who makes the plastics and 'disposable' nappies? Who makes the cars and the planes and the tankers? Who builds the war machines? Who makes all the useless junk you can buy at the mall? Some of these things we need. Most of them we don't. Corporations spend billions creating demand where before there was none and convincing us we need more when, in reality, if we spread things around a little, we – all 8 billion of us – would already have more than enough.

The minds behind global consumerism could use their influence (for influence read obscene mountains of money) to reverse the processes they initiated. They have the power. They have the resources. What they lack is the will to pursue anything other than profit, market share and the vicelike grip on government that it gives them.

I have no doubt that many super-smart, super-creative innovators around the world already possess the technologies that will help us to clean up our mess. However, none of these people and none of their brilliant, planet-saving designs will see the light of day whilst a mindset of growth at any cost governs the world's economies.

For now – and how much now we have left is uncertain – all we can do as individuals and communities is make considered choices about how we live our lives, what we consume and how we dispose of things that are no longer useful. The kinds of caring choices we would make in any loving relationship but with the planet as our partner.

The people are waking up but the military industrial corpocracy rumbles on; deeply unconscious and ceaselessly acquisitive at the expense of the rest of us – and, crucially, at the expense of the world that supports us all. The next phase in human evolution cannot be a step; it must be a vault, a leap into enlightenment. Otherwise, our fate will be to commit planetary matricide and self-genocide. All that will remain is a dumping ground that was once a paradise called Earth.

On that cheery note, I hope you'll enjoy *Garbage Man*.

And remember, it's only a story…

Joseph D'Lacey
April, 2019

"The Earth and myself are of one mind. The measure of the land and the measure of our bodies are the same..."

Nez Percé chief Hinmaton Yalakit (Chief Joseph)
1830 - 1904

Prologue

The two figures stood, close enough to touch but not touching, in the midsummer moonlight.

A man.

A young woman.

Around them the bounties of his garden slumbered on the ground or on their stalks or in their pods. Their surfaces shone luminous grey; their bulk cast blacker velveteen shadows on the already black earth. A tiny breeze, barely the breath of an infant, touched every leaf and stem, stirring them to sigh in their sleep.

There was a dragging ache deep in Agatha's abdomen.

'Are you certain this is what you want?' Mason asked. His words made puffs of mist, slow to dissipate. They were so quietly spoken she wasn't even sure she'd heard them. The vapour from his lungs was the only clue. Yet another chilled English summer, she thought. Another thing she wanted to be free of.

'Yes.'

A cloud dampened the moon.

The man watched her. Even by this insufficient silver light, she knew he could see her well enough. Not her face, not her eyes, but what she held behind them. She had to make it convincing. She, in turn, could see his eyes and not much else behind the bramble of his beard. His pupils were black pearls, lost in the deep, dark wells of his irises. She would never see into him, no matter how hard she looked, no matter how long.

The cloud thickened. Her belly cramped. She hesitated.

There was still time to change her mind. All she had to do was walk away. She needn't even speak. If she turned and tiptoed back up the garden, along the side wall, out onto Bluebell Way and back to the house where her family slept, if she merely did that and said not another word to Mason Brand, he would know what it meant. He would understand. And they would never talk again.

But she'd come this far, hadn't she? Risked being caught outside late at night with a man old enough to have fathered her. A few more minutes and she'd have done it, given him what he wanted. In half an hour she could be snuggled into bed. There was no sense in leaving now, was there? It was so nearly complete. She almost had what she'd come for – his promise to give her what she needed most. And once he'd fulfilled his end of their agreement – sometime in the next few days – she would be free. Free of her family, free of the Meadowlands Estate, free of the dead-end town of Shreve and away into a decent future. A real future, not just some girl's fantasy.

Perhaps he saw all this and mistook it for commitment and conviction. For a man so awkward and hesitant by day, he was suddenly very direct.

'Good. You have what I asked you for?'

'Y… yes.'

'Let me see it.'

She supposed she could have carried it here some other way but what would have been easier than the method she'd chosen? Besides, it would be fresher this way. He'd made it clear that was important.

She turned and stepped away, far enough that he'd see her shape and movement perhaps, but nothing more than that. She unzipped and pulled down her jeans and used the fingers of her left hand to tug the gusset of her underwear towards her left thigh. It was a cold night and her skin roughened to the touch of the air. With her right hand she took hold of the soft tassel of cotton thread and gently drew the obstruction from herself. Her flow was heavy; the cotton wadding brought partially coagulated strings with it. They struck and clung to her bare thigh, black lightning against a sky of white skin.

'Shit,' she whispered. She held it out to him. 'Here.'

'I can't touch it.'

'Don't be pathetic.'

'No. I must not touch the blood.'

'I need to get myself sorted out.'

She heard him take a few steps away and quickly return. He held out his palm to her. On it was a runner bean leaf. She dropped the tampon onto it. Steam rose from it like Mason's breath, adhered to the platinum-edged shadows of his garden. When she'd cleaned herself up with a tissue as best she could and renewed her protection, she pulled up her jeans and went to stand with him. He returned her offering. It warmed her palm through the delicate leaf.

'Over here,' he said. He knelt on a patch of recently dug earth. When she didn't follow suit, he took her wrist and pulled her down beside him. 'Dig,' he said, pointing to a place in the centre of the bare earth. 'Right there.'

Aggie looked around for something to use.

'Have you got a trowel or something?' He turned to her slowly.

'Use your hands.'

She placed the blood-burdened leaf to one side. Disgusted that she would get muck under her manicured nails or chip the varnish off, she fingered the grainy soil, brushing it out of the way. There was little progress.

'If you're not serious, there's still time to forget all this. You must act willingly or not at all.'

Aside from her blood and this midnight tryst, Agatha Smithfield didn't intend to keep her side of the bargain. Not the commitments he wanted later – not a chance. No matter how much what he'd asked her to do in the future frightened her, no matter how much gravity he'd attached to her 'responsibility'. She would go through with the actions he demanded right now, detached and cool. And that was all. She would give nothing more of herself after this. When she possessed what he promised her – just a few hours of his expertise – she would be long gone and he would never find her.

'I am willing,' she lied.

'Then dig the earth like you mean it, girl. Like you *love* it.'

Her anger flared unexpectedly, fuelled by her passion to escape Shreve.

I'll show you some fucking digging.

She heaved at the earth, scooping up double handfuls of Mason's loose, fertile soil and dumping them to one side. If he was impressed by her endeavour he didn't show it. He merely knelt there, nodding solemnly. Her fingers struck something smooth and yielding in the dirt. She brushed away some granules and recognised pieces of an image she'd seen before. Just like the one she'd seen on the wall of his stairs.

'Hey… Isn't that the pho—'

'Put your blood into the earth.'

'I was only as—'

'Do it now.'

I'm not going to miss you at all, Mr. Mason Brand. I'll take what I need from you and you'll get nothing in return. When I get out of this town, I'm never going to think about you again.

She dumped the leaf and tampon into the hole. The blood-logged cotton stuck to the matt photographic paper with a damp thud. She tried to cover it all over but he stopped her.

'One last thing,' he whispered.

He was holding out an index card. There was writing on it. Right in that moment the moon pulled free of the clouds, illuminating them and their midnight labours in mercurial brightness. Years later, she would often think of that moment, how the moon had showed her the words, conspired to make them clear and give her one last chance not to go through with it. Of course, in the actual moment that it happened, she merely cursed the moon for assisting Mason in his madness. She was suddenly more than able to see what he'd written:

I, Agatha Smithfield,

– thank God he doesn't know my middle name—

give my word that I will study the ways of the Earth from Mason Brand. In time, I too will find a student and pass the knowledge to them.
Signed,

The index card awaited her touch.
'In blood, I suppose?' she asked.
He passed her a pen.
'Biro's fine. Make your mark.'
She hesitated again when the tip of the pen touched the card, and almost as quickly dismissed her foolishness. All of this was bullshit. Mason was full of lies and neuroses. The Earth was not alive and the moon was not their witness. There was no creator to keep a tally of deals done, deals broken. When she had what she wanted, she'd be free.

She had one final point to make. Might as well pretend to be part of his delusion.
'There's no time limit.' She said.
'No.'
'So what happens if you die?'
'I'm not going to die for a long time. But whatever happens, you must fulfil your promise before that day comes.'
'What if you... you know... have an accident or something?'
He reached into his trouser pocket.
'I've already thought of that. This is the key to my back

door. If I drop dead or get hit by a bus, go up to the cupboard in the spare bedroom. In there you'll find a small pine chest about the size of picnic basket. In it are my papers. They'll tell you eighty percent of what you need to know. The rest you'll have to learn without me.'

He handed her the key, still warm from his thigh. She slipped it into her jeans pocket. Before she could give the whole stupid issue any more thought, she signed the index card.

'Put it in the ground,' he said. 'Bury everything.'

'Can't you get your hands dirty for a change?'

'It has to be you who touches the Earth.'

'Fine.'

Testily, she pushed all the excavated dirt back into the small hole and patted it down. She brushed her hands off against each other and began to stand. Once again, Mason pulled her to the dirt. He held her there while he whispered among the cool silver shadows.

'Great Mother, we thank you for your gifts and comforts. Daily we serve and respect your ways. Witness our offerings and oaths to you this night. May we fulfil them honourably. Blessed be.'

When he let go of her hand she ran from his garden, not caring how much noise she made, not caring who might see a schoolgirl running home through the streets of the Meadowlands estate long after midnight.

Part I

'The Earth can heal you...'
Statement taken from Mason Brand's journal, dated
27th April, 2001

1

Tamsin Doherty took a taxi back from the clinic knowing Kevin wouldn't be around when she arrived home. She'd memorised the advice leaflet so there was no need to hide anything when she got through their front door.

Expect slight bleeding to lessen over the next few days. Cramping was normal – painkillers had been provided and she'd already chewed two of them down. Anything out of the ordinary (what the fuck was ordinary about this?) and she should contact her GP. Emotional fluctuations could occur. That she could handle. If there was one thing she was glad about, it was her almost sociopathic self-control. No one – *no one* – would have any idea what she'd done. Especially not Kevin. Even though all this was his fault, she would never say a word about it. Not even on her deathbed. And if it happened again she'd do exactly the same thing. Oh, she'd find ways to hurt him, of course. Kevin Doherty was not a man, he was a representation of a man. She cared about her two Staffies more than she cared about him. And, whether he was aware of it or not, she would humiliate him, belittle him behind his back at every turn.

Marriage was like everything else in the World. It revolved around money and power. Kevin had the money, she had the power and ever more it would remain. There was an adjunct to that. Whoever was the best keeper of secrets had the most power.

Christ, I'm a bitch. A hard-faced taker.

No, not a taker, Tam. A winner. Life is short, beauty doesn't last. Take what you can get while you can get it. Make the most of every moment. Smell the fucking roses.

Who was that talking? Her mother? Probably, God rest her. She was a woman who'd had everything a man could provide. She'd lived like a queen to the end of her days. Tamsin planned to do the same.

Smell the roses? Oh, she smelled them alright. Nothing was sweeter.

The taxi's motion made her nauseous. The drugs still in her system, she assumed.

'Slow down, would you? It's not a fucking track day.'

The driver glanced in his rear-view. She saw his eyes assess for talent first, danger second. If only he knew. The ride got smoother and she relaxed a little. Once she was through the door of her house all this would be behind her. Life, her blissful suburban wet-dream, would continue. She smiled. Satisfaction. Anticipation.

The smile fell away, though. She had questions. She could fend them off and distract herself eternally but she knew the questions would never leave her alone.

What would they do with it? Experiments? It was such a tiny thing – more like a rat or a mouse than a human. Would they burn it? Perhaps it would be buried. She imagined there was a job in the hospital for some minimum-waged minion who did nothing but burials. Judging by the number of women in the recovery room, both too young-looking and too old-looking, her fantasy interment worker would be kept very busy.

Yes, burial.

That was what happened. It was the proper thing, after all. Bury it. Let it rot. Let it be forgotten forever in the earth.

Her smile returned and she slumbered slightly, still drugged and comfortable. Her dreams were snippets of manipulated chaos and well-planned destruction. So much to look forward to.

Richard Smithfield sat in front of his computer and wiped his sweaty palms on his trousers. Moments later the slick had returned. The computer's drive whirred and ticked. His wireless router whined at the edge of his hearing. An LED flickered, suggestive of the high-speed transfer of information. The fan kicked in to cool the circuitry.

Pam and the children were asleep and the house was quiet. It was three am. His study door was locked from the inside. But still. He was always like this. Heart rate elevated. An untrustworthy sensation in his guts. Breath caught at the top of his lungs.

He swallowed loudly. The download continued. This was the last one. He swore it to himself.

When the download was complete his media program opened the new file automatically. He turned the volume down to the lowest possible level, expanded the footage to full screen. He watched, an audience of one, the rush of blood inside his head louder than the grunts of satisfaction and the cries of denial and pleas for cessation. He didn't understand the language but he didn't need to. The tears were real. The contact was real. No make-up, no CGI. No actors.

He could not take his gaze from the salacious thievery in front of him. Didn't want to blink when the surface of his eyeballs dried and demanded it. He was there with them; hurting, taking. And soon enough he used his own hand to give himself the release he so terribly wanted to experience, not in fantasy, not on the screen, but in real life.

Richard Smithfield couldn't drive past a playground or school without giving them a sidelong glance. Sports days and matches had always been the most exciting and most testing times for him. Pam thought he was a proud father, watching Agatha swim and Donald play soccer but he was only ever on the lookout for that one opportunity; the one he most wanted but would never, ever take. Like a lion assessing a herd, he was waiting for an unusual animal to separate from the others and make itself known to him. It was a game, of course, and games needed more than one player. He watched for the ones who recognised themselves in him without even knowing that was what they saw.

And that was where the game ended. It was enough for him to know he was able to find prospects out there. He could not allow such investigations to become actions. Even though he thought about it every single day of his life. He loved his family too much. If he hadn't met Pam and had the kids, he supposed he might be locked up by now. Making a family hadn't come naturally to him. He'd had to imagine other things in order to succeed with Pam. But he had them now and he cared very deeply for them.

He imagined a time of freedom when he was older, somehow believing there would be less at stake when the kids had grown up and moved away. Such a time would probably never come. For now, and forever probably, pornography would have to suffice. It was dangerous enough like this. Stories about rings being smashed by the police and men like him being dragged into court were in the news all the time. He knew because he watched for those stories more than any other. He hadn't allied himself with other people, though, and he hoped that would be enough to keep him safe.

As soon as he'd ejaculated, guilt flooded every cell of his body. He sweated it, smelled it on himself. It was always the same. He cleaned up carefully, even down to picking up moulted pubic hairs from the carpet. Everything would be flushed away down the toilet. He checked his file system and saw how much footage and images he'd accumulated. It made him nauseous to think of what might happen if his computer was seized.

Suddenly he was finding it a struggle to breathe. His heart was labouring but this time in a different way. It was beating like a baby bird's heart but it didn't feel like it was pumping enough blood. The rushing sound came back to his ears and rose in volume. The study seemed to go grey and all he could see was what was right in front of him. The computer. The files full of digitally-recorded exploitation.

It had to go. All of it.

This was the last one. He'd promised himself and he was going to make good on that promise this time. There was no untraceable way to erase files from a computer. He knew that. There were programs that would write over the disks hundreds of times but traces could be found no matter how many times the data was erased and overwritten. And the obvious question to be asked by the authorities in such a case would be: what on earth was so private it had to be concealed with such obsession?

Tomorrow he would see to the problem and make his home and his family safe. Then it would be time to buy himself a brand new, totally 'clean' computer. A computer he would not befoul with his fixation.

My name is Ray Wade. My username is The Survivor. It is a world of nightmares now, worse than anything I could have imagined.

I spend the day collecting useful items and clearing out houses one at a time, one street at a time throughout the city. Houses are easy; they yield bounties for a minimum of effort at minimal risk.

I've been scratched a few times but bitten only once. Not the sort of damage I need to worry about. However, while I've managed to collect ammunition of many kinds and plenty of medical items in various packs, the entire day has been fruitless because I have discovered no firearms. No rifle. No shotgun. Not even a pistol.

Daytime is never too bad, never too dangerous. It's my chance to recuperate and stock up on necessities. Take rest, drink a supplement, raid the silent town for anything that might be useful. Minor scuffles are usually the worst I encounter while the sun is up. At first I only had a flick knife — for use at very close quarters. It's all about technique; dodging bites and grabs and lunges, darting in between these, scoring a single wound and getting back out of reach again. With patience, striking with precision, this is the way to overcome them.

Dozens of them lie motionless around the town in my wake. Dead again. Dead for good and ever.

That first day, with nothing but my flick knife, had been difficult. The first night which followed it was worse. Many was the time I began to believe I wouldn't make it, that I'd lost too much blood or carried too much infection in my system. Somehow, eking out my meagre packful of possessions, I stayed alive. Every new house I came to, every storeroom I found, was a bonus. I lived from one moment to the next, thinking only of what I could salvage and how best to destroy those who assailed me.

This night, though, I know in my heart it will be worse. Somehow, the sunsets hold a clue to how the night will be and here I am, not ready. Not ready by a long chalk, with the sun slipping behind gangrenous clouds, casting ochre and meat-toned shadows everywhere. The clouds lump up into intestinal creases, promising rain and possibly lightning.

And what do I have to get me through a night I know will be the leanest yet for bounties, the roughest yet for attacks and ambushes? My pack contains two bottles of protein supplement shakes – one strawberry, the other pineapple, for what little that's worth. For the dark I've been lucky enough to discover a miner's headlamp and spare batteries. I have syringes, antibiotics, needle, thread, bandage and scissors and one large bottle of topical disinfectant. In case of a real emergency, I have a single shot of adrenaline that might buy me enough time to find a hiding place where I can rest up for a while.

Problem is, while I am the hunter in the daytime, at night they come looking for me. Finding somewhere with a strong enough door to keep them out, even a lone determined one, will require a major stroke of good fortune. I don't hold out much hope. One wound tonight, one serious bite or cut, and I will be sharing the dirt with the rest of them.

I have one thing going for me.

In the three days I've been here, I've found good handheld weapons. After using the flick knife I arrived with, I discovered a length of hefty pipe. A couple of well-aimed blows to the head with that was enough to take any of them down. At least so far. Then in a really tight spot, badly wounded and needing to tend to myself, I found a fire axe – lightweight haft and sharp as the day it was made. Get the swing right and it removed heads in a single swipe. Using it had almost been a pleasure after that.

Accordingly, my hand-to-hand skill increased. In one house I bested an unusually fast and deft assailant. Killing it had been a major undertaking until I found its weak spot. When I subsequently searched the house, I found manuals on martial techniques and then, completely by accident, I discovered a false section in the bedroom wall. Behind it had been built a small alcove and altar. On this altar, next to the statue of some eastern deity I didn't recognise, was a sheathed katana. I wasted no time strapping it to myself and making a few test strokes in the air of the bedroom. As if I'd been born to hold that very weapon, the strokes from the manuals came to me like inspiration.

It was the confidence that weapon and those skills gave me that made me so careless of the time. Feeling unassailable and swaggering into every house on every street in search of booty, I've passed a whole day without making any real progress.

And now the darkness is coming; bruised, aching nightfall over a dead town full of sickness. I have my pack, lightly stocked by any standards, and I have my head-lamp, which I now put on. And I have my katana; the one thing that might surely cut through this night and lead the way to morning.

The RefuSec Waste Management truck pulled up to the gates of Shreve District Council landfill at 6.05 mother gates were locked and the staff car park was empty save for a dust covered and dented Ford Mondeo. It was dark and an uneasy breeze agitated the gates causing them to clang softly on their hinges.

On the other side of the entrance, a light was on in one of the prefab buildings. Another, taller block of light appeared as the door of the building opened. Briefly it was filled by the silhouette of a man pulling on a coat. The door shut behind him. As he approached the gates, the truck's headlights picked out the day-glo stripes on his workwear.

A light mounted on top of the fence began to pulse orange and the gates slid open with a minimum of noise from their well-maintained runners and bearings. The man in the coat waved the truck in. There was a hiss of brakes being released and a cough of diesel. The truck pulled inside the perimeter and stopped again. Behind it, the gates were already closing.

The figure from the building approached the cab. The window was open. A tattooed face looked out, grinning and chewing.

'Alright, Stig.' said the driver through crackles of gum.

The gate-man nodded, not missing the open-mouthed smacking.

'Still trying to pack in the cigarettes?'

'Nah. Given up giving up, mate. Addicted to the bloody gum as well now. Fackyin'… look at this.' Chewing all the while the driver with a bad painting for a face rolled up his sleeve. His eyes were open very wide. 'Nicotine patch, that is,' he said pointing as though the gate-man might miss it. 'A fag's just not the full bifter without the patch and the gum. I have to take a couple of beta-blockers with a few swigs of scotch before I can think about gettin' any kip at night.' The driver stared out into the night. 'Fackyin'…'

The gate-man considered a light-hearted jibe about rehab and let it pass. The driver was lean and had a reputation for getting out of his cab to settle slights. Instead the gate-man said:

'Know where you're going?'

The driver nodded. Too fast. Too many times. Like a viper-strike his hand came out of the cab window. The gate-man flinched but he needn't have. The hand was thin and grimy, fading turquoise webs and dots extending down from the wrist, a swallow near the thumb. Between the long fingers a wad of dirty twenties. The gate-man smiled and took them, flicked through, and pocketed the lot.

'Who's overrun their quota this time?' he asked as the hand withdrew upwards.

'It's not that,' said the driver. 'The incinerator at the hospital's bust, innit. Fackyin'… can't burn up the cut off arms and legs and lumps of cancer an' that. Amazing how much "waste" they create. I ain't going in a hospital, Stig. Not ever. I'd come out half the man I am now.' The driver looked down and grinned, eyes chalky, already thinking about something else. Briefly, he came back to the moment. 'Tell you what else, Stig. It stinks. The worst stink of anything I've ever had to shift. Shit and disease and rotting meat, all from people like you and me. Went into hospital in one piece, left with bits missing and a super-bug. Never going in there, mate. Fackyin'… never.'

The gate-man nodded and stepped back.

The driver slammed the truck into gear and ground away along the temporary road leading to the landfill cells. Very soon, when the canyons of trash were all filled, the whole landfill would be sealed and covered with soil. They'd turn it onto a public park or sports centre or playing field and, in time, no one would remember the network of feeder roads that led the trucks to the huge mouths in the earth that swallowed the town's muck silently and willingly. All this would be gone but the gate-man would be doing something similar somewhere else – at least for a while. There would always be waste and there would always be a need for waste managers and refuse engineers. He smiled because he knew he'd never be out of work.

Until he wanted to be.

The sound of the truck's engine receded into the darkness along with the glare from its headlights. The gate-man half wished the driver would make an over-stimulated miscalculation and bury himself and his truck as well.

Fackyin'... forever.

But where was the charity in that kind of thinking? Besides, without the hyperactive driver, whose name he still didn't know after years of after-hours interactions like this one, there would be no backhanders for burying the town's unauthorised waste. Not to mention the loads brought in by other drivers from other towns in other counties all around the country. Landfill space was running out fast. At two-hundred quid per unauthorised load – and there were several of those every week – the gateman was amassing a serious retirement fund. He looked through the chain link fence at his battered car and smiled. No one would ever guess he was a wealthy man. Only when this job was long behind him and he was living in a country where the weather and the people didn't bring you down every single day, only then would he allow himself to live the way he wanted to.

It was going to be a lot of fun.

2

To anyone else it would have been the filthiest place on Earth. To Mason Brand it was a place of power, even more sacred and essential than his precious vegetable garden. He broke in there most nights to make contact with the land.

He stood barefoot on a layer of freshly-dumped soil. It was about a foot thick, just enough to keep the smell down and the animals from digging through overnight. Below the thin, yielding earth millions of tons of compacted waste rotted. Through his soles he could feel the warmth of it rising up like living radiation. The warmth came in the form of gas – noxiously sweet-smelling methane mostly – and in a simple emanation of heat; a subterranean fever.

The expanse below, filled with every kind of rubbish so compressed it was solid enough to build upon, was alive with decomposition. Tiny bugs were multiplying and eating the waste, breaking it down a particle at a time. Even the metals were being oxidised and consumed. All manner of human leavings and discarded materials were locked below him in cells the size of canyons excavated deep into the earth. Tramped down, by huge machines with toothed wheels, covered with soil to be forgotten and ignored. An entire county's dumping ground. A place no one ever thought about unless the wind was blowing the wrong way.

But Mason Brand thought about it a lot.

There was something very dangerous about Shreve's landfill. Here, after all, was the most poisonous site in the Midlands – in the country perhaps. More polluted than the run-off from any of Shreve's factories. More pregnant with disease than the sewers. Cut yourself on a piece of rusted metal here and the wound would corrupt your entire body with sickness, end your life in a few days. These were the things the people of Shreve might have thought about the landfill, if they'd had a spare moment. And, of course, if they thought about it a little more carefully, they might have realised they were incredibly fortunate such a place existed; a place of severance and forgetting, a place of great convenience where all their waste could be covered over and ignored.

Mason would have been the most optimistic of all of them. For him there was something very beneficial about this place of gathered mess and heaped destruction and filth. Something almost holy. He had a gut feeling about the land and about its influence. This instinct was something which came from generations who'd existed long before him, woodsmen and wanderers, the generations who'd lived close to the land. Mason had lived exactly like them for a time, like a neolith. It was a part of his past he tried hard not to think about.

He had a sense of the Earth's ability to heal and transform. This power came in the form of a pull or draw – not gravity exactly but a force of similar quality. The body of the planet, its soil and dust, was something like a living poultice. He had used this quality to cure himself of various ills over the years. A pack of wet soil wrapped in muslin and applied directly to his skin had cleared him of an attack of boils five years previously. Two years later, the same treatment, combined with crushed herbs from his garden, had relieved him of scabies.

For deeper maladies, wounds to the soul, Mason Brand was in the habit of digging a shallow trench, lying down naked so his skin would touch the loam and covering himself with earth up to his chin. There in his own back garden, hidden among his fruits and vegetables, he would lie awake all night with the worms and the slugs progressing around him. The Earth would draw the spiritual sickness from him and by the dawning he would be clean. Clean as the day his mother had expelled him, innocent and unprotected, into the filthy world of men.

It wasn't something he talked about with his neighbours. Mason Brand rarely talked to anyone if he could avoid it. The landfill was a place where, by necessity, the Earth's drawing was very strong indeed. And that was why, at night, when the compactors stood still as drugged giants and the rest of Shreve slumbered within their clean brick walls, Mason would climb through the hole he'd made in the perimeter fence and stand barefoot in this place of entropy and rot.

A quarter of a mile away, near the workers' huts and the contractor's offices, a small tower stood like a black candle against the light-polluted sky and at the top of this candle a flame, only visible at night, burned soft blue: the ignited exhalations of the earth, the collected methane being burned to save the atmosphere from its deleterious effects. But it wasn't possible to collect all the gas and sometimes Mason would see violet will-o-the-wisps flash and shimmer and disappear as a small pocket of vapour ignited spontaneously. He saw these flashes as signs of the Earth's life, blips on a monitor, pulses and heartbeats, messages of goodwill rising from deep within the body of the world. And from these portents he took faith in the way of things and experienced a simple gladness about the rightfulness and righteousness of decay.

He curled his toes into the soil, gripped the Earth, held on to her. She took away his leavings too; bad energies, bad thoughts, sickness before it had the chance to take root in him. Wrongfulness was pulled down through him, leaving him pure.

A sickle of moon rose up from the opposite horizon, as if to balance the disappearance of the sun. It was nothing but a cool glow at first, indistinct and pale behind the low, filthy clouds. As it rose it shrank and its edges became honed until it slit the fleshy vapours near the ground and floated free. A crooked smile, a slash in the night sky where the light from a pure universe seeped through.

Mason was hypnotised. He had no way to measure the slippage of overlapping moments. He might have been doing no more than focussing on an object through a lens or he might have been standing there a whole season, growing roots through the veneer of loose soil and deep into the landfill. Finally, he blinked and looked around him, feeling it was time to go home. He needed to rest. Even the Earth slept, half of it slumbering through darkness as it rotated its spherical face to the blessing of the sun.

Every part of his body was cold but the soles of his feet, still receiving warmth from the ground, still bleeding out his darker energies. He would never be completely pure – nothing and no one could be. For then an absolute state would be reached and the motion and flow of things into each other would, therefore, have ceased. Such a state, he believed, was synonymous with the end of the world and, no matter how well he felt he understood these things, he was not ready for that.

But the moon held him, its bright blade incising his eyes, the hook of it snagged into his mind. He could feel its draw on him too, coaxing his water, pulling him up. He closed his eyes a moment and hauled himself back taking a deep breath. Yes, time to go home.

His feet were welded to the ground and came away reluctantly. He stumbled and almost fell over trying the take his first couple of steps. Then the grip of the moon and the grip of the Earth were eased and he was liberated.

He didn't get far before stopping again. There was wetness underfoot. Strange. The weather had been changeable but there'd been no rain for a few days. No puddles or muddy troughs belonged here, especially not on newly scattered soil. He looked down and scanned the darkness where only his feet were recognisable, fungus white against the black humus. Around them, oily liquid blackness was spreading out. The viscous fluid reflected the scalpel-sharp moon and even the yellow glow of the streetlights coming from Meadowlands, the estate where he lived.

All manner of possibilities sprang into his mind. A water main had burst nearby and was flooding the landfill. A blockage had caused the canal to burst its banks. Something in the landfill had burst and its filth was seeping upwards. None of the explanations fitted what was happening. They came and went in a sliver of a moment leaving only fear behind. Something was wrong here; profoundly, unnaturally wrong. The longer he looked at the welling of black fluid around his feet, covering them now, the stronger became this conviction.

Without taking another step, he crouched a little and put his hand to the surface of this rising flood. It was warm and slightly greasy between his fingertips. He held the substance below his nose and inhaled. It smelled rusty. This made sense to him. The landfill was full of oxidising iron and steel. Perhaps the leachate from the landfill had been blocked somehow and was backing up. Just as soon as he had this notion, it too was dismissed. The fluid should have smelled of things other than metal decay. It should have smelled of shit and rot. It didn't.

He walked now, suddenly and with purpose, away from the newly covered area of landfill and back towards the fence-line. The substance under his feet was tarry and when he reached a place where the fluid no longer welled, the loose soil stuck to his tacky soles. He collected his shoes and socks by the gap in the chain-link, bent low and stepped through. He turned and used his pocketful of wire ties to sew the fence breach together again.

The way to his back garden twisted through low shrubs where small, well-used tracks had been made by badgers and rabbits. It led out onto an expanse of brownland where the grass that grew was sparse and clumped. Underfoot was coke and slag from the open cast coal mine that had been there before the days of the landfill. If this wasn't hazardous enough to bare feet, much of the waste ground was littered with shattered glass from discarded bottles and other litter. Mason didn't care; whatever was on his feet, he didn't want to get it on his socks and in his shoes. He kept waiting for the substance to itch or burn the skin of his feet but it didn't.

And so, as he did so many nights of the year, he crossed the brownland like a shadow returning to its sleeping owner. He was lucky, he believed, to reach his back gate without cutting himself. Instead of letting himself in through the back door of his house, he unlocked the garden shed, stepped in and switched on its single bare bulb. After the darkness of the landfill, forty watts was like staring at the midday sun. He blinked until his pupils adjusted and sat on a woodwormed pine chair.

Then he looked at his feet.

'Agatha, come and get your tea.'

Agatha Smithfield hated her name.

'Witch,' she whispered to the walls of her room. 'Witch-bitch-cunt.'

There were footsteps on the stairs; her mother padding in her stupid, ugly pink slippers, a pair of flesh-tone pop-socks barely hiding the broken veins in her ankles. Her mother scuffing along the upstairs carpet; the footsteps of a very minor martyr. She could see it all without looking.

'Aggie? Your tea's ready. Are you coming down?'

The voice was breezy, masking concern. Agatha swallowed her rage, stuffed it back down into her stomach to smoulder and pressurise.

The only other Agatha she knew of was Agatha Christie, a boring woman – long dead – who had written boring murder stories populated by boring toffs from a boring age she had no interest in.

Boring, boring, boring.

'Yes, mother. Of course, I'm coming. Don't rush me all the time.'

'Sorry, dear.'

And don't fucking apologise for everything.

The soft footsteps retreated, a wound in their rhythm. Agatha felt guilt and disgust uncoil in her throat.

The name Agatha was synonymous with boring. It was also synonymous with ancient, grey-haired people. It was no name for a seventeen-year-old woman of the third millennium. Plenty of other girls her age had used their middle names to escape the stigma of their first names. But Betty Smithfield sounded so similarly awful there was no point. Shit, what had her parents been thinking about when they named her? They'd refused her entreaties to let her change her names. She vowed to do it anyway as soon as she left home. It would be goodbye Agatha Betty. Maybe she'd even change her surname, begin a second life. In the meantime, the contraction 'Aggie' was the best she could do.

Downstairs, they'd all be sitting there already. Waiting. Don would have started eating even though their mother and father would have told him not to. Whenever she saw her brother, he was eating but there was no sign of it on his frame. The way he looked he might have been wandering the streets for a month. Nothing on him but sinew and gaunt, tight muscle. If she ate half as much as him she'd turn into a walrus.

She swore softly and swung her legs off the bed. She smoothed down her clothes, feeling the gentleness of her own curves and enjoying it. She looked in the mirror. She was beautiful and she knew it. She had no idea why she was stuck here in the suburbs of a town where the future held no promise. There was no existence here which she could aspire to, other than single-motherhood and government handouts and daytime TV. Gossip and jealousy, binge drinking and bitter tears as life stole her looks. She wasn't so stupid as to believe her beauty would last forever. If she wanted to use it, she had to get started. The sooner she left, the sooner her second life, her real life, could begin.

It was the way out she hadn't quite found yet. She knew it wasn't as simple as hitching a ride to London and hoping for the best. She'd heard of other girls who had done as much. Some came back, beaten by the city and its takers, happy to sink back into the mould society had prepared for them, glad to be safe and obscure. Others had not returned but by the silence they left behind them, it was clear they had not succeeded. Not succeeded at anything except deviating from their grand schemes, succeeded instead at being exploited, succeeded at failure. It was no wonder they never came back, dragging the miasma of their filthy misadventures behind them like the smell of sickness. What family could live down such prodigality around here, where everyone talked and anyone could be destroyed by rumour without even knowing they were falling from grace?

No. She was not going to follow that path. She was going to plan it and she was going to achieve her goals through careful preparation. There was a right way of leaving town and she would find it. She would leave Agatha Betty Smithfield far behind and she would transform. When she did finally come back, it would be with her head held high and against the odds. Those who weren't proud of her would be nauseous with envy.

Knowing this made it possible to walk down the stairs of her family's uninspiring house, a house like too many others on the estate with an uninspiring family to match. Knowing this, she could take her place at the table and smile and eat the bland shit her mother cooked each day. She could do it because it was all part of her plan. Her time was coming. In months or weeks or days, the opportunity she was waiting for would present itself. There was a shiver of excitement in her stomach.

Richard Smithfield looked at her over his glasses, a toad of a man – not sweaty; oily.

'Finally, the queen arrives.'

She sat down at the table. Donald looked at her out of the corner of his eye and put his fork down but he was already chewing something. Her mother, Pamela Smithfield, smiled but it looked like a wince.

'For what we are about to receive,' she said, 'may the Lord make us truly thankful.'

They muttered Amen.

Donald resumed eating, everyone else began.

Aggie put lumpy mashed potato and dried out chicken in her mouth. The gravy was brown but had no flavour. It didn't even smell of anything. The only smell seemed to be wafting in from the waste disposal unit in the kitchen sink. It was always getting blocked. Either that or the wind was blowing the wrong way from the landfill again. She ignored it and chewed. Under the table, Sasquatch the golden retriever waited beside Aggie for his share of the meal – most of which would arrive from her surreptitious fingers long before it could be considered leftovers.

'Gosh, mother, this is lovely,' she said.

Pamela Smithfield's smile returned, uncertain, faltering. She said nothing.

Nor did anyone else.

Not only did it smell like rust, it looked like rust. He picked off a dried flake of it. It came away reluctantly like a new scab. Crumbling this between his fingers, it even felt like rust as it disintegrated.

Suddenly, more than anything in the world, he *wanted* it to be rust.

But it wasn't.

He left the shed, locked it, let himself into the silent house through the back door and went upstairs to scrub his feet in the bath. Only when they were scoured red and no trace remained, only when he'd washed the tub out thoroughly three times, only then did he allow himself to run a proper bath.

He lay there, knees poking up like strange tall islands, their dark hair matted flat to his white skin. Steam rose; the mist surrounding his anatomical seascape. He tried not to think about what had happened. All the evidence was gone now. It would be easy enough to let time pass and convince himself he'd made a mistake or that he'd stared at the moon for so long he'd hallucinated the rest of it. He became uncertain of his own judgement and was immediately glad for his fallibility, his untrustworthy perceptions.

There was comfort then and his eyes closed against the knee-atolls and the glare of the bathroom bulb. It lasted only moments. His eyes snapped open. This matter would not lie. He could not ignore it.

Mother Earth was bleeding.

I consider my options.

I can stay holed up in a room all night, recuperating and staying safe but I am wasting precious time by doing so — outside the situation worsens. I also run the risk of my scent being picked up by hungry assailants out on the hunt. One or two I can manage and, if the door is strong enough, I might keep them out until morning. But if one or two become three or four, there won't be any door strong enough to keep them at bay.

I can continue raiding houses but the strength and agility of the assailants is far greater once the sun is down. I risk losing more than I might gain from the plundering.

The only real option is the bold approach: to take my katana onto the streets and hope I make it out of suburbia and up to the facility. There are routes, I know there are. Some of them will be almost uninhabited, even by assailants. But knowing which route to take is mostly luck. Stumble down the wrong alley or break through a fence in the wrong back garden and I'm likely to encounter odds I can't match — not even with the weaponry of the Japanese warrior class. Not even with the skills I've developed, so hard-won over the last three days. The assailants have ways of moving, habits of attack and I've studied them well. Against one or even two at a time it gives me a big advantage. But against greater numbers I don't think I'll survive for long.

This leaves a final possibility but it's the coward's way forward. I can use stealth. Creep from doorway to doorway, sidle along walls and stay in the shadows of alleyways. I can crouch and crawl on my belly in the dirt. It will be slow. It will drain me. But it's safer than walking into God knows how many skirmishes and risking my life.

While I consider all this, I stand with my back to a brick wall which forms the side of a three-bedroomed house. Opposite me is the wooden fence dividing this property from the one next door. I notice I'm panting, my adrenaline levels rising at the prospect of what lies ahead. Whatever I do, I will not sleep this night. I will not rest unless injury forces me into hiding.

I drop to a crouch and creep along the wall towards the back garden. It's unlikely there will be anyone back there. I can't see too far ahead but to turn my head-lamp on will attract attention. I have to do this almost blind. I come to the end of the wall and I'm about to sprint over the back lawn to the rear fence of the house when I think I notice movement to my left, by the back door of the house.

I turn to look.

Assailants. Three of them.

Heads cocked to listen, clothes torn or missing, decay visible everywhere. Ribs showing through ripped tee shirts. Lipless mouths grinning. Lidless orbs swivelling maniacal, unfocussed.

They make a papery sound as they keep vigil. It is not breathing but the movement of their desiccated dead skin. They are agitated, hungry.

Three.

More than I can deal with even using surprise.

I'm going to have to get on my face and slide over the grass. I'll have to stop regularly to turn and check they haven't discovered me. What are they doing here? So many in one place. In the wrong place. Gardens like this should be empty. They should be safe.

Sick with fear, hands shaking, I put my face to the ground and start forward one stolen hand-span at a time.

Tamsin Doherty twitches in their bed. Beside her is an expanse of linen across which she and Kevin rarely meet throughout the night. On the other side of this gulf is the cliff face formed by his back. Her eyes are closed. There is a waxy patina of sweat darkening her hairline, transparent pinheads above her lips. Her closed eyelids are two pregnant bellies in which twin eye-foetuses kick. She takes a sudden in-breath, fingers gripping the sheets.

There is a tall building, a building made by the hands of men but one which reaches up very high. Some days the upper parts of this building are hidden by clouds. She knows there were people here once but now they are gone. There is only the building. It stands tall and alone in a silent landscape as if it is the last building on Earth, as if it is the first.

She sees the building from above and notices something there. Something moving on its bare, flat concrete roof. She knows what this thing is long before she is close enough to really see it. All the people have gone and they have left behind a poor denuded baby. She feels she may have lived many lives but never has she seen such a solitary being. Perhaps, like the paradox of the building, this is not the last baby on Earth. Perhaps, somehow, it is the first.

The baby crawls on the sky-scraper's flat roof. There is a small wall and railing around the top of the building but the baby will fit through the rails easily if it finds them. It crawls well too. It might easily haul itself over the edge. She wants to go closer and help the baby, bring it safely to the ground but she cannot. She is here merely as an observer. The more the baby crawls, the more determined it becomes. It is naked and its hands and knees and feet, where they scrape over the cold concrete have developed thick pads, thick as the paws of wolves and lions.

The baby finds the door to steps that lead down. But the baby does not know about door handles and even if it did it would not be able to reach. It bashes its head against the steel door and when the door does not open, it crawls on, dogged.

The baby does not cry.

Sometimes this is as far as Tamsin's dream goes. Nevertheless, she wakes dripping, swallowing, one hand clamped over her heart, the other clasped over her abdomen.

Both places are empty.

Beside her, Kevin Doherty sleeps on.

3

They lined the surface of every wall in Mason's house, so much like wallpaper he barely noticed them. They were like memories of someone else's life, someone else's history, not his. Indeed, that was exactly what they were, for his bearded face appeared in none of them. Sometimes he caught himself staring at one of them, trying to recall if the moment had really been the way the camera had trapped it. He knew profoundly that cameras were like people; they never told the truth. There was so much happening in each of these kidnapped snaps – all he'd had to do was press a button and the theft was complete – but most of it the camera missed. The camera missed the hearts of these people he photographed but told you instead – insisted – that it had captured them faithfully. The picture convinced but the picture recorded only a fraction the event, a shard of the person, a shadow of the scene. It was like trying to catch and preserve snowflakes and this impossibility was what he had come to detest.

In those moments when he lost himself in remembering, or at least finding his memory as fallible as the camera's, he also found passion. He had taken pictures with a kind of anger and frustration and it was that, perhaps more than anything else, the camera had recorded. Mason was one of life's observers, the kind of man who spent parties watching and judging the guests instead of talking to them. Or, if he did talk to them, their words only reinforced his condemnation. London life, photographic life and all the parties that accompanied it, had therefore not suited him. And yet, it was at many of these gatherings that he'd shot his finest work – what others classed as his finest, at least. It was in the times he felt most alienated by his own inability to participate that he caught that fraction of a face or gesture which made a subject so interesting to look at later.

Rock stars, film stars, West end stars, critics, debutantes, lords and ladies, journos, paps, escorts and rent boys, dealers, pimps and spies. He'd caught them all at one time or another and in doing so he'd achieved three things. Fame, money and a nervous breakdown. It was inconceivable to Mason that his work could be seen as so influential. They called him a genius and this brought him more than a reasonable share of hate and adoration. For the years he spent on the London scene, he was 'known' everywhere. To him it was the ultimate irony; he had no personality and yet London turned him into a personality. In those days, he'd even appeared on late night chat shows where most of the guests and even the hosts were too stoned or pissed to be working. Back then, such things had seemed like good, highbrow arts programming. In reality it was egotism and bullshit of the worst kind. No one should have been paid to do it but they all were.

Mason had watched and snapped his way into photography's hall of fame in just three years. Within another two he had disappeared from London and the photographic scene forever. And no one knew where he'd gone. The rumour was he'd entered rehab on a long-term basis but the truth was Mason never had the stamina to be an abuser of substances. Too much of anything introduced to his system made him ill. Also, it clouded his photographic eye, and so he'd steered clear of every narcotic.

What he'd really done was move out of his flat, sell everything he owned including the bulk of his photographic equipment, and bought a tiny mobile home. The vehicle had space for a single occupant to sleep in the back. He drove his new home away from London and didn't stop until he reached the north coast of Scotland. He had money in the bank enough to live comfortably until he died. Instead he lived like a hermit, eating little, walking miles each day before returning to his four-wheeled home, still hating himself and everything he'd become and still not having any way to define who or what he was.

The barren Scottish wilds hurt him with their emptiness almost as much as London's overpopulation and amorality had affronted him. There were no trees to speak of, only vast, layered ranges of hills and mountains, blasted by wind and carpeted with heather. His eyes needed more than this and so he left, driving down the west coast to the Lake District and onwards until he crossed into Wales. On the far side of Snowdonia, near the coast, he found oak-lined hillsides from where he could both see and smell the ocean. The hillsides were silent and the oaks there were ancient and twisted. He spent several days exploring the smallest tracks until he found a remote farm at the centre of a huge, unpopulated stretch of land. The farm was lost at the centre of the property, so rundown it was becoming part of the hillside. The land comprised high, steep hills inland, sloping down to densely wooded valleys so overgrown it seemed no man could have walked there for centuries. Below the woods the land levelled out towards the sea.

He parked beside the rusted skeleton of a tractor. A crooked woman opened the door to him when he knocked and the farmhouse exhaled the smell of living human decay. Mason had stepped back. The woman left it to him to speak.

'I'd like to park on your land.'

'We don't allow camping.'

'I'm not camping.'

'What would you call it then?'

'I just need some… quiet… for a while.'

'How long's a while?' she'd asked.

'I don't know. I'll pay you. I've got cash.'

She'd looked at him more closely then. Noticed his lengthening beard, his yellowing teeth – not age but neglect. Seen the sick caverns of his eyes and the closeness of his skin to his bones. She saw his posture. She was a judge of animals not men but she must have seen he was carrying some burden. He found her assessment uncomfortable.

'You committed a crime somewhere, have you, boy? You on the run? We don't want you bringing your problems here.'

'I've done nothing wrong,' he said and he was able to look into her eyes as he spoke.

The crooked woman had squashed her already juiceless lips together as if deciding.

'My husband's sick. I don't need more troubles.'

'I'm not in trouble. I just need quiet. I just want some time.'

'I'll have to ask him.'

She'd shut the door then and he heard her scuffle away along what he imagined to be a dark, claustrophobic passageway. Then there was silence.

Mason turned to look at the hills and the rugged dry stone walls hewn from those hills. All around were dilapidated fences with rotting posts and broken barbed wire. The farmhouse was falling apart. Slates were missing from the roof. In the steep fields sheep cropped the grass. Shit matted their rear ends and many of them limped with foot-rot. Far on a hillside he saw grey-beaked rooks pecking at the torn open carcass of a ram. It began to rain, lightly at first which he found refreshing. The rain became heavy and determined. The water dripped from his unwashed hair into his collar and down his neck. He stepped under the broken porch which kept him dry, but the wind took lively and sprayed the water sideways onto him. He walked back to the minute campervan and got into the driver's seat. From there he watched the rain distort and obscure the landscape through his windscreen and he thought about how the way he saw things didn't really change what they actually were.

He fell asleep.

It was still raining when a rap that sounded hard enough to break the driver's side window woke him up. His heart was out of control at the shock of it and he couldn't catch his breath. The woman's face was smeared and deformed by the rain. Her presence so close by frightened him. She held beside her a shepherd's crook. To him it looked like a black iron hook. Rain fell hard and loud on the roof and the windscreen. She rapped the glass again even though she must have been able to see he was awake. He returned to himself then and opened the car door.

'You'll be coming in,' she said as if the rain meant nothing to her. 'He wants to see you. See your face.'

'Shouldn't you be revising?'

'Fuck off, dork.'

Donald Smithfield stood in the doorway of his sister's bedroom. Aggie was trying so hard to be a woman but she was still a girl. Even though he was only fifteen, he knew this. And she knew he knew it. This, he supposed, was why she acted like she hated him all the time. But then, even with only a few moments of hindsight, he knew he probably could have come up with a better opener.

'What I mean is, I could help. You know, test you on stuff.'

She knew him too well. These things, these family understandings, they worked both ways.

'What do you want?'

'Nothing. What do you mean? I just thought we could…'

He watched her measuring him up. He couldn't hold her gaze under such conditions and he looked away. Then he looked down. That was a mistake.

'It's about a girl isn't it?'

'Course not.'

But now her mood was different. She was curious. She was – miraculously, and there was no telling how many seconds it might last – not pissed off any more. This change made him think twice about the wisdom of coming to her for advice.

'A boy then?' She asked, knowing the power of her words.

Perhaps they'd shared too many secrets already. Though, now he thought about it more carefully, it had probably been him who had spilled his guts four-to-one over the years. Why was he so stupid? Why did he keep trusting her when she used her power to crush him?

'I'm not into boys.'

'Not this time.'

'Just forget it, Agatha.'

Using her full name was one tiny weapon he could employ. All it would do, though, was let her know for sure that she'd needled him deep; giving her more satisfaction, if that was what she wanted. He turned away from the door and pulled it closed, hating to break the connection but knowing he had to save some part of himself, keep something intact if he was going to work things out on his own.

Before he'd taken two steps she was standing in the open doorway.

'Wait, Don. I'm sorry.' He stopped, his back to her. 'I shouldn't have said that, I know. I'm… look, it's just me, okay? I'm in a rat. I'm pissed off with everything. I just want to get out of here and I can't. Can you understand that?'

He supposed he must have nodded.

'Come in. Shut the door and we'll talk. I'll help you, I promise.'

She sounded genuine enough but she could still have been reeling him in. He turned to look at her. The malice was gone. The need to dominate was gone. She wanted him in her life again. God, how stunned he was by the necessity of his sister's love. He didn't know what he'd do when she followed her dreams away from home and he never saw her. Who would he talk to then? Who would understand him?

She stepped out of the doorway to allow him past but he hesitated. He didn't move because he knew that to walk into her room now was to walk into that future, the one in which he had to grow up and survive without the protection of Agatha. She loved him. She cared for him. There was no one else he could talk to about things. Stepping into her bedroom was stepping closer to that time when she would be out of his life. Where all this emotion was coming from, this passion, he didn't know. All he knew was that everything he thought about hurt. Life was a rainbow of pain and he wasn't sure he could live with any of its colours.

'Don't stand there crying, Donny. Come in.'

He hadn't even realised but now he reached up and found the dampness on his cheeks.

'Shit,' he said, walking through the door.

The first thing she did was take hold of him and hug him tight. And he was weeping and weeping and he didn't even know why.

Pictorial fragments of Mason's memories coated the walls. He peered now at one of the only colour photographs he'd ever kept.

The light source came from the small window in the picture and it barely lit the scene. A flash would have killed the daylight, though, what little there was, and destroyed what he'd seen in that moment. This was the nearest he – or his equipment – had ever come to apprehending a moment fully and honestly. It had nothing to do with the fact the shot was in colour – there was barely enough pigment in the room to make that clear. The walls were almost grey, the furniture so faded it too might have been charcoals and ashes. The wood was dark enough to appear black at first glance and even the face the picture showed was drained of the bloom of life.

The man sat in an armchair that must have been as old or older than its occupant. It had certainly moulded itself to the sick lines of his body. His hands gripped the armrests and the veins on them stood out like wiring. He wasn't looking at Mason. He was staring out of the window at a landscape he must have known better than the contours of his own gnarled body. The man's grey hair was thin but long and pushed back as though by an invisible wind. It looked like his chair was a flying machine and he the pilot. Only the profile of the man's face was visible but even so, anyone looking at the photo would have known that this man had sight beyond the power of normal human eyes. He was looking at the landscape, only part of which was visible in the photo, but he was seeing more than anyone else could see. He was seeing beyond.

That was it. An old man; a dying man as it turned out, his knees wrapped in a torn and threadbare tartan rug, his fingers spread like claws into the worn upholstery, in a room in a crumbling farmhouse cupped in the palm of the land. It wasn't much of a subject. It wasn't like the photos he'd taken in London. Critics would not have understood it and if they had they might not have wanted to give Mason much credit for it. It was too simple. Too unusual. Too real.

It was probably the only photo he'd ever taken that had any true value and it was not a value measurable in money. When he took it, he'd been living in the woods a mile from the farmhouse for almost a year.

Richard Smithfield was having trouble breathing. The problem had started when he realised his computer contained enough evidence to destroy his life.

He stood in the cold of his workspace at the back of the garage, wheezing slightly and unable to completely fill his lungs. In the kitchen Pamela was doing her best to make a tasty evening meal for the family. No doubt she would be unable to achieve such a thing. Aggie would be inspecting herself in the mirror or texting her vile girlfriends about, well, God knew what. Donald, if he was anything approaching a normal fifteen-year old boy, would be wanking himself braindead in his bedroom.

He sighed in the gloom and switched on the fluorescent strip-light above the work bench. It illuminated what he was holding. The flattish, grey metal case was heavy in his hand. It contained the weight of his secrets. Not only that, it was designed to take punishment, to withstand knocks and accidents.

This wasn't going to be any kind of accident.

Patiently, Richard Smithfield peeled off the metallic stickers identifying his product and set them aside. Using several sizes of screwdrivers, he separated the two halves of the dense casing. Another metal plate was riveted over the disks of the hard drive – there was no way to remove it without force. He levered the plate off, snapping and shearing small pieces of steel.

There inside, pristine and unmarked by a single particle of dust lay the stack of five cobalt alloy disks. They were the colour of blue slate but mirror bright. At certain angles they gave off a rainbow shimmer. He removed the steel spindle holding them in place and lifted them off. Hard to believe so much information could be stored on these beautifully simple looking components. Hard to believe such engineered matter held enough information to condemn him to prison and the life of an outcast.

But they could and they had to go.

He placed the disks on a large old rag and folded it around them several times. He turned this bundle over so that it would keep itself closed. He pounded the bundle with a claw hammer until there was nothing inside but shards and powder. He placed all the dismantled and shattered components of the drive in a black bin liner and put it in the boot of the Volvo. Early in the morning he would drive out, ostensibly to fill up with diesel, and drop the bin liner into the huge compressor at the tip. In a few days it would be untraceable at the bottom of Shreve's vast landfill.

Then, and only then, he'd be able to breathe again.

The sensation of floating is wonderful at first. She feels giddy, light in her core.

Then she sees the building, far in the distance, piercing the sky to some degree but failing to attain heaven. She begins to fly towards it, not wanting to. She has no control. She is not flying, she is being carried, forced to fly. Perhaps then, she could also be made to fall. The earth is very far below, she would fall for a long time. She has a sense of being on a precipice, held there by something untrustworthy. A clip which might be faulty. A belt which might be old and frayed. Or perhaps something worse, the whim of a tormentor. Some entity she must trust to hold her even though it has the power to destroy her.

Like this, always on the verge of losing her balance or being pushed, she is propelled towards the building.

Reaching it and seeing how it thins to a thread as it extends downwards, she realises how tall it is. Miles, perhaps ten miles, from roof to foundation. Steel and glass and concrete. The entity holding her drops her and she begins to understand the true nature of falling. Wind pushing up at her but not enough to slow her down. The feeling that she's left part of her insides behind. No net, no parachute, no safety line, no jutting branch or handhold.

The entity is not ready to let her die yet. It wants her to

see something. She stops falling. No deceleration, nothing below to catch her, she just stops. It hurts at such velocity. And now she is hauled high again, flying against her will, back up towards the roof of the building.

She sees the baby and feels as though she must have seen it a thousand times; the crawl-leather on its hands and knees and feet, the bruises on its head. The entity has brought her here because no matter how many centuries it has been searching this roof, the baby's journey is only just beginning.

Something new now. It looks so familiar but she can't remember if it was there before or not. Now that she sees it, she supposes it's always been there. The baby has found a sky light. It is made of angled panels of glass which meet in a shallow apex. The baby does not know what a sky light is. The baby knows nothing but the will to crawl and search.

It thump-thumps up onto a glass panel, eager now that it has discovered something new. Its hands and knees slap against the glass as it climbs the gentle gradient of a sheet of glass many times its size. This is a new feeling beneath its fingers. Cold, yes, but smooth and comfortable.

A crack appears. It makes a scratching, creaking noise and the baby stops crawling for a moment. Sound. A sound other than the slip and slap of it patting its leathery limbs on concrete day after day, year after year. She can see the crack is right under the baby. If it keeps crawling, it might leave the crack behind, make it to the safety of the apex or even that of a stronger sheet of glass.

The baby laughs, just once, a sort of gurgled 'Ha!' of triumph. It knows it has definitely discovered something new.

The glass breaks.

She flies through it with the baby.

Follows it down.

4

There was a photo of the farmer's wife too, also alone, and taken on another day.

Somehow the opportunity to photograph her and her husband together never came up. This time he was using black and white again. He'd found her in the kitchen peeling potatoes at the table. He had his camera with him but not because he'd planned to take her picture. He stood in the doorless entry to the kitchen seeing that everything about the scene was right and his hands went automatically to the camera slung around his neck. Only when he had his hands on it did she look up at him.

He'd asked her husband's permission to take his photograph in his armchair by the window. This was something different, an opportunistic moment. He was about to ask her if it was all right when she looked back down at what she was doing as though he wasn't there. He'd been around the pair of them long enough to understand how much they spoke without using their mouths. He relaxed a little, checked the light reading and brought the camera's eye to his eye and when they were both seeing the same thing in the same way, he took the shot. But in the moment he'd found his composition, in the moment he'd committed himself to the shot, she looked up at him and her face opened.

Here, take it all, she seemed to be saying, like a rape victim going limp with compliance, that passivity taking all the power from the rapist. This wasn't a rape, of course, not in any sense. She wanted him to see what was in her face and she opened it for him. Just then and never again.

Mason looked at that photo now. There was nothing in it to give it a date in recognisable time, except perhaps the quality of the picture itself. It could have been a hundred and fifty years old. There she sat at her table, a half peeled potato in one hand, a short knife, half worn away with sharpening in the other. Her fingers were crooked and had painful-looking arthritic nodules on them. The joints were swollen but still bony. A pile of peelings lay to one side. In an aluminium pan of cold water with a loose handle lay the clean, skinless potatoes. She looked up from her work and in her eyes there was history: the transition from carefree girl to practical farmer's wife to widow-expectant in a single glance.

Every time he looked at the photo, Mason thought he could see bitterness but there was no bitterness there. Only experience and tolerance; not resentment but forbearance. There was a solitude there too, the seed of which must have been growing for a long time. She did not have her husband's sight and so could not share his view of the world. Not even his view from the window where he sat. Being with him, loving him so quietly as she did, had made her a lonely soul living firmly in this world while her husband looked into the next.

Oh God.

There was no help in staring at these fragments from the past – good work though they may have been. He wasn't looking at the photos to remember who he was or feel better about the past. He was looking for guidance, for answers.

The farmer would have known something about the bleeding Earth but he had long since followed where only his gaze had penetrated before.

Mason severed the connection with the photos, disorientated by the clarity of the memories that accompanied his staring. Such was the power of photography.

Little use it was to him now.

The farmer and his wife had helped him back then. He would have said they'd helped him to regain a missing part of himself but the truth was, the missing part was one he'd never been connected to until he arrived in on their land. He had to lose the rest of himself on that stretch of ancient hillside before he discovered the part that had always been missing.

I make it to the gates of the facility but it's been slow going. Assailants stand everywhere in twos and threes. Watchful, sensing the air at all times, the merest whisper of my passing makes them turn their heads my way. I want to leap up and draw my sword, at least take out one or two groups, but I know the noise will attract more and still more of them until I am swiftly overcome. Again and again I've had to lie perfectly still and pray I haven't roused them enough to come and investigate. I've pushed it, pushed it because my advancement has been so slow, but I've made it all the way to the facility car park without a single encounter. I am healthy. I am strong. I have weapons and skill. Dawn is only an hour or two away. All I have to do now is find a way inside the facility.

It's the perfect moment. Better than I could have hoped for.

Ray Wade saved the game to his memory card and looked at his watch.

Christ.

4.45 am.

There was a rotten smell in the house that the dope smoke barely disguised and his eyes were red and sore. As usual, the bin needed emptying and the late-night screen-watching was burning his eyes. Or it could have been the worsening stench from the landfill – a toxic gas, so the papers said.

Tomorrow – well, later today – was another day of lectures and classes. If he was lucky he'd get three hours of sleep. Jenny had been in bed for a couple of hours already – bored by his lack of attention. Either that or too stoned to stay awake any longer. Ray rubbed his face, dropped the controller and switched off the console and TV.

His skin was still puckered with goose flesh. The zombies in Revenant Apocalypse gave him the *serious* creeps. Perhaps because of this, and the tension the game created, he was completely hooked on it. They were so… watchful. So awake. Sniffing the air like dogs, vigilant eyes backlit by disease. And the way they attacked was merciless. Shit, it was fast too. You couldn't turn your back and stroll away. If you engaged them, you had to put them down. God, he'd wanted so badly to use that katana on the fuckers.

That would be a treat for the following night.

Well, really it was this night, wasn't it? He smiled in the skunk-spicy darkness of his tiny living room. Not too many hours to go until he let slip the samurai blade.

The baby chuckles, the first emotion it has ever shown other than determination – if that could ever count as an emotion. It has found its little hill of glass and scales it with confidence, with more strength than an infant ought to possess. She hovers above it unable to scream a warning even though she tries. The entity won't allow her to interfere, only to observe. No, that's not true; the entity allows her to feel everything, to empathise utterly with the chubby bundle, so hardened and bull-headed in its quest. She already knows something of the pain that is to come.

But only something.

There is no time here, she has decided. When she is here she recognises everything. When she wakes, all she knows is that she has dreamed this before. How many times, she has no idea. But when she is here, with the building, with the baby, she knows she has visited a thousand times. A hundred thousand. Revealing and discovering each part of the nightmare incrementally.

It will never be over.

There's a squeaky cracking sound as the fracture creeps across the pane of glass. The glass gives way to the baby's weight and it falls through. She's right behind it in slow motion. So she sees how easily the edges that touch the baby open its unprotected flanks. The cuts are slow to respond, perhaps because they are the first wounds the baby has ever known. Or perhaps it's simply because the entity wants her to see the details. Edges a mere molecule thick stroking innocent, flawless skin and revealing the flesh below. Then, finally, the wounds are obscured by a welling up of the baby's life fluid.

It falls in silence. So sharp are the blades which have cut it that it doesn't even know it has been opened up. It is also still a relative stranger to pain. She knows this state cannot last. She knows worse, much worse, is to befall the innocent.

Silence.

They fall together in silence. The baby first, she following closely.

Concrete welcomes them with cold inevitability and unyielding hardness.

The baby hits the floor in a rain of transparent razors. She does not. She is the witness.

The baby is not dead. But it should be. It is still but for its breathing.

Its left arm is broken. Not a simple greenstick fracture but a break. Radius and ulna snapped like tiny sticks of rock. Despite the hard pads on its hands and knees, glass shards have penetrated every part of the baby's body which have made contact with the floor. Its mouth is a wet, red mess. If it had any teeth they would be gone. Instead the mandible is cracked and flattened. The upper palate is crushed somewhat, making the baby's bloody face flatter, wider. It bounced when it hit, from its face onto its side and she can see the many places where the glass has pierced it ventrally and exited dorsally. It has developed spines of glass.

They have landed – no, the baby has landed – in some sort of corridor or hallway with many doors leading off to either side. She is dismayed in a way that she is not able to express. She is not allowed to express it. The entity makes her hold her feelings in.

The baby opens its eyes. It is looking up. For a moment she thinks it sees her and her guilt deepens, colouring her very soul a warm red. But the baby does not see her. It looks through, beyond. And besides, she sees now that the baby only has one eye that still functions. From the other, the broad end of a glass lancet protrudes. This does not prevent the baby from trying to blink. One blink works, the other meets resistance.

And now, finally, the baby is waking up to pain for the first time. It feels its wounds; all of them, and its solitude and it howls for all of this. She would love to be allowed to hear its scream; she deserves to, she believes. But the entity permits her only to imagine what this scream must sound like. The baby howls and weeps, the hot sting of its tears no sensation at all beside its abandonment and wounding. It cries like this for a very long time and she is not allowed to give the baby comfort. Cannot approach to lay a mothering hand upon its torn, dying body.

But the baby is not dying.

When it realises this, when pain and crying are unanswered, it stops its grizzling. The broken baby turns from its side onto its hands and knees again. Leaving etches of blood in grooves made by the glass that is now part of it, it crawls along the corridor. At each door it discovers, it raises its broken arm and flails for entry. For response. When there is nothing, it crawls on, scratching along the concrete in cherubic agony, in saintly silence, still searching.

The photos were always evocative.

Mason remembered how he'd driven his camper down a rocky track toward the trees. It was steep enough to make him wonder if the camper would ever get back up. His very next thought was:

Who the fuck cares?

The ancient track stopped being rock and became rutted dirt and shale nearer the trees. But the way was still clear and the gradient had eased. He supposed the farmer must have kept the track open with a tractor or quad bike – if not the farmer, then someone he hired to help. Under the trees it was darker, the unending grey of the Welsh sky not making much impression beneath the low leaf canopy. The track ended at a gulley where no vehicle could go any further.

He walked out from his camper that day and into the rain, much gentler then than when he arrived at the farmhouse, and explored the area.

The gulley was small, nothing dramatic but it had to be negotiated on foot. On the side he descended were small boulders and rocks, all wearing a thick fur of bright moss. He lost his footing several times as he clambered down. At the bottom of the gulley was a tiny stream, black water flowing over coal-dark peat. It was probably no more than a footstep across the widest part. He crossed it. Beyond, was the opposite slope of the miniature valley. There, the grass was fuller and greener than the place where Mason switched off his engine. There were no rocks to slip on or trip over.

There, on the far side of the gulley, protected by moss-covered oaks dripping fronds of lichen and tears of rain, in the clean damp air he felt himself go silent inside. His mind stopped replaying his fears and insecurities. It stopped questioning the validity or lack thereof of who and what Mason Brand was. It was as near to true peace as he'd ever come. Given to him in a single moment. In that same moment he decided he would stay in those woods until he was ready to go back to civilisation.

And if that time never came, he knew he could remain there. Just *be* there until the end. Like the farmer.

In his bed, Don Smithfield held the memory of the woman he lived for in his mind's eye and wanked until his prick was sore. Three ejaculations later and he still couldn't rid himself of her, couldn't sleep. Instead of memories he tried a fantasy, took their fragile new love to an unexplored level. He couldn't come. His prick was chafed so raw there was no more pleasure in the pursuit. And anyway, this lonely stroking only left him empty, sorry and bereft.

He lay on his back in the darkness and wondered what to do. No answer came to him. Telling Aggie had probably been a mistake. She was incredulous at first and then, he thought, pretty impressed, though she hid it well. He made her promise, swear on their parents' death, that she would tell no one. He thought she'd taken it seriously but there was no way of knowing for certain. She might blurt it to a girlfriend 'in confidence' or she might announce it in her class just to embarrass him. Maybe, just maybe, she would do as she'd promised and keep it a secret.

In a way, it would be cool if his mates found out but if it went any further there could be serious trouble. Police kind of trouble.

He'd had sex with a woman twice his age. That made her thirty years old.

And it made her a criminal.

None of this made it any easier to sleep. He slipped out of bed and sat at his desk, wincing as his pyjamas brushed the skin of his prick. The touch, though it stung, was enough to arouse him once more. He nudged the mouse on his desktop and a soft light filled the room. As his erection flared and reheated the skin was so dry it almost crackled. Then there was a sudden warmth and dampness in the crotch seam of his pyjamas. He looked down at his lap. A blot of blood was spreading across the cotton. Terrified, he fumbled his prick out for an inspection. The wound wasn't serious, just a split in his raw foreskin, but it bled enthusiastically. His erection went down fast. All he could think about was what he would tell his mum when the PJs went for a wash. He decided he'd throw them out.

I have to get my mind off all this.

Instead of surfing for porn, he looked at the online news. Shreve had been on national TV today but he'd been too preoccupied to listen properly. He looked up the story on the BBC.

– Doctors blame poor waste management for rise in health problems – read the headline. Apparently, Shreve's residents were suffering a far higher than average incidence of migraine, asthma and eye problems. Some hospital consultants in the area were blaming waste-leakage and fumes from the landfill site. During the day, Donald could see the huge dump they were talking about from his bedroom window. A local obstetrician had gone on the record to say he believed a recent and sharp rise in birth defects and childhood leukaemia to be directly related to the landfill.

Don blinked and rubbed his eyes. He looked away from the screen for a few moments until his vision cleared. Perhaps it was all the worry. Maybe he was highly suggestible. Out of nowhere a mean pounding was building up behind his right eye.

He could have sworn there was a smell of rot in his bedroom.

Ray took off his clothes and slipped in beside Jenny. It was after 5am now. He was exhausted and involuntarily replaying the scarier scenes from Revenant Apocalypse over and over again. His eyes hurt and the smell of rubbish from the kitchen bin had found its way into the bedroom too. Tomorrow, he promised himself, he would empty it and bleach it. Somewhere between getting back from college and switching on his console there would be an opportunity.

He was high and wired, his skin super sensitive. Feeling Jenny's warmth beside him created current through his whole body. The current flowed towards his groin and in moments he was fully aroused. He lay down beside her and caressed her sleeping body, sparks from the dope igniting his fingertips. He could hear his heart and the whoosh of his blood in his ears. She pushed his hand off and rolled away before he could really get started.

His electricity coagulated into bile and frustration. Did she have something better to do? She could sleep any time. Where was the passion? Why didn't she want the comfort to be found by fucking in their private darkness at five in the morning? There were the lectures of course but he had a knack for absorbing information no matter how tired or stoned he was. Jenny, on the other hand, worried about every missed fact.

Fuck you, Jenny. You can sleep at your own place tomorrow night.

But he didn't say it out loud.

The thought that they might not be particularly compatible had been sky-written across the blue of his mind many times but, like most forms of advertising, he ignored it. Most of the time he was too high to be bothered with the responsibility of facing the facts.

He sat up in bed and lit a cigarette. Though it ought to have had the opposite effect, it unwound him. His erection collapsed, his frustration seeping away with it. The electricity in his skin turned off. He watched the glow of his fag brighten with each drag and the pulse of it soothed him. Tomorrow was another day. Another chance with Jenny. Another batch of classes he didn't need to worry about. Another opportunity to get wrecked.

And, in all likelihood, it would be the day of the katana.

He crushed the butt out and fell asleep with a smile of anticipation not quite relinquishing his face.

Mason lived in the woods like a hermit for several months.

Occasionally, he walked to the nearest village for basic supplies. The farmer's wife gave him eggs from time to time. He drank the water which flowed from the hills and nothing had ever tasted sweeter or cleaner. He imagined it was purifying him.

He awoke when the light came and slept when the sun was lost behind the hills. There was nothing to do with his days and so he did nothing. The only activity was to watch the animals and birds around him and wander the forest of stunted, warped oaks.

Often, he wrote his thoughts and observations in a scrappy journal. This was the only thing he could consider to be an 'activity'. The rest of his existence was the twig of his mind and body bobbing slowly along time's river. But the writing was something which had an intensity to it. He allowed anything in his mind to come onto the page without ever thinking to censor it. There was no one else to see it, nor had he thought far enough ahead to think there might ever be such a person in the future. These moments of writing were like fugues. He would lose himself to the wearing down of a pencil and its re-sharpening as he wove words onto a cheap jumbo pad he'd found in the village co-op.

Pages later he would look up and find the light of the day had changed. Whether hidden by cloud and rain or not, the sun might have shifted far across the sky and he would flip back through the indented sheets barely remembering what he'd put there. Nor did he ever read carefully over his scrawl. It didn't seem the words were his. They came through him like a voice. He came to think of it as a kind of calling. Though he wrote the words of the calling every day, he worked hard to ignore what they told him. All he did was marvel at the amount and strength of it and the way the activity excised him from time and reality for however long he did it.

The pages and the doing of nothing mounted up in comfortable drifts. He watched the animals. He watched the seasons. The tyres on his camper went flat.

He didn't care.

5

Mason looked out of his kitchen window into the back garden. Soon he would begin this season's planting.

All the produce from last year, even the over-wintering vegetables, were used up or preserved. The garden, with its many beds was a featureless patchwork of exposed earth where his fertiliser was melding with the soil and strips of variously faded and dirty carpeting he'd employed to smother down any and all weeds. He felt excitement as a rising jitter in his stomach and a vague urge to move his bowels.

Every year it was the same, a childlike eagerness to help the earth bring forth food for him to live on. He sniggered to himself at his overreaction but he felt no embarrassment. This was who he was now. Not a photographer, not a bold visual 'genius' who owned all of London at the winking of his camera's shutter. He was simply a gardener. In fact, he believed himself to possess the soul of an agrarian. Even though he was no such thing now, he planned to be so in the future. Alone and remote on the land like the farmer he'd come to see as his teacher.

This period in suburbia was temporary but necessary. Before he retreated for good, he wanted to give people one last chance. He had changed and so he hoped he might see another side to everyone else, not be so deeply critical of every other human being on the planet. So far, though, his solitude here on the Meadowlands estate was almost more complete than it had been on the farmer's land. His time of living so close beside the earth was already years behind him. He was getting stuck again, as he had in London. He had to accept that soon the moment to move on would come.

Just one more season. Just one more season of being among people, even though he chased them away from his front door and did not speak to them in the street. Just one more year of being human before he became once more a creature of the land and of the forest.

He realised, as he surveyed his garden, that he was holding his breath.

He let it go.

He knew what the problem was. He could even admit it to himself. But he couldn't overcome it. He thought he'd been alone in London but he'd been wrong. His true solitude came during his time among the trees. It was so difficult. Life in the woods had been so tranquil and so restorative to him that it was painful to admit how much the loneliness of it hurt him.

As much as he wanted the peace, he was terrified of making the final decision to live alone again, even though it was probably the happiest he'd ever be.

It wasn't just the loneliness, of course. The depth of solitude was the obvious thing, the thing he would have talked about if anyone ever discussed it with him as a friend. There was another issue, however. The one he'd come to suburbia to avoid. Most of the time it was noisy enough that he didn't notice it. He missed it and feared equally. The land and the trees and all the animals he'd shared the woods with had a voice, one voice, a calling. And they talked to him as though he were their closest confidant. They talked and the land talked and they never shut up. His papers were full of their ramblings and even now, years later, he dared not look back over them to see what they'd said to him.

As though he'd created a moment of the perfect silence into which speech might come, as though he'd petitioned it, the calling came through the babble of suburbia's white noise right in that instant:

you're being a coward

'I'm not finished,' he said, placing his forehead to the chill of the window pane and staring at the expectant garden. 'I'm not finished with people. Not yet.'

have courage, Mason Brand

only the act which requires courage is the true act

He closed his eyes tight shut for a moment.

When he opened them, the face startled him so much he jerked away from the glass with a pounding heart. Like a man caught thieving. There was no time to recover himself. He stood there, red-faced, chest thudding, not knowing where to look. Could he have looked any fucking stranger than with his head pressed on the glass like a mental patient? Anger was the only response but his ire was hesitant like his words. He wasn't used to speaking.

'This is private... ground. Land, I mean to say. It's my land and you shouldn't be here.'

'Maybe I've got the wrong house. You're Mr. Brand, aren't you?'

He blinked at the girl, looked around, recovering himself, coming back to the room. This was his problem; too stuck in his head and his memories. Not *present* enough.

'You shouldn't be back here. Can't you ring the front bell? Knock? Like... normal people?'

It was ridiculous. They were talking through the glass with raised voices, almost shouting. The girl – she wasn't a girl really, more of a... she smiled at him.

'Look, I'm not here to steal your veggies, Mr. Brand. I just wanted a quick chat. Could you open the door?'

The part of Mason which remembered how to behave was screaming at him to act sensibly and open the door, offer tea and biscuits or a glass of wine – was she old enough for that? Of course she was – to do something, anything, and stop acting like a bloody psycho before she walked away.

But the back door, even with its six dirty panes of glass in peeling frames, was a barrier between him and the world. The world had come into his back garden, without any sort of invitation and she stood there now, still not leaving but with her expression fading from mild amusement at what could just be shyness and eccentricity into concern about her safety with such a man. He noticed her glance from side to side, probably checking if anyone was within earshot or working out how quickly she could run –

'I remember when you moved in here,' she said. 'It was my eleventh birthday. I saw your knackered old camper pull in and watched you go around the back. Thought you were a tramp or a gypsy or something. I fell off my pissing bike watching you. Only time I ever cried on my birthday.'

'You'll have other birthdays,' he said, trying very hard to… he wasn't sure what he was trying to do but he knew he was failing.

'Uh, right,' said the girl. 'Listen, I can tell this isn't a good moment. I'll come back.'

She turned to leave and all kinds of panic leapt inside him, yanked him into action. He opened the door and put his head out. Already she'd reached the corner of the house.

'Wait.'

She turned back.

'I mean… I'm sorry.' Something kicked in from the past, from a thousand failed social interactions. 'I've got a lot on my mind right now. What's your name?'

'Aggie Smithfield. I live just down—'

'I know where,' he said and immediately decided he sounded creepy rather than informed about the community. He followed up quickly, holding out his hand which, for once, was not soil-blackened. 'I'm Mason.'

He watched her hesitate. Something in her eyes, some need he couldn't decipher, made her overcome any nerves she might have had. She walked back to him, boldly enough to make him retreat a fraction. Keeping his hand out was an effort. She took it before he gave in, squeezed it with adult formality.

'It's good to meet you,' she said and he believed she meant it. Not like the people in the old days. This one was too young to hate him or envy him or try to drain him.

He realised he was still holding her hand and he let go

quickly. He'd come too close to blowing this simple – there was nothing simple about it – interaction too many times already.

'I just wanted to talk to you,' she said. 'Only for five minutes. Could I come in?'

He didn't move.

She gestured with her head over his garden fence, towards the landfill site.

'I wouldn't mind chatting out here but,' She wrinkled her nose. 'You know… wind's blowing the wrong way.'

She was right but he wouldn't have noticed without a reminder. To him the smell of the dump was normal. More than that; it was a comfort.

'Of course. Sorry.'

He retreated and opened the back door of his house to a stranger – to any person – for the first time since arriving six years previously.

For a time he stood there wondering what to do next. Where should they stand or should they sit down? What should he offer her or was that too forward, too much like… something? He saw the kitchen with new eyes now, her eyes, and realised she was looking at the state, not only of his house, but of his mind. This was what happened when you let people in.

After a few moments he laughed – pure nerves – at a total loss for how to continue.

'What?'

'Oh, God,' he said, finally relaxing just a little. 'I'm very…'

'Used to your own company?'

He laughed again, exposed and suddenly not minding. Not from her. She seemed so natural about it.

'Yes, that's it. That's it exactly. Would you like a mug of tea? I make it quite strong.'

'Do you have coffee?'

'No. Sorry.'

'Tea's fine. I'm not stopping long, honestly. I only wanted to ask you about…'

She was looking out to the hallway and stairs. She'd seen the photographs. How could she not notice them? They were everywhere except in the kitchen. He couldn't stop himself this time. He pushed the door closed, severing her view. He didn't know what to say. He went to the sink, feeling scrutinised, and put water in the kettle. As soon as he went to plug it in, he realised it was only enough for him; he went back to the tap to double the amount.

'Actually,' she said. 'It was the photos I wanted to talk to you about.'

He spun.

'What? What do you mean, the photos?'

'Well, about all of it. You know, what you did. How you did it. I want to know about photography.'

He stood there shaking his head. He didn't stop shaking his head. Even after he'd said:

'I don't want to talk about that.'

The kettle ticked, slow at first and then faster. A sigh began inside it, rising and rising. The sigh became a rumble. There was a click. Mason stopped shaking his head but didn't turn to pour out the water.

'I don't want to talk about it.'

She'll go now, he thought. Back to her house and her family and I will not have to go through this.

'Please. I really want to know. It's the only thing that interests me.'

'I can't.'

She took a step closer to him and he wondered what that boldness signified.

'Just tell me about one photograph and I promise you I'll go. If you still don't want to talk about it after that, I'll never disturb you again.'

Before he could stop her – how could he have stopped her without touching her? – she'd pulled the kitchen door back open and walked into the downstairs hallway. Every wall was covered in framed monochrome photographs.

There was no space between them. None of them were straight. He saw them with her eyes, the way he'd just seen his kitchen, terrified by her scrutiny – still quite casual at the moment but deepening, lengthening with every moment that slipped by. He had to get her out.

'Will you do that? Just tell me about one. I'll go then. I really will.'

What choice was there now short of pushing her out by force?

He clasped a hand over his beard, squeezed the rough hairs until they pulled the skin of his face.

'Okay. One only. Then you go. And I don't want you coming back here. Do you follow me? Not ever.'

'Fine.'

She was all business now. So close to what she'd come for. A vampire, just like all the rest of them.

Now she looked closer, roved and stopped, moved on again. Drinking his moments – they were his moments even though he never talked about them that way. His moments. His partial realities. His misrepresentations, therefore, of the real world. They were dangerous, photographs, they told lies about the world.

She was on the stairs. She'd stopped.

No.

'Okay. Tell me about this one.'

She was pointing at the farmer.

It was difficult to make it short but Mason did his best. He left out as much detail as possible, used terms that would elicit scant curiosity. He also lied: It was a farm he'd visited once. They'd asked him in for tea. When they saw his camera they asked if he would take a few pictures. This was the only one he'd kept. The shot was a fluke.

The girl was quiet for a while and he could see what

was happening. The lack of information itself was causing her to have questions.

'That's all there is to it,' he said. 'Time for you to go. Please.'

She turned back to him. Whatever she'd come here for it was clear she hadn't got it. She didn't look angry. She looked sad. Defeated. She walked past him and back out to the kitchen without making eye contact. Two tea mugs stood empty on one of the surfaces, curls of steam still rising from the kettle. She reached out for the back door handle and hesitated, turning back to where he still stood in the hallway.

'I want to be a model.'

His mind flooded with responses:

Silly bloody girl. No idea what you'd be getting yourself into. It doesn't stop at photography no matter what your principles are. She could do it, though, she's got the build and the grace. She's got the blank, clean face. Whether you make it or not, that life will suck you dry like it did to me.

None of it came out. Instead he gave a kind of snort. It might have sounded like a laugh to her but that wasn't what it was.

'Why does everyone assume you're going to fail before you even start? I'm not stupid, if that's what you're thinking. I won't be taken advantage of.'

'Really?' This time he did laugh. 'How will you avoid it?'

'I'm a good judge of character.'

'If that was true you wouldn't be in this house.'

'I can trust you, Mr. Brand. You're a recluse but I know you're all right.'

'Do you? How do you know that?'

She shrugged.

'Listen to me,' he said, 'You're too young and too inexperienced to know who you can trust and who you can't. Do your parents know what you're up to?'

'It's nothing to do with them.'

'Give me one reason why I shouldn't tell them what

you're thinking of doing. Do you think they'll approve?'

'Don't do that.'

'Then don't be stupid.'

'This is such *bollocks.*'

She was crying. The little girl had been unmasked. She governed herself quickly, wiped the few tears away.

'Mr. Brand,' she said. 'I came here for your help. I know I can trust you so don't mess me about. I need a portfolio. A really good one.'

Mason shrugged, not understanding.

'I want you to photograph me. I know who you are. With your name all over my photos, I'll bypass all the sharks when I get to London.'

Mason held his hand out towards the door, gesturing for her to open it.

'You have to leave. Now.'

The farmer wasn't as sick as he looked.

He came to visit Mason often. Sometimes walking down the steep, treacherous track with help of a long, warped stick. Mason would hear him coming long before he arrived. The diseased wheezing and the knock of his staff finding purchase on stones, the uneven footsteps of a limping man, the footsteps of a determined man. Stealing over the greasy stones, over the mossy stones, through air hanging wet even when it wasn't raining, he came. He came through woods either angered by wind or resisting the unmoving light above them. He passed through the mug and cling of summer and through the nerveless hands of winter with pain in its bones. To him the world was a gateway. He need pay no fee for entry, showed no fear of departure. Bearded, ragged, staring, he walked like he was already a soul slipped from its shitty human moorings, a living man with the knowledge of the dead. And then he would be there, beside Mason and silent, watching the world with him, leading Mason's eye to what he saw, *how* he saw.

Other times he came in Mason's dreams. No less cumbersome or telegraphed an approach. No less fanfaring of his power. No less a shell of a man and still no less a mage.

Whether conscious or not, the farmer tutored Mason. He was a demanding master, a cruel one, and yet occasionally more caring than Mason's own parents. His lessons were stories sometimes, tales of people who lived in times lost to memory and history. His lessons were visions of those ages and visions of the future. He taught about the Earth and the land.

'You came here to forget who you thought you were,' he'd said one day. 'That was the right decision. You thought you'd find yourself here but you won't. That would be an insignificant pursuit, a waste of very precious time. You must learn about how things are, not what you believe them to be. You must become a blank, a forgetting.'

This hadn't been what Mason wanted. He'd wanted only to be left to himself.

'It doesn't matter what you want, fool,' said the farmer.

'But I'm *paying* you to let me stay here. I came to be alone.'

'I don't need your money. Leave if you want. Leave now. But if you want to stay here, if you want this sweetness—'

He'd made the woods silent then, like a conductor, and creature by creature, sound by sound, mood by mood, he'd brought it back to life and Mason's soul was enchanted.

'– you'll heed me. You'll work hard to discard what you thought you knew and who you used to be. You'll understand – the way the old ones did.'

Mason didn't even see the farmer's hand seize the back of his head. The old man knelt and Mason was forced down with him. The hand, like the claws of a huge falcon, pushed his head onto the ground. Fallen gorse needles punctured his face. Moss and weeds mingled with his beard. Plugs of damp peat entered his nose. He panicked, tried to push back. The claws were too powerful. Trying to avoid suffocation, he opened his mouth. The farmer pushed harder. His mouth was stopped with the oozing of soft soil. His eyes went black against the engulfing mire.

'You'll learn to love your mother, boy. Smell her, taste her, listen to her. Respect her. This is what you are, boy, your mother's reek and muck. Everything you are, she's given you.'

The claw pulled him gasping from the ground. He was lifted by his head until his feet lost contact with the earth. He felt the most nauseating whirling and disorientation, a disconnection from everything, a free-floating terror.

'Open your eyes, boy.'

The soil was gone from his mouth and nose and face. Gone was the fecund stench of endless cycles of becoming and destruction. He could see. And so he looked. What he saw was the sun. It burned everything else from his vision. It scoured his mind of all distraction until there was only eye-whitening heat and purity.

'Simple enough for you? Mother Earth. Father Sun. Learn it. Embody it. That's why you're here.'

The claw had disappeared and Mason found he was sitting beside the farmer on the rocks as they had been before. The farmer was looking out of the woods towards the other side of the estuary or maybe he was looking into other worlds than this. Mason's heart was arrhythmic and loud, his breath laboured. He touched his face but there was no trace of soil there in his beard, no burnt skin.

The farmer had stood up, his joints creaking like wet timber, and begun his walk back to the farmhouse.

'Stay or leave. It's your choice.'

That was the first lesson.

Mason stayed.

That was exactly the kind of detail he left out of his brief explanation of the photo on the stairway. As he sat, drinking the tea he'd been about to make for both of them. He sifted through the events of the morning trying hard to ignore all the parts in which he'd acted like a little boy. It didn't leave much.

Maybe he should have been less concerned about someone judging him to be crazy, worrying about what a seventeen-year-ld girl might think of her heroic, meal-ticket photographer. Maybe if he'd gone ahead and told her the whole story she'd have left without him having to ask her and without any intention of ever coming back. But his woodland history was too delicate for him to spill to anyone, least of all the too-young-to-care and destined-for-the-streets Aggie Smithfield. If he was ever going to tell it, it would have to be to the right person. Someone who would embody it the way he had. Someone who would pass it on.

Knowledge, he'd discovered, came with certain built-in responsibilities. First off, once you knew something to be true, acting in ignorance or against that knowledge would always be a kind of sin. There was no way to un-know what he had learned. He carried it in his blood now, he supposed. That was the other problem. Knowledge existed to enrich the world. To help people make sense of their existences and help the world make sense of its people. How the people behaved affected the behaviour of the world. Mason knew he was one of the very few individuals left who understood this and used it as their guidance system. His morality was based upon such understanding now. To allow himself to reach the end of his life without propagating his knowledge would be the most ignorant and irresponsible thing he could do.

He thought about that every day; woke each morning, pure from the Earth's drawing, and wondered how he could disseminate what he knew. When he'd reached full consciousness, in other words, by the time he'd finished his first cup of tea, he was convincing himself that this world he now inhabited, this cushioned, blinkered suburbia, could not take the truth. There was not one person left out here in the places where tarmac and concrete separated people's feet from the ground who would listen long enough for his words to make any difference at all.

He'd be sectioned in a heartbeat.

Aside from that, Mason felt no sense of authority conveyed upon him by his knowledge. He had stumbled across a heavy burden in the woods, picked it up and shouldered at the behest of the farmer. Now he couldn't put his load down without condemning himself. His only option would be to share the weight. It was an option which didn't exist.

Other than the issue he'd brought back with him from the forested valley in Wales – that of his responsibility – Mason was unused to having to solve any kind of problem. This was one advantage of living alone and steering clear of people. He only ever had to think about or deal with himself. Most of the time, because he stayed in tune with the Earth and the seasons, there was little to concern him. Occasionally, his memories troubled him. Those from the woods and occasionally those from his time on the London scene. All of that was manageable stuff.

Now, in the space of a few minutes, he had a real problem. One that wouldn't just go away without him doing something about it. This was what happened when you talked to other people. Every word uttered, every gesture employed in expression and the concealment of expression led to complexity. He didn't need this girl hanging around. He didn't need to talk to her about the farmer. He especially didn't need to take photos of her – that was the kind of activity which would lead to him being run off the estate whether he'd decided to leave or not.

He drained his tea mug and stood up. Moments later he was standing on the stairs again looking at the picture.

It was mesmerising. All you wanted to know when you looked at it was 'who is this man?' and 'what is it that he sees?'. No matter how often he looked at the photo the effect was the same. He could only imagine the effect it would have had on the girl. Intrigue was not the thing to arouse in someone like her. She was tenacious and determined. He knew she'd be back. What he didn't know was how he would handle her return.

He looked away from the picture with an effort. The truth was he didn't need the photo. It didn't need to be framed there on his wall. Everything about the farmer was inside him now and firmly in his memory. It would all stay there forever. The physical photo itself was unimportant. It was time for change – something the farmer had always told him was important to accept, even to welcome. He had also taught Mason ways to encourage such change.

He snatched the frame off the wall. The space it left was like a hole in his armour but he ignored how that made him feel. He unclipped the frame as he walked back down to the kitchen. He removed the rear panel and exposed the photo for the first time in several years. The frame had kept it clean and bright. The back of the picture was still white. He took the picture out carefully and turned it over. It seemed a fragile thing now, its power diminished. It was vulnerable in his callused hands.

Photos were lies, he reminded himself. He knew it so well and yet he still found it hard to make his body do what his sprit knew was right.

'I don't need it any more,' he whispered.

He opened the back door and stepped out into the cold air. When he reached the shed, he hesitated, fumbling for the padlock keys in his pocket. He stopped and withdrew his fingers without retrieving the key. He wouldn't need a shovel for this job. Sometimes it was better to dig with your bare hands, let the earth taste your skin and smell your wishes.

6

'I can't believe we live in such a shit-hole.'

'It's not that bad.'

'It's a fucking pit and you know it.'

Aggie Smithfield and her friend Moira sat on the swings shivering and smoking. The last hour and a half of school was a double revision period, self-supervised, so they'd left early. The recreation ground was a natural gathering point for the children of the estate and there was no better time to be there than when school was still in and they had it to themselves. Aggie turned her legs from side to side, assessing the shape and the length. It was too cold for the short skirt she was wearing but her legs were too pretty to keep covered. She could feel Moira looking too.

'I don't know why you hate it so much,' said Moira. 'My family's lived around here for generations.'

'That doesn't make it a nice place.'

'They must have stayed here for a reason.'

Yeah, because they're all too stupid to leave. Aggie liked Moira enough to know better than to say it.

'Maybe they didn't have any choice,' she said instead.

Moira blew out smoke. The wind bent the stream and snatched it away.

'No. They like it here. They know everyone. Everyone knows them. It's home.'

'What about you?'

Moira pulled her jacket tighter against the cold blow.

'I'm happy enough.'

'Don't you ever think about leaving?'

'I'd miss them all too much.'

The conversation was going nowhere. At least, not to the place Aggie wanted it to go. Why was there no one she could talk to?

'You'll keep in touch, won't you?' asked Moira.

'What?'

'I know you want to get out of here. Just promise me you'll text me sometimes, eh?'

Aggie looked at Moira but she'd turned her head away. She was putting her hand out to take hold of Moira's when she sensed movement behind her. Too late to evade them, she felt fingers close around her ribs and a shout by her ear.

'RRAAA!'

She leapt off the swing with Don still clutching her. Her heart hammered, she'd nearly wet herself. Don was laughing.

'You twat,' she shouted. 'You juvenile fucking twat.'

Moira was laughing too. The idiots. It wouldn't be like this in London. People would respect her.

'Alright, Moira.'

'Alright, Don.'

'What are you doing here, Donald?' asked his sister. 'Why aren't you at school?'

'Why aren't you?'

'You haven't skipped the whole day have you?'

'Got a sick note.'

'Real or imaginary?'

'Real, I think. Doctor says I might have migraines or something. I had this pain inside my eye. Really bad it was, like someone was pumping it up with air. Felt like it was going to explode.' He eyed his sister's cigarette. 'Give us a fag, will you?'

'No way.'

'A drag then.'

'No, Donald.'

Moira leaned over with an open packet of ten Benson & Hedges.

'Here you go, *Donald*,' she said.

As he took it, she caught his eye and smiled. He looked away quickly. She passed him her cigarette and let him light up off its tip. Aggie looked disgusted.

84

'If they smell it on you, I'll get the blame,' she said.

'Spray him with a bit of perfume,' said Moira. 'Works for me.'

Aggie ignored the suggestion, concentrating on what Donald had said about his sick note.

'I suppose your eye just got better, did it?'

'Mum got a prescription for some painkillers. They work too. Make you feel… I don't know, far away or something.'

The pissed-off wrinkles of Aggie's face dropped out as she caught sight of something over Don's shoulder. His instinct was to look but she stopped him with her hand.

'Drop your fag and crush it out,' she said. 'Don't turn around.'

Don grinned.

'Dad home early, is he? Out walking Sasquatch?'

'Seriously, Don, I'm not kidding. Do it now.'

He took only his third drag and dropped the butt, squashing it under one of his Vans.

'Happy?'

Then he heard the sound of steps approaching on the tarmac footpath leading to the play area. Now he turned around.

They all recognised the approaching figure. A woman of forty-five dressed as though she was sixty. Flat brown shoes, grey tights and an ankle length woollen skirt. She wore a drab cardigan and a padded green jacket over the top. Her hair was black but she styled it like it was already grey in unflattering, homogenous curls. Around her neck was knotted, as always, a plain silk scarf. The scarf made her look like a sailor.

'Shit,' said Don. 'The vigilante.'

Moira giggled, catching his eye again. Don appreciated the attention.

The vigilante approached at a march. This was how she walked everywhere. She had a message to deliver, a mission to the darker limits of society. Don found himself giggling too but it was nerves in his case. The woman actually frightened him.

She was still twenty yards away when her tongue leapt forth.

'Why aren't you children at school?'

None of them said anything. The marching quickened and she arrived.

'Have you got cloth ears? Answer me, why aren't you at school?'

It fell to Aggie.

'We've got a free class.'

'Rubbish, girl. I'll report you to your headmaster.' Aggie sighed.

'My name is Aggie Sm—'

'I know who you are, child.'

'I'm in the sixth form and we have a free class. Go ahead and report us if you like. The head*mistress* will put you straight.'

It was a risk. The vigilante wasn't beyond making the call and then they'd be in proper trouble. But Aggie was banking on the woman's most obvious frailty – she hated to be wrong. Especially in front of 'children'.

'You should learn to speak to your elders with some respect.'

'What? The way you respect us, you mean?'

The vigilante looked at their faces individually.

'What about you, young man? You're not in the sixth form.'

'I'm off sick.'

'You don't look sick to me.'

'The doctor made me better.'

It was true but it came off like backchat and he regretted it.

She scanned their faces harder. She wasn't going anywhere yet.

'You've been smoking, haven't you?'

She said it more to Don than the girls and Aggie answered quickly to shut it down.

'*We've* been smoking,' she said gesturing to Moira. 'We're seventeen so it's perfectly legal behaviour. He can't because he can't afford it. Besides, he's too young.'

'Filthy girls. Filthy habit. How can you sully yourselves that way? Don't you care about your... bodies?'

That tiny hesitation was enough to lose the battle for the vigilante. Now they all knew she wasn't talking about their 'bodies'. She was talking about their ability to bring forth children. She was talking about sex. It was a wrong turn.

'What do you mean?' asked Aggie.

'I mean it's unhealthy for you. You should stop.'

Aggie capitalised.

'What have our *bodies* got to do with you, Mrs. Ahern? What do you want to know about our bodies for?'

The vigilante stood straighter, moved her intense head away from them. Staying clear.

'I'm only concerned for your health, girls.'

'Don't you know it's inappropriate to talk about *bodies* with *children*, Mrs. Ahern? There's a special word for it nowadays. What is it that word, Moira?'

Moira's smile was all sharp teeth.

'Grooming,' she said. 'Yeah, grooming's the word.'

'Grooming,' repeated Aggie. 'You could get put away for that.'

The steel went out of the vigilante's mission.

'I feel sorry for you,' she said. 'I really do. You walk through this world with sin as your companion and the devil for comfort. It could be paradise. Heaven on Earth and you won't give it a moment's attention.'

'I think you ought to leave now, Mrs. Ahern. You're making my little brother upset. He's not even sixteen, as you know. All this abusive language could have a damaging effect on him. He might need to go for counselling. He'd have to tell them all about you.' She looked at her brother. 'Wouldn't you, Donald?'

She had more power over him than the vigilante. She'd make his life hell if he didn't side with her. So he nodded and the counter-attack was complete.

Mrs. Ahern couldn't resist one last try. As softly as she could manage and using all her energy to restrain her utter affront she said:

'Why don't you come to church this Sunday, the three of you? Try and see things another way?'

'Why don't you get lost?' said Aggie.

Mrs. Ahern's lips tightened over whatever more it was she'd wanted to say. She nodded to herself almost imperceptibly and turned away. The retreat was more of a hurry than a march. When she was out of earshot, they all released sighs. Aggie took out her cigarettes and offered them to Moira and Don. Such inclusion was not wasted on him. He swelled up to their stature.

'Fucking curtain-twitching bible-bashing Nazi bitch-bag,' said Aggie.

The three of them went slack with laughter.

Mason replaced the photo of the farmer with one of tens of thousands of others he'd taken. It was very similar; this time a wistful model staring through a window on a rainy day, her fingers holding the nets so she could see out. It was for a catalogue selling floaty, hippy outfits. The model had no soul. The picture had no soul. It was black and white. It was perfect. Now the walls were sealed with lies again, not a true moment among the jigsaw of framed images. He stood back and smiled.

That night he travelled back across the barren brownland to the landfill. He hurried to keep out the chill. Once through the disguised hole in the fence he found the freshest area of soil. This was where they'd been dumping and compacting that same day. Now the 'cell' was filled and covered with earth. He removed his shoes and socks and stepped onto the soft warm humus. He flexed his feet and gripped the earth, let it get stuck between his toes and under his toenails. It was like coming home. He gave himself to the sensation of being 'drained'. All the worry over the girl, the memories of his time in the woods, they seeped away like pus into a clay poultice.

His mind slipped its mooring.

At first the vibration was in his head. He felt giddy with it and his teeth buzzed where they met. It was like having the cone of a super-woofer placed against his occiput. A subsonic noise shook his cranium at some wavelength that threatened to unpick the sutures of his skull. Even this was not unpleasant in the state of consciousness he'd reached.

Then the buzz extended to the rest of his body and he came back to himself. He opened his eyes. His entire body was oscillating. It wasn't in his head at all, it was rising up from his feet. He looked down. It wasn't so dark, he couldn't see that his feet had already sunk in to the ankles. He didn't move.

The vibration became a rumble – he could hear it all around him now. He could feel it in his chest. His heart stumbled over its own rhythm. The Earth was shaking now. His knees responded like shock absorbers. And then the shaking became too strong for his legs and he fell to the soft earth. There was thunder under the ground. His hands sunk through layers of soil. His body followed them. There was soil in his mouth, grit forcing its way under his eyelids, trickling into his ears. He would have screamed if it hadn't been a waste of the only breath he had left. The world itself tremored and he feared he would either be buried or flung off into space. Anoxia made sparkles behind his crushed-shut eyes. He had to breathe but if he did he'd breathe the earth into his lungs and suffocate. The sparkling became brighter and he began to relax, knowing it was wrong but not being able to resist.

All movement ceased.

Mason pushed his way back out of the soil, trying to spit out dirt and breathe at the same time. Particles stuck in his throat. For several minutes he believed he would still die, only above ground. But each in-breath revived him and each exhalation cleared the earth from his airways. He cried mud; shook soil from his ears.

When he was able, he stood up, wiping his face and blowing his nose onto the landfill's covering of clean soil. The touch of his bare soles against the earth held no comfort for him now. Before he was able to walk clear of the newly covered cell, he felt the welling of treacly warmth rising through the topsoil. There was no need to stop and examine it this time; he knew exactly what it was.

Feeling only guilt and not knowing why, he made the darkest shadows his companions all the way home.

Ray woke, eyes wide, fully conscious. The whole flat was shaking. He could hear the glasses rattling in the kitchen cupboard, the cutlery shivering in its drawer. His mobile phone chattered towards the edge of the bedside table and fell off.

Seconds later the vibrations receded, to a tremble, to a buzz, to nothing. Heart racing, he reached out to Jenny and squeezed her hand

'Did you feel that?' He whispered.

She took a few seconds to reply.

'Feel what?' she said eventually with a sleep-weighted tongue.

It took only a few minutes for him to get back to sleep, such was the level of dope in his system. In the morning, all he retained was a vague sense of anxiety.

Tamsin's dreams lengthen and intensify. Sleep becomes exhausting, and yet, come the morning, she remembers nothing. Sometimes, she notices Kevin looking at her over his paper at breakfast but he never asks if she's all right.

Since the true agony of the fall – the baby's awakening as she thinks of it whilst dreaming – the scenario is different. When she arrives at the sky-penetrating building the baby is gone. The roof-light is already broken.

She flies in, feeling something close to panic. She must find the baby. She is responsible for it. Here in the dream, feeling responsibility is perfectly natural. Down through the broken-toothed mouth of glass. The corridor is dim now that the only illumination comes from the skylight. There is no electricity in the building. No need for it because there are no people. She knows the building is empty from top to bottom and that the baby should not hurt itself with fruitless searching. But, just as she knows the building is uninhabited, she knows the baby will never stop looking.

There's a zigzag blood trail in the corridor, still wet, and she remembers the baby's injuries. There's a spike of glass the size of a knife blade piercing its eye and embedded in its brain. It really shouldn't be alive. It has crawled over the broken glass, apparently injuring itself further, in order to test every door. She follows the blood trail, still floating, still controlled by the entity. The meandering red smear on the never-carpeted concrete widens, wettens. There are scratches in the stain where the glass it's dragging with it cuts into the concrete, occasionally snapping off and leaving a bloody fragment. There can't be this much blood in the tiny child's body, can there?

She follows the trail around a corner.

Somehow the baby has found an open door. The blood leads through it. She follows. She comes to a bathroom. The baby has found nothing but a small pack of razorblades. It plays with them as though they are cards, lacerating its fingers to the bone until every blade is sticky and slippery. Some of them are stuck in its palms. The baby stops for a moment and looks around. Does it hear her? Does it know she's there? She prays it will see her with its one good eye; acknowledge her at the very least. Then she knows the baby won't be lonely any more. But the baby doesn't see her. It isn't looking for her. It's looking for other toys to play with. The baby smiles through its broken mouth, dribbling cherry saliva. It turns to crawl out of the bathroom pushing the razorblades deeper with every shuffle. One lodges in its knee, opening up the leathery pad there to bring a fresh welling. The blood lubricates its progress towards the kitchen.

There's something in there it wants. She sees it first, precariously positioned at the edge of a work surface. The baby crawls right to it. It looks up and sees the knife-block but it cannot reach.

Don't do this, she pleads. Why are you doing this to yourself? No words are allowed to come forth.

The baby begins to bang on the cupboard doors below the surface. Its broken arm has knitted but at an unnatural angle. The tiny sharp-edged bones still protrude from a wound which will never completely heal. With the second 'elbow' of its broken arm and the other hand variously pierced by razorblades, it beats the cupboards hard. The vibration affects the knife block, bringing it nearer to the edge.

No, baby, don't do that. Her scream is cave-silent.

The inevitable happens. The knife-block tumbles spilling its seven blades out as it falls. The block hits the baby's head and bounces away heavily. The knives enter the baby's body easily, as though it were made of fresh cake. They slide in deep. Deep enough to stay. The baby pauses, turns. Some of the longer knives have passed right through it. She sees the points poking downward from its chest as it screams. She can't hear the screaming. She only feels it, deep inside, her spirit being murdered by the baby's pain. She wants to weep and cannot.

The baby is crawling again. Back out through the open door. Back into the corridor where it resumes its wounded seeking.

She is with the baby at the top of the stairs. The stairs descend a square shaft in flights, with landings on each floor. They lead down into darkness. They look eternal but this is only because she loses sight of them somewhere very far below. There is a railing but the baby could easily slip through. It has stopped bleeding now but that barely seems a mercy considering the many impalings which are now part of its existence.

It hesitates at the top step. It is clear the baby does not understand stairs. She notices the baby isn't as chubby as it was before. She can see its ribs when it breathes and there's a squeezebox wheezing coming from the places where it was penetrated by knives. It tries to crawl down anyway and topples forward, smashing its nose on the corner of the second step before it gathers momentum and begins to roll with real force. Each bounce hammers steel or glass deeper into the baby's body. It hits the wall at the bottom of the first flight which slows it but does not stop it from rolling down the next flight.

And the next, and the next.

The entity compels her to follow.

Down into the darkness where, for a long time she is aware only of her own descent and the vibration of flesh and bone and glass and metal being resisted by man-made stone. She is blind for a time and then the entity forces her to see in night vision – grainy black and white and only directly ahead of her eyes. All the rest is a tunnel of darkness or shadow.

The baby has been falling for hours. It is thinner and every part of it has been smashed ragged. It retains its piercings almost possessively but its once-angelic roundness is now all broken corners and snapped edges.

They reach the ground floor. She is right behind, unable

to weep with relief for the infant. She would cry a dead sea if the entity allowed her but it won't. There's not much flesh left on the baby now. Mostly it is a crawling pile of broken bones, already fusing into crippled angles and deformed shapes. One hand is now only a stump of broken razors. Its toes are tiny sharp bonelets. Bones which should have been ribs grow like spines from the baby's back. Its other eye is gone now.

Blind, shattered, emaciated, the baby still searches.

Many, many times she follows the baby on its journey down from light to shadow to darkness.

On the ground level, everything is dirty, messed up, abandoned looking. As though people were here once. Everything is broken as if a bomb exploded. She is back again, watching the bone-baby, the razor-baby, crawling. The only sound is the scrape of its knife-points and bones over the concrete. The baby has still not found what it seeks.

There has been a pause in the dream for what feels like decades when she's here. The baby has reached the ground floor but has found nothing. If anything, it is searching with even more determination now.

This time, it finds something.

Right in the centre of the ground floor there is a square opening. The hatch is open. It looks like some kind of maintenance shaft and she is able to peer down while the baby skirts its edge. It's deep, too deep for her to see the bottom.

Don't do it. Don't go in there.

The baby hooks its crippled razor hands over the lip of the hatchway and pulls. She falls right behind it. It is in these descents through the air that the bone-baby knows its greatest and most short-lived pleasure; weightlessness means no pressure on its fractures and punctures. When it falls, it is free.

She sees a ledge below them. The baby hits it, crushing both its legs before bouncing slightly and falling again. This happens many times. She would weep if her eyes weren't as dry as dust.

Finally the baby hits a dirty, debris-strewn floor. It hits with the sound of splintering. With her monochrome night-vision, she sees the bone-baby lying still and she feels a welling of terrible sadness and terrible relief. She wants to touch the dead bone-baby but the entity won't allow it. Then there is movement. The rising and falling of crush-damaged lungs, the beating of a torn but resolute heart. The bone-baby lifts its broken skull, lolling dislocated but still attached to its neck. It scents the darkness and begins to drag itself along through the rubble. Its metal and bone protrusions catch on corners and tear its body open further. It crawls on.

Then she can see something ahead. It's a faint glow, rusty looking beyond the shadows. The bone-baby is eager. It crawls faster, scraping along like forks on china, like fingernails on a blackboard. She is suddenly afraid. More afraid than she has ever been before. The bone-baby makes progress towards the light. The passage grows tighter around them. Soon the baby's spikes and breaks are catching the walls above and below and on both sides. She finds it hard to breathe as the space grows narrower. The baby gets stuck at the end of the passage. It is only inches from the light. She sees it straining its broken body, more glass and razor and steel and bone than flesh now, straining towards the red-orange glow.

She knows the baby is crying in frustration but the entity won't let her hear it.

Then the bone-baby is gone. It has passed through. She tries to follow but she too gets stuck. There's a huge warmth coming from the tiny hole at the end of the passage, huge and powerful. Eventually, she squeezes through.

This time the fall is short. She lands on a stone floor on her feet. The entity has finally put her down. She feels solid, feels her own weight at last and knows she can fall no further. The heat and brightness are coming from a giant blast furnace which occupies one entire wall of this cavern she's standing in. Inside the furnace, molten rock and metal bubbles and spits. She takes a few steps back and turns all about, looking for the bone-baby. The bone-baby has gone.

For a while she thinks it has crawled into the furnace to extinguish itself forever. Either that or to live in the most intense agony it could find. Surely the furnace was the worst torment of all in this damned and forgotten building.

Then she looks down and realises she can't see her feet. At first this makes no sense to her. She looks and looks, not understanding what she sees. There's a misshapen lump of flesh in the way. She steps to one side and the lump comes with her. It's attached somehow. She still can't see how or why.

Something moves within her. Deep inside her abdomen. Buried there.

No wonder the shape makes no sense. It is the flesh of her belly as she has never seen it before. She is pregnant. The bone-baby is inside her. Her shape is unrecognisable because it is her once-smooth, naked belly-flesh stretched over the now foetally-coiled baby with all its wounds. Razors and knives and shattered glass and fractured bones made one with her. Already, its points and breaks, its shattered edges and grimy barbs are tearing through the walls of her womb. She can feel the bone-baby feeding off her insides, draining her strength. She is suddenly exhausted.

The first contraction is a mind-ripping shock. Enough to send her insane in a moment. She understands now what this will do to her. Her uterus shrinks, gripping the bone-baby, trying to force it out. Instead of beginning the baby's journey through the birth canal, this clenching forces the baby's weapons of self-harm into her body. Her liver, spleen and kidneys are skewered in the first few seconds of labour. The amniotic sac is punctured in many places and the fluid washes her legs in a shower of watery gore and mucus. The damage of its downward passage will be her destruction.

The bone-baby has completed its search. It is ready to be born.

And she will be the one to bear it.

Tamsin wakes, sweat-soaked, two fists pressed deep into her belly, biting back the scream. There is warmth and wetness between her legs. She puts her fingers there and brings them to her eyes expecting to see the dark signature of blood. Instead she smells urine.

7

The binoculars were handy but she didn't always need them.

Many of the things Mavis Ahern saw happened right outside her house or across the street. Sometimes it was necessary to pretend she was on her way to the paper shop in order to find out where people were going. That kind of surveillance was tricky. She knew she already had a reputation as a meddler. When she followed someone, she had to be absolutely certain they either didn't know who she was or didn't know she was there. She was God's eye in the Meadowlands Estate; she couldn't afford for His eye to be put out through her own carelessness.

The Smithfield girl was up to something. It was obvious to Mavis if not to anyone else. Three times now – each occasion was clearly marked on the Agatha Smithfield record sheet, pinned to the fridge with a suffering Christ magnet – the girl had walked alone along Bluebell Way, passing Mavis's house on the opposite side of the street. There was nothing in that direction worth walking to as far as Mavis could tell. The recreation ground was the other way. The post office, co-op and chip shop were on the far side of the rec. Even The Compass pub, where the youths bought and sold their drugs in the car park, was back past The Smithfield's own house.

Following the girl was impossible; Aggie would notice her immediately, especially after their last encounter. The best view she would get if the girl came past again would be from around the side wall dividing her property from the next door house. She glanced at the times of the sightings; all three were Sundays, one mid-morning when Mavis had not long been back from church, the other two shortly after lunch. It was simple then; the following Sunday, she would be ready. She would devote the day to this one matter. There had to be a way to bring the girl back into the flock but first she had to know the nature of the girl's sin. It would be the power this knowledge gave her that would provide the impetus for the girl to comply with her wishes. Yes, it was blackmail but the ends utterly justified the means.

Mavis would teach the girl about the love of God first. Then she would teach her about prayer. Right here in the living room. On their knees. Mavis would show her the way. It was time to bring the sheep back into God's pasture. One at a time at first and then, as the flock grew, she would lead them home in droves.

It seemed as though winter had no plan to end. Until the weather began to change, any kind of change, Mason knew there was little he could do in his garden.

Other things kept him occupied.

Upstairs there were two spare 'bedrooms' neither of which he used for sleeping. The larger one contained a wardrobe left by the previous owners. When he had spare items or clothes, he put them in this room in boxes. The air in there smelled of damp cardboard and perspiration. There was a set of free weights in the corner. He used them occasionally to 'hurt' himself back into his body when the calling he'd first heard in the woods wanted to speak to him again. Lifting weights helped to dampen the effect. If he worked hard enough he could stumble to his bed and fall asleep, still dripping sweat, and wake up clear and silent-minded. Recently, he'd been spending more and more time up there. The way he lifted weights didn't enlarge his muscles, it had the effect of bringing grooves and curves into relief as his fat burned. A vain man would have spent time admiring the effect in the mirror. Mason Brand never bothered.

In the smaller of the two spare rooms he fitted a blackout roller-blind. Testing it in the middle of the day with the door shut threw the room into complete darkness. He changed the bulb in the light fitting for a 25 watt red bulb. From the boxes in the next room he brought four tray-baths, an indoor clothes line, some tongs and developer, stop and acid fixer. He hadn't worn a watch for many years but now he would need one. All he could find was a wind-up alarm clock in one of the boxes. He gave its key a couple of twists and it ticked immediately. There was no work surface so he brought the kitchen table upstairs. It wouldn't be for long, after all. For the moment he could eat standing at the kitchen counter.

As he worked he found he was excited. His hands trembled ever so slightly and it made him laugh to himself. Like a kid again. He mastered the emotion quickly. This was not something he was going to allow himself to get used to. Nor would he do it again once this task was finished. When the room was ready, he pulled down the blackout blind and tested the light levels. It was perfect. He left the room in darkness.

As he shut the door his telephone rang downstairs. He did not recognise the sound. Its tone was strange in the silence of the house. A message coming in from somewhere. A message for him. There was no answering machine. The phone rang and rang.

As if breaking out of a trance he hurried down the stairs and picked up the receiver. He didn't know what to say. Finally the voice at the other end took the initiative.

'Hello? Mr. Brand?'

'I… yes.'

'Shall I come round?'

'No.'

'We need to find somewhere.'

'I know.'

'If I pick you up, we could walk there together.'

'No.'

There was a short, tense sigh. Words snatched back before they were out.

'You can't come here again,' he said. 'People will notice.'

'I don't care. I don't give a fuck.'

'I do. I'd like to live here a little longer.'

'Have you got a mobile?'

'No.'

'We'll meet then? Somewhere…'

'Outdoors. Trees and sky for depth and background. Texture and skin. It has to be…'

'What?'

'Natural.'

'I wanted some modern stuff too, you know.'

'Nature is modern. Nature is ancient. It's all the same. You'll get what I give you or you'll get nothing.'

'Fine. Where then?'

'Shreve Country Park. Off the beaten track.'

'I know a place. It's where people go to—'

'That's no good. On the other side. By the landfill. There's a quieter spot.'

'It stinks like shit over there.'

'It's a quieter spot. Take it or leave it.'

'Fine. What time?'

'Before dusk.'

'What should I wear?'

'It's not important.'

'Where is this place?'

'There's a concrete pumping station by the rock dam.'

'I know where you mean.'

'Behind that, there's a track leading off the footpath. The gate is broken and overgrown. You'll find it to the left of a hollow tree.'

There was silence on the line for a while. He listened to quiet white noise. He thought he could hear her breathing. Suddenly, he didn't want her to change her mind.

'I'll have a can of mace with me, you know.'

'Bring whatever makes you feel safe. I don't care. Before dusk tonight. That's not long from now. Don't be late.'

He placed the receiver down and stood unmoving in his hallway for a long time.

The old camper van hadn't moved from its parking place on the block-paved frontage of his house since he'd arrived six years previously. The tyres were long since flat, there was green and yellow mildew growing on the rubber sealant around the windows and windscreen. Rust expanded from several sites like a skin disease. People had made their complaints from time to time but it was his property and his car. There was nothing they could make him do about it unless someone proved the vehicle was a danger. Most people had learned to simply leave Mason alone and that was how he liked it.

The only part of the camper that still worked was the rear door through which the tiny living space was accessed. Some nights when he couldn't sleep he would take an A4 pad and sit on the dampening foam cushions by candlelight and imagine he was back in the woods. It was a dangerous pastime because it was the kind of activity that opened him to the calling. Some nights he missed the woods so much he was happy to take the risk. And, if he heard the calling, he wrote what it said.

If he needed to shop for anything or go anywhere, Mason rode a bicycle. The bike came from the recycling centre at the Shreve tip and that was the place he was most likely to go when he needed something. Winter was giving way, releasing its grip, weakening as the Earth progressed around the sun. Although it had held Shreve tight in its clamped fist this year, time was prising its fingers free. Perhaps no one else would know the change was coming for another few days –

when the weather began to soften – but Mason felt the changes in his blood the way he felt the phases of the moon affect his mood. He needed new tools and new pieces for his old tools. The tip was the place to find them.

He cycled off early to miss the traffic, cold morning light gleaming on the speckled chrome of his handlebars.

The tip was a great place. It opened at 7am and closed at 6pm in winter, 8pm in the summer. People took their bags of garden waste and old furniture and broken TVs and all manner of leavings. Most of it went into the crusher ready to be taken to the landfill. There were bays for separating items out of the rubbish; places for wood, glass, cardboard, electronics, broken domestic appliances, hardcore, soil, green waste and metals. But many people still dropped items for separation into the main waste bay.

As Mason cycled past the entrance to Shreve Country Park he was unable to stop himself from glancing in and smiling at the memory of what had taken place there. He had done a good job, a professional job. In spite of the guilt he felt over letting himself be manipulated into working again, he had the girl's word that she would receive his knowledge. He pushed the smile away quickly when he saw someone leaving the car park on foot. It was a man walking two panting, salivating bulldogs. It looked more like the dogs were walking him. Mason didn't make eye contact, he never did, but he recognised the man from Bluebell Way. There was a faintest waft of cigarettes as he cycled by; that and the odour of the overheated mutts.

His journey took him around the town's small ring road and off on a dead-end road leading to the tip. As he cycled along this road, three trucks full of collected waste turned out of the tip's entrance and grumbled past him. He was buffeted by dust, diesel and the smell of waste – something he almost relished. So sensitive was his nose that he could put a fair guess on what each truck contained.

The staff knew him and knew also that he wasn't one

for conversation. Instead they nodded to him and smiled. Mason liked to think he had the respect of the people that worked at the tip. He doubted they were very well paid, but they, like him, could see the value of all the things the rest of the town threw away. He was quite sure they capitalised on it whenever they could.

Mason parked his bike outside the office where it would be safe and walked around to the portakabin where they displayed dumped items ready for resale. He spotted a box of books and went immediately to it. Here was something more for his shelf in the shed. He looked for classics mainly but sometimes a modern thriller would catch his eye. As he rummaged, a car pulled up at the main bay. Mason glanced up and saw Richard Smithfield's Volvo pull in. He edged quickly to one side. This was a man he had no desire to talk to or meet. Ever.

The man got out of his car, wearing driving gloves. He went to the boot of the car and opened it. Mason shrank back as Richard Smithfield *looked around* before removing a single black bin bag and walking quickly towards the dumping hatch. The bag looked heavy but barely filled. He threw it in. The sound it made was a kind of crash and clink. A metallic percussion. Mason expected Mr. Smithfield to take more bags out of the Volvo but he didn't. He slammed the boot shut, jumped back into the car and drove away. There was a five mile an hour speed limit around the tip. Mr. Smithfield must have been doing fifteen or twenty. Dust rose in the vehicle's wake as it sped away along the access road and back to the main ring road which looped the town.

Aggie Smithfield walked along Bluebell Way trying not to hurry. It was hard not to break into a run. Her mouth was dry with anticipation and, for the moment, she wasn't thinking about Mason Brand at all, only what his name on her photographs could do for her. He'd given them to her in a simple, plastic-coated cardboard folder with elastic drawn over a steel bobble to keep it shut. He wouldn't let her look at the photos while she was there.

'Open it when you get home. Not before,' he'd said only moments before.

'Fine.'

She'd tried to keep the hurt out of her voice. Had he noticed? It was hard to see his face through his beard. Hard to see his mind through his eyes. She had no idea what he was thinking. One thing she'd realised: he wasn't as old as the beard made him look. And he was all muscle. His downcast demeanour and his rumpled clothes hid a lean, strong man rippling with quiet energy. It was hard to admit to herself that something about him aroused her interest – her sexual interest. He was hairy. He seemed dirty. He wore no sprays or aftershave, made no effort at all to look… nice. But the orbs of his eyes were the purest white she'd ever seen. The whites of a fundamentalist. Somehow she knew this meant his body, his *insides*, were clean and unpolluted. No cigarettes. No booze. No skunk. And all he seemed to eat were the vegetables from his own garden. His irises were a gleaming brown-amber, somehow lit from the inside. Whenever he looked at her she had to look away.

Right now, none of that mattered. What mattered was getting home to her bedroom and locking the door. Then she could—

'Where do you think you're going in such a hurry, young lady?'

Fuck. Not now.

She took a few more steps.

'I asked you a question, girly.'

She stopped, turned and faced Mavis Ahern across the street. The hag was standing on the pavement outside her house. God knew how long she'd been watching for –

Aggie hadn't been concentrating. She didn't want a confrontation this time.

'I'm going home,' she said, trying to keep her voice from betraying her excitement, and now this unexpected frustration.

'And where have you been?'

That was enough, right there.

'None of your business.'

'It is if you've been up to no good. If I think you're getting yourself into trouble, I'll have no choice but to tell your parents.'

Aggie stood with her mouth moving and no words coming out. Was this woman for real? Why did the old bitch think she had anything to do with her life? Why was she even on this planet? Her mind made up to settle things for the last time, Aggie approached the Ahern woman directly, staring her out. There was some fanaticism in this woman's eyes too but nothing like the power in the gaze of Mason Brand. He saw things as they really were. This old bitch saw them through a fractured, opaque lens. As Aggie neared her, the older woman appeared to back up. Only a fraction but it was enough.

'Someone should have told you this long ago, Mavis. You're a sad, lonely, old woman with nothing better to do than poke your nose into other people's lives. I'm sick of it. If you've got something to say to my mum and dad, you come with me and say it. Right now.'

Mrs. Ahern had lost her voice for the moment.

'Come on, you curtain-twitching bitch. Come and tell my parents all about it.'

'What did you call me?'

'You heard.'

Aggie grabbed a hold of the woman's wrist and started to pull her along the pavement. The woman was stronger than she looked but she didn't let that stop her.

'Come on, we'll go and talk to them right now. I want to get this over with.'

'Let go of me. This is assault.'

'You don't know the fucking meaning of the word.'

Mavis Ahern snapped her arm out of Aggie's grip making Aggie stumbled away. The folder flew out of her grasp. When it hit the pavement the steel bobble caught the kerbside and bent. The elastic snapped off. Silky sheets of monochromatic images slipped into the gutter. For a slice of a second, Aggie stood in hesitation, her secrets disgorged in the street. Then she dived to retrieve the spilled guts of her brand new portfolio. Mavis Ahern beat her to it. She had grabbed two sheets from the folder before Aggie could collect the rest up and shuffle them back into their protective shell.

For some reason, Aggie didn't try to take them back straight away. Here, for the first time ever, someone was seeing her as she had always wanted to be seen. It was her vanity that caused the hesitation, not the fact that she wanted Mrs. Ahern in particular to see her that way. She regretted it immediately. These things were still... private somehow. Aggie hadn't even seen them herself and now this psycho harridan had her sticky fingers all over them.

Still Aggie didn't move. She watched the vigilante's face. What she saw there gave her satisfaction. The woman was awed by the art and struck by Aggie's beauty. She was envious and disgusted. Aggie saw the flame of self-hatred rise into the woman's face before she denounced the images she held in her hand.

'Filth. Degradation. What is wrong with you people?'

That was it, wasn't it? The vigilante believed herself separate from the rest of the community – at least from those who didn't attend church or live by her painful, joyless morals. To her, Aggie was some kind of heathen invader in her perfect, religious world. Aggie took her chance and snatched the photos. Mavis Ahern was far quicker again than she'd expected. Aggie's fingers met empty air.

'Give them back.'

'I shall be keeping these for your parents to see. Possibly for the police.'

'They're mine,' said Aggie. 'My property. If you don't give them back to me I'll call the law myself.' She pulled her mobile from her pocket and stated dialling. 'All I've got to do is hit dial and I'll be talking to the police. Do you want them to come down here and interview you in the street over an accusation of theft? How's that going to look in your precious church, eh?'

'These are illegal.'

'Believe it or not, Mavis, I know the law about this because I plan to make it my profession. There's nothing illegal about these images. The police will agree with me. All I have to do is get them to come here and look for themselves. Now, give me back my property.'

The vigilante didn't seem able to hand the photos back without her glance being drawn again and again to what she saw on those two sheets of black and white photography. Aggie's removal of the photos from her hand brought her back to something like full concentration.

'You're damned,' was all she said.

Aggie snorted.

'I'm not damned. I'm liberated.' She placed the photos carefully back inside the folder with the others. She'd have to hold it all closed with her fingers now that the bobble was so bent. 'I'll think of you,' she said to the crazy, lonely woman who stood before her. 'I'll think of you often when I'm living far from here and you're still rotting alone with nothing better to do than pray and spy.'

She turned her back to the vigilante and hurried on. The anticipation of examining all the photos in the privacy of her room was only partially diminished by the confrontation. Some of the shots were dirty from landing in the gutter – those she would get him to reproduce for her. The sooner she got out of Meadowlands and Shreve, the better. She was one step closer now, a huge step closer to breaking free of this shithole forever.

Part II

'Everything is alive...'
Statement taken from Mason Brand's journal dated June
19th, 2001

8

To Mason Brand the cycle of the seasons was the kind of certainty you could stake your life on.

Predicting the actual weather, on the other hand; that was an idiot's pastime. Especially this spring. For days there had been extremes that no forecasts had prepared people for. Monday had been cold, bright and crackle dry. Tuesday, the rain was as warm and heavy as a monsoon. The chill had returned on Wednesday and the rain had turned to snow – four inches of it that soon became a depressing brown slush.

Reports said storms were moving in.

Mason ignored forecasts. Each day he took a broad-brimmed, brown wax hat and a coat of the same material into the vegetable plot with him. Under the coat he wore three more layers, just in case. In his weathered, padlocked shed at the far end of the middle strip of his three planting beds, he kept his tools and a reclaimed pine chair. On a narrow shelf were the few hardback novels salvaged from the tip's recycling centre. The dust jackets were long gone and many of the books were stained and warped by damp. He read them in breaks between digging or when it was raining too hard for him to be outside. He was comfortable in the shed, a thinner skin between him and the free air.

The days smelled clean and blue. An insistent wind scoured the slumber out of the countryside and relieved the trees of their dead branches. Between the clear days and the gales there were showers that came and went as easily as children's tears. Nature puffed and cried and smiled its resuscitation attempts, impatient for the land to respond. In surreptitious moments, when it thought no one was watching, life returned.

It always did.

First, he rolled back the wet, mildewed strips of carpet that had kept the light from the soil below.

Beneath it were satin-backed beetles and slaty woodlice, beating their legs in panicked rhythms and scuttling for cover. Pale orange centipedes twisted and writhed as if the exposure was burning them. Ants, their bead-black bodies reflecting pinpoints of sky, marched in the crazy corridors they'd constructed throughout the winter. Worms, previously safe, nosed their way downwards away from his eyes. A few white strands and rootlets had survived the darkness but had failed to grow. The sudden light would finish them off. The earth was tamped and flattened by the weight of the carpet but it was clear of weed and ready for Mason's fork and shovel. It begged to be broken open and sown. A dirty richness rose up to meet his nostrils and it was enough to make him salivate and smile. This unveiling, this undressing of the land was his favourite moment of the year.

In his shed there was a small window over which he had placed a tough wire mesh to prevent break-ins by opportunists after his tools. The window framed a view of Shreve's landfill site, beyond the garden wall of his house, far across the Meadowlands recreation ground and the brownfield land surrounding it. When he glanced up from his novels, what he would notice first were the distant seagulls. They turned in the air in their hundreds like particles trapped in a slow liquid whirlwind. In unpredictable moments, the twister would evaporate and drop them. They would fall to earth, their white backs disappearing into the camouflage of waste.

There wasn't really that much to see; the landfill was specifically designed not to be an eyesore. What was visible was a laterally-spreading volume of multicoloured trash. Each evening, the machines covered the newest waste with soil. In the direction that this solid river crept were man-made canyons – once an open-cast coal mine – awaiting the growing flood. The landscape changed so gradually it was impossible to define, even in the space of a day, what it was that had altered. But alter it did, and constantly. This kind of dumping was going on all over the country. What couldn't be dumped here was shipped overseas. He wondered how long it would be before the world smothered itself beneath a crust of refuse. Then, like a tightly crumpled ball of tossed scrap paper, Earth would spin through space, useless and dead.

He turned the soil. He read. He planted his seed. He watched the seagulls slow-whirling between the clouds and the creeping tide of waste.

When the wind turned, it bore upon it the odorous ghosts of a billion used objects – some degradable, others not. Mason's nose recognised it all. He smelled the composted tops, tails and skins of fruits and vegetables – none as wholesome as the ones he grew. He smelled greasy leftovers – inedible animal bones and fat. He smelled the soured excrement trapped in wadded disposable nappies and feared for the health of the children that had worn them. He smelled the owners of discarded clothes and shoes, knew them a little. He smelled old blood and tissues, the acid of batteries, smelled the abandonment of broken toys, the obsolescence of outdated computers and other electronic devices.

The run-off from these and many other articles, washed, rinsed and dissolved by rain, seeped downwards. Somewhere below it all was a warm, living broth – a kombucha of liquid filth festering and decomposing. Leachate was what the industry called it. This too he smelled or, at least, believed he could. It was supposed to be sealed within the landfill by plastic liners but he didn't believe for a moment that the leachate didn't escape into the water table.

That spring, with the fickle wind changing its mind daily, the smells came to him often. He thought he noticed something different, a vibrancy that didn't belong. Or was it merely that this spring was so much more eager than so many others he could remember? Perhaps he was smelling its expectancy on the air. He sensed that the growing season would be a fertile one: there would be a surplus of produce he could pickle and make into chutneys. There'd be enough to give to charity. For the moment, he was still living well off his crop of over-wintering vegetables.

He put in broad beans and garlic, leeks and potatoes. He sowed carrot and parsnip seed. He planted delicate broccoli and Brussels sprout shoots in regimented lines. Radishes, onions, beetroot, celery and lettuce made up his salad plot. Under cardboard boxes, to keep it sweet, he grew rhubarb. In their own corner, where there was more room to spread, he placed marrows and courgettes. On his fruit trees, like clusters of tiny white satellite dishes, blossoms sprang open ready to guide in their insect helpers.

Mason sweated over the land, no matter how cold the days, and his saline fell upon the soil.

The storm was savage and wilful. It was easy to see why the ancients believed it meant the gods were angry. That evening they were furious. It approached from a long way off like a giant travelling many continents for vengeance. Mason watched it come.

At first, early in the afternoon, white clouds multiplied upwards from the horizon. Like vaporous spawn, like rising balloons of fungus. The sun caught these clouds and they were so pure white they reflected it. Mason shielded his eyes. They reared up, swelled and loomed: mountain ranges breaking from the ground. Nodding at their appearance, Mason turned his attention to the earth once more, raking the larger stones from one of his beds. Each time he looked up, the clouds were higher. He stopped to watch and see them grow but his eyes could not catch the movement. Too slow to be noticed, too fast to be caught.

The storm strode across the land.

Within an hour, its bulk filled half the dome of the spring sky. Its highest point was anvil flat, the whole mass coming straight towards Mason's house. The whiteness of the clouds had gone. Now they were armoured grey and bulbous. The sun no longer beamed back from their surface but was swallowed there. The amorphous cloak of vapours darkened and deepened, spread its influence ever wider. Silent, cold-smiling, it came.

Mason stowed his tools and stopped work to watch the beast stampede his way. The clouds began to stretch over him and his garden. He felt his tininess and knew the storm could crush him under its boot heel. Every day, no matter how careful he was, he mashed insects under his own soles just as unknowingly. Even with the first clouds high over his head, the base of the storm was still beyond the horizon. The size of it drew a primitive response from within him. He retreated from the shed to the back door of his house, ready to go inside at any moment.

There had been a breeze all day, blowing towards Mason whenever he looked up. Now it died as though the storm had stolen the wind's breath for itself. The storm had been inhaling and expanding for hours; now there was pause. Mason smelled ozone on the air; a dry, dusty, charged smell. Far beyond the horizon and barely audible, paper thunder rippled across the sky. The hair on Mason's arms and legs lifted. A chill penetrated his stomach. He saw knotted expressions in the tempest's clouds and thought he could sense the skirl it was preparing to unleash.

The storm approached still nearer.

Its black base cleared the horizon. It walked on feet of darkness strapped into boots of night. The horizon disappeared. The clouds over Mason churned and twisted, boiling upside down. The wind returned, gently at first, like a hand pushing at his face, tugging his beard, urging him inside. He heeded the warning. Without taking his eyes off the storm, he backed into the kitchen.

Before he shut the door, the storm let go. It spat white teeth that bit into the earth. The after image was still glowing when the storm screamed, finally exhaling its first rush of gathered zephyrs. Mason clasped his hands to his head to block the pain from his eardrums and used his body to slam the door. He didn't move from the back window of his house for an hour.

Outside, the storm stopped moving and stabbed the land all around with crooked white swords, skewered it with blue fire-tridents, whipped it with electric silver birch. It shrieked at the land. It trampled it. It beat the ground with hammers of light. While the Earth was silent, it screamed, and raged and swore.

And though it raped and brutalised the land, the storm wept at its own unstoppable cruelty and the soil beneath it turned to mud.

It was six forty-five in the morning and still quite dark. Ozzy and Lemmy strained against their leads.

Their hanging tongues dripped saliva and twitched as they panted and choked. Their cheeks were drawn back, wrinkled into determined grins. Black claws dragged and scraped at the paved footpath. Like squat twins, the bull terriers leaned into the future. Two taut leashes attached them to Kevin Doherty, who was inclined backwards and walking forwards at the same time in an attempt to keep control. Just a few more metres and they'd be at the entrance to Shreve Country Park. Then he could relax.

Before they even reached the gate, the two Staffies were

close to asphyxiating themselves. Kevin didn't think that eating long grass, sniffing strangers' urine and running yourself to the point of collapse was anything to get excited about, but he didn't pretend to understand dogs. Not like Tammy, whose 'boys' they were.

Why it was him that had to walk them every day was another thing he didn't understand.

The car park was empty, but he still checked there was no one else with a dog in the immediate area. Ozzy and Lemmy hadn't been 'socialised' but, while they'd never actually fought with other dogs or bitten anyone, Kevin was fairly sure it was only a matter of time before they gave in to their breeding and committed a multiple murder. He knelt down to the dogs to reach for their collars but they pulled away, dropping him to his knees in a puddle left by the previous night's storm.

'Fucking hell. You hairy, stinky bastards.'

He rocked back onto his heels, reined them in and flicked them free of their leads. They shot off like a pair of short-legged missiles with spinning tails and snap-flapping ears. Into the trees, into the undergrowth, gone. Twenty seconds later there was a rustling and they reappeared, sprinting back to him and occasionally looking at each other to see who was winning. They split as they reached him, skidded into a tight turn behind him and raced away again. For the first twenty minutes or so, that was how it would be.

Kevin sat down on a bench, his knees cold, wet and dirty. He took out the cigarette he'd hidden in his glasses case and lit it with a small pink lighter. The rare rush of smoke flooded his bloodstream, dizzying his vision. There were *some* compensations for walking the dogs.

The roads wore a skin of dirty water which split and resealed with the passing of cars.

In a tired and dented black Rover, Ray Wade touched the brakes for a moment and then placed his foot back on the accelerator.

'What?' said Jenny.

'Nothing,' said Ray. But he didn't want to lie. 'Thought I saw something on the grass verge. Light us a fag, would you?'

'I saw it too. Looked like a—'

'A body. I know.' Ray speeded up. 'It was a bin liner full of rubbish. That's all.'

'We should check,' said Jenny.

Ray looked across at her to see if she was serious and knowing that if she was he wouldn't get any peace until he did what she wanted. It was the same with everything. They watched the DVDs she wanted to watch, went to the clubs she wanted to go to, hung around with her friends, did sex the way she liked it.

Maybe he could defuse her this time.

'It's somebody's trash, Jenny. The gyppos fly-tip along this road all the time.' He looked at his watch for effect. 'Anyway, we're late as it is. Can I have that fag, please?'

Jenny had her arms folded, her lips pushed forward. Ray could tell she was thinking. Not a natural talent. She was more fun when she wasn't thinking.

'What if someone's lying there? Hurt or unconscious? We should definitely check, Ray.'

'*Jenny*. We can still make half of Bodger's lecture. If we stop, we'll miss the whole thing.'

'No. Everyone's doing that.'

'Doing what?'

'Everyone's driving past and seeing something there. And they're all going "Oh, it's just a bag of rubbish. Oh, I'm too busy to stop." How would you feel if you were hurt and everyone was ignoring you?'

'I'm telling you. I saw it. It's nothing.'

'Go back.'

'Je—'

'Do it, Ray. I'm not kidding.'

Ray despised himself for not standing firm yet again. But this was different, wasn't it? This really could be someone in trouble. Knowing that, weren't they morally obliged to go back? He swore to himself and started looking for a place to turn around.

'If it turns out to be a black bin liner full of rubbish, you owe me. Big style.' he said.

'I don't owe you anything for doing what's right, Ray.'

'If you make us miss this lecture for no reason, you owe me.'

She shrugged.

'Fine. I'll owe you.' Ray smiled.

'Two dogs.' he said.

'What?'

But she knew what he meant.

'Next time we do it. I want it like two dogs.'

'What*ever*.'

He looked over, gauging her mood. Was she… thinking again? Nah, not twice in one morning, surely.

'Give me that fag, Jenny.'

She crushed the empty pack in her fist, rolled the window down and threw it out into the damp morning.

'We're out,' she said.

'Quickly. You have to be so quick. Please, Don, he'll be back soon.'

Half terrified and half limp with abandon, Tammy let Don batter her against the beige carpeted stairs. He was standing on the parquet hallway floor, uniform trousers and underpants piled over his shoes. He held her hips as she knelt on the third step. The force of his lunges, the panic in them, hurt and delighted her. He was inept but that made it all the more delicious.

She imagined Kevin coming home, letting the dogs in, standing for a moment in the doorway not believing, taking the first object to hand – a thumb stick from the brolly holder – and smashing Don over the head, swiping at his ribs, driving the tip of the stick into his throat and mashing his windpipe as the poor boy tried to pull his trousers up and explain. Sweet, giddy mayhem.

She came.

When the boy was gone, red-faced and furtive out the back door and off to catch the school bus, Tammy weighed the rumpled condom in her palm. It was still warm with his semen. She slit it with a paring knife and flushed it away in the downstairs toilet. Then, already aching for more risk and the boy's utter devotion, she showered.

In the kitchen, over strong coffee, she read the paper Don had delivered. Catching sight of the wall clock as she glanced up from the singles pages – sad fuckers – she noticed Kevin was taking longer than usual. Christ, she thought, I could have milked the kid a second and third time. Teenagers were like that: endless enthusiasm.

There was a noise from outside the back door and she looked over, expecting to see her boys, Ozzy and Lemmy, thirsty and spent. It wasn't the dogs. Through the glass door she saw some other kind of animal, rolling and struggling on the back steps. It seemed to be covered in rubbish, as though it had spent the night in a dumpster. Its weak thrashing suggested it was wounded. She let the paper drop to the counter of the breakfast bar and stood up slowly to take a better look.

The path at Shreve Country Park took a two-mile route around a reservoir and bird sanctuary. It passed through wooded areas and fields, and across a dam-like embankment. Only in some areas did it follow the shoreline of the water. Their warm-up races over, Ozzy and Lemmy now danced on their hind legs around Kevin. Tongues lolling, eyes rolling, foam around their jaws, they begged for him to throw the rubber ball. It was hard, red and heavy. Kevin drew his arm back and hurled it as far as he could, hoping to lose it in the long grass and weeds. That would keep them searching for a while and give him a few moments free of their dirty duo mania.

They raced away at less than knee high and disappeared into the sea of grass. He watched dew drops sparkle off the tasselled grass tips as the dogs tunnelled through below. Knowing there was plenty more time, he wished he'd brought extra cigarettes. Quitting was the second hardest thing he'd ever done. Pretending he hadn't taken it up again was the hardest. But walks were the best time to indulge because the fresh air blasted through his clothes and took away the smells. Between the outdoors and his gold-top breath freshener, he'd managed to keep his relapse a secret from Tammy.

He reached a stile leading to the next section of footpath and turned back to see where the dogs were. There was no movement in the field. The throw had really tested their retrieving skills. That was a joke, of course; when the pair of them *did* return with the ball, neither of them would let go of it and yet they would prance around and hassle him to take it and throw it again. He'd have to wrestle it from their slimy, spittly mouths. Dogs. He just didn't get them.

He looked around before he shouted out:

'Ozzy! Lemmy! Here.'

He hated calling their ridiculous names – Tammy's idea, naturally – and withered inwardly if anyone was near enough to hear.

On the other side of the field there was movement in the grass and then a single line of disturbance approaching fast. Lemmy appeared from the hip-high jungle with the red sphere plugging his mouth. Ozzy was right behind him. Their coats were dark-streaked with fallen dew. Lemmy stood quivering in front of him, offering the ball, wagging.

'Clever boy, Lemmy. Want me to throw it again?'

He reached down to take it and Lemmy turned away. Ozzy tried to steal the ball from his mouth so he turned the other way. Kevin reached again. They both started to bounce and cavort around him.

'Right. Piss off then.'

He stepped over the stile. Delighted – laughing it looked like to Kevin – Lemmy and Ozzy went under it, dropped the ball and sprinted away up the path.

He caught up to them a few minutes later. They were sniffing at a split bag of rubbish.

'Hey, get out of it, you two!'

Bloody hell, he thought. Why did people dump stuff this way? And in a nature reserve of all places. He clapped his hands twice.

'Oi, OUT! Come on.'

They looked back, guilt on their faces, and ignored him. It was a big bin liner and much of its contents were strewn out behind it into the water. It looked like it had burst open when someone tried to drag it out. He stomped over to the dogs, sick of being disobeyed. As he bent down to grab their collars he saw that the rubbish wasn't rubbish at all. It was moving.

It was alive.

9

Ray and Jenny left the car on the other side of the road.

Now they stood on the grass verge with the traffic slashing past over the wet tarmac. They were close enough to the road that some of the spray from the cars sprinkled their legs. Ray had his arms folded across his chest. He felt stupid standing there. People would drive by and think that they were the ones dumping stuff illegally. But he was half happy too: Jenny owed him. Big style. Doggy style.

'What did I tell you? It's just someone's unwanted crap. I can't believe we're doing this.'

Jenny didn't answer. She was looking at the elongated, comma-shaped pile of junk and black plastic as though it had hypnotised her.

'We're late,' said Ray. 'Let's get going.'

Jenny walked around to inspect it from a different angle. He couldn't understand why; the stuff stank of rot and shite. She crouched down.

'Jenny, this is mental. We're leaving.'

'No.'

'What do you mean "no"? We need to get to lectures.'

She turned her head and stared up at him.

'Ray, look at this, will you?'

She was pointing at something near the fat end of the trash pile. Ray hadn't seen it until then. It was the body of a rabbit but it was flat, like it had been run over. The eyes were missing from the head. It was a patch of grey, fur-covered bones.

'Road kill. If I stand here much longer, my breakfast is going to make a reappearance.'

'I don't think it was hit by a car.'

'Jenny, I don't care if it was assassinated or died in its sleep. I'm going now. If you don't want to come with me you can hitch to college.'

He said the words but he didn't leave and Jenny didn't stand up to come with him. Typical, he thought, his self-respect leaking away as it so often did when dealing with her. On the road the traffic was decreasing, the rush hour almost over.

'Ray?'

'What.'

'Is it me or is this moving?'

'If that rabbit's moving, it's because it's got a skinful of maggots.'

'No. Not the rabbit. The rubbish. Look.'

She pointed to the oddly shaped lump of debris. Ray looked more carefully. It seemed to rise and fall as if it were… breathing. The thought of missing lectures suddenly lost its importance. Ray became mesmerised by his concentration, his attempt to recognise what he saw. Jenny beat him to it.

'I think there might be someone stuck inside all this,' she said.

She reached out and began to remove items of refuse from the pile but each thing she took hold of – an old noodle carton, a crushed nine-volt battery, a piece of rag – remained attached to the whole as if fused. She pulled harder, tried to dig her fingers through a section of black plastic. The rubbish rolled towards her and she fell back onto her bottom in the waterlogged grass.

'Shit.'

She still held the tongue of an old tennis shoe in her hand. She attempted to get back onto her feet. Ray, watching it all, saw the bulk of the rubbish pile in a different way now. It seemed heavy, muscular. He saw the eyes before Jenny. Two tiny brown eyes that glittered. They were charged with a life and intelligence far superior to that of the rabbit they had once belonged to. With unreal speed, the mass of rubbish surged towards Jenny, knocking her flat on her back. Before Ray could move, it had swamped her legs, humping its way over her like some junkyard walrus.

She screamed: fear and disbelief. Ray couldn't move.

She screamed again: pain.

'RAY. It's BITING me. Get it OFF.'

He looked at the thing, still not understanding it. Not knowing how to begin to save Jenny from a living, breathing pile of litter. Another scream. She looked at him, eyes wide and beseeching.

'*PLEASE*, Ray. DO SOMETHING.'

Finally, the animal in Ray surfaced from below the constant haze of spent marijuana. Wrathful and vicious, he put the boot in like a rioter kicking a downed policeman. The steel toe-cap of his Dr Martens hefted into the rubbish again and again, penetrating the black plastic, forcing crumpled cans and crisp packets deep inside the thing. It ruptured easily and liquid filth spilled forth. The stink made him retch and still he kicked, fear and ignorance devolving him into a savage. He kicked and choked and kicked again, tearing the thing open. It had covered Jenny to her chest by this time but the damage Ray's boots had inflicted had overcome it.

Soon he was kicking a deflated pile of rubbish. Pieces of it flew away with each new shoeing, sending litter and paper across the verge. He kicked and kicked. Jenny pushed the bulk of the thing off her body and rolled away and still he kicked it. The eyes, the tiny clever rabbit eyes, watched him as if interested in what he was doing to the rest of its body. He saw them and stomped them out, stomped them dead into the wet grass until they were mud and mucus. Tears streaked his face and then, exhausted, he coughed up his breakfast amid the strewn trash.

Jenny was standing awkwardly and weeping in shock and pain. As she cried, she scanned the ground and limped through the scattered remains of the creature. Ray saw the torn end of her shoe and the way her blood ran so freely from the wound there.

'We've got to get you to hospital.'

'Not yet,' she said.

'Yes, Jenny. We have to go now. You're losing blood.'

She looked at him, pleading again, yet somehow still in control.

'Please, Ray. We have to find my toe first.'

Mason found the thing early on the morning after the storm.

He'd seen something moving around the bottom of his runner bean canes and thought initially that it was a cat taking a dump or a sick rabbit looking for refuge. Neither would have bothered him much. He'd have moved the cat shit – no telling what toxins might be in it – to a place where it wouldn't affect the purity of his crops. If he'd caught the rabbit he'd have ended its myxomatosis misery or put it back out in the scrubland beyond the garden. It only took a few seconds of watching to see that it was neither of those things. The colours were too man-made. The movements were wrong.

With a mug of tea he'd only taken one sip from in his right hand, he shuffled barefoot into his wellies and flop-footed his way out to the bean canes. His mind worked hard to make sense of what he was seeing but there was no context for it. Partially obscured by the lower leaves of the runners, it was the contents of an overturned dustbin, it was the run off from a sewer, it was the scum that forms over drains, the pin mould of the cellar. He smelled it before he reached it and knew immediately where it had come from. He stopped, feet chilled in his Wellingtons, right hand hot from the tea mug.

The thing was an accident. It was an abortion. Yet it lived. The shape of its body was that of a huge, bloated tadpole. He could see echoes of embryo, attempts at foetus, but it was all wrong: plastic and cardboard and glass and paper did not live, could not move. He had to be seeing it wrong. He had to be looking at an animal or newborn baby which had somehow entangled itself in waste. Perhaps some underage girl had given birth in secret and then thrown away her child. Perhaps it had survived.

He experienced a ripple of guilt rising along his spine. It passed immediately. He'd done nothing wrong, broken no trusts or taboos. He'd looked, passed time, taken the photos. He'd been professional, as he'd been in his old life. That was all. And this was nothing to do with it.

And still, he felt responsible. Even if it was nothing to do with the girl, it was something to do with him, was it not? He knew it was.

Mason trusted himself. He trusted his eyes. What he saw clenching and twisting on the fertile ground of his garden was neither human nor animal. It was something new, something *more*. Not only did he know where it had come from, he knew exactly what it was. Suddenly the calling he had recorded in pencil in dozens of pads in the woods and since then on those occasional nights in his dead camper van, suddenly all of it made sense. The blood, the earthquake, the rising of new life. He had written all of this down years before. It was a message about this time, this era. If he hadn't wanted to believe before, now he was obliged to.

Something swivelled in the 'head' of the thing. It was a child's marble, rainbow swirls of colour rippling within it. The ball was covered by a layer of transparent plastic, part of a clear supermarket weighing-bag for fruit or vegetables. The plastic crackled as the thing tried to look up at him. Then the tiny body swelled up. A split, formed by the opening of an old polystyrene burger box, appeared below the eye. The thing deflated, venting a wail of need and perdition more heartbreaking than the cry of any child.

He knelt down and reached out to it.

A moment after she opened the back door, Tammy Doherty's coffee mug hit the top step and broke into three uneven shards. Her screams started before the impact and finished long after, so the brief, sharp sound of shattering china was swallowed and lost.

Kevin Doherty took a firm hold of each collar and hauled the dogs away from the thing. They each had their jaws embedded and so it moved with them. Frustrated, Lemmy and Ozzy shook their heads, trying to rip into their prey. The black plastic tore and rubbish spilled out accompanied by a viscous brown slop. Kevin, smelling shit, turned his head away.

'For fuck's sake… LET GO.'

He wrenched the dogs backwards and they lost their grip. They spat out the trash from their mouths and licked their lips in disgust as though they'd only just realised what they were doing. The torn tube of refuse rolled away down the small slope towards the water. Kevin watched it, not certain of what he'd seen.

He laughed.

'I must be going soft in the head.'

The rubbish was just rubbish. It wasn't living. With the dogs chewing and tearing at it, of *course* it had been moving. And now that they'd let go, gravity had rolled it back down the incline to the reservoir. He shook his head, finding it hard to believe what conclusions the mind would draw given the right circumstances. He didn't make any attempt to clear up the rubbish, though. That was the responsibility of whoever had discarded it in the first place. He told himself that if he saw the park warden, he'd report the dumping. He clicked the leads onto the dogs' collars and turned back towards the car park.

Mason lined an old mushroom box with rags from under the kitchen sink and placed it in the corner of his shed. It seemed the best place. He certainly didn't want the smell in his house. The thing's weak mewls made him feel a kind of panicked accountability. He didn't want it to die. It was inevitable, wasn't it, that sooner or later something like this would happen?

The more he thought about it, the more it excited him. Something new had been born from the badness and unwantedness of the world. There was something natural in that, something logical and right. Didn't compost make his garden grow better? Didn't the grass eventually grow thicker and greener from below an old cowpat? The thing wept. Mason recognised the cry of hunger, a cry that without him would soon become the miserable tears of starvation.

He went to fetch a saucer of warm milk.

It was hard for Kevin to ignore the spilled pile of rubbish at the back doorstep. The dogs were so muddy and smelly after their walk that he'd tied them up to their post in the garden before letting himself in through the back door. The sight of the trash disturbed him. It would have been different if he'd known it was from their own dustbin – Tammy might have dropped it whilst taking it out – but Kevin didn't recognise any of it. They didn't eat microwave quick-rice for a start. They certainly hadn't thrown away an old radio. And the smell of the sewers that rose from the slack pile was worse than any odour that had ever come from their house.

There was a broken coffee mug on the top step and a pale stain where the contents had splashed the stone. One of the broken pieces was sticking into the rubbish pile. To Kevin it looked like a blade buried in a strange body. He touched the trash with the tip of his shoe but it was inanimate. Once again, he found himself laughing at the hair trigger of his imagination. He stopped laughing when he looked through the back door into the house and saw Tammy crying at the breakfast bar attended by a neighbour.

He stepped inside.

'What happened, babe?'

Mavis Ahern from across the street looked up with accusing eyes. As though he had caused Tammy's tears, as though he was a guilty man. She tightened a protective arm around Tammy's shoulders and answered for her.

'She's had a shock. Might not have happened if you spent more time here.'

He'd never liked the woman; younger than she looked and dressed, but a good deal more fucked-up than any close neighbour ought to be.

Mavis Ahern was Tammy's friend – well, more of an acquaintance really – but did she really have the right to talk to him that way in his own house? Her gall took him by surprise and he was silent too long to react spontaneously. Instead he thought about why Miss Ahern would take such an attitude. A spinster to her marrow, of course, but was that deliberate or accidental? Did she really hate men or did she just like women more? There was more to the way she held her arm around Tammy than simple shielding; she was milking the physical contact somehow and fearful of its ending. Kevin was that end.

He approached the breakfast bar and when Tammy saw him, she reached out leaving Mavis the way she looked like she belonged; standing alone. He drew Tammy tight, holding her head to his chest and allowed his eyes to meet their neighbour's.

'Thanks for coming over, Miss Ahern. We'll be fine now.'

He smiled at her, barely sincere, knowing she had no option but to leave. The woman left by the back door, stepping with care around the spilled rubbish. He comforted Tammy in silence for some minutes, her degree of upset puzzling him. She wasn't the type of girl to freak like this. She was tough, hard-edged. It was one of the few things he still admired about her.

Eventually, he stepped away from her and opened the cupboard under the sink. He took out a roll of black bin liners and snapped one free. From the utility room he picked up a dustpan and brush. As he made towards the back door Tammy spoke,

'Don't touch it. There's... something... in it.'

Unmoved, Kevin said,

'It's rubbish, babe. That's all. I'm going to get rid of it for you.'

'But it was...'

'It was what?'

Eventually she shook her head.

'Doesn't matter.'

Kevin, lips clamped tight, stepped outside.

Its wailing drove nails of guilt into his heart. Guilt for not satisfying its needs. Guilt over what he might have to do if he decided to fulfil those needs.

A few minutes before, he'd placed a saucer of pure white liquid, still warm from the microwave, in front of its rag-box cradle. It had turned its single glass eye upon him as though he were torturing it. It had vented a moan of bleak destitution that punctured his chest.

Milk was not to be its nourishment.

Crying without tears, he'd left the shed and stood in the fertile surroundings staring through the newly-forming fruits and vegetables. Pods, gourds, edible flowers, seed heads, nourishing green stalks. All had grown up from the ash and dust of the earth. All had taken strength and vitality from dead or decaying matter, from things that had once lived.

The answer had to be here somewhere. He'd never known a problem that couldn't be worked out by spending time in the garden. His eyes focussed on the runner beans he'd planted a month earlier. Some of their flowers had already formed and dropped away leaving the tiny precursors to the long flat seed carriers that he would eat. The ones he did not cook or freeze would ripen and dry and he would keep the speckled purple beans inside them to plant the following year. Generations of runner beans had come and gone right here in his garden.

Miniature kidneys; that was what the beans reminded him of.

Below ground, potatoes were forming in clumps under flowering tops. In the miniature glasshouse, tomatoes were appearing in tiny green rows on the vine. They grew from a special compost that he'd devised over the years. Dead things fed the living. That was the natural way. And flowers, fruits and seeds were the organs by which those living things reproduced and flourished.

The thing in the shed was not living in the strictest sense. It had been born amid the slime and ordure of human waste. It had come from dead, discarded things and it had crawled away from its birthplace in its attempt to survive. Clearly, whatever it needed wasn't in the landfill. The dead feed the living. That was the law. But it was an old law now. This creature was something new; nature's new vision. A break from evolution. Something that would perhaps save the world from self-destruction if it had the chance to survive. He knew it was important. It was beyond important. The creature was the key to a fresh nature in the world, a new living logic that would reverse the destructive appetites of humanity.

Only one new logic made sense in this case: a reversal of

the old natural laws. The creature's survival depended on it.

For a moment he smiled in understanding but it faded with the implications of what he had to do. He wanted to think of himself as the midwife of the new nature but he'd been too late for that, merely witnessing the birth from a distance. But if the creature survived, he might be remembered as the nursemaid of the new nature. Perhaps even its governess and teacher. He was half surprised to find he wanted the responsibility.

The guilt was something he would have to learn to live with.

Explaining what had happened had been impossible. They knew there was no way anyone would believe the truth but coming up with an alternative story had been almost as difficult. As Ray drove and Jenny held her mutilated foot against the dashboard they'd had a surreal conversation. Blood and effluent had smeared the moulded plastic.

'You slammed a garage door on it.'

'I'm not strong enough to do this to myself.'

'All right. I slammed a garage door on it.'

Jenny, who had shown surprising stoicism since the 'accident' started to cry. Ray pressed a little harder on the accelerator hoping to pass the van in front of them. Traffic appeared in the opposite lane and he had to ease off. All the time they spent between here and the hospital meant more time for Jenny's wound to be exposed to the filth of the thing he'd killed.

'We dropped a manhole cover on it. Those things are heavy.'

'What the fuck were we doing carrying a manhole cover?'

'Uh… we were… going into the sewer to retrieve some

keys. That will explain the, uh… you know, the smell and everything.'

Jenny had stared across at him then and Ray had felt a real rift open up between them for the first time. Or perhaps it was just the first time he'd admitted it to himself. When it came to handling things together, handling life, nothing worked. Stoned, they were fine. They were company for each other. Adequate company. He didn't know why it suddenly hurt to see it that way. She looked sick of him. Sick of everything.

'A dog bit me, Ray. It bit my toe right off. We were by the river and there was a lot of rubbish strewn around. That's what we'll say.'

Ray had shrugged. Fine. It was her toe. It would be her story. As suddenly as the jab of emotional hurt had come, it vanished. He couldn't wait to get the odour of blood and shit out of his car.

Now, two hours later, he dropped Jenny off at her place. She was dosed up with painkillers and he'd bought her a half bottle of brandy for the shock. She didn't ask him in and he was glad. He held the door open for her and she thumped inelegantly past him on her borrowed hospital crutches. She still smelled terrible because there was sewage all over her jeans and jacket but the doctors had told her not to get her foot wet. Still, he hoped she'd have a bath.

'Want me to come in and make you a cup of tea or something?' he asked, feeling obliged to make some kind of gesture.

'I'll be fine,' she said. She collapsed onto her untidy couch, unscrewed the cap off the brandy and took a couple of large sips. 'Don't you worry about me.'

She managed an ugly, forced smile and all Ray wanted to do was leave.

The doctor who stitched her foot up hadn't believed their dog story. They stood by it, though. Even when he pointed out it was unlikely a canine bite would look like this. He'd given her a tetanus shot and a week's course of antibiotics. He never even mentioned rabies. The doctor wasn't much older than they were and looked exhausted. Maybe that was why he hadn't involved the police. Either way, they were both relieved to get away from Shreve A&E without having to answer any more questions.

Now Ray looked at Jenny and thought about how this might be a story he'd tell his mates or his next girlfriend. One day, perhaps but not yet. For now, still not understanding what had happened and the shock of her mutilation would keep the event a secret.

'You sure you'll be alright?' He asked.

She took another sip of brandy and nodded without looking up.

'I'll see you then,' he said.

'Yeah. See ya.'

He shut the door and walked slowly back to the car. Next stop was the pub. College would have to survive without him for a day or two. Ray had some forgetting to do. After a couple of pints in the snug of The Barge had released some of the weird tension that had built up inside him, he couldn't help a grim smile and a stifled giggle which drew a glance from Doug, the landlord: they hadn't found her toe.

10

Mavis Ahern kept an eye on her street and as much of Meadowlands as she could see. Not a neighbourhood watch so much as a Christian vigil. This was the tiny corner of God's no-longer-so-green Earth where she was His sentinel. There were misdeeds to be seen most days if she watched carefully enough and long enough. The binoculars were essential to her task, as was the swivelling piano stool which allowed her gaze to sweep smoothly between the windows and pathways of Bluebell Way.

She saw cars keyed by children too young to be out after six o'clock. She saw drunken youths urinating against the swings in the corner of the playing field visible from her bathroom. From there she could also observe the space behind the pavilion and lavatories where old and young alike believed they could not be seen. She had views into the bedrooms of several houses on the street and also into some of the lounges and hallways. From her own bedroom she could see plenty of back gardens too. What others considered private, she considered her business; God's business.

Wickedness flourished in Bluebell Way.

But nothing so far had topped the goings on in one particular house, the house opposite her own in which she believed she had a friend and at least one fellow Christian. Now she knew how wrong she had been. Not that she'd ever liked the husband and his flash car nor his secret smoking habit, observed on a couple of mornings when she'd followed him down to Shreve Country Park. She didn't much like the dogs either, but in the lady of the house she saw a wayward, vulnerable, potentially salvageable Christian girl who just needed a little bit of herding in the right direction.

Now, though, Mavis merely saw herself as incredibly

naïve and, despite the dubious education her watchfulness had bestowed upon her, completely unprepared for the depths of iniquity that lay beneath the suburban veneer of middle-class life in her town.

She'd watched the boy on his paper round for months and, as plain as his presence was, he'd always been invisible to her. Then, one morning, the door had opened just as he pushed his paper through the letterbox. She'd seen a glimpse of Tamsin Doherty in her white dressing gown, hands clasped around a cup of black coffee. There was an exchange on the doorstep she couldn't hear, both the boy and the woman motionless as the words passed between them. Somehow, Mavis knew what would happen even though she could barely believe such a thing possible. But she must have been able to imagine the outcome otherwise how could she have had this premonition?

She often wondered what the words were that had been spoken by the woman and the boy that morning. What on Earth could they have been? How did two such ill-matched people begin these things? Along with the vague foreknowledge of the sin to come, Mavis also knew she would never understand the answers to her questions even if she found them. The relationship was from the realms of some deranged fantasy, dreamed up by the kind of minds she would never penetrate.

She found it hard not to hate Kevin Doherty, despite the fact the woman's sin was greater – in anyone's eyes. Even the boy seemed wiser than his years. He ought to have known better. Boys were such filthy creatures and they had no hope of growing into anything other than vile men with wills honed for domination and a desire for badness in all things.

She would somehow have to put it all straight. What was the point in watching for the Lord if you didn't labour for Him too? This would not be evangelism. It would be the saving of three otherwise lost, damned souls. She would bring them back from the cusp of ruination.

Mason tested his theory first to be sure.

There was something sacred in the act for him. He was the first one whose life the creature would gain from. He wasn't scared of the knife or of making the cut but his stomach leapt and fluttered as he knelt in front of the weakening newborn and put the blade of a small penknife to a vein on the inside of his elbow. It must have been a kind of excitement.

The air in the shed smelled of excrement and decay but he ignored this, likening the task to changing a child's nappy: it was the natural function of a carer or guardian. The creature knew what Mason was about do and its mewlings changed from pathetic whines to expectant, urgent growls. It squirmed amid its rags in anticipation. Leaning down so the drops from his arm would run into the clean saucer, he punctured his skin with the tip of the knife. Quick and sure he split the vein.

The clinical way he did it prevented the incision from hurting much. Dark blood trickled down from the cut and dribbled off the tip of his elbow. It pattered warmly into the white saucer. He flexed his biceps tight to squeeze more from the neat wound until the saucer was close to overflowing. The cries of the creature were insistent. He laid the knife down and placed the saucer on the floor beside the rag box. The creature leaned out and a crumpled plastic straw appeared from its Styrofoam flap of a mouth. The straw darkened as the creature drew Mason's living fluid in. The creature swelled.

A midnight light expanded behind its glass eye.

The studio was more like a warehouse. Aggie arrived at

seven in the morning, running from Stepney Green tube station. Most of the others were already there – not a great start. A gruff ogre of a woman had prodded her along a corridor muttering in Czech or Polish.

She and six other girls – some of them younger than she was, she was fairly certain – had prepared for the shoot in what she thought must once have been a cold storage room. The thick vertical strips of plastic still formed the 'door' between the dressing room and the large bare space where the photographers and sets were. The work happened at a frenetic pace, the photographers working to some kind of deadline she didn't understand. The pressure was constant. Everyone was impatient and rude and she couldn't risk admitting to a lack of experience. There seemed to be a lack of staff too. One make-up girl ran between the seven of them. A barely coherent boy about her age gestured to outfits hanging in flimsy dry-cleaning wrappers on a chrome clothes rail. She was so cold her nipples stood permanently erect and she had a sense the photographers quietly enjoyed her discomfort. She'd expected all the staff to be Italian or French but instead they had names like Grigor and Dobry and Janek.

She tried to think of it as bohemian but really it was sleazy. No denying it.

It was only her second week in London and already she felt like she'd been there two months. The smell of the city was in her skin now, didn't come off no matter how hard she scrubbed. She was at the bottom of the pile and there was a long way to climb over the sharp hip-bones and elbows of thousands of other models. Every one of them would do what they could to thwart her. The dressing room atmosphere was not one of camaraderie and understanding, it was chilly and toxic. Most of the girls didn't even speak to her. Aggie was horrified to realise she was getting used to it.

By eleven the shoot was over. Aggie checked her tiny

diary for the address and time of the next shoot. There was no way she was going to make it on schedule. She hadn't eaten breakfast and there was no opportunity to grab a snack. Running from the warehouse, and thanking God she'd worn flat shoes, she skittered down into the underground and caught a District line train to East Putney. She studied her A to Z as she travelled and ran to the next address arriving in a sweat.

The location was utterly different from any she'd seen so far. She rang the bell of what appeared to be the top floor flat of a very smart-looking Victorian town house. No one replied but she heard a buzzer and pushed the door open. Inside was a lift shaft running up the centre of the stairs. She was too frightened to go inside in case she got stuck. Once again she found herself running.

She arrived outside the top floor front door out of breath and knocked.

No one came immediately and she was about to knock again when a woman opened the door. She was small and dark-haired with a languid voice and manner.

'Welcome, cherie,' she said and moved out of the way.

At last, a French accent and a decent venue.

Aggie stepped past her into a private London paradise. The flat was lined with paintings and free-standing sculptures. Tropical plants and flowers sprouted from lavish pots wherever there was a space. From a room she couldn't see, a dreamy kind of music she didn't recognise wafted out.

'God, this is lovely,' she said and then regretted it. Learning to hide her ignorance was one of the hardest lessons the city had to offer.

The woman shrugged, smiled a little and gestured for Aggie to move deeper into the collision of art and jungle.

'The door to the left, cherie.'

When Aggie reached the door the woman was suddenly right behind her.

'What would you like to drink?'

'God, I'd love a cup of tea. Milk and two sugars.'

The petite woman tilted her head, her brow wrinkling slightly. Then she laughed.

'You're a vodka girl,' she said. 'I can always tell.'

Before Aggie could protest, she'd receded away down the overgrown corridor. Not knowing what else to do, Aggie turned the handle and pushed open the door. She didn't understand what she saw.

The room was painted black. A darkroom, she thought, at first. Then, by the light of the bare bulb in the centre of the ceiling, she saw the wooden rack lining the wall to her left, the chains and cuffs hanging from it. A chair with a high back, like some kind of Gothic throne, occupied the centre of the space. From its arms and legs hung thick leather thongs and buckled straps. On the wall to her right hung rows of paraphernalia. Some of them she recognised – whips and restraints and masks among them. Other items tested her imagination. It was as the purpose of some of the objects began to make sense that she felt a bulky presence behind her.

She turned.

A man stood in the corridor. His physical intimacy forced her inside the room. The French woman followed them in and closed the door behind her.

'I don't do this kind of… work.'

She didn't know what else to say.

'No one officially does this kind of work,' said the man.

He was squat and muscular with a flattened face. His accent was almost aristocratic. It silenced her for a few more seconds.

'No,' she said eventually, looking from one impassive face to the other, 'I don't *ever* do this kind of work.'

The man stepped past her into the room. He leaned on the chair back. The woman handed Aggie a nearly full high-ball – vodka, ice, lemon. She held it but did not drink. The woman took her place beside the man. Aggie glanced towards the door and the man shrugged.

'You're not under any obligation,' he said. 'Leave if you want.'

Aggie's heartbeat swelled in her neck. Her chest hammered. She was sure they could hear it.

Sooner or later this was going to come up. All I have to do is turn around and walk away.

She didn't move. Her own stubbornness frightened her. Why didn't she just leave? she wondered. She wanted more. Something was telling her she wasn't in danger. All she was doing was walking the wild side.

Do I really want to succeed so badly that I'll stoop to this?

It's not stooping, Aggie. It's work. That's all it is.

Christ. All the promises I've made to myself.

She watched the man and the woman watching her. How many times had they done this? Dozens? Hundreds?

'Seeing as you're still here,' said the man, 'let me explain one very simple thing to you.'

He reached into the back pocket of his jeans and placed a stack of twenty-pound notes on the hard seat of the chair. She tried to count how many were there. It looked like more than the agency would pay her in a whole week. Cash. No questions asked. Suddenly, she could see a crack into the future.

No, Aggie. This is not the way.

The man laid several more notes beside the first stack. A sweat broke on Aggie's upper lip, even though the room seemed cooler than the rest of the flat.

'What exactly would I have to do?' She asked.

Her words came out dry and cracked.

The man put a few extra twenties on the chair but didn't speak.

Aggie took a long drink from her glass.

Donald Smithfield was in love. There was no other way to explain it.

Being in love was more painful than pleasurable. That had been a surprise. Now the holidays had come, he'd had plenty of time to think about it – usually while he lay in bed before sleeping and after he woke in the morning.

Mrs. Doherty was breaking his balls and his heart one hot, lonely day at a time.

The heart problem was caused by Mr. Doherty, the smug bastard who could have her any time he wanted, spend all his time with her. The man took her for granted, that much Don understood.

God, I swear if I lived with Mrs. Doherty I'd make her feel like a queen every day.

He'd look after her and give her everything she wanted. Anything. Could Mr. Doherty say that? Don doubted it. The man didn't care about her. That was why she'd been so vulnerable.

Seeing her with her husband, imagining her with her husband, knowing that he, Don, had no real right to be with her and yet every right because he loved her, that was what hurt his heart. He smelled heartbreak when he smelled black coffee – that was what she was drinking on the three mornings he'd been there. Heartbreak was the smell of a newspaper, like the ones he delivered around the neighbourhood; the ones he'd delivered the day he'd seen her crying and asked if she was okay. Walking past his sister Aggie's bedroom door he smelled heartbreak. She used the same perfume as Mrs. Doherty. All these things knifed his heart. The wet scent of freshly cut lawns filled his nose every day. Even summer smelled of heartbreak.

Thinking about her for more than a few moments, remembering what had happened each of those times, turned his fifteen-year-old prick to flaming iron. It leaked throughout the day. Either he left it alone or he didn't. Either way, his leaden balls ached constantly.

From his bedroom window, he could see the corner of the Doherty's house across the estate, but there were no windows visible. He sat there for hours waiting to see her, just to catch a glimpse of her for a few moments as she entered or left. She wore summer dresses and high heeled sandals; she wore tight shorts and clinging tee shirts that showed off her breasts and behind; she wore her blonde hair in a pony tail; sometimes she let it flow free. He often cried with frustration as he masturbated. He didn't want his own pathetic, insufficient hand. He wanted her.

He wanted nothing else.

A yearlong week into the holiday, he began to grow up. It was time to stop wanking and do something. If he wanted her that badly, he told himself, he had to find a way to see her.

Gone were the moody days, the indecisive days of frost then sun then rain. The world had bloomed and now, day after day, the sun stared at the greenness of it all through cloudless skies. Rain, when it did come, fell at night and was a ghost before people began their mornings.

In Mason's garden, the fruit and vegetables filled and fattened, drawing strength and goodness from the soil and his rocket fuel compost. He'd eaten all the new potatoes and as much of the broccoli as he could manage alone. The rest of it he canned and stored in his pantry. The garden helped him cut out many of the costs of living. He fed it and in turn, it fed him.

However, there were two mouths to feed now, one of which wanted nothing the garden had to offer.

He no longer sat to read in the cool of the shed or rested there when his energy flagged – he was tired most of the time these last few days. There wasn't enough space any more and the shed-thing was so ravenous that Mason didn't like to be near it for a moment longer than was necessary.

At night he put drugged cat food out to attract animals into the garden. Long before dawn, he would collect them while they slept and throw them into the shed. There wasn't always an animal to give to the shed-thing and on those mornings, to keep it from making its increasingly louder groans of hunger, he was obliged to give of himself. The neighbourhood was running out of hedgehogs and stray cats. When Mason looked at himself in the mirror in the mornings, he was pale beneath his tan. There was no way he could give this much blood and remain strong and healthy. Maintaining the garden was becoming a struggle. Keeping the shed-thing properly fed was becoming impossible.

And, pretty soon, someone was going to knock on his door asking if he'd seen their pet moggy.

On the nights after it had engulfed an animal, the shed-thing scratched at the shed door and Mason would let it out. It would slip and slummock its way over to the back wall where he would open the gate for it. Each of these nights it went back to the landfill and returned with extra parts. Blood was enough to keep it alive, but it needed bone and soft tissue in order to grow. The first time it absorbed a sleeping cat, it returned from the landfill with a second eye and a replacement for the first one. The eyes were made from a discarded pair of spectacles and caused the creature to look bookish and short-sighted. Everything it added to itself was made of garbage. Inside, Mason imagined it creating amalgamated organs that grew as it grew. Three hedgehog livers and four cat livers to make one shed-thing liver. Each brain adding to the ones already in its ever-changing head.

So far the shed-thing still looked like a developing foetus, its reclaimed limbs made from anything it could find – old chair and table legs, the wheels from the corners of sofas, joints made of rusted hinges or ball bearings fitted into approximated sockets to give it a greater range of movement. Flimsy carrier bag or bin-liner skin was exchanged for cloth and leather and sheets of flexible plastic.

It went on all fours, like the living creatures it had taken into itself, but it was no animal. Mason could see the growing intelligence behind its glass eyes. There was a blackness within that shone from its reconstituted lenses, a depth Mason had never seen in a human eye.

As exhausting as nannying and suckling the newborn shed-thing was, Mason couldn't stop himself from doing it. There was such sound *reason* in keeping it alive. He could find no argument against it. There was something else. He was fascinated by its development. He cared about it. It was not his pet. It was not his child. It was the future.

And yet, sometimes he talked to it in mock-scolding, motherly tones.

'One of these days the starving puppy routine is going to stop working, you know,' he told it.

There was no animal to give it that morning so Mason reopened what was now a wound that would leave a deep and visible scar. He placed a quarter of a pint of his blood in the doorway of the shed and the creature seemed to smile at him as it lapped up his warm sacrifice. Gone was the burger box mouth and the pathetically crumpled straw proboscis. Now it lapped with a suede belt tip. Its mouth was formed by the opening of a plastic purse.

'Don't worry. I'm just fooling. You're meant to be here. There's a reason for it. I'll make sure you're all right. I'm going to help you grow up straight and strong.'

The lapping paused, the belt dripping darkly. The shed-thing looked at him from far behind its glasses-for-eyes. He thought he saw the corners of the purse turn upward in a synthetic smile.

Kevin Doherty realised his marriage was over the day he lost the dogs. Ozzy and Lemmy had very little to do with it and yet, without them, it would never have happened.

At seven fifteen, he was halfway round the reservoir and two cigarettes poorer. It was then that he saw a girl sitting on a bench overlooking the water. She was wearing jeans and a black leather motorcycle jacket – it must still have been cool when she'd ventured out into the morning and he wondered how long she'd been there. Even from a hundred and fifty yards away she looked sad. The next thing he noticed was a cast or bandage on her foot and a pair of grey crutches leaning against the bench beside her. He'd known he would speak to her, that something was going to happen.

As he approached, Ozzy and Lemmy tumbled out of a hawthorn hedge ahead of him. When they saw the girl on the bench they raced towards her barking in penetrating stereo.

'Bloody hell,' he muttered, knowing he was going to have to call them back and that she'd hear their stupid names. He started running, vainly trying to close the distance to the bench before them. It wasn't even a contest. The girl turned to see what the dogs were barking at and saw them inbound at high speed. Kevin watched her reach for her crutches.

'Shit.'

And then he was shouting,

'Ozzy, Lemmy, come here. Hey, HERE boys.' He whistled and watched them ignore it. They were yards from the girl who had struggled to her feet and realised there was nowhere to go. 'OZZY! LEMMY! HEEL, NOW!'

He was there but not in time. Sensing the girl's fear, the dogs now ran around her in opposite circles, hackles spiked, white spittle scattering from their jaws. He caught Ozzy by the collar and fumbled around after Lemmy who hid behind the girl every time Kevin lunged for him.

'God, I'm really sorry about this,' he said. 'They won't hurt you, honestly. They're just a bit… exuberant. Come here, Lemmy, you stunted bastard.'

When he'd put them back on their leads he took them over to the fence that bordered the fields beyond and tied them to it.

'Don't you show me up again or you're both going into kennels. Forever.'

He walked back over to the girl who was leaning on her crutches and trembling. Her head was turned away.

'Listen, I'm ever so sorry. Are you going to be all right?'

He didn't know whether he should put out his hand and take hold of her arm. He decided not to. She turned towards him then and her face was wet with tears. She'd been laughing.

'I'll be fine,' she said through a giggle.

'I thought you were traumatised,' he said stupidly.

'Yeah, well I was to start with but watching you handle your highly-trained dogs helped me get over it. That and their heavy metal call-signs.'

Kevin's lips went tight. The girl was long-haired, kind of a rocker herself with all the leather and denim, and this close to her he realised why it was inevitable he'd talk to her. Even without the help of the dogs he'd have stopped and said something to her. What was that? Pheromones? She charmed him now, as he stood next to her, but he had no idea why. She was attractive in a way that made no sense to him. Not a single stereotypical beauty-feature in sight and yet he could hardly keep his eyes from exploring her.

And here she was taking the piss out of the dogs' names. Taking the piss out of him.

'Not my idea,' he said and saw her glance at the ring on his left hand. He hadn't planned to admit he was married.

Too late already.

'Uh huh,' she said, as though she didn't believe him. 'Well, they could really do with some obedience training.'

'I'm sorry,' he said again.

For some uncomfortable moments, there was silence. The kind of silence that ought to have clarified the conversation was over. He didn't want that, though.

'I feel terrible about this. They drive me nuts those two. Are you sure you'll be okay?'

'I'm hard. I'll handle it.'

Before he could stop himself he said,

'Do you smoke?'

'I do, as it happens.'

Kevin reached into his pocket and drew out his glasses case. There were two cigarettes remaining, both a little wrinkled and bent. He offered one to her.

'Here. It's the least I can do.'

She smiled and shook her head, drawing an almost full pack of Camels from her own jacket pocket.

'I couldn't possibly take one of your last fags. Besides,' she said, catching sight of the Silk Cut logo, 'it'll be like smoking hot air. I need some serious tar.'

She held the pack out. Kevin sighed, shook his head and took one, his humiliation complete.

'Don't worry,' she said. 'I appreciate the offer. And the dog thing, it wasn't your fault. Just forget it, okay?'

He sighed again.

'Okay.'

She cupped her hands over her lighter, a pink Bic just like his, and flicked it for him. The first rush of 'real' smoke made him dizzy.

'Been trying to quit?' She asked, noticing the look on his face.

'Kind of.'

'Not many of us around these days.'

'That's how it looks,' said Kevin, 'but none of the tobacco companies seem to have gone out of business.'

She sat back down on the bench and once more leaned her crutches against it. He joined her. As soon as they were sitting, the conversation died and he was left thinking he shouldn't be there. If anyone from the estate saw him, the rumours would spread like plague. He rushed the cigarette, heating and lengthening the glowing end in the process and crumpling the diminishing shaft of white.

She smirked.

'That's quite an addiction,' she said. 'Maybe you should just let the tobacco companies take your money. Looks like you need the nicotine.'

She was kidding, he knew, and it was good of her to be so pleasant natured when his – correction, Tammy's – dogs had just scared the crap out of her. He also knew she was right about the smoking. Her simple observation had an equally simple but unsettling inference. Kevin Doherty isn't allowed to be himself, he thought. Kevin Doherty does the things his wife wants him to do and he does it to keep the peace. Kevin Doherty's marriage exists beneath a patina of lies: two unhappy people share the same house and bed. Both of those people would like to be elsewhere doing other things with other people. Living other lives. Being themselves.

It was so obvious it was depressing. Why couldn't he have admitted before?

The thoughts had stopped him smoking and the ash had caught up with the rest of the cigarette. It toppled in a grey column onto his navy blue Ralph Lauren chinos. It broke up on impact and some rolled onto the gritty dirt under the bench. He could have brushed it away but he didn't.

'Everything all right?' asked the girl.

'Fine.' He took a deep breath. 'My name's Kevin, by the way.'

He put the butt in his mouth and held out his hand, squinting as the smoke stung his eyes.

'I'm Jenny,' she said and shook it.

He relaxed then, finding happiness in this other world,

this real world that suddenly existed outside his marriage. He nodded towards her bandaged foot.

'How did you break your foot?'

'I was hoping you wouldn't ask me that.'

Shit, he thought, can I possibly get this any more wrong than I already have? But she continued and he could see her trying to save him from his newfound gift for crashing and burning:

'What I mean is, it's difficult to explain. Maybe I could tell you about it another time.'

She allowed her eyes to meet his and he was both elated and terrified to arrive at this moment out of nowhere. What he wanted. What he shouldn't have. What he deserved?

He dropped the cigarette and crushed it out under his shoe.

'I'd like that.'

He stood up and held out his hand again. Another lame-assed gesture that felt all wrong. She took it with a smile and a barely noticeable shake of her head.

'Will I see you around here,' he asked, 'or...' he didn't know where to go with the suggestion.

She was already writing down her telephone number.

'Here,' she said. 'Why don't you call me sometime.'

'I will.'

He looked around as he accepted the scrap of cardboard from her Camel packet in case anyone was watching. It was then that he noticed the lack of activity over by the fence.

'Oh shit. No.'

The leads hung there abandoned, each with the collar still attached. Tammy always insisted they not be too tight so that they didn't choke the dogs. Taking advantage of her thoughtfulness, the rock and roll Staffies were gone.

11

The cliché of seeing light at the end of a dark tunnel came nowhere near to describing the experience of soaring from life into death. It did even less justice to that singular moment in which she'd found salvation. For Mavis Ahern those two experiences were indivisible.

Now, as she sat and examined the photographs she'd snapped, she was taken back to the person she'd been before her illumination. Her old life had been similarly earthly, similarly uninspired. Yes, there had been lust, but not like this. Hers had been a lust for some other kind of connection; lust born of spiritual isolation.

Other than the occasional movement of her fingers, the room was still. Dust particles migrated slowly through rectangular blocks of sunlight like nebulae rotating through space. The room was silent. She held the stack in her right hand and when she'd seen enough she placed the top photo to the back and studied the next one. A china cup of black coffee had been cold beside her for a long time. Her eyes drilled each of the images before she moved them from front to back. Over and over again she analysed what she saw, trying to understand. She could not.

All the photos could do was remind her of the 'life' she'd known before finding her Saviour. There had been a void in her existence then – no, that wasn't accurate – her entire existence had been a void, even in childhood. She had never participated, she had only ever observed. The world revolved and its people willingly danced. The old Mavis – the *young* Mavis, as she'd been – did not like the music. Nothing in the dance held any meaning for her. Until she found Him, even the natural spin of the planet seemed powered by random, purposeless clockwork. The world was a toy, its people were puppets; the whole of creation pirouetting ceaselessly in an absurd oblivion.

Reaching nineteen without any change in her outlook and concluding her arrival in the world was equally without meaning, Mavis hung herself inside her mother's huge antique wardrobe. She didn't understand the principles of a hangman's noose and so she asphyxiated slowly rather than snapping her neck. Her body's will to survive had been stronger than her mind's inability to find a reason to keep on living and she kicked and hammered the old cupboard to pieces around her. It collapsed, setting her free.

And it was in that moment, cheek by jowl with the reaper's blade, God had entered her life. It was like standing in the stream of a flamethrower. All her ignorance was burned away. At last, she began to understand. She did not feel welcome in the world because she was His special scion. Of course she felt alienated and excluded – she was of the very divine fire that now flayed away the last of her human stupidity. Through the flames came God's voice so clear and direct that the sound hurt more than the blaze around her.

You are my child, my instrument. Love me as I love you and I will always guide you, always protect you. Do as I ask, and you will dwell forever in my house.

She'd never felt alive before that moment. Now she was alight with sensation; explosions of brightness and colour lit up death's night sky.

-I'll do anything you ask of me.-

I ask only this: Be vigilant.

There was a terrible moment of doubt. The conflagration dimmed.

-How will I know what to watch for?-

Trust me. You will know.

In a moment her faith was total. She had a relationship, a *personal* relationship, with the creator. It was like a direct line to his wisdom and love. He never spoke to her again – not in words – but he communicated with her in signs every day. Whenever she asked for His judgement or help on a matter, the answer came. All she had to do was *be vigilant* and she would see His reply. The sign might come in a newspaper article or from a television advert. It could arrive as a phone call from someone or an odd coincidence that had very specific significance. Since sharing in God's love everything had become significant. She was constantly in conversation with Him.

Though she wore a silk square to hide the scar the rope had left on her neck, when she was safe and alone at home, she uncovered it. For, though it was a shameful thing she would never let another human being see, it was also the mark that made her His child forever; her mark of salvation and redemption.

And she was constantly watchful.

It had become her duty, not merely to spread the good news, but to watch for sinfulness and wrongdoing in her small area of the world and to make things right in His name. Where she'd previously seen meaninglessness in every deed, now she saw the playing out of the battle between good and evil. Increasingly, the world looked like Satan's domain. Greed, selfishness and an unquenchable desire for instant satisfaction were tearing the Christian world apart. Morality – the simple, common sense goodness outlined by the Ten Commandments – was a fraying thread. It no longer held anything secure. God's creation was falling apart around her. Though she was frightened by what the world could do, by what ordinary people could stoop to, she stood squarely beneath the responsibility to show no tolerance for evil. She shouldered it gladly.

Everything had its purpose. Even the unpleasant altercation with the Smithfield girl outside her house had yielded something. It gave her the idea of using her old camera. Now, studying the pictures she'd collected from the camera shop that morning, she realised she was in a position not only of responsibility but also of power. This, again, was part of His message to her. Not only must she watch, now she must act. Her camera was dated. It contained film which needed to be developed, but it did the job well enough. Not all the photos were clear and few of them 'proved' anything.

One or two, however, had the power to set things straight.

The question was how best to use them and whom to show them to. She had two options:

She could go with her anger, her desire to do damage to the guilty party, and show them to the person she had, until very recently, favoured. Or she could show them to the one who, in her eyes, had done the greater wrong. The more she thought about it, the more she realised that much of her thinking was based on her prejudice against young, good-looking, self-assured men. She had to let the Lord be the judge.

When it came right down to it, the woman had done much worse and had been doing it for longer. It shocked Mavis that such things were occurring on the very estate where she had lived for the last twenty years. It was a sure sign of where the world was heading – into the welcoming jaws of Armageddon. Mavis didn't want the judgement day to come, though she had no fear of it on her own account, and maybe by getting just these two young people to see the wrongfulness of their behaviour, getting them to reconcile their differences and start again, maybe that would keep God's wrath at bay just a little bit longer. There had to be love in this world and there had to be respect. Most of all there had to be faithfulness to God's plain but holy laws. Righteousness and Goodness and Sacrifice above all other things.

And forgiveness. It was difficult to bear that in mind. If

Mavis could not forgive their actions then how could these two, who had strayed so far from the Christian path of marriage, forgive each other? Her decision could not be made lightly or without the help of the Lord.

Mavis Ahern laid aside the wedge of amateurish but incriminating photos. She slipped off the sofa and onto the carpet. There she prayed and meditated and cried for His guidance. She petitioned for a sign that would make her course of action clear.

An hour later, her knees sore from kneeling on the thin carpet, she opened her eyes and struggled to get to her feet. Numbness and tingling in her calves threatened to take her balance so she let herself fall into the armchair that looked onto the garden. There she saw her rose beds and how sweetly the roses bloomed from their foundation of manure. She saw how unforgiving the spikes of the roses were and how they all existed together in a natural harmony. From muck came beautiful things, dangerous things. Marriage was like those roses, wasn't it? God surely meant for her to do something rather than nothing and the roses were His sign to her.

A magpie flew down from her pear tree. One for sorrow, she thought. What did that mean? A moment later she saw a separate pair, still flicking their tails and rattling their calls to each other up in the branches. Three for a girl. She looked around carefully but there were no more. And no other obvious signs.

So, then: she would tell Tamsin. Show her the pictures. Her part would be done then – unless they asked for further guidance from her – and the two young people would have to mend their marriage in their own way.

From the muck good things would come. That was the Lord's message.

The drinking part was easy, as was the not turning up to college. In the space of a day, Ray Wade had developed an uneasiness that made him want to avoid everything. Including his higher education. It wasn't an important term to complete – he'd already taken the exams and thought he'd done well enough. Lectures had seemed far more important before Jenny's accident. He'd let Shreve Tertiary College know he was sick and then stayed sick until the term had finished. Now it was the summer holiday, a time for long lunchtime pub sessions. For late nights smoking weed, watching DVDs and playing Revenant Apocalypse on his game console. There was Glastonbury and Notting Hill Carnival to look forward to and, since Jenny was no longer running his life, he could do whatever he wanted.

He had the feeling though, that some things remained unresolved. For a start, he knew he was staying bombed all the time because he missed her. He hated himself for being so weak when all he'd wanted to do was to get away from her and live his life the way he wanted to. And then there was the incident that had happened at the roadside.

He thought about that more than anything.

He thought about it even when he thought he wasn't thinking about it.

It was this constant obsessing that led him, not back to Jenny's door, but to the grass verge where it had happened. He had to know what it was he'd seen. Put it behind him once and for all.

It was a different day when he drove out to the ring road, the quickest way from his place to College – the way they'd been going when it happened. Day by sweltering day, the sun had burned away all the moisture from the earth and now the verges were hard, dry and yellowed. Ray had both the front windows down in the Rover to counteract the heat – there was nothing hotter than the interior of a black car in a heat wave. He might as well be driving around in a pizza oven. The smell of synthetic leather and moulded plastic oozed from the seats and steering wheel as Fleetwood Mac thrummed out 'The Chain' from the only thing of value in the car, Ray's Pioneer stereo.

Neither the sunshine vibe music, nor the glaring presence of summer were enough to make him feel good about revisiting the spot where Jenny had 'lost' her toe. He pulled off the road in the gateway to a field waist-high with brightly-flowering rape and walked the final few yards to the spot.

A month of weather had changed the place from the damp, blood-streaked verge he remembered to an arid, dusty scrub. As he reached the spot, he slowed down and took in a long, careful view of the strip of stubbly grass lying between the ring road and the fields. There wasn't a single car passing in either direction. Across the rapeseed field a silent gang of crows loitered in the dead outer branches of an oak tree. The ground in front of him was dry and empty. No blood, no litter, no sign of anything except drought.

He stopped on the place where he thought the 'attack' had happened and giggled at the memory of Jenny being knocked over in the rain by a bag of damp rubbish. He shook his head at himself. How could he be laughing? Some other part of him answered, *how can you not be laughing*? The bag of rubbish hadn't been moving. It hadn't been alive. They'd both had very little sleep the previous night. They'd both been so stoned on a new batch of weed that they'd taken most of that sleep in a tangled pile on the sofa. Nothing had bitten Jenny's toe off. Inside the bag of rubbish there must have been a shard of broken glass, an old carving knife or razor. Shit, there could have been an animal trap hidden inside it deliberately by some evil-minded sicko.

And why was there nothing here to prove that

anything had ever happened? Because the environmental services would have been along in the meantime and cleared up the mess. A crow or magpie had probably hopped away with Jenny's big toe and fed strips of it to its brood of hungry chicks. Ray released a sigh.

'What the fuck am I wasting time out here for? I've still got all ten tarsals.'

Astounded by his own stupidity, worried and amused in equal measure by the kinds of paranoid fantasy he was prepared to accept as true, he turned away from the spot and trotted back to the car.

His mind eased by his review of events, he made a deal with himself:

He wasn't going to think about stupid Jenny and her stupid toe anymore. He wasn't going to believe in slithering hungry garbage. He was going to enjoy the rest of the summer.

His aching heart and his aching cock led the way. Her front door was a terrifying magnet he could not avoid, though the rest of his body protested. Even his brain told him he was crazy.

Don't do it like this.

Think about it first.

Make a plan.

The voice of his heart was louder. The voice of his heart commanded.

Donald's feet walked him down the stairs of his house and to the front door. None of his family was up yet. Knowing exactly how to open the front door and close it again without a sound, Donald's body let him out into the warm bright morning. His paper round took about twenty minutes. That was all the time he had in the worst scenario. In a better scenario, there might be longer but only if he didn't dawdle now. Faster than he was prepared for, his legs took him and all his pain on a direct route to her. He cut the corners off the streets, walked across other people's driveways, stepped through the edges of gardens.

His mind screamed at him to stop, turn around, go home, think it over.

His heart battered away making it hard to breathe. His throat dried out and he knew he'd have no voice, only the expression on his face when he saw her. That would be enough, said his heart, more than enough. Then they would touch – a spark to the high-octane fuel – and he would enter a painless ecstasy.

For a few minutes, his mind said.

That will be enough, replied his heart.

He was there somehow. Without remembering a single step that brought him. His chest hurt. He knew when he opened his mouth all she would hear would be the drum and bass of his heartbeat. A hand reached up to knock, he saw it and couldn't believe it was his. It was. The hand knocked an urgent double-rap on the white-painted wood.

Footsteps in the hallway. The door opened and he saw her
fucking hell
husband standing there in his dressing gown. Unshaven, bleary eyed. Unhappy.

He couldn't speak. He couldn't look the man in the eye. He was sure his face was the colour of the scarlet roses in her front garden. The man looked confused and impatient.

'What can I do for you?' asked Kevin Doherty.

But Donald heard the barely veiled 'piss off, squirt' in his tone. His throat locked.

Mr. Doherty opened his eyes wider, craned his neck forward in a we're-all-waiting-and-we've-all-got-better-things-to-do gesture of encouragement. Then Donald saw recognition on the man's face. There could be nothing worse.

'You're the paper boy.'

'Uh...' said Donald.

...

'I'm s-sorry,' he added.

...

And finally,

'No papers today.'

Mr. Doherty shrugged.

'Thanks for the warning, but who cares? There's nothing in the local rag worth reading about. Do me a favour, son, will you? Cancel our subscription.'

The words stopped Donald's heart. The paper was his only connection to her.

'It's all right, son. I'm sure you won't lose your job over it.'

The husband closed the door. Donald's legs turned him around and took him away as fast as possible. A shout from behind stopped his heart again.

'Hey! Come here a second.'

Donald stopped walking and considered sprinting. His body wouldn't do it. He rotated towards Mr. Doherty like a robot and took a few reluctant steps back towards the door. The man's voice dropped to a whisper.

'I want to ask you something.'

Donald started thinking up the frantic denials, lies and excuses. None of them were believable. Mr. Doherty was going to smash him into unconsciousness. Maybe strangle him to death right there on the doorstep.

Mr Doherty looked from side to side at the quiet neighbourhood and beckoned Donald closer. Two steps were all he could manage.

Mr. Doherty's voice became even quieter.

'You haven't seen a couple Staffordshire bull terriers, have you? They're easy enough to recognise – got these stupid grins on their faces most of the time. Thought you might have noticed them on your paper round.'

Ray Wade's days took on a lethargic monotony that was utterly comfortable and utterly safe. He arose some time in the hour before midday and would see the pile of books that needed to be read before the end of the holidays. Bypassing them he would spend fifteen minutes or more frowning over a month-old crossword as he sat on the pot. Breakfast at Luigi's café varied a little, but not much – some version of the full English highlighting his favoured fried food of the moment – and then back to the flat for his first spliff of the day. There was no hurry in any of this.

He made a mug of tea and set it on the coffee table while he constructed a complex pattern of cigarette papers, licking and ripping until he had the shape he wanted. Then he crumbled hash over the innards of a Marlboro, made a roach from the dwindling packet and rolled the whole lot into a pristine cone. The first blast of hot, tearing smoke hit his lungs like spicy fog and jammed his brain with sparks and dizziness a moment later.

When he'd recovered from the first rush, out came the games console and in went disc 2 of Revenant Apocalypse, the scariest and most satisfying game he'd ever played. There on the rumpled couch he would stay for the next three or four hours, moving only to make tea, relieve himself or roll new joints.

In the late afternoon, both spaced and creeped-out by his one-man war against the undead, he would rediscover the world of sunshine outside the flat and walk through Shreve to The Barge, a pub overlooking the canal. There, in the gravelled beer garden, he would sit and stare at the ducks – cold pints of cider taking the edge off the build up of game-induced paranoia.

The walk home would include a stop at Rockets Video Rental for a couple of DVDs – comedies usually – to counteract the terror of half a day spent hacking zombies to pieces with a sword. The final leg would then depend on which takeaway he required and whether or not he needed to visit Monkey Man for a new block of hash.

Ray intended to make the most of the student loan he knew he'd spend many miserable years paying off.

And at three or four in the morning, too stoned even to masturbate, he knew that all the things he put into his body and distracted his mind with each day had only one purpose. No amount of brain haze could hide it: they helped him not think about what was missing in his life.

It became Mason's ritual to rise at around half past three in the morning and sit in the kitchen with the back door open drinking tea until he heard something. He sat there now, halfway through his third mug, cold between his cupped palms. A night breeze teased his bare ankles in the darkness and he shivered, put the tea on the window ledge. It was out there right now, far across the scrubland, sifting waste while Shreve slept.

It was impossible for Mason to sleep when he knew the shed-thing was at large in night's obscurity, picking over the landfill for better parts. He didn't fear for the animals or people it might find while it searched for augmentations. He worried he wasn't taking good enough care of it, that it would get lost or hurt or buried out there on its own in the middle of the night. He thought of it as an orphan whose guardian he had become.

The noise he waited for was a scratching on the wooden gate at the bottom of the garden. It was an unmistakeable sound. It had that presumption to it, the way a child might knock on its own parents' door. The scratching said so much about the shed-thing, this creature which could not speak a word. It telegraphed the shed-thing's vulnerability: *let me in, give me sanctuary, I need to be safe now.* It communicated urgency: *I'm hungry, sustain me.* It wordlessly spoke of a terrifying solitude: *I do not know what I am or why I am like this, let me see you, let me be with you again.*

Sometimes he worried he was putting words in its makeshift mouth, that it was nothing more than an abomination, death rekindled into living death, trying mindlessly to survive.

Each night he let it out and each morning, long before dawn it returned; larger, altered. It developed itself. The process made Mason think of hermit crabs discarding shells they'd outgrown in favour of something more spacious. But there was so much more to it than that. The shed-thing didn't merely make itself larger. It improved itself, it self-modified. It appeared to learn as it went what the best combinations were for a strong, resilient frame. This was not the behaviour of senseless, dead matter.

It was using some of the flesh it had taken as muscle and sinew to hold its newest parts together. Corroded copper pipes, pieces of garden hose and bicycle tyre inner tubes had become its veins and in them, judging by the smell, flowed the filthy biochemistry of recycled bloods and the slimy leachate from beneath the landfill. It was a more complicated thing to look at now. Mason found it bewitching in the way of sunsets, for, like them, the creature was never the same two days in a row. It was mysterious; Mason knew what was in it, what it was *of*, but not how it fitted together. Not how it lived. The shed-thing was animate; sentient, junkyard mechanics. It was improvised biology melded with reclaimed human wreckage. The shed-thing defied entropy – more than that, it opposed and reversed it. It was beautiful and new the way the shimmering fur of a tiny wild fox cub was beautiful. It was as feral as a wolf, as intelligent as…

Mason tried not to think about that.

Every day the creature budded in some new way, reliant upon the amount and nature of the live flesh and organs he fed it. It added to itself continually. What remained obvious, despite its many flaws and deformities, was its unceasing intent to evolve from its quadruped form. It was trying – and it was failing every time – to become humanoid in shape. There were aberrations, of course – vestigial limbs that survived for only a day, extra toes and ears which disappeared or dropped off and rotted so quickly they appeared to evaporate. Many mornings the creature had a tail but by the end of the day it would have vanished.

It was no animal, even though it had the nature of an animal and the vitals and ligaments and tissues of an animal. No. What it aspired to was humanity.

Since the bounteous day that two stray bulldogs had been drawn to the food in the garden, the creature had added a great deal of body to itself. He'd come to think of it affectionately as the shed-thing but it barely fitted inside the shed any more.

And that, if nothing else, troubled Mason deeply. For, if it was no longer a shed-thing, what would it be?

The noise came. It was not a scratching.

It was a knock. A soft, surreptitious knock on the garden gate. Three taps. He almost didn't hear it over his own breathing. The spacing and the volume were a code and, once again, Mason heard the inference from the speechless shed-thing. It was a signal meant only for him. *I'm back, let me come in.* All of this was their little secret. *Come quietly, don't let anyone know.* There was something else. Something he hadn't heard before. Usually the scratching was insistent but somehow fatigued, as though the shed-thing had exhausted itself in its nocturnal seeking.

The three taps came again. A little louder. A little faster. Urgency.

The shed-thing was excited. There was something it wanted to show him.

In his slippers and worn-through pyjamas, Mason crept quietly to the bottom of the garden. The fronds and leaves of his vegetables left dew on him as he passed, raising chicken-skin from scalp to toe. He saw the lighter coloured square of his back gate and beyond it a shape. He had the impression of something crouching there and for a moment he lost all his confidence. He stopped on the paved path a few steps from the gate. Beyond it a shape moved in the darkness. There was no way to identify it except that it was no shape ever seen before. Not by him. Not by anyone.

It did not tap again. It knew he was there.

Why couldn't he step forward and open the gate?

The answer was in his heart rate, his life-pump swelling in his chest. Mason was afraid.

The silence of the shed-thing was full of patience. It was full of excitement. That was what scared him.

He stepped forward and reached for the latch. He pressed the thumb lever, the black metal cool in his fingers. The well-oiled workings made no sound as he lifted the latch and pulled open the gate.

There was a moment of mental safety in which Mason reasoned that what he now saw beyond the gate was all in his imagination. There was nothing new here. Rationality helped in this brief delusion. The shed-thing was still just a pile of trash and animal parts which crawled on four legs. In the darkness, all he could see was the jumble of mismatched structures and appendages he'd come to expect when the shed-thing came home each night. Similar but larger, exactly as it usually was.

Then the shed-thing did something it had never done

before. It moved in a new way. Instead of crawling towards him, it *uncoiled*. Upwards.

Mason took several steps back up the path. It rose up to show him what it had become. It was proud to display itself, he could see that in the way it moved, turning a little to each side so he could see it against the wall of night behind. The shed-thing stood now on two legs, swaying like a toddler taking its first steps.

Mason put his hand over his mouth to keep the gasp inside. The gasp which might have escalated into some louder expression of disgust.

The shed-thing had found enough pieces of furniture and angle iron to make itself a pair of legs. But these new limbs, although larger and longer than before were insufficient for the task. It had used the bull terriers' limbs as a template and so it stood now, only partially upright, on limbs with thick rounded haunches, skinny-looking 'tibia' and 'fibula' and elongated, front-flexing ankles. And, just like dogs, there was no way it could stay standing on these hind legs for very long. Still, Mason noted the sense of achievement the shed-thing was displaying. It had found a kind of confidence in itself he hadn't seen. Before, it had laboured for itself with a will and a sense of urgency. Here was its first moment of a more human emotion, something approaching self-belief. Mason despaired; it had built this pride on sandy foundations.

Even as Mason thought these things, the shed-thing's ungainly swaying worsened. A tearing came from one if its new legs as the weight of the rest of its body overcame the poor structure. The shed-thing's left leg snapped at the ankle. Not understanding what had happened, it tried to take a step towards Mason. Instead it fell through the entrance to the back garden, forcing Mason to sidestep into his cabbages. The noise the fall made was loud, like someone had dumped a small skip onto his path. For a moment there was silence, the silence after a child falls over and before it fully realises it's hurt. And then came a keening wail from somewhere deep inside the shed-thing, a moan of failure and pain and frustration.

A light went on in the bedroom of the next door neighbour's house.

Mason's voice was a harsh whisper:

'You've got to be quiet.'

The bedroom window opened and a man looked out. He seemed to scan the night blindly at first and as though he expected to see thieves making off with something from his own garden. As his eyes adjusted after the glare of the bedroom light he must have seen something on Mason's side of the fence.

'Don't move,' hissed Mason to the shed-thing.

Thankfully, it lay completely still.

The neighbour saw him in the light emitted from the bedroom. There was no need for the man to shout. The night was otherwise utterly silent.

'You're a fucking lunatic, Brand. Leave your pissing rubbish alone until morning. If you wake us up again, I'm calling the police.'

The man withdrew and the bedroom window shut behind him. Mason imagined the brief explanation the man would have shared with his wife. The light went out.

After a long time, so long his knees had stiffened, he began to haul the shed-thing to safety. As soon as he touched it, it pushed him away. He felt the anger in the gesture. It began to pull itself along with its three remaining good limbs, dragging the broken leg behind it. Mason unlocked the shed and let it haul itself in. He had to lift the useless leg over the threshold but then it was whipped away from him onto the blackness. He stood in the cave-hole of the doorway for a few moments listening to the forlorn whimpers of the failed creature and wondered at the nature of its tears.

12

Jenny wasn't great in bed but it was almost worth it just for the cigarettes that followed. Delicious, biting lungfuls of high-tar fags that made his scalp tingle and gave him a rare reason to smile. These thoughts gave him an immediate and physical rash of guilt across the back of his neck. Too many years spent with the wrong woman had deepened his cynicism. The truth was, for the first time ever, the quality of the sex didn't matter. He felt something for Jenny he didn't remember feeling for Tammy, even when they'd first met.

He would never tell the girl – and girl she was compared to him – but the simple fact was that Jenny was an amateurish fuck. Either she didn't like it much or she wasn't very experienced. More surprising than this to Kevin was that he didn't care. In his experience, sex improved as a relationship lengthened. It was a small matter and there was plenty of time. When Jenny was beside him, in her bedroom or anywhere they met, Kevin felt like he was in the right place. Such a simple state of mind. A sensation he didn't recognise but one he delighted in.

He assumed Jenny must have been used to having things her own way because she often said manipulative things. His response was to smile and tell her to piss off. Compared to Tammy, she was a beginner at mind games too – ironic, considering she was studying psychology at Shreve College.

There would be no more inference or atmosphere or undertones in his life. Just honesty.

'If you've got something to say, Jen, just get it off your chest, eh?'

The first time he'd said something like that she went quiet for a while. Now she was learning the art of being up front:

'I don't like the way you look at every woman that walks past.'

'Tough. It's my programming.'

'Change it.'

'Alright. I'll try.'

Or

'Do you have to eat spaghetti that way?'

'Yes.'

'It's embarrassing me.'

'How would you like me to eat spaghetti?'

'By cutting it up first.'

'No chance.'

She won some. She lost some. At least there were no misunderstandings.

Her missing big toe bothered him. It didn't turn him off or revolt him but there was something about it that wasn't right. At this stage, he didn't feel he could ask her any more without upsetting her and that was the last thing he wanted. But wasn't he doing the very thing he disliked in himself and others by not coming out with it?

She'd said she'd lost it using a hover mower at her parents' house. The scarring around the remaining knuckle was still purple and shiny. When she moved her other toes the scar tissue turned white where the bone stump pressed out from inside. Something in the way she'd answered the question 'how did you lose that?' made him think she was lying and he couldn't understand why. He didn't ask her about it again.

Had it been something embarrassing? Something that would make her look like an idiot to him? If so, he didn't care. He liked her laughing, stupid ways. Accidents happened to everyone and none of them ever looked cool. Maybe it had been an act of violence. Kevin's mind ran with that one. Had she been kidnapped? Her toe sent as a sign of the abductor's seriousness before she was rescued or the ransom paid and she was freed?

Other things gnawed at him. Where was her toe now? Perhaps she'd had an infection and it had been amputated.

He assumed that hospital waste was taken somewhere very safe and burned but he could only guess. If the toe had been severed in the lawnmower accident, perhaps it was too damaged to be recovered. In that case the flesh would have rotted on a lawn somewhere, the bone stolen by a fox or left to sink into the earth. Two small bones, one joint between them. Lost, discarded, stolen, who knew?

One day, when they got to know each other better, when there was more trust, he'd ask her again. But he knew he was a traitor to himself by putting it off.

The next time Don visited Mrs. Doherty, he made sure Mr. Doherty was out. It took three more days of surveillance for the moment to appear. He saw Mr. Doherty back out of the driveway in his BMW Z3. Unaccompanied. Don didn't care if it was for just ten minutes. Or only five. He had to see her.

He sprayed his ripe armpits with Lynx, what his dad called a gypsy shower, and did the same inside his Vans before he slipped them on and hurried out of the house. It was impossible to make it casual. Anyone looking out of a window nearby would see him, see where he was going. They would notice the purpose in his pace. He no longer cared. He walked fast but without panic straight up to her door and rang the bell. His heart was banging, fit to escape the prison of his ribs. He ignored it. What he was doing would put everything right. No more heartache. No more misery. A sore prick perhaps, but a fulfilled one. A few moments. That was all he needed.

He saw a figure through the frosted glass. He chewed back his heart, swallowed it down.

This time she answered the door. She.

They stood in the kitchen. She leaned against the breakfast bar with a coffee. She seemed to have a lot of make-up on. Her eyes looked tired. Something about her was different but Don didn't know what it was. Worse, he knew that if he was older, with just a little more experience, he probably could have worked it out. He cursed his insufficient years.

She was wearing white cycling shorts and a tight blue running top. He didn't know if it was just fashion or what – he'd certainly never seen her out jogging or returning home from anywhere looking sweaty. All he knew was that the outfit left plenty of skin bare and clung to her curves like latex. He put his left hand in his pocket to shield his erection.

Silently, she appraised him, as though waiting for him to explain why he'd come. He didn't know what to say. She'd merely turned and walked away leaving him to shut the front door and follow. He glanced from the floor to her breasts, feeling like what he was – a kid. He knew his time was running out.

'Sorry to hear about your dogs.'

It was the only thing that came to him. It would have to do. Immediately she was animated, shocked.

'Why? What's happened? Have they been hurt?'

'No. I don't think so. I heard you'd lost them.'

She flashed a look of angry impatience at him.

'Tell me something I don't bloody know, Donald. Christ, I thought you were going to tell me they'd been run over or something.'

Donald shook his head.

'Nothing like that, Mrs. Doherty. I was just sorry to hear about it. If we ever lost Sasquatch, mum would be…'

There it was. Out before he'd even thought about it. He saw Mrs. Doherty as similar to his mother in some way. Not quite as old, but still, he'd even said it out loud and –

'Two things, Don. First, don't call me Mrs. Doherty.

Coming from you it makes me feel like an old hag.'

Donald blushed. How pear-shaped could this go? He didn't want her to feel old. He wanted her to know that she was beautiful and that he—

'Second, what kind of a name for a dog is Sasquatch?'

'What should I call you?'

She topped up her coffee from a cafetiere.

'You should call me Tamsin. Don. Answer the question.'

'What?'

'Why on earth did you call your dog Sasquatch, for God's sake?'

'When she was a puppy, her feet were huge compared to the rest of her body.'

'And?'

'So, I named her Sasquatch.'

'Christ, Don, what does it mean?'

'You don't… it's the Native American name for Bigfoot. The giant ape that people keep seeing.'

Tamsin blew on her coffee.

'Well, I never knew that. You're quite bright, aren't you?'

Donald was confused. The fact that she didn't know what Sasquatch was made her stupid or from another planet. It didn't make him smart. Suddenly, he preferred her when she wasn't talking. Talking was raising barriers between them instead of breaking them down. But, right now, talk was all he had.

'Do you think you'll find them?'

'I don't know. Kevin says he's put a poster up in the post office and knocked on a few doors but I doubt he's really asked anyone. Bloody useless man.'

Though it cheered him to hear her say it, Donald didn't think what she was saying was fair.

'He asked me. That's how I know you lost them.'

'Really? Well he ought to be asking a lot of other people too. He ought to be out there now going house to house.

Instead he's gone to some bloody weekend business meeting. Probably just playing golf and drinking. Christ, we might as well be retired the way we go on.'

The whole weekend? And *she saw Mr. Doherty as useless?*

Donald jumped all over the opportunities.

'I could find them for you.'

'You?'

'Yeah. I know my way through Meadowlands like no one else. I know loads more of the people than you do. I could ask around. Someone's bound to have seen them.'

'Would you really do that?'

'Sure. Why not?'

She threw her coffee in the sink.

'Come here.'

On legs like stilts he went to her. She stroked his cheek.

'You're very sweet to me.'

Her long nails traced the side of his neck and disappeared into the hair at the back of his head sending tight, flesh prickles all the way to his feet. She drew him close and pressed his head into her throat. He felt her breasts pressing flat between them. He took his hand out of his pocket and put his arms around her. He didn't see her smile and close her eyes as she felt his erection spring free.

'Do you have to rush off, Donald, or can you spare me a few minutes?'

He tried to answer but his throat was clogged dry. Some kind of noise came out but it didn't sound like his voice.

'That's good. You haven't seen upstairs yet, have you? We've just had it redecorated.'

Ray arrived at The Barge at one o'clock and ordered a pint of cider to quench his thirst – the short walk from his flat was enough to get him sweating. He could feel the heat reflecting up from the pavement. It was a good day to have chosen his cut-off denim shorts and an army surplus shirt, the sleeves rolled well above the elbows. No matter what the weather, Ray Wade never wore sandals or showed his feet. He would never admit it but to show the skin of his feet made him feel utterly vulnerable. He'd have preferred to strip in public than take off his shoes. His favourite footwear was boots and even the unusually hot weather hadn't changed him – he was wearing the least booty boots he owned, a pair of green Converse hi-tops. A creased leather bush hat kept the sun off his head.

The Barge was already humming with people enjoying the suddenness of summer. Families with kids ate outside near the small playground. Students from Shreve College attended in large numbers, so there was no shortage of people to talk to. Ray fell in with a crowd of psychology students as they discussed Big Brother. These were people he'd met through Jenny but their chosen subject hadn't made them better judges of quality TV. Ray thought Big Brother stank of voyeuristic exploitation.

'That programme's a fucking carnival,' he said. 'It's exactly the sort of freak-show the government wants to distract us with while they levy stealth taxes against us and steal our privacy and liberty. All the contestants should be executed.'

Up until that moment, the talk had been, if not positive, then at least interested in the reality show. After Ray spoke there was a silence. Maybe it was the third pint of cider that had loosened his tongue. He didn't care. He grinned around the table challenging any of them to disagree. They were all two years younger than he was anyway. The quietest of them was a Goth chick with long purple-streaked black hair and heavy make up. Her skin was china white next to her long black garb and her piercings glinted in the sun.

'Lethal injection or firing squad?' she asked in the lengthening pause.

Ray grinned.

'What about a good old-fashioned hanging?'

The Goth – her name was Delilah, though he didn't believe that for a moment – shook her head.

'Public execution would play into their hands. They should all be made to live alone and unobserved knowing they'll never get any attention again.'

Ray lifted his pint to her.

'Nice one.'

Any girl that wore a full-length black dress in thirty-degree heat was alright by him. He tried to gauge the size of her breasts through her clothing. They seemed fulsome. But it was difficult to tell. You never knew with these Goth chicks. They dressed that way because they had something to hide. Obsessive compulsives, bulimics and self-harmers most of them.

Delilah smiled back at him while the conversation resumed and went in a different direction. It seemed to leave him and her behind. He wondered if he'd been staring and quickly found he didn't care. Ray stood up.

'Anyone for another?'

He only asked because he knew they'd all just bought a round. All except Delilah who'd arrived later than everyone else. She was thirsty.

'I'll have a pint of cider, please.'

She started to dig out a grimy looking purse.

'You can get the next one,' he said.

That was when it all went to shit.

As he turned for the bar he caught sight of a couple sitting on the grass by the canal. He stopped, an empty pint glass in each hand. The couple were kissing deeply. He could almost taste their mingling saliva. The girl was Jenny. Seeing it hit him in the chest physically, like a bag of lead. It took his breath away. Something was different about Jenny; he'd never seen her look so good. She'd lost weight, cut and dyed her hair. He could see her usually bitten nails were long, manicured and painted. With them she held the back of the man's head as she kissed him. Who the hell was the bloke?

Ray realised that he was staring and made his feet walk to the bar while the rest of him seemed to stay behind in the beer garden.

He placed the glasses on the bar.

'Two pints of cider, please,' he said to Doug the landlord.

'You alright, Ray? You look weary.'

'Fine, Doug. Too much sun probably.'

'Too much cider, more like.'

Ray squeezed off a smile and made an announcement.

'Today, cider will be the cure for my weariness.'

It was as hollow as it sounded. Doug ignored him while he pulled the drinks.

Outside, Ray handed Delilah her drink and took his seat at the other end of the table. But now he was morose and he knew it showed on his face. He wanted to flirt with Delilah but suddenly he didn't have it in him. He stamped the sparks out by avoiding her gaze and ignoring her comments. His contribution to the chat around the table dried to a trickle. He surrendered himself to the larynx-ripping chill of the cider a mouthful at a time, welcomed its effect.

This is my habit, my coping mechanism, my panic room. And it fucking works.

He slipped into the safe alcoholic mind-fog a little deeper than usual for a lunchtime session but he didn't care. There was nothing important that needed to be done. Not thinking about Jenny was hard; the image of her face welded to the face of a stranger wouldn't quite leave him alone. He grunted his way through the next hour, only half paying attention to what was said. Then, very suddenly it seemed to him, the group was breaking up and leaving. He looked at his watch. It was almost three.

Rather than putting her off, Ray's ignorance of Delilah had served to make her more determined to connect with him. When everyone else had gone, she reappeared from the pub and sat next to him.

'You look fucked, Raymond.'

'No one calls me Raymond. It's Ray.'

'So, you *are* fucked then, I take it.'

'I'm on my way.'

'Fancy a joint somewhere?'

Ray focussed. The girl was talking his sweet holiday language. Immediately, he realised she probably knew his reputation – that he always had a decent sized stash. She was just in it for a free toke.

'Why not?' he asked. And then, testing her, 'What've you got?'

'Some nice sticky buds from my mate on the Crowthorns estate.'

Crowthorns? This was a dealer Ray hadn't heard of. Even though he was fairly drunk he took in the information and retained it. Some things had importance. This was one of those things.

'Sounds good to me. Where shall we go?'

'Outside, I was thinking. It's too nice for indoors.'

'That's fairly radical thinking for a Goth, isn't it? Aren't you allergic to the rays of the sun? Turn to dust or something?'

Delilah's disappointment was plain. She looked like she was thinking about leaving.

'I didn't think you'd be one to judge by looks alone. Not like everyone else. Was I wrong about that?'

'Hey, come on. I'm not serious.' He smiled crookedly. 'I mean look at me. Do I look like the sort of person I look like?'

'You sure you won't pass out? This weed is really strong stuff.'

'I bet I've had stronger. I'll be fine.'

He watched her a little unsteadily for a few seconds, not caring how obvious was his stare. She seemed to make up her mind.

'Okay,' she said. 'Let's go.'

'Great.'

Ray stood up from the bench and swayed pleasantly. He had made full contact with the cider goddess and he loved her.

They walked around the outside of the pub to leave and Ray couldn't resist scanning the grassy bank for Jenny. She wasn't there. The thought of her made him so totally miserable he could barely feel the sunshine.

I'm not going to let you spoil my day, Jenny. Or my summer. I never cared about you that much.

He straightened himself, tried to walk with assured steps and failed within a few yards. He giggled.

'Hey, where did you say we were going?' He asked.

'I didn't.'

'Fine. Where *are* we going?'

'Into nature. I know a lovely spot where no one ever goes.'

'Cool,' said Ray. 'Supercool.'

Tammy had always thought of Mavis as a sweet, well-meaning old lady. A little bit lonely, a little bit dotty, perhaps, but otherwise harmless and always nice to have around for a cup of coffee and a chat. She was even able to ignore the occasional evangelical hint in return for some harmless company. Recently, however, Tammy had noticed that the woman had begun to look tight of face, sharper somehow, and more intense. The word fanatical sprung to mind. There were rumours of disputes in the street with neighbours and more than one tale of Mavis being seen at her window with a pair of binoculars. Apparently she'd tried to drag some local youths to church. Physically.

The obvious conclusion was that the lonely, dreary hag was losing it. Everyone who mentioned her now believed Mavis to be, at the very least, a little cracked.

At first Tammy couldn't help but feel sorry for the woman. Mavis was still young really, even though she neither looked nor acted as though she was. She didn't appear to have any family nearby and if she really was developing some kind of mental problem there wouldn't be anyone to look after her. She'd probably end up drooling and ignored by under-paid, under-trained staff in some psychiatric ward with rotting mortar and peeling green paint.

It was a sad thought. It made Tammy think carefully for the first time about what she would do in those circumstances. Something similar would probably happen to her when she got old. Everyone seemed to end up in some kind of 'care' home. Would she even know she was losing her wits or did crazy people hold on to the belief that they were sane even when their minds were porridge? It was too terrifying and depressing to contemplate. Especially because Tammy knew she would never allow herself to have children.

So, when Mavis knocked on her door one morning while Kevin was out, Tammy was all welcomes and smiles.

'Good morning to you, Tamsin,' Mavis said on the doorstep. 'Might I have a word?'

'Of course. Come in and have some coffee. I've been wondering how you've been. Seems ages since we had a nice chin-wag.'

Tammy caught the look on Mavis's face. Sternness wavering and then returning. She didn't understand it.

As brightly as she could, Tammy said,

'Seat at the breakfast bar or a comfy chair in the lounge, Mavis?'

'Oh…'

The hesitation went on as Mavis followed her through the hall. They both ended up in the kitchen while Tammy put the kettle on. So the decision was made.

As she took out cups (always with saucers for Mavis) and brought out the real coffee and the cafetiere, she wondered what to say.

Mavis took care of that.

'I've brought you something, my dear,' she said and placed a large, recycled brown envelope on the breakfast counter.

'That looks exciting. Shall I open it now?'

'Why don't you wait until you've got your cup of coffee?'

Again, Mavis's expression didn't match the words coming out of her mouth and suddenly, Tammy realised that this probably wasn't going to be a pleasant morning of coffee and chit-chat. It would be the strain of talking to a woman who was adrift from her mental moorings. She chided herself for being so selfish. Mavis had always been a caring support for her – even though Tammy was independent enough not to need anyone's support – and the strange woman had no one else. She would make the most of their time together. Her sudden charitable feelings surprised her.

'Here you are, Mavis.'

She placed everything on the breakfast bar between them and sat opposite. She even put out the special ginger shortbread biscuits she usually reserved for herself. Then she reached for the envelope, slid a table knife under the flap and slit it open in one deft swipe. She tipped the contents onto the counter.

Snapshots of her and the boy. Not explicit but explicit enough. Her face flamed.

'I don't understand, Mavis. What is all this?'

'I would have thought that was obvious.'

'But why? Who took these and where did you…'

Christ, it's her. She's *done this.*

No. It couldn't be. Not sweet, quaint Mavis from across the street.

Across the street.

That was where the photos had been taken from. Shots of the front door and hallway. Shots of the bedroom.

'You're a jezebel, Tamsin. A Babylon whore. I've been so wrong about you. It hurts me to think I've spent time trusting a woman capable of this kind of deceit. This kind of… *filth.*'

It was a moment or two before Tamsin replied. The volume and pitch of her voice rising as she found her words.

'Don't you judge me, Mavis. Don't you come into my house and pass judgement on my life. What about you? How many people have you spied on? How many dirty little secrets are you party to? Do you get off on it, Mavis? Is it because you've got no one to talk to? Christ, I don't care if you do end up locked in some dungeon for the insane. How dare you come round here and do this as though you're some kind of moral watchdog? You're just a sad, curtain-twitching nutter looking for a way of getting some kicks.'

Tammy threw the pictures across the breakfast bar.

'Take these and fuck off, you depraved cow.'

She stood up and walked round the counter to Mavis's seat. The woman looked shocked. The fingers of one hand fluttered at the silk neck scarf she always wore. She looked frightened and Tammy was glad. Tammy pointed to the front door.

'Out. And don't come back.'

Mavis cleared her throat but didn't move.

'I think you should listen to me before you turn your back on this.'

'I'm not listening to another word from you, Mavis Ahern. You're not welcome here any more.'

'I'm going to tell your husband, Tamsin. I've got the letter ready to give to him.'

Tammy exploded.

'You do that and I'll fucking kill you.'

She turned away and drew a carving knife out of the wooden block beside the sink. She held the point in Mavis's face.

When the doorbell rang, Mason was in his back garden as usual. He wouldn't have heard it if he hadn't been bending down to the outside tap for a drink of water.

The sun was high and even though he was only checking things over in the vegetable plot, he was sweating. People didn't come calling at his house too often. Perhaps a pair of Jehovah's Witnesses – Jehovah's Nitwits he called them; to their faces if they hung around too long – or the occasional cold-caller who hadn't heard to keep away.

Now he had more reasons to turn people away than simply not being a 'people person'.

The doorbell rang a second time. He shrugged to himself and walked quietly along the side pathway to the front of the house. He wasn't pleased to see a teenager from the estate dressed in baggy cargo trousers and unlaced skateboard trainers. The kid had a fervent look, determined somehow, and Mason immediately wondered if he was out of his head on drugs or desperate for the money to buy some more. But Mason wasn't scared of the boy. He was a tall man and strong from all his garden labour and lifting free weights. Strong from the pure, simple food he ate and the outdoor air he breathed. Not like these burger-eating, computer-fixated kids with nothing but slackness in their muscles and no hint of steel in their bones.

'What are you doing here, boy?'

The kid jumped, not knowing he'd been observed.

'Sorry to bother you, Mr. Brand. I'm looking for two stray dogs. Staffordshire bull terriers, they are. Have you seen them?'

'How do you know my name?'

'I deliver your papers. Post office always writes your name in the top corner. Have you seen the dogs? Two brindles called Ozzy and Lemmy.'

Mason acted like he was thinking about it.

'Why do you want to know?' he asked. 'They your dogs?'

The kid looked exasperated.

'No. They belong to Mrs. Doherty at the other end of Bluebell Way. I said I'd ask around.' The kid was losing interest and turned to go. 'If you do see them, maybe you could let her know. She lives at number twenty-seven.'

Mason let the boy get back onto the pavement before he spoke.

'Didn't have any collars on, did they? Shouldn't let dogs out like that.'

'You've seen them, then?'

'People who don't look after animals properly shouldn't be allowed to keep them, I reckon.'

The boy walked back towards him. He seemed unusually committed for a youngster, unusually concerned.

'They haven't been hurt, have they? Tam... Mrs. Doherty'll be heartbroken if anything's happened to them.'

Mason opened the gate to the side walkway of the house and sauntered away into his back garden. He heard the kid scuffing along behind him, lace tips clicking and bouncing along the flagstones.

'Have you got them back here?' The boy asked.

Mason walked down through the rows of leafy

vegetables to the shed that was now partially obscured by a small square of tall maize plants. He reached into his pocket and took out a key, jiggled it into a heavy old padlock on the shed door and snapped it open. Inside there was heavy movement and scratching. The boy heard it too.

'Blimey,' said the kid. 'Managed to catch them, did you? That can't have been easy. They're a real handful that pair.'

'See for yourself,' said Mason and opened the shed door a few inches.

It was midday, the sun almost overhead and bright enough that they were both squinting. Mason knew the kid couldn't see what was in the gloom of the shed. He would see what Mason saw, something moving in the shadowed space.

13

The snapshots Kevin found in the large envelope were poor quality and rushed-looking. He studied them whilst sitting at the breakfast bar with a cup of coffee. Some of them were smeared by movement. Others had out-of-focus leaves, branches or other objects in the near view, partially obscuring the two figures beyond. They weren't going to win any photographic competitions.

But they were meticulous and they were telling. Somehow, the inexpert handling lent authenticity to the secret moments the camera had stolen. They were secret no longer.

Kevin stared at the shots of him sitting with his arm around Jenny Chapman on the bench in Shreve Country Park. Holding hands over a table at The Barge. A kiss – on the lips – beside his BMW. There were no images more intimate than that but, taken together, it was enough.

What he noticed most strikingly was the ease of their togetherness. Unless he was imagining it, it came through even in these hurried photos. The pictures made him realise something he hadn't been able to fully admit before he'd seen them. He wanted Jenny, wanted to be with her, and he was ready to do anything to make that happen.

There was also a letter in the brown envelope, written in a fastidiously neat style. Certain he was being blackmailed for money, he hadn't understood it at first. The letter implored him to see the sin in what he was doing. It told him he was one diseased microbe in a world drowned by a moral plague. Did he not understand the seriousness of the vows he'd made in the sight of God? Did he not realise what would become of his soul? The letter told him to confess everything to his wife, end the affair and make good on his marriage vows. If he did not tell Tamsin, she would be the next to receive a brown envelope.

He had to read it three times before he realised there was no demand for money or anything else. The letter said he was not alone in sinning and that he would find out why soon enough.

It was signed Mavis Ahern.

Kevin folded the letter in half and replaced it and the photos inside the envelope. It was pure luck that he'd been there when the post arrived and Tamsin had been out. Otherwise she'd have opened his mail for him like she always did. The photos weren't a bad thing. Not a bad thing at all. In the space of a few minutes, they'd helped him make a very simple decision.

He took out a pack of Camels – no more low-tar nonsense – and lit one with his pink Bic. The kitchen filled with smoke. He flicked the ash into his half-full coffee cup and waited.

She'd taken his hand somewhere along the way and it struck him as a gesture of innocence. He imagined how they looked together, him in his shorts and hi-tops and hat and her in her long dark gowns, her piercings concentrating the sun to bright pinpoints.

We make it look as though love transcends boundaries.

He smiled to himself.

I must be really drunk.

She didn't speak much as they walked and Ray was so relaxed with the drink and the heat that he didn't feel uncomfortable. Sometimes he looked to the side to take in her strangeness again, to remind himself who he was walking with. It was very clear he didn't know who she was at all. He didn't care. The near anonymity of it was exciting. In those moments she would look back at him, quite unashamedly assessing his eyes and they would both smile. That was enough for Ray to be happy. If that was to be the extent of their afternoon together it would be a very simple and good thing.

Tomorrow, he already knew, much if not all of this walk would be unremembered history, at least on his part, so he sank himself into their shared moments totally like a man stopping swimming and letting himself sink to the bottom of a lake. There on the bottom, he found he could still breathe.

They passed people and shops and the ends of streets and old Victorian houses and estates. They walked along A roads then B roads and then on rural footpaths and finally, as an agitation began to niggle Ray's booze-soaked nerves, they were in a wood. She'd passed through a stretched gap in a badly-maintained barbed-wire fence, holding her skirts and sleeves about herself to avoid tearing her clothes. Ray stooped and followed.

The noise from the road receded. Soon Ray could hear nothing but the sound of their footsteps on the brittle grass and last year's desiccated oak leaves. Much of their progress involved crouching or pushing branches out of the way and it took only seconds for Ray to be lost. Pleasantly so. It was like being on an alien world. He felt a euphoria he knew it would be difficult to recreate and he realised that coming here in the future – if they had any kind of future together – would never again be the surprise it was turning out to be. Imagine, he thought, a Goth out here in all this free air, this absence of all things urban. As he watched her creep between trees, over fallen logs and under branches, he saw that she fitted this landscape. She looked like a witch in her natural habitat; the wilds.

They stopped in a tiny clearing, not much bigger than a room in a house. It was an accidental den, it seemed, where there was nothing but grass – dry and yellow, with the ground showing through its bald patches. Five twisted oaks formed the perimeter and between them high bushes of sloe and hawthorn.

'Nice place you have here,' said Ray.

'I'm trusting you not to tell anyone about this,' she said. 'It's a secret.'

He dropped to his haunches and collapsed against a tree. His feet were hot in his All Stars. He decided to remove the canvas boots, hesitating only for a moment when he realised this would leave him exposed.

'Do they stink?' she asked.

He shrugged.

'Not really. I'm a nice clean boy.'

'That's a shame.'

'I'm easily influenced.'

Delilah grinned and then turned away. She knelt with her head in the bushes. There was a shaking and rustling of branches.

She dragged an old wooden ammunition crate into the clearing.

'Where'd you find that?' he asked.

'Same place you got your shirt. Army surplus.'

'What's in it?'

'Luxuries. You'll see.'

She brought out a couple of tartan car blankets with ragged edges, an opened, half-empty bottle of vodka and two cushions.

Ray was impressed.

'You're a woman of… hidden attributes,' he said.

'You don't know the half of it.'

The last item out of the crate was a clear plastic bag scrolled into a neat cigar and secured with rubber bands. She unfurled it and handed it to Ray. He inhaled the aroma of the contents with his eyes closed.

'Bloody hell,' he said. 'that is fresh and strong and good in the extreme. Want me to skin up?'

'I prefer a pipe. Got one in my bag. You don't mind do you?'

'Not at all. Long as I don't go comatose.'

'It'll give you a serious kick in the head but you've had a chance to sober up a bit after the walk. I think you'll manage.'

'I will, I will. I will manage.'

From her velvet patchwork handbag, she withdrew a short, olive-wood pipe. It was intricately decorated with tiny figures. The way she handled the pipe was reverential.

'What are the carvings?' He asked.

'They're tree spirits.'

Tree spirits. Right.

She loaded the pipe with the sticky-looking weed, put a lighter to it and took a long toke deep into her lungs. She coughed but managed to hold on to all but a single snort of smoke that puffed from her nostrils. She passed Ray the pipe and he followed her lead.

The grass vapour rose up like a cobra and bit him in the mind. For a few moments he came loose from his body and soared. Soon the rush settled and he felt the vibration extend to the tips of his toes and fingers. His head cleared and the drunk was suddenly gone, replaced by clear-sighted, enhanced awareness.

'Enlightening,' he said.

'Isn't it.'

They sat on the blankets with the cushion behind them propped against a squat oak. She took his hand again and it seemed he could feel her communicating with him from her aura to his. They turned towards each other and kissed with taser lips, sparking tongues. Delilah came alive. She pushed away from the tree and swung a heavily skirted leg over Ray's lap. Kneeling there she kissed him harder, inhaled him as though he were the magic smoke. He was shocked to begin with. This was not what he was used to. This was not Jenny, waiting for him to make a move before anything would happen. This was a woman who desired. Delilah needed. He could taste it in her saliva – a clean elixir on his tongue. He could feel it on her bloated lips and in the heat that seeped from her crotch. She was confident of her sexuality, easy in her longing, fluid in her drawing.

Her garments became a restriction and she struggled against the clinging length of her dress, the numbness of her spurred motorcycle boots. She stood up from Ray and caught hold of the dress's hem, lifting it and freeing herself. She flung it to the dusty grass and stood naked before him. Black at the armpits, black at the crotch, black at her boots. Ray stared at the dark manliness of her sexual hair and the paleness of her strong hips and heavy breasts. His erection crystallised into hot glass.

Delilah took her boots off and she was the witch of the woods then, still pulling him in with her eyes.

'I'm going to come just looking at you,' he said.

She knelt between his legs and cupped a hand to the seam of his shorts.

'Judging by the size of your bollocks, that's not going to be a problem.'

She helped him undress.

There was a thing in Mr. Brand's shed, something twice the size of a man with the face and jaws of a dog. Donald wasted precious seconds trying to understand what he was seeing and in that time, the thing rose from a crouch to a hunched standing position. It placed a limb against one wall to support itself. It was taller than him but looked crippled and thin. Donald knew the difference between real and imaginary, between the living and the dead but this creature, this beast, didn't fit any category.

The thing in the shed looked like a child's primary school project, a collage of useless, broken items. It was the melding of animal flesh and bone with the flotsam of the dump. Tiny veins ran into hollow electrical flex then disappeared beneath fur or bristle or skin. The hollow legs of plastic classroom chairs made for its femurs, hundreds of tiny mammalian ribs bound with wire formed the cavern of its chest. Coils of innards pulsated within – all visible because there was not enough skin to conceal it. Flattened rusted cans were its shoulder blades. The eyes and jaws of a dog protruded from the front of its amalgamated skull.

Mr. Brand had definitely seen the Staffies.

The thing made the insistent snuffles and squeaks of foraging animals. It creaked and grinded as it moved its improvised joints. It smelled of diseased excrement, of bleach and ammonia, of sulphur and dried blood.

A hand made of an old weeding fork took hold of Donald's throat so tightly he could neither scream nor breathe. It was far stronger and quicker than he could have anticipated. A desperate intelligence forced itself out through the insufficient eyes of the dogs and searched his face, scanned his body. The expression of the thing was one of utter desperation and yearning. It was single-minded and yet it was contrite.

For a moment, Donald wondered why such a tormented thing would ever feel such remorse. It was only for a moment.

The hand forced him down to the splintered, dirt-covered floor of the shed.

Donald saw Mr. Brand's bearded face looking in through the mesh-covered window with his hands cupped around his eyes to keep out the brightness of the afternoon sun. It was all too unreal to make any impact on Donald. It had happened so quickly and was so outside his experience of the world that he was still waiting for it all to end as a practical joke or, at worst, some sick lesson Mr. Brand wanted to teach the youths of the community by making an example of him.

He only accepted the reality of the situation when the

thing in the shed began taking him apart.

Mason watched the creature pinion the boy on the floor.

There were long moments in which the shed-thing assessed and gauged the supine teenager. Its cobbled-together skull, reminiscent of a dog's but moving in some robotic imitation of a human head, swept up and down the length of Donald Smithfield's body, making calculations Mason didn't want to guess at. The shed-thing was frantic to perceive the bounty it had received but it did not yet possess the organs necessary to fully sense its captive. Its inadequate eyes roved and explored face and neck and chest and limbs while the boy silently choked in its grip. It sniffed the boy too, eager to measure the wealth of materials his body might offer.

It stopped for a moment and turned its head up towards the window to meet its guardian's stare. Never yet had Mason seen so much life behind those eyes, so much intelligence and potential. The shed-thing was on the cusp of becoming, perhaps in the way the boy must have been close to becoming a man. The shed-thing nodded to Mason, or perhaps it was more of a bow. In thanks, in deference, in awe.

It sheared off Donald Smithfield's left hand with filth-dripping bolt cutters which unfolded from its chest. Its own fork hand had the boy's throat so tight he was barely breathing; nothing more than a high-pitched rasp escaped the boy's mouth. But no grip was strong enough to stop the expression of shock and agony creasing the boy's face as he felt his hand severed.

The moment it separated, the shed-thing forced the bleeding stump into its own chest. Its entire body appeared to expand. The boy went pale, his eyes widened. Mason saw Donald's thoughts playing out for a long time in those perfect irises, irises which screamed in glistening crystal blue. Hope and passion and belief in a world of choice and freedom – all this was taken from the boy a piece at a time. The shed-thing didn't seem to understand that by not killing the boy outright, it was extending his agony; bringing the child to the precipice of sanity and hurling him over still conscious. Or, if it did, it didn't appear to care. While Donald still breathed, it opened him up from pubes to sternum. It began to select and remove his organs, holding them up for inspection in the angled bars of sunlight penetrating the shed, before thrusting them into itself through the many openings and unmade sections of its own body. When it began to clip through the boy's ribs, Mason had to look away.

The clattering of metal against wet bone emanated from behind him. The shed-thing was trembling as it worked. Mason sensed its eagerness and excitement. As soon as it could finish, it would return to the landfill with its new brains and bones and skin, with the fine, healthy organs of a young human. There would be no slowing it down now. Risking daylight and detection, it would collect more garbage and redesign itself. It would be more powerful. It would be larger. It would have a suitable vehicle for the innate intelligence it had displayed since the morning Mason found it.

Mason had no idea what he would do when it returned.

14

Steel panels and shattered glass; plastic bags and shitty, rotten nappies.

Old shirts and mouldering dishrags; torn corduroy trousers and moth-eaten jumpers. Crushed, jagged baked bean cans; short loops of flex; plastic cartons, plastic packaging, broken plastic toys; tubing, stuffing, plasterboard, bricks; oxidising springs, hinges and wire; splintered planks and bent nails; light fittings; smashed picture frames and burnt things; peelings, leftovers and cooked bones; raw bones; dead rats, guinea pigs and hamsters; aborted foetuses; grease, fat and oil; upturned drawers and their unwanted contents; retired desks and lamps; keyboards, mice, PCs, laptops, hard drives, monitors, TVs, satellite dishes, speakers, mobile phones, SIM cards, software.

Blood.

Rust.

Lightning.

Intent.

These were the things of which the fecalith was wrought. He grew swiftly.

He moved as though falling through space when swimming in the landfill. Though its contents were crushed almost solid by the daily stomping of the heavy compactors, to him it was a private aquarium and he moved through it with the ease and grace of a dolphin. Nothing impeded him. He was drawn, called to certain places where useful parts were to be found – the glass from the door of a washing machine to form a new eye, an old radiator panel to gird his exhaust-pipe ribs, empty beer barrels and oil drums from which to fashion his vertebrae. When he passed below, the dry and jagged surface of the landfill rippled like the swell of a polluted sea. Within hours the fecalith reached maturity.

The old man's offerings – the hedgehogs and cats and rabbits, his own blood and the mind and body of the boy – all these flowed and lived within him, as aspects of his vast and growing consciousness, as did the blood of the boy's sister. They formed the templates from which inanimate things became living. Parts of him bristled with approximated fur or spines, his teeth were copies of dog canines, human incisors and herbivorous molars – but huge now and made of hard junk. His jaws were hinged girders, his fingers, jointed railings. He walked on legs of reclaimed iron and in his rubber and copper veins flowed a new blood of commingled effluent and living plasma. In this blood moved the soul of the fecalith and the fecalith's will. In his steel-cased skull processors, motherboards, hard drives and software grew and evolved. Awareness seeped into the circuitry, code flowed into its assembly of brains. In the slime at the bottom of the landfill, the fecalith philosophised and meditated as he swam.

Like all sentient beings, he contemplated the reason for his becoming, the purpose of his existence. The where of it, the when of it, the how.

And the why.

Unlike most sentient beings, the fecalith began to understand why he existed, where he had come from and what he had come to do.

There had been many created like him, born on the same day, animated by the same elemental forces. Fashioned by the immense power and anger of the storm, they had risen at its will. Of all of them, the fecalith was the only one to have survived and he was growing fast now, almost into his maturity. But the same potential from which his kin had risen still existed here in this fertile lake of garbage. He could be their mind. He could be their general. If only he could bring them back.

The shed was an empty space now.

Neither the boy nor the creature might ever have existed.

Mason sat on the dirty floorboards, the sun knifing a deep angle into the gloom but not touching him. He watched the dust specks turning in the bright shaft. Dead atoms, floating but inert. Mindless, discarded chips and fragments of the world.

Things had changed.

Muck and blood flowed in the veins and improvised tubules of the creature, death and life mingled to make some third state – newborn in the world. Newborn and abroad.

The creature had left the same night he gave it the boy and had not returned.

Mason felt the splintery wood beneath his hands. There was no trace of Donald Smithfield. Neither stain of his blood nor rag of his clothes. Not a page of skin or partial bone. Not a hair. The creature had absorbed him totally. Mason's tools were gone too. The fork and the shovel, the trowel, the hoe and hedge trimmers. The scraps of paper and cloth that had been its bed. Even the old books on the shelf. All taken.

There had been a purpose to all this, Mason was sure of that, but now that he tried to remember it he found it impossible to justify. In some part of himself he didn't even believe it was real. Had something gone wrong in his mind? Had he dreamed up an adventure to end his solitude, wished the creature into existence to bring some purpose to his life? It was hard to believe it could have come to this – Mason had always believed he was content with simplicity. Now, with the creature gone, he felt a loneliness worse than any before.

In the immense inner fields of his emotions, where happiness had grown like a bounteous golden crop in time with the growth of the shed-thing, now grew tares of doubt and guilt. They choked everything. He'd had a mission or a fantasy perhaps – it didn't matter – and now that mission was finished. There was no trace of it. He was left with nothing but the knowledge of his crime. He could now contemplate his slaughter of the child at his leisure. Were it not for him, the boy would still be alive.

Nothing else remained to make concrete his reasoning. The shed was *utterly bare* inside. He had acted with great conviction, believing in a new age for the world. Now, there was nothing left to show that he'd acted well. He might merely be insane, having concocted a wild fantasy. Or he might be a killer of animals and children for no good reason. Surrounded outside by the abundant growth of his garden, of ripe fruits and vegetables aplenty, Mason sat staring and desolate at the inside of the shed door.

There was nothing to make him move. No reason to stand or eat. No meaning in anything he might or might not do. Not any more.

The light moved with great patience and stealth across the worn and bare shed floor, over his splayed legs and crept up the opposite wall. It turned rose gold then pink; all the while losing it's brightness. Finally the light slept and darkness rose.

The shed was black inside and still Mason waited for something to stir him, some prompt to make him live again.

None came.

Ray woke in the cool of the evening.

He opened his eyes and stayed still for a few moments as his mind stitched reality back together. The first thing he remembered was the last thing that had happened – Delilah sucking an unprecedented fourth orgasm from him. His cock was pleasantly raw and deep inside his balls there was a constant, flat ache. He lay on his side, his head on one of the pillows. Delilah had laid his shirt over him. His hip and leg were sore from the hard ground.

He raised himself into a sitting position, his back against the tree, and looked around. There was a note sticking out of his Converse hi-top.

> Ray,
> Had to go. Put the box away. Keep our secret!
> Call me.
> Luv D
> XXX

There was a mobile number written below it.

He folded the paper up and put it in his shorts pocket before dressing.

Standing up, he felt the weakness in his legs. This was from their two knee-tremblers. When the ground felt too hard, they'd stood up and used the tree for support. He put his hand to the rough bark of the oak.

'Thanks. You were great.'

His voice sounded weak and out of place, the levity inappropriate now he was alone. He finished dressing, suddenly wanting to be away from the place. The sun was still up but it was low in the sky and he couldn't see it through the trees. A coral pink haze was gathering and reflecting off the gnarled skin of the trees. It made the tiny grove other-worldly once more but not in the same way it had appeared to him before. He'd have enjoyed it if Delilah was still with him. Alone, the place felt wrong. He put the cushions and blankets back in the ammo box without bothering to shake them and shoved it hurriedly back into the undergrowth out of sight. All he wanted to do was leave, get out of the woods and back to his place before it got too dark.

After a minute or two of walking through the trees, he knew he didn't recognise where he was. It seemed like the right direction but he couldn't be certain and he didn't remember any landmarks. How long had they walked through the trees for before they arrived? Surely not more than two or three minutes. He should have been near the fence by now. There were trees in every direction. Nothing looked familiar. The pink light deepened and darkened.

Paranoia and fear crept over the back of his head like insects. He turned from one direction to another looking for some sign of their passing, a hint of a path. Something that looked like a passage through the trees became visible. He followed it. Moments later it was blocked by a fallen branch. They definitely hadn't come this way. Turning back he began to trot towards the clearing with the idea that he would start again. It didn't take long for him to realise he'd lost the way back to their little grotto too.

Unable to control his nerves any longer, Ray started running.

He stumbled over branches and half stepped in a rabbit hole.

Could have broken my bloody ankle.

Realising the extent of his panic, he slowed down and took more notice of where he put his feet. He knew how stupid he was being but he couldn't stop himself from running. It was the bloody dope; the high was long gone leaving him nothing but freaked.

And then, up ahead, he glimpsed the sun; red now, through a straggly mesh of branches. He had to be nearing the edge of the woods. Relief surging through him, he sprinted towards the visceral glow. The woods ended but not where he'd entered them. There was no barbed wire fence here. Instead he found he was standing on a raised bank with a huge view of the countryside. The ground sloped steeply away from him into smaller trees and brush. Beyond the dense shrubs was a meandering gravel path and a little farther on, the edge of a lake. Far to the other side of the lake a heat haze rippled over Shreve's notorious landfill, blurring the horizon.

Of course, it wasn't a real lake he was looking across. He had his bearings now. This was the reservoir in the centre of Shreve Country Park. From here he knew he could find his way back to town. There was no need to run any more. Now he knew where he was, there was plenty of light and lots of time. He could turn his mind to what he really wanted to do – get home and phone Delilah.

The sun rippled as it touched the horizon and sank fast. He'd been glancing at it from time to time and dozens of after-images glowed on his retina. When the sun was gone, leaving the sky a deep dusty pink, the after-images remained. They obscured his vision of the patchwork fields and the pylons marching single-file across the country to diminish into the distance. Nothing in the expanse before him looked real. The shimmer from the landfill made the entire horizon look like a fake backdrop, a gaudily painted banner fluttering in a warm breeze. Movement caught his eye on the far side of the reservoir. Once and then a second time. It was towards the middle of the landfill. At first he assumed it was the residual blobs of sunlight in his eyes but then the movement took form, a very recognisable form.

Something huge heaved itself out of the landfill. Ray recognised the action, that of a swimmer leaving a pool. This shape was far, far too large for that though. It must have been at least half a mile away. He could only see the shape in silhouette – what was left of the daylight was right behind it – but when it stood to its full height, he knew the outline very well. It was the figure of a man. A giant man with jagged, rough edges. It stood for a long time dripping effluent and pieces of junk, only its head turning slowly from side to side as it surveyed the land all around it. It was taller than the trees nearest to it. Taller, perhaps, than a three storey building. Ray didn't have time to make a more accurate estimate of its height. He heard the tendons in the giant's neck groaning like strained steel guy wires. Then it strode towards the lake, towards him, each footstep slow and lumbering but full of purpose. He felt the throb of its progress like a fat heart beating deep and slow beneath his feet. He smelled the wafted rot of re-forged detritus and reanimated filth.

Despite the fading haze of cider and the clearing marijuana fog, Ray knew he wasn't imagining it this time. The trash from the landfill was alive. The garbage man was coming. Ray couldn't move.

When it reached the perimeter of the landfill, it stopped and scanned its surroundings again. Its gaze fell on something to its right. Ray held his breath – stupid really, there was no way the thing could have heard him breathing from this distance. The urge to crouch back into the trees was strong but his desire to see what the creature would do next overcame it. It turned in the direction of its stare. Ray tried to see what it was seeing. There was nothing there but open fields and power lines. The garbage man began to walk again, that in itself was spectacle enough. Ray wished he could see better how the thing worked, what it was made up of. It stepped over the perimeter fence of the landfill and approached one of the pylons. It was about the same height as the structure, almost an inanimate skeletal version of itself. For a moment, Ray felt pity for the giant garbage man. It was merely searching for a companion. In the pylon, it had found a false friend, one that would burn or destroy it. Ray found himself on the point of calling out, even though it was already too late and there was no way the giant could hear him.

He didn't get the opportunity. The garbage man had taken hold of one of the power lines and yanked it free of the towering skeleton's grip. There was a blue flash which left Ray blind for a second or two, then the sound of a distant electrostatic snap reached his ears. The garbage man held a writhing snake of raw voltage in its hands. Blue sparks poured from the snake's severed neck in a bright arcing fountain. Parts of the garbage man's body lit up red and orange and yellow. It juddered, rooted to the earth. Then it clumped back to the perimeter fence, hauling the live cable behind it. It bucked in his grip like a thin black eel, spitting neon poison. The cable just reached the edge of the landfill. The garbage man knelt and thrust the power-spewing ligament deep into the rubbish.

For a few moments, nothing happened.

Then the surface of the landfill began to pulsate and liquefy. It began to boil. Embryonic shadows, too small and distant to define, began to slither and crawl from the deep pits of trash. They left it from every side, in every direction. And all the while, the garbage man knelt at the edge of his domain like a rain god siphoning water into a desert. He brought forth life.

Ray was down the bank and onto the path before his mind registered he was running.

He didn't stop until he'd reached his flat. He double-locked the door behind him, dived into the bathroom and bolted that door too. He sat down on the toilet, his legs shaking with exertion. He held his head and in between his gasps for air he cried like a little boy.

15

Kevin watched Tamsin open the door, catch the smell in the air and march towards the kitchen. She stopped in the doorway, hands on hips.

'What do you think you're doing?'

He was more nervous than he'd hoped to be. Her voice hinted at nothing but total self-belief, her face showed no cracks. Already he was wondering how he was going to win this war; win it and finish it in a single engagement.

'Smoking cigarettes.'

It was, at least, obvious she knew something was up. That much showed in the flicker of her eyes as he tapped ash into his second empty coffee mug. It was a stupid habit he'd picked up at college and never quite lost. Stupid because, while it was temporarily convenient, it meant he had to strain soggy fag-ends out of the sink when the dregs of coffee were finally thrown away. Tammy hated it and had told him so the first time she'd seen him smoke at home. It had mattered back then, what she thought. It mattered now, too, but only because he knew how much it irritated her. She was seeing the challenge in his actions, the rebellion. That was exactly what he wanted.

'When did you take that up again?'

'I never stopped.'

Something there. A pause. Another flicker of – what? Calculation? Hesitation? – then she was normal. A placid lake. She shrugged, dropped her handbag on the kitchen counter and swept out of the kitchen without saying anything more.

She should have bitten by now. Snapped, more like. She had every right to lose her cool; he'd deceived her. She was holding back. Why?

She trotted up the stairs. Unusual. She was fit, of course,

but her gestures, her way of moving was in general more leisurely, more regal. Tammy didn't trot.

Kevin wasn't used to chain smoking. He dropped the half-finished cigarette into the half-finished coffee. It died with a hiss. He lit another, beginning to feel a little light-headed, a little nauseous.

Upstairs he heard water running. It was the shower. Again, unusual. Too brisk for Tammy. Baths were more her style. Perhaps she felt more distant in the shower cubicle with the glass door pulled shut. More separate.

Fine.

He took his cigarette and the rest of the pack with him and followed her up. He didn't take an ashtray.

He opened the bathroom door, breaking another marital protocol. He took her towel from the hook while she was turned away from him and sat on the toilet. He pushed the door shut with his foot. Smoke and steam mingled. She knew he was there but he watched her ignoring him through the glass.

Ignoring him.

While she must have thought it was the greatest act of nonchalance ever performed, Kevin found it half amusing and half disturbing. There was only one reason she would pretend not to be bothered by this. She had something to hide. The kind of secret that came out when non-smoking husbands started smoking again. The kind of secret that would come out in an argument.

What had the letter said? Something about him not being alone in sin.

He was suddenly dead certain that Tamsin was afraid of confronting him. Tamsin thought he was smoking and belligerent because he'd already discovered something about her. What could it be?

What the hell else? An affair. That was definitely her style.

The water in the shower stopped running but she didn't get straight out. He could sense her tension now even through the cloudy glass. First she'd felt safe. Now she was trapped.

She stepped out and reached for the towel that wasn't there.

Without her usual poise and confidence she stood, naked and dripping on the shower mat. He blew out a long stream of smoke in her direction.

'Got the smell of his spunk off now?'

'*What*?'

'Who is he?'

'Can you pass me my towel, please?'

'No. I can't.'

She lunged for the door but he had his foot against it and her wet hands failed to even turn the handle.

'Give me the fucking towel, Kevin.'

'Answer the question.'

'I don't know what you're talking about.'

He sighed deeply, acting far more laboured and weary than he really was.

'We've been married six years, Tammy. Not bad really, when you think about it. Not bad in this day and age. So, I'm going to give you one more chance to be honest with me. I think I owe you that much.' He drew on the cigarette. 'Who is he?'

He watched her carefully. There was a lot going on behind those eyes. Computation, assessment, analysis of risk. She looked like she might have thought in this way a lot. All her life, perhaps. He couldn't understand why he hadn't noticed it before. Or maybe he had and had mistaken it for intelligence. But this wasn't benign intelligence. This was deviousness. It took split seconds, that was all, but he could see it nonetheless.

'Open the door and let me out or I'm going to start screaming.'

Part of him wanted that. Yes, screaming. A struggle. Something worse. Ignoring her threat, he said, 'I've seen the photographs. They're not very good but they show everything. What you fail to understand here, Tammy, is that I'm not giving you the opportunity to deny this. We're way past that now. All I want is an answer to my question: Who is he?'

It was a crazy bluff but he was past caring. He'd seen no photos but it was reasonable to assume that if Mavis Ahern had pressured him with visual evidence, she'd done the same to Tamsin. After all, her motive wasn't to squeeze them for money; it was to bring them back together in the sight of God.

He was looking forward to telling Mavis Ahern that they'd been married in a registry office, in a civil ceremony, without a Bible in sight. That would keep, however.

Meanwhile, he was watching Tammy. Every move. Every twitch. The gooseflesh had risen on her now that she was beginning to cool in the larry bathroom air. The calculations inside her head seemed to have slowed and become more specific.

'You can't hurt him.'

'No? Why not?'

'Because he's just… you know why.'

'No, I don't. Tell me why I shouldn't hurt him, Tammy.'

'He's only a kid.'

'Only a…' Kevin put a hand to his forehead, touched it ever so lightly. 'It's the paper boy, isn't it? You've been screwing the fucking paper boy.'

He stood up and took hold of Tammy's wet hair in his left fist. With his right hand, he put out his cigarette against the wet strands. He wasn't absolutely sure what he was going to do with her, all he knew was that he wasn't going to hold back.

'I can't believe how long I've put up with your bullshit. You know,' he said, 'If you really want to start screaming, now would probably be a good time.'

She watched the silver Z3 pull up outside her flat and knew that everything was about to change. Something about the way he slammed it up beside the kerb. When he got out, she saw a mark on his face for a split second. Then he turned away, walked to the passenger side door and hefted out a large sports bag. Her stomach fluttered as she ran to the front door of the shared downstairs corridor to let him in.

There was a fresh cut across his cheek bone, the blood only just dried. For a few moments he stood on the doorstep without speaking. She lost faith then, wondered if he'd really go all the way.

And then:

'I've left her.'

Still, he didn't move forward.

She stood out of his way. The tension dropped out of his shoulders, the pinch left his mouth and eyes. He stepped over the threshold and dropped the bag in the hallway. He was shaking his head, not understanding what he was doing, moving by instinct not thought.

She led him through her front door to the sofa. Returning to the entryway she collected his bag and dropped it inside the flat. She sat down beside him.

'What happened?'

'It got... physical. I wanted to hurt her. Really hurt her. I dragged her into the bedroom. I don't know what I thought I was going to do. And then, suddenly, all the anger went out of me. I knew it would be crazy to give in to the rage. I thought about the future. I thought about you. I didn't want... didn't want... to jeopardise it. Us. So I just stopped. And when she realised it, she spun around with the nearest thing to hand – our wedding photo, as it happened – and hit me in the face with it.'

'But why, Kev? I mean, what had she done to make you so angry?'

'She was having an affair.'

'So were you.'

'I know. But…'

'There's no justification. You're as culpable as she is.'

'There's more to it than that. Years of her… disdain. And control. It was so typical of her. And the poor… it doesn't matter. He was just such a mark, such an easy target. She's evil. She gets off on chaos.'

He was quiet then and she went to the kitchen to make coffee. She didn't believe he was a violent man. Despite what she'd said to him, she knew his rage was appropriate – who wouldn't be angry in that situation? But if he'd acted on the emotion, that would have been unforgivable. She'd have thought differently of him then. But he hadn't. He'd risen above it. Because of her.

As she splashed boiling water into the two mugs she became aware of him standing behind her.

'What?' she said, pouring in the milk.

'Can I stay?'

She kept her back to him as she stirred the sugar into her cup. Finally, she turned and held out a mug.

'I was hoping you'd ask me that.'

There were other people Ray could have phoned; the authorities perhaps. But who else would believe what he had to say? And who else did he owe this knowledge to?

Ray pressed dial. The phone rang several times and cut to voice mail. He hung up and dialled a second time without leaving a message. Same thing again. His heart was still banging hard and his breathing nowhere near recovering. It didn't matter. He hung up and dialled again.

Please…

This time she answered.

'Ray?'

He had no idea what to say.

'Yeah, it's me.'

'What is it? You sound… are you all right?'

'No. Not really.'

'Look, Ray, I don't want you thinking you can just phone me any time. As far as I'm concerned you and I are finished.'

'I know that. This isn't… about that. It's…'

He heard a man's voice in the background; he assumed it was the man he'd seen her with at The Barge. Unless she'd gone completely… He didn't want to think about it. Still, despite the terror he felt, despite the sensation that something was yanking the rug of reality out from under him, he recognised jealousy rising up through all of it. *Was* that the real reason he'd phoned her?

'Make it quick, Ray, this isn't a good time for me.' He took a deep breath.

'There's no easy way to say this, Jenny. I'm not even sure I believe it myself. But I had to tell you. I wanted you to have the best chance to get away.'

'Get away?'

'The thing we found. By the side of the road –'

Her voice tightened.

'No, Ray. Don't do this.'

'Jenny, please listen. I've spent every day since then pretending it didn't happen, that it wasn't real, that somehow you just had an accident or that something bit you. Just like we told them in the hospital. But I never believed that.'

'Ray, please—'

'You have to listen to me. Just for a few more seconds and then I promise I'll never call you again. That thing was alive. I haven't been able to face it until today but it was. I think we killed it but there's more of them out there. Worse things. *Bigger* things.'

He could hear Jenny crying now. He didn't want her upset, he wanted her to listen. She needed to concentrate.

'You never took any notice of me, never heard me. If you only ever do it once, it has to be now, Jenny. I think your life depends on it.'

'How can you do this to me, Ray? It's so sick. You were always weak but I never thought you'd stoop to this.'

'Thirty seconds more, Jenny, that's all. I was out at the reservoir this afternoon, not so far from where we stopped that day. I saw something rise up. I've never seen anything else like it except on that day with you. And then it made more of them – too many to count. I swear, Jenny, I swear to you now I saw it. Saw *them*. I had to call you. I had to let you know. So you could be ready. So you could… leave… if you wanted to.'

At the other end of the connection. Jenny seemed to have sniffed her way back to some kind of composure.

'You can't have me back, Ray. No amount of bullshit or scare tactics is going to make me want a weak man like you ever again. You're scum, Ray Wade. You're garbage.'

The line closed.

'Jenny. Jenny? Be there. For God's sake, still be there.'

He dialled the number and it cut straight to voice mail. He waited for the prompt to leave a message, then changed his mind and hung up. What more could he say to her? How could he even be certain she would listen to his message? He dropped the handset back on its base station and collapsed onto his sofa. He'd had his chance. He'd done his best to warn her.

Now he had to think about himself.

Mason Brand began to decay along with his post-harvest crops.

Though he'd always had a beard, he'd always kept it trimmed. Now he never touched it. It obscured him, hid his face the way ivy hides old ruins. He preferred it. He stopped cleaning his teeth and bathed even less than he had before. He knew he smelled bad but it didn't concern him. The cornucopia of fruit and vegetables the garden had yielded rotted, much of it unpicked. He ate rarely and made no effort to pickle or preserve any produce.

He no longer understood the nature of things.

He would allow himself to die like a spent vine.

Except that he knew it wasn't time yet. He was waiting for something. Something would happen. He knew that much. It *had* to happen sooner or later. When he'd seen this thing, this *happening*, then he would stop living. It was proper that he, Mason Brand, be allowed to end and to rot. He no longer deserved a place in the world.

Autumn arrived less eagerly than the spring had come. The stifling, long days hung on an and on. Everyone else saw it as the most marvellous summer of heat hazes and broad, crimson-orange sunsets that graced each evening's horizon. People lay on the grass in parks and kissed languidly. Parents took their kids on picnics and bike rides. Students, emboldened by beer and cider, leapt into the canals and rivers of every college town.

No one believed the summer would go on forever, not truly, but no one wanted it to end. On the warm nights, muggy with moisture and the promise of rain that never seemed to come, the world, and Shreve in particular, was lulled by a sense of eternal youth.

When the first leaves turned and dropped in drowsy breezes, Mason Brand was the only one smiling. But it was a chill-bitten smile, a smile ahead of its season.

The very meat of him longed for the pressing of the earth all around him, its weight pushing down from above, its healing power drawing down the poison from his bones and transmuting his evil.

Ray waited two days for something to happen.

In that time he stayed at home. He ate baked beans and tins of soup instead of walking to the take-away or calling for a delivery. He didn't want to see or talk to anyone. Instead of hiring DVDs, he watched TV. He replayed Revenant Apocalypse instead of buying new games. At dusk and dawn he peeped through his curtains expecting the giant to thunder down his street and smash through the wall. He watched people put out their rubbish and waited for it to come to life and ooze out of their black wheelie bins.

He smoked as much dope as possible, achieving a permanent, medicinal high.

Nothing happened.

He watched the news. There were no reports of undead rubbish or towering landfill zombies. The world continued to devour itself in war; people still murdered their lovers and children; plane, rail and road accidents claimed their usual quota of victims; the prime minister still lied through his smiling teeth while he raped the nation.

Nothing had changed.

Finally, he picked up the phone and dialled the number he should have called the night he ran back from the woods. She answered after one ring. His stomach lurched with unexpected joy at the sound of her voice.

'Hi,' he said. 'It's Ray.'

There was a silence.

'I didn't think you were going to call.'

'Sorry. I've been… studying. Fancy a pint?'

16

Mason Brand couldn't remember the last time he'd eaten. He didn't care. There was no hunger anyway, no desire other than for the blackness to hurry up and take him.

His skin was petal pale. Even his day-burnt face and forearms had faded. He couldn't remember the last time he'd been outside. He didn't know what day it was nor the time. He had no television, no radio, no computer.

Life had become a condition of two states: light and dark.

In the light he tried to sleep to pass the hours. It had worked for the first few days but then his body no longer required further rest. Instead of sleeping, he hid in the twisted sheets and blankets on his bed.

Then the darkness came, like a kidnapper slipping a black hood over the day's head and pulling a cord tight around its neck. He would sleep then because of his body's clock, its understanding of what the night was for. But then his body woke, no more than an hour or two after the light had gone and then Mason was awake in the most awful way.

Something about the workings of his mind was different at night. Some aspect of him was more alert than it was during the day. His veins itched with it. His mind's eyelid was peeled by it, left raw and staring. And with that eye he viewed his waking dreams of guilt and saw visions of the destruction of the world. Destruction that he was responsible for.

Under dark crimson skies, heavy with suffocating cloud, the Earth was changing. Upon its skin had grown many organisms in its long history. They had tunnelled and burrowed and lived and died without troubling it. In its waters they had swum for incalculable generations, keeping harmony all the while with the world and its rhythms. Then had come a new creature, similar at first to many of the others. The creature was wily and smart, outwitting its predators despite its physical weakness. The creature spread rapidly and successfully to all parts of the world's vast body. It became a parasite, feeding from the world, sucking on it, mining it, scorching it, flaying it alive.

What choice was left to the world but to respond? She was slow at first, merely showing the signs of her anger and disgust. She spun a little wide from her axis, shed her protective layers, became lean. The mountains ground against each other like determined teeth. The winds shrieked and whirled, throwing the parasite's dwellings to dust. The waters rose up and drowned the parasites, washed away their homes. Fires swept the dry climates.

But the parasite survived it all. The world's mere anger was not enough.

So, she shifted her shape.

And this was what Mason saw in his dreams.

Where the land had been flat, blades of rock thrust up. Where the land had been solid, rifts tore open. The winds of the world joined forces and swept her in unison, one mighty gale that blew from West to East forever. The fresh waters of the world became poison. The sea waters grew into impassable towers. Everywhere the world grew eyes to watch the parasites die, grew mouths to eat them, ears to hear their screams and then their silence. The world consumed her parasites because it was the only way she knew to survive them.

Each night, awake or sleeping – he could not always tell – he watched the world eating humanity as she tried to save herself.

Why had it come to this?

Was it really his fault?

He knew, of course, that much of the evil of men was nothing to do with him. He had lived in harmony with the Earth and her cycles and seasons. He had loved her the way only a farmer can love the world. He had tended her, respected her, exchanged with her.

Now this.

Perhaps that was why she had chosen him.

Eyes shut or open, Mason saw what he believed was the future or a representation of it. The world was not ending but humanity was. He had not been the nursemaid to a new way of life, he had been the trafficker who gave the assassin free passage. He had aided the executioner of all mankind.

He had not seen the fecalith for many days. Weeks, perhaps – he wasn't sure. What would it be like now? How much would it have grown? What and who would it have devoured and added to itself?

Would it still recognise him and if it did, would it even matter?

He'd led that poor boy to the most horrible end. The first human death in this new and dangerous world. His own end could not come soon enough.

It was in the middle of the night when he realised that waiting for the end was pathetic and cowardly. He should kill himself swiftly, mete out the justice due to him and have done with it.

He slipped from the filthy second skin his sheets had become and stood naked in front of the full length mirror in his bedroom. Moonlight filled the room with luminous silver light.

He was thin now. His ribs showed – he could count them all. What little fat he'd carried had gone from around his waist. His abdominal muscles were a ridge along the centre of his stomach. Inside, all his organs would have shrunk to fit this smaller cavity. His pelvis protruded like a small shelf. Everywhere the guy-wires of his body, the sinews, showed tight and proud beneath his thinning skin.

A razor would do it.

A blade across his skinny neck and his blood would pool blackly in that silver light.

There was no razor in the house.

He went to the kitchen. There he took out a tiny paring knife and his whetstone. The sound of grinding, slippery steel was loud in all that quiet. For five minutes he stood, his right hand sliding up and down, up and down; a sandy, gritty movement vibrating in his bones, raising the hair on his forearms and neck.

He tested the blade against his thumb.

Sharp as a razor. Sturdier. Surer.

He moved in the direction of the stairs but sensed something outside the back door. He stopped and turned. Was there movement out there among the quicksilver shadows? He stood for a long time, watching. Stood until his vision greyed out and he had to blink it clear. It was so long since he'd looked outside that the shapes out there, the rotted-down stalks and stems and vines, made no sense to him. He recognised none of it in the insufficient moonlight.

The knife became a weapon of self-defence and he clutched it, blade upward, in his weak fist. The sense of a presence outside the back door grew and spread. A dark tide had flowed all the way to his back step, covering everything, a living black ocean.

But that could not be.

He stepped closer to the glass in the back door until he could see his own breath on it. The ground seemed to be rippling in the moonlight as though his whole house were at sea. His grip on the knife loosened because his palms were sweating.

He listened, turned an ear towards the glass.

Whispers across the lake of his garden in a language he did not understand.

He told himself he did not understand it but in truth he knew every word. The calling had returned.

Something scraped against the bottom of the door and he stood back.

The waves in the garden were rising, a squall getting up out there. Crests began to obscure the only shape he did recognise – his shed. The level outside was rising.

He backed away still further.

What could his knife do against all this?

And could he really kill himself now when tomorrow would no doubt bring the strangest dawn the Earth had ever seen?

He waited there for a long time, trying to discern some shape, anything recognisable in the flood of movement beyond the glass. He could not.

He waited for it – for them – to come and take him as he so deserved to be taken. He waited for them to separate him into vein, muscle and bone, lymph and blood, to dissociate his various organs and reuse them in accordance with their new way. They came no further than the threshold.

An hour must have passed wherein he entered some staring trance, as though contemplating a mandala. Then, finally, he was tired. Tired enough to sleep. He turned from the black ocean in his garden, disconnected and trudged upstairs to his bed. He placed the knife in the drawer of his bedside table next to his grandmother's Bible, a book he never read.

Before he died there was something he needed to do.

Aggie stood naked in the tiny bedroom of her shared flat in Wandsworth.

The landlord had made a poor job of turning two bedrooms into four – there was barely enough space for her to walk around her bed and the walls were like cardboard. Somewhere in the house there was damp rot and every room smelled of mould and sweaty decay. She hated it and barely spoke to her flatmates. Maybe it was because she believed she was worth so much more than the existence she'd found. Maybe it was because she was becoming exactly the person she swore she'd never be.

The mirror showed her who that person was.

She had lost weight trying to stay as skinny as the other girls. After finding the job in East Putney and quitting the money-grabbing modelling agency, she'd found it impossible to put the weight back on. She remembered how she'd looked when she studied herself in the mirror of the bedroom in her parents' house. She hadn't been fat then, but she'd had curves and a fuller bust. Now her ribs showed just a little too much. The gentle, attractive mound of her belly had become a definite concavity – still desirable in the world of modelling but a difference she didn't welcome. And yet, there seemed nothing she could do about it. She tried to eat but the hunger wasn't there. Her skin had taken the grey out of the city air. Her sweat smelled stronger, sourer than when she'd lived at home.

These things were a source of constant anxiety but her skin told other stories. Tales not necessarily about the lonely single girl trying to make it in the world of fashion. The bruises on her wrists and ankles never quite had the time to fade now and so she wore clothes with sleeves that draped to her hands or fingers. The whippings were more for show than for pain but occasionally the leather did leave weals. Sometimes the marks took several days to disappear.

She no longer had any pubic hair and the hair on her head had been shorn to a crew cut allowing her to wear a variety of wigs. Before she'd left home she'd always worn clip-on earrings, not having any desire for the real thing. Now she had piercings in places she would never even have considered. The one consolation was the balance of her bank account. All of a sudden she had savings. Soon she would move to better accommodation – she promised herself a nice place on her own nearer the centre of the city. She'd clean herself up. Get pretty again. And then she'd get back into the kind of work she'd always dreamed of doing. She had enough experience now to shop around for the right kind of jobs.

Just a little more money and she'd move on. She'd move *up*.

The mirror was straight with her. More honest than she was being with herself about where her life was headed. It was one thing she couldn't ignore. There was no disguising the changes. She was a different kind of girl now. She was a different kind of animal.

Her phone rang and she flinched at the sound. It could only mean one thing: more work. She grabbed it out of her handbag and pressed accept. No one spoke.

'Yeah?' she said.

'Agatha?' It had been a familiar voice once but now, like her own body, she barely recognised it.

'Mum.' She had no idea what to say. 'How did you get this number?'

There was something wrong with her mother's voice.

'You've got to come home, poppet.'

'Don't start this. I'm never coming back.'

Her mother was trying not to cry.

'You've got to. You've got to come back.'

'Listen, I'm nev—'

'Yes, you are, Agatha. You're coming home right now. Donald's…' The tears Pamela Smithfield had been holding on to escaped. Her next words came out as a kind of howl. '… gone missing.'

Delilah held Ray's head against her breasts as they lay beneath the oak tree.

She liked him unshaven, his stubble scratchy and prickling to her skin. She liked the smell of sebum that came from his unwashed hair and the sourness of his underarms. From all of him came a musky fuck-odour. She'd smelled it the first time they'd come to the secret clearing. Since then, the more sex they'd had, the stronger the smell became. It was as though his hormonal system had responded to her at a chemical level. The more they touched each other, entered each other, the more of this smell he produced and the more magnetic he became to her. Even when they weren't together she could smell a trace of him. She never wanted to lose it.

Ray had changed in other ways. He was more of a man. Still a feckless dreamer. Still a person who found it hard to live in what other people called the real world. Inside him, though, something had hardened, locking another thing deeper inside. She sensed a fear in him and she knew not to ask him about it. Not yet.

Spent, he dozed beside her. They'd brought sleeping bags to the clearing so that they could spend the night outdoors. Now the weather had turned a little cooler, the bags were ideal for day-time trysts too.

Ray twitched, making her jump.

He sat up and she saw in his eyes the hidden thing that had returned from sleep with him. It faded quickly.

'Shit.' He said.

She touched his arm.

'What is it?'

'A dream, thank God.'

'What happened?'

Ray looked around at the oak trees as if gauging their strength.

'Do you think we're safe here?' he asked.

'Completely. No one knows about this place. No one else has ever found it.'

He wiped his face with both hands.

'That's not really what I mean, D. I thought it was coming here. Coming for us.'

'What was?'

Ray rubbed his forehead hard and shook his head to clear it.

'Sorry. I'm still half asleep. Or stoned or whatever. You

know that feeling when you think you've woken up but you're still dreaming? That's how I feel.'

'Are you scared?'

'I'm fine. Just need to arrive properly. Is there any water left?'

She passed him the canteen and he took several small sips. Then he lay back against the tree and put his arm around her.

'I love this place, D. Being here with you, it's like being on a better planet. A place that only you and I understand.'

'I feel the same way.'

'Did you bring other blokes here before me?'

She held her breath for a moment. They'd known each other long enough for this.

'My first boyfriend brought me here when I was fourteen. He was three years older than me and that seemed like a lot back then. I didn't tell my parents about him. At school, the other girls were jealous. Boys my age wouldn't come near me when they realised who I was seeing. His name was Simon Pike. Everyone called him Spike. He'd already left school and had a job in what used to be Manny's Spares and Repairs. I had a thing for all that grease and grime.'

'Dirty girl to the bone, aren't you?'

'To the marrow, Ray. Anyway, he brought me in here a few times. It was Spike who put the ammo box here but there were other things in it back then. The first few times he was nice with me, took it slow. I lost my virginity right here under this tree. It wasn't bad, really.' She paused, remembering. Not smiling. 'Pass me the water, would you?'

Ray handed her the canteen. She could tell he knew there was more to the story and she was glad.

'We came here one Friday evening after he finished work. He didn't even go home to change. Just took off his overalls, washed his hands and brought me here. It was like he was in a hurry. We made love and then he stood up. I heard some laughter in the bushes and I realised straight away what he'd done. Either he'd bet his mates he'd do it while they watched or they'd paid him. I never found out. They'd all been drinking hard when they walked out into the clearing. Spike was angry, so I suppose they must have promised to stay quiet so I wouldn't know. The funny thing is, I wasn't that angry. I knew they'd watched us and, from the looks on their faces, they'd enjoyed it. That made me feel good. I must have been born kinky, I suppose.'

She watched Ray's face. He could have laughed or commented but he didn't. Again she was pleased. She continued.

'They raped me. Spike tried to stop them but not very hard. In the end he just joined in. By the time they'd all had a go, the first one was hard again. It took hours before they were finished. You know what the worst of it was?'

Ray shook his head, watching her carefully.

'If they'd suggested it to me, if they'd let me have a drink and if they'd just asked me, I probably would have said yes. But for them, the pleasure was not in the asking, it was in the taking, the forcing. It was after dark when they left me. I heard Spike being sick a little way off. Back then, I really believed it was me he was disgusted with. He'd fucked me and he'd hated it so much it made him ill. That was what made me so introverted for so long, thinking I was the kind of girl that made men puke.'

She checked Ray's expression again. It was his opportunity to tell her that she didn't have that effect on him. He didn't take it. She already knew how she made him feel and he knew it. Nothing needed to be said. They were good together. She was falling in love with him.

'I squatted under this tree and their sperm poured out of me onto the dirt. It just kept coming and coming and I remember thinking "I'm going to be pregnant and I won't have any idea who the father is". But I didn't get pregnant and all those billions of sperms died here on the ground. It was that that brought me back here in a way. This was the place where I'd faced men and survived. This was the place where their power had fallen into the ground, impotent and wasted. This was my place, not theirs. I used the dirt where I'd squatted to perform cleansing rituals on myself. And then I fell in love with the outdoors. I'd rather be outside than in the most beautiful palace in the world.'

'What about the Goth image? It doesn't really fit, does it?'

'No. But it keeps people from getting too close.'

'Hasn't worked with me, has it?'

'It's worked perfectly. You saw through my disguise. You're worthy of me.'

'I'm not so sure about that.'

She seized his face between her palms and looked into his eyes.

'Ray. No matter what you may think of yourself, I can see who you really are and who you can become. I wouldn't have told you any of this if I didn't have the greatest trust in you and the greatest belief.'

'D, I've dropped out of college. I don't have a job. I spend every day stoned and I waste most of the hours of daylight playing video games. I'm not worthy of anything.'

'I could slap you for saying that. I believe in you, Ray. You're only like this because you're afraid. When you conquer your fear, you'll be capable of anything.'

'What fear?'

She put a finger on his heart.

'The one you have locked away right here.'

His tears came from nowhere. It was as though her finger had pressed some kind of release mechanism. He knew she was a real witch then, a powerful white witch with the keys to open him up. He turned his face into her breasts again and wept there until his tears rolled onto her belly.

When the tears finally stopped he told her everything.

He told her about the garbage man.

Part III

'Respect your mother and father above all things…'
Statement taken from Mason Brand's journal,
dated September 21st, 2001

17

Together, Ray and Delilah watched for the garbage man and his followers.

They looked for signs of him in the back alleys of Shreve and along the winding pathways of the Country Park. Sometimes Ray drove them to the local tip and recycling centre where they threw small bags of rubbish they'd brought from their homes – merely as a reason to be there. All the while, they watched the skips and bays for signs of movement.

Telling Delilah about what he'd seen felt like a confession. He'd been surprised by her reaction. She'd listened closely and nodded from time to time as though she understood something he did not. She seemed to draw meaning from what he said as though interpreting a dream for him. She was silent for a long time after he finished. When she finally responded he was terrified she was going to tell him he was a psycho and she never wanted to see him again. He compared this fear to the feelings he'd had for Jenny. Not even the jealousy he'd felt at The Barge had been as strong as the fear that Delilah might no longer want him. Before she said a word he realised he loved her.

It had started out as fun, a kind of accident.

And now, well, here they were: pleasantly, nakedly tangled in her bed. She was explaining Gaia theory to him and almost welcoming the rise of a new supernatural force. He wasn't fully concentrating; he wondered if he had the guts to ask her to marry him. He didn't, it appeared. Not right at that moment. But the idea was now never far from his mind, the unspoken words lingering around his lips.

'It's such a privilege to be alive now,' she said, stroking his shoulder.

'What do you mean?'

'In times like these. When elemental forces are manifesting on our plane.'

'Huh, I thought that was the cabin crew handing out the headsets.'

She cuffed him over the head.

'It's a new era, Ray. The long-awaited age of Aquarius.'

He reached to the bedside table to retrieve a Marlboro and her matches. He lit the cigarette, took a pull and passed it to her.

'Isn't the age of Aquarius meant to be a time of peace, love and harmony?' He asked.

'Sure. But these things never come without a struggle. This is the dawning. The garbage man and his kind are some kind of message to us. A catalyst perhaps.'

'But they… you know… they're hungry.'

'I'm not saying it's going to be pleasant. Change never comes without pain. Things are not born without the agony of labour. But afterwards…'

'What then?'

'Who knows? That's up to us, I suppose. We've gone fairly far astray. Look at how we live these days. It would take a hell of a wake-up call to get people to change. Even a little bit. Everyone's too comfortable and too removed from the outdoors. They've forgotten how to touch the Earth.'

'You're losing me now, hippie-chick.'

'I'm serious, Ray. You need to understand this.'

'It's a little difficult to take it all in.'

She stopped caressing him.

'Yeah? Well make the effort.'

'Ok. Sorry. But, come on, D, what do you mean by "touch the Earth"?'

'Almost exactly that. Living in a house with double glazing and central heating, and sleeping in a bed raised up from the floor, and buying food in packets instead of growing it or hunting it; all these things disconnect us from the Earth.'

'But why should that matter? We're all still healthy – healthier than we've ever been. Besides, wherever we go, the Earth is all around us. We can't get away from it.'

She regarded him with a playful contempt.

'I don't have to explain this to you, you know. Not if you're not interested.'

He thought about it.

'I want to understand. I'm just playing devil's advocate for a moment. I mean, I see myself as fairly broad-minded but do you think anyone else will listen when you start talking about connecting with the Earth? If you can't persuade me, what hope have you got?'

'That's easy enough. It won't be me explaining it. It'll be your friends. The ones I haven't met yet.'

Ray knew she had a point. No one was going to listen to a voluptuous Goth girl – except him of course – but they might listen to a thundering, man-shaped tower of scrap and living tissue. Especially if he was backed up by the 'friends' Ray had seen.

Or maybe the prime minister would simply call in the army and blow it off the face of the Earth everyone was so averse to touching. Destroy it, like people did with everything else they were too stupid or too lazy to understand.

He was still puzzled though.

'When the one I saw with Jenny bit off her toe, it was *ravening*. Do you think it would have stopped before it killed her if we'd just let it carry on?'

'Absolutely not. It wouldn't have left a scrap of her.'

'How do you know?'

'I don't *know* for certain but I'm fairly sure. This thing – *these* things – it sounds like they start out as small groupings of waste. I bet they don't survive long if they don't consume living things. But if they get enough of what they need, they grow up like the one you saw coming out of the landfill. God knows what that one's had to eat.'

'Then they're evil,' said Ray. 'Predatory, carnivorous, evil beasts. We've got to stop them.'

Delilah pushed him away.

'You can't mean that. They're not evil, Ray. Are bears evil? Or lions or crocodiles? All of them are capable of killing people and many of them do. But does that make them evil? They're just trying to survive.'

'Maybe,' he said.

He took the cigarette back and smoked it quietly. She watched him.

'I haven't convinced you, have I?'

'To a degree, you have. But you haven't seen the bloody things, D. Maybe they're not actually evil but how will they know when to stop... adding to themselves? What if they don't? Ever?' He turned to look at her. 'What will happen to us?'

He knew she would try to make light of it. She wanted a future with him too – he could read it in her face. As glad as he was of that, he began to experience a clean and simple dread. Here was something real and valuable, right here with him now. Real love. He recognised it because his mind and body were hard-wired to recognise it. Upon the strength of this emotion, the lives of human beings were built. But with this wonderful, joyful thing – intertwined with it – came this new possibility, the possibility that he could lose it all before he'd had the chance to truly be part of it. He couldn't accept the cruelty of it.

But whatever witticism she'd hoped to use never came. Perhaps she didn't want to dishonour what they were feeling with jokes and avoidance of the truth. She took the cigarette away from him and put it in the ashtray, still burning. She slipped down the bed a short way so that their heads were level. She held his face and kissed him. He gave himself to the kiss without thought. Lost himself to her.

What choice was there?

The canal towpath was overgrown with weeds only just beginning to die back after the long summer. Nettles leaned in from both sides of a narrow green corridor, kept open only by the regular passing of walkers and fisherman. On the walks Kevin and Jenny had taken since he'd moved in, they'd seen kingfishers, woodpeckers and even a few grass snakes. Over the last few days, however, the incidence of any wildlife seemed to have diminished. He assumed it was the onset of cooler, shorter days making the animals less active.

They kept away from Shreve Country Park. Kev didn't want to be anywhere near his old home and he'd assumed Jenny wouldn't want to run into Tamsin. She'd protested, though.

'Why should we change our routines? What's she going to do?'

'It's not that, Jen. I need the space for a start. And I could do without a nasty confrontation. I want some time to get my head together, plan something for us.'

She hadn't pushed him further.

Now, as they walked in single file to avoid nettle stings, Kev felt that all things were in place, life was simple and good. He reached behind and Jenny took his hand for a few paces. Not far beyond, the path broadened. On their left was an ancient hedgerow and on their right, growing out of the canal, were crowds of rushes. As soon as there was space, they walked beside each other. Kev put his arm around her shoulder.

'I've been thinking, Jen. Why don't we move? Somewhere that's got countryside all around it. Miles and miles of land and trees and rivers and hills.'

'What's wrong with Shreve?'

'Nothing's wrong with it, as such. But what have we

got? We've got a stinky, silted up old canal. We've got a reservoir disguised as a park. And we've got one of the biggest landfill sites in the country. The rest of it is industrial estates and council houses.'

'What about all these fields?'

'Yeah, but we've had to drive to get here. And all this land is cultivated. I want to go to a place where you look out the window and it's wild. You step outside your front door and you're surrounded by nature. Untouched. As it was meant to be.'

'What about your sports car?'

'I'll flog it.'

'What about your wife?'

'She could use a good flogging too.'

He watched Jenny's smile and thought that it was reserved somehow. A little cautious. He stopped walking and turned to her.

'Listen to me, Jen. This is not one of those situations in which the husband has a long-term mistress but never leaves his wife. Tamsin is out of my life forever as far as I'm concerned. She'll do everything she can to take half of everything I've got but I don't care about that if you don't. I want to be with you, Jen. Full stop. End of story. Start of new book. Whatever we've got – love, money, dreams – let's take it all and go somewhere we can enjoy it. Somewhere beautiful. I don't know how it's happened but being with you has opened me up to seeing the world in a different way. I feel alive like I never did before.'

If he'd expected a teary, joyful acceptance of his outpouring, he didn't get it.

'Is this the "something" you've been "planning"?' She asked.

'I suppose it must be. I didn't really know what it was until it came out.'

'Look, Kev…'

Jenny trailed off and looked away.

He'd hoped that it would go so much better than this. That she'd be keen to escape with him. Escape what, though? Was that all he'd come up with in the time he'd been thinking about all this? Was he just finding a way to run away from it all? To avoid it?

'Jen, I'm sorry. Maybe this is all too soon. I just thought… I mean I really believed that we were…'

Jenny wasn't listening to him any more. She was staring at something in the rushes. He was about to lose his temper with her for taking no notice when he realised that her face had drained pale.

'Jenny, what's wrong?'

The rushes were shifting, rustling. Something in the canal was making them do that. Something large and heavy. Jenny was backing away.

'Babe, hold on. It's probably just—'

Her scream, disgusted and terrified, cut him off.

He stepped in front of her to see down from her angle into the rushes. Something writhed there, trying to heave itself up from the water. Its movement reminded him of a seal or walrus that was close to drowning. The thing had no grace of movement. It merely rolled and floundered, *pulsated* almost, in its attempt to be free of the muddy canal water and the clinging reeds. He had the feeling he'd seen something like this, something he could make no sense of, before.

But this was no déjà vu. Down in Shreve country park that morning, months ago now, the dogs had attacked something similar. This coiling, juddering shape gave off the same rank odour of effluent and trash. This time there was no mistaking the facts. It really was moving. The thing was alive and independent in its own right. Unless someone was playing a practical joke on them – he wanted so much to believe that was what this was. The thing's movement was so jerky and so mechanical; it could easily have been some kind of home-made machine. He glanced around hoping to catch sight of someone with a remote controller, someone else with a hand held camcorder. They were alone.

And the thing was making progress. Part of it was on the towpath now. Shit. What was it? He could see eyes. Too many of them and none of them the same. He could see skin and animal pelts. He could see polythene bags of various colours, wrinkling and stretching taut as the thing heaved itself up. And then he saw an opening that could only have been a mouth. And in it he saw two horizontal, parallel knife blades, one in the upper part of the opening and one in the lower. The mouth hole closed and opened again. A shearing sound came from the blades.

Finally, Jen spoke in a whisper:

'Run, Kev.'

'What?'

'RUN.'

They slept as they lay when it was over, tangled, sticky, elated. But Ray knew they'd both felt the first wounds of impending heartbreak. Their love, their lives, were fragile. Never more so than now.

A scream woke Ray. His eyes flicked open and he listened. For a very few seconds he was able to indulge the idea that he might have dreamed it. He'd dreamed so many in the last few days. Then he heard another. The first had been fear. This one was pain. Delilah was awake too by then. They both jumped out of bed.

There were other screams now, further away. Shouts of panic and shock nearer by. The sound of people running in the street. Ray looked out of the window as he zipped up his jeans. For a moment he was absolutely still. Delilah joined him.

'Fucking hell,' he said.

Delilah was more specific.

'It's started.'

All along the canal side of the towpath, there was movement. The weeds shook and trembled and the water rippled.

Out of the corner of his eye, Kev thought he saw shapes swimming in the murky water. Up ahead, Jenny was sprinting. He'd never seen her move so fast. There was an unevenness to her running gait because of the missing toe but it didn't slow her down. Every few paces she hurdled some agglomeration of rubbish that had squirmed into her path and moments later he was forced to do the same.

Bloated black worms of rubbish overflowed from the canal every few feet. Kev thanked God they were so cumbersome but he was afraid too that their lack of mobility was some kind of bluff and that, at any time, they might lash out and bring both him and Jenny down.

They reached the canal bridge where the towpath let up onto the road. Jenny hammered up the slope and he followed, already fishing for the car keys. He pressed the fob, the locks sprung open and they shut themselves inside. He fumbled the key into the ignition with shaking fingers, started the car on the third attempt and left rubber on the tarmac as they screeched away.

There was no sustained sense of relief. As Kevin drove, he saw more crawling, writhing shapes in the fields and, as they neared town, in the alleys and streets of Shreve. Groups of kids poked some of the bags with sticks or laid into them with booted feet. In other places people backed away when the numbers of trash things seemed too great.

'Where the hell are they all coming from?' he said, not really expecting an answer.

'From the landfill,' said Jenny.

'How do you know that?'

'I just know it.'

He was about to ask her again when she said,

'Kev, where are you taking us?'

'Home.'

'Why? Don't you think we should be trying to get as far away as possible?'

She was right, of course. She was thinking. He was panicking.

He took a left turn, heading for the ring road. From there they could reach the motorway and go north or south. Anywhere, as long as it was away from Shreve. But the traffic was mounting. Kev didn't think anyone in the cars and trucks had realised yet that it was time to leave town, but the sight of the trash things invading Shreve was causing accidents. In front of them two cars had smashed into the back of a local bus. The driver had got out to dispute whose fault it was but now all parties were merely watching the laboured progress of the landfill creatures converging from every direction.

Kev drove around the knot of gawping drivers from the accident, almost colliding head-on with a speeding Land Rover. They both braked and Kev pushed through the gap, ignoring the horn and abusive shouts from the other driver.

They hit the ring road and the driving was better. There were no landfill creatures to distract anyone. Kev took the slip road that led off the bypass and out towards the motorway. Up ahead another car had done the same. The driver had seen the pile of 'rubbish' spilled all across the road and had tried to drive over it. Kevin imagined the man's annoyance as the nails and blades hidden inside the self-sacrificing creatures had punctured all his tyres like a stinger trap. The man had stepped out of his car and was screaming now. Something in the mass of trash at his feet had a hold of him. He was trying to tear his leg out of its grip. Kevin saw blood welling through the man's trousers, a whitening of the man's face. The man stumbled and fell to his knees. He put out one hand to stop himself going down all the way and when he regained his balance he brought the hand up again. All four fingers were gone.

Jenny stifled her scream with two hands over her mouth.

'We've got to help him,' said Kev.

'No. It's too late. Turn around, Kev. Turn us around before we get stuck out here.'

He checked his mirrors. Another car was pulling up behind them on the slip road. He flicked on his hazard lights and put the Z3 into reverse. A second turn put him onto the hard shoulder. He passed the approaching car of a woman making wank signals to him through the glass. Down on the ring road he rejoined the flow of traffic to more blaring horns.

'I'll try the next exit.'

Jenny said nothing. She didn't even nod.

Half a mile further along he signalled and pulled off the ring road again. This time he was ready for the road block and saw it long before they came close. A moving tide of rubbish had stretched right across the slip road. None of it moved. It was waiting. He turned the car around between the hard shoulder and the gravel verge.

Back on the ring road traffic was building up.

'Where the fuck are we going to go?'

'I'm thinking,' said Jenny. 'Just give me a minute.'

'I'm not sure how many minutes we've got.'

Mavis Ahern lay in bed with damp cotton pads over her closed eyes. She was dressed in a white blouse and navy cardigan, a calf-length grey skirt, tights and flat shoes. The curtains were drawn shut to keep out the light.

She'd come back to bed and lain this way since the sparkles at the edge of her vision had begun that morning. The sparkles had become streaks of blue lightning. Thunder followed in the form of pulses of agony that burst inside the entire right-hand side of her head. Her coffee and cornflakes made a swift reappearance. Traces of them stained her cardigan. She didn't care. After seeing herself in the mirror; her face grey, the vein in her right temple raised by internal pressure, she'd gone directly to bed.

It was years since she'd had a migraine. She thought she'd outgrown them. This one had started as she watched two boys kissing behind the pavilion. They couldn't have been more than eleven years old. One boy had unzipped the other's baggy cargo pants. Put his hand inside. Flash. Crackle. The auras had begun.

Why had the migraines returned? Was it some kind of punishment?

Maybe it was because Tamsin had gone as far as threatening her with a knife. Perhaps the shock of that was only now sinking in. Her plan to reunite the Dohertys in the sight of the Lord had failed utterly. Kevin had left the marriage home. It could not have gone more wrong.

She was filled with doubts.

Had God deserted her? Left the neighbourhood? The whole town? Given up and abandoned it to eat itself away from the inside?

She was so sick now, she hadn't the energy to look for a sign that He still loved her. The room pressed in around her. Icy sweat dripped from her head, palms and armpits. Her sense of smell was enhanced to the point where the insides of her nostrils felt stripped raw. She tried to breathe only through her mouth because the slightest smell made her nausea worse.

Her pulse was erratic. Each beat was a clap of agony

inside her head. The irregularity of it was frightening; her heart not beating the right time, losing its rhythm. She tried not to worry about it. She tried not to think. Thinking only made it all worse. Keeping the image of the two boys from her mind was almost impossible. It hung there at the edge of her consciousness, waiting for her guard to come down. Whenever she drifted close to sleep, instead of being released from the pain, she saw the boys. The furtive glances, their innocent, inexpert hands, their trembling excitement. She would snap back to wakefulness and sickness and pain.

She didn't know how long she'd lain there. Hours, it had to be, but how many she didn't know. She ignored the urge to urinate at first and even succeeded in convincing her body it didn't need to go. Twice she'd managed the trick of it but now the urge had returned, insistent and demanding. She would not be able to trick herself again nor sleep through it. Sooner or later she'd have to get up and face the agonies that a sudden change of blood pressure would cause her.

It was time.

She turned her palms to the mattress, ready to ease herself upright.

From downstairs came the muffled sound of glass breaking and wood, the door-frame perhaps, being – what? – kicked?

More glass shattered. There was a scraping sound. She recognised it: the back door had been opened.

Strange how both the urge to pee and the intensity of pain receded as she listened. From downstairs she heard thumps and dragging sounds. Deliberate, determined movements. She imagined a man, deformed somehow, limping from the back door across the lino in the kitchen and onto the hallway carpet. Was someone hurt perhaps? Mr. Siscombe from next door having a heart attack and struggling to find help? She couldn't just lie there. She had to check.

More quietly than she would have done minutes earlier, she pushed herself into a sitting position and swung her legs out of bed. The pads fell from her eyes. Her vision turned gritty white and the room spun away from her. The pain struck her like a tsunami. For several moments she didn't even know if she was still sitting or if she'd fallen back onto the bed. She couldn't stop the sickness then. She just sat forward and let her stomach clench and cramp. There was nothing in it and she racked one dry spasm after another until finally a dribble of pale green bile rose and slipped from her lips onto her grey skirt. This seemed to satisfy her stomach and the retching ceased. The chartreuse liver-mucus seeped into the rough fabric.

The white-out must have robbed her of a few seconds because now the noise of dragging and stumping was on the stairs. Nearing the top. There was definitely an urgency to the movement. A kind of desperation.

Her bladder was a bag of needles. Even so, she didn't believe she'd be able to stand.

The smell of sewage and rot hit her and her eyes widened in utter revulsion. The vomiting began again. This time the bile was dark green and coagulated. Its bitterness made her nausea worse. She heaved and heaved until it seemed her head would burst.

And then the thing that had broken into her house and dragged itself up the stairs came into view and she knew what it was. God had sent His retribution. She had failed Him despite every effort to serve. Now He had sent a creature to escort her downwards, away from Him forever, unblessed and discarded.

She didn't know what it was. It had no name. It had five 'arms' which it used as legs. It was fashioned of junk and animal parts and filth. It dragged a long fat body and left a wet trail of excrement on her carpet. A long-bodied spider without enough legs to move properly. It was searching for something. It used its arms to point its front end in one direction and then the other – hers. Its eyes were the loops from the handles of scissors. Its teeth were the ends of dozens of knitting needles. They clicked as it saw her. It dragged itself into her bedroom.

The thing was almost comical. It was impossible to believe it was real. The pain had elevated her awareness and reality had become a kind of farce now. Here came the shit spider with its stunted arms and comedy teeth. Here came its leaking body behind it. Clickety-click went the shit spider's chattery teeth. Snip, snip went its scissor-hole eyes. It was no higher off the ground than a small terrier. Along it came and she watched. She might have giggled if she knew it wouldn't have hurt her to do so.

The shit spider crawled closer, all the while blinking its eyes and clacking its remnant jaws. It took hold of her left leg with surprising strength; the grip was as sudden and strong as a sprung animal trap. The comedy went out of it all when it bit off half of her left foot. Until then, there'd never been pain worse than a migraine. The scream that had been waiting in the wings like an actor with only one line made its entrance.

The shit spider was hungry.

It bit and swallowed but did not chew.

She watched all this with inquisitive terror. The smell of waste filled her nostrils until they burned ammonia white.

Both her feet were gone.

Mavis Ahern allowed her bladder to release.

She thought of her roses. How from the muck good things would come. She had been wrong. So very, very wrong.

18

He wasn't happy with her decision but he couldn't think of anywhere better. Time was the only factor and so he agreed.

The Shreve Tertiary College car park was only a quarter full. It was Saturday, a day mainly for adult learners and weekend courses of a less academic nature. Kev pulled up right outside the front entrance and Jenny got out. When he didn't follow her, she walked around to the driver's side. He lowered the window.

The sound of sirens came from every direction. Smoke rose from various points on the horizon. Whether people realised it or not, Shreve was beginning to come to a halt. On the main steps of the college, students stood in frowning groups, not yet aware of what was happening.

'Aren't you coming in?' She asked.

'Yes. But not yet.'

'You're going to get her, aren't you?'

He looked away.

'I can't just leave her there with these things. I can't just let her die, Jenny. I'd never forgive myself. Trust me, babe. I love you but I have to do this. I've got no choice.'

'Kev, please… I know she's your wife… I know you probably still love her but—'

'Jen, it's not that. I just—'

'What I'm saying is, I don't care about her or what happens to her. I care about you. You've got to come back to me, Kev. Promise me you'll come back.'

He took her hand.

'I'm coming back, Jen. I swear it.'

Morning found Mason Brand shaved and dressed in clothes that had not come out of the wardrobe for several years. They smelled musty at first so he'd aired them on a ladder outside the back door.

In the predawn light, the garden was nothing more than untended fruitfulness turning into waste ground. Nothing moved out there. Whatever tide had drawn so close to his shore had ebbed far, far away.

The shaving didn't go well.

He cut off as much of his beard as he could with scissors. Then he used the only thing sharp enough in the house to finish the job – the knife he'd honed intending to kill himself. It did not lack for keenness – it was merely the wrong shape and several times he poked himself with the sharp end, eliciting a wince and a very willing blood flow. Finally, he managed to get most of his face smooth. He left long sideburns and a tuft under his chin where he'd nearly taken the top off his adam's apple.

The brown suit was loose because he'd lost weight so he punched extra holes in an old Swedish army belt and pulled the trousers tight around his waist with it. He wore a white shirt and an old, broad-ended tie. He had no dress shoes so he wore his walking boots, also brown, and pulled the bottoms of his trousers down to cover them as best he could.

Standing dressed outside the back door it was easy to believe that he'd imagined or hallucinated the things he thought he'd seen out there. It was such a long time since he'd eaten that his mind might have played any number of tricks on him. One thing it hadn't done was let him forget his morality. He had done wrong – ultimate wrong – and he intended to do something about it before the end came. What exactly he would do, he wasn't certain, but he felt a small power left within himself, as though he'd discovered a final crusade worth pursuing.

He neither drank nor ate anything. When the sun came

up, it burned into his eyes for several seconds before he turned away. Something made him take off his boots and for several minutes he stood barefoot on the soil of his garden before brushing his feet clean and putting the boots back on.

He walked away from his suburban lair with determination.

Kevin's drive back to Bluebell Way was worse.

Small accidents had occurred on many roads, mostly because of the distraction caused by the animated waste that crawled or slithered in every street. But some people, the small and the slow, perhaps the overly inquisitive, had already been unlucky. He passed a mobility scooter on which sat an elderly man. The man wore a flat cap and a dirty coat but his face was obscured by a creature half rabbit and half spoilage. Evidently the man had been trying to scream for help when the rabbit thing had extended a pseudo limb of some kind and thrust it up through his exposed palate. Now the old man stared ahead while the rabbit educated itself on his aged brain and other limping chimeras of junk and flesh crawled over him. They disassembled him, added him to themselves.

Too occupied with the fate of the elderly man, Kevin himself almost hit a cyclist who had wobbled into the centre of the road. He resolved to keep his mind on the journey.

Armed police had arrived at the top of one terrace where the rubbish seemed to be invading in force. He remembered that this street had both a home for the elderly and a day nursery. He wanted to stop then and do something to help. The thought of the rubbish cannibalising parts from children barely old enough to stand made his stomach turn over and his anger ignite. But what could he do?

He pulled onto the kerb to watch the police operation. It was clear that though they had their routines and training, it didn't fit the situation. The group converged on a large knot of resurrected debris, their rifles and pistols aimed downwards into them. Officers glanced at each other and shook their heads. Someone gave the command to open fire and the street echoed with the unfamiliar sounds of war. Automatic bursts and single shots popped and clattered into the rubbish. Here and there Kevin saw puffs and bursts and tears in the amalgamated flesh and plastic, the tin and bone. But the majority of the rubbish kept moving, seething forward. It was slow because it lacked the limbs to propel itself properly. But it came forward without fear, unaffected by the threat of bullets that could rip through it so easily. Many of the individual creatures that had been hit were still moving – evidently, the bullets had missed the vital components or hadn't torn big enough holes in their 'skins'.

Kevin remembered the way Ozzy and Lemmy had chewed open the fat tadpole-shaped thing he'd seen at the reservoir. That had been enough to end its life. The bullets were making only small holes and probably passed right through their targets. They'd need something less precise to stop the landfill creatures. He pulled back into the road and put his foot down for home.

Correction, my ex-home.

Bluebell Way was an invasion site. Kevin couldn't believe it.

It looked as though the landfill had been airlifted in ten tons at a time. But looking closer he could see dozens of individual landfill creatures moving in their hesitant, fumbling way. Christ, he thought, they're so much more dangerous than they look.

Dozens of them were besieging his house. Tamsin was upstairs looking out of the window in pale-faced terror and disbelief. Before he parked, he turned the car to face back the way he'd come. If they made it back out of the house they needed every advantage. Lumbering, crippled assemblies of rubbish and animal flesh assailed the door, climbing over each other to break in. One of the panels in the frosted glass had already shattered and something was *pouring* itself in through the space. Kevin had no weapons.

He spent several valuable moments thinking before he jumped out of the car. Tamsin had seen him by now and was jumping up and down at the window in desperation. She looked like a child. He saw another look on her face too, one he'd never seen before. Remorse. She was sorry. Sorry for what she'd done or sorry for what he'd done, he couldn't tell.

The garage was clear of creatures; it was the living they craved. He ran to it, unlocked it and hauled the door up. As soon as they sensed he was there landfill creatures converged on him from every direction. Panic rose and swelled in him. It was like an urge to piss with time running out. How long could he hold himself together? He hauled the door down behind him. It creaked as they pressed themselves against it.

In the garage he grabbed the tool with the longest handle, a rake they'd never used – it still had the price sticker on it. In the corner there was a five-litre plastic petrol can in which he kept the two-stroke fuel for the lawn mower. He picked it up and shook it. It was less than half full. Would it be enough? Was two-stroke even flammable without a wick? He couldn't remember.

Something scratched the leg of his jeans and he shook his foot violently. With a pathetic mewl, something unrecognisable crashed back against the wall. Whimpering, it began to crawl back to him. They'd lifted the door enough for some of the smaller creatures to slip under. More of them were working their way through the gap.

He let himself out the side door of the garage, shutting the things inside, and went to the back of the house, watchful and twitchy. There were two or three landfill creatures crossing the garden towards the back steps but the main body of attackers was still at the front door. He crept quietly to the front of the house, now, along the side wall. Several of them had already found him. They swarmed down the alley formed between the house and the garage but they were all small fry. He pushed them back with the rake as though sweeping. Some of them tore badly and a filthy plasma leaked out. Kevin choked on the smell but kept pushing.

Most of the landfill creatures were slow moving and ungainly. He knew if he was nimble enough, he'd be able to do enough damage to buy some time.

At the front of the house he risked hopping over several of the things to get closer to the main entry. Fumbling and shaking, his knees jittering as he stood on the spot, he unscrewed the lid of the petrol can and splashed the fuel out towards the front door and all over the converging landfill creatures. They shivered at the touch of the liquid as if knowing what would follow. Darting between other creatures on the lawn he spilled fuel out behind him as he sprinted back to the side wall. He hoped the trail of fuel was unbroken and he tried to douse as many of the creatures in his path as he could. When he reached the back garden he took the pink Bic lighter from his pocket and thanked God he hadn't quit smoking. It was so low on gas he couldn't hear any fluid inside when he shook it. He flicked it beside the fuel-glistening grass but there it had no effect. He flicked it again and again.

'Come on. For God's sake, come ON.'

The fuel caught, not from the lighter's flame but from a spark hitting it. It leapt to life burning his eyelashes and the front of his hair. He fell backwards onto the grass. The fire was already around the corner to the front of the house. Every landfill creature the flames touched caught light and began to melt. Every one of them made such desperate, haunted cries he almost wanted to turn the hose on them. The leaping flame and the writhing of the dying creatures mesmerised him for a few seconds as he lay on his side. The sound was hard to bear. It interrupted his concentration.

There was a searing pain in his ear and then he was screaming and rolling away from it. He struggled to his feet and put his hand to the side of his head. Most of his left ear was missing. It had disappeared inside the razorblade mouth of a tiny trash freak.

'You dirty fucker,' he screamed.

He used the rake to tear it apart. Scattered and broken it was soon still. There in the liquid shit of its blood, lay his severed ear. He didn't dare touch it.

Crying at the pain, he went to the back door and used the rake on the other creatures that were scrabbling at the glass, killing them easily. Then he let himself in and locked the door behind him. Terrified that the wound would be infected, he turned the tap on, bent down and bathed what was left of his ear under it. The water made the pain worse but he gritted his teeth. With the damage had come a kind of hyper-clarity. The creatures outside were an obstacle. He would find a way around them. Getting Tammy to safety was a problem he would solve. The insanity of the situation no longer screamed at him and slowed his thinking down. Everything was simple now.

Pressing a clean tea towel to the side of his head he ran up the stairs.

She was waiting at the top, tearful and overjoyed.

'Oh Christ, Kevin. Thank you. Thank you so much.'

'I only came back for a change of boxer shorts.'

She noticed the bloodstained tea towel.

'Was it… one of them?'

He nodded then pushed past her to the bathroom to search in the cabinet. The things he didn't want he threw on the floor. When he found what he was looking for he unscrewed the cap and handed it to Tammy. This was the feared and respected remedy his own father had put on all their cuts when they were little – hydrogen peroxide.

'I won't be able to do this to myself.'

'What do expect me to do?'

'Just tip a bit on when I take the towel away.'

Their eyes met for a second and he saw she'd have no problem doing what he'd asked. There was still enough hate in her to power a city. He took the towel away and she upended the bottle over what remained of his ear.

'Aaaarrgh! Shit, shit, shit, shit, SHIIIITTT.'

The exposed flesh turned white as it fizzed. He forced the urge to hit her back down again. They had to concentrate on getting out. But it did cross his mind to wonder again why he'd come back for the bitch.

Never mind, Kev, just keep it moving.

He dropped the tea towel and when he looked at her again, she was crying.

'What is it?'

'I don't want us to hurt each other any more, Kevin. I've had enough. Enough for a lifetime. And I… I can't believe you came back. I know I don't deserve it.'

'We're not out of this yet, Tammy. The whole town's infested with these things.'

'The whole t—'

The sound of smashed glass and something heavy landing on the kitchen floor came from downstairs. It was a terrifying sound. The sound of an intelligent action, part of the landfill creatures' plan.

Kevin took her hand.

'Come on, we're leaving.'

He ran from the bathroom to the spare room. He looked down into the back garden but couldn't see anything out there. From the front door came the sound of writhing, moaning creatures on fire and the smell of burning plastic and charred meat.

He led Tammy to the top of the stairs. At the back door, he heard the lock being turned and the handle being pushed down. He cursed himself; in his haste, he'd left the rake in the kitchen. There had to be something in the house he could use. If the creatures weren't very strong, keeping them at a distance would be enough. Perhaps they could reach the recess under the stairs. Then he could use the sweeping brush to keep whatever was in the kitchen at a safe range until they got out.

He descended the stairs more cautiously than he'd come up them, bringing Tammy by the hand behind him. Smoke was seeping in around the frame of the front door. It smelled like the paint and wood had caught fire; the whole house would catch soon. He didn't plan to hang around long enough to see their home go up in flames.

At the bottom of the steps, he looked over the rail and into the kitchen. In the middle of the floor, surrounded by shattered glass, was a flower pot. It had also smashed when it hit the floor, scattering compost and jettisoning a geranium. But there was no movement in the kitchen and no sound inside the house other than his own breathing and heartbeat.

He motioned to Tammy that it was safe to move and together they stepped down into the front hallway. He signalled for her to stay behind him and then edged forwards towards the door of the storage recess under the stairs. He had to turn his back on the kitchen to open it. Even though he was stealthy, the hinge creaked because the wood had warped. It took three tugs to get the door open. Inside it was too gloomy to see what he needed.

'Where's the broom?' he whispered.

Tammy shook her head then remembered.

'Outside the back door.'

'Shit. There must be something else in here.'

Tammy leaned across and flicked the light switch for him.

Vacuum cleaner. Dustpan and brush. Bleach. Feather duster. Flimsy plastic mop.

'Come on, come on.'

Then he saw the tool box.

'Thank you, Lord.'

He crouched down to unsnap the latches. Inside was the nearest thing to a weapon he was going to find, his claw hammer. As he reached into the tool box he heard Tammy's scream cut short. He leapt up with the hammer in time to see Tammy being dragged into the kitchen by her throat. Not all the creatures crawled any more. Not all of them were slow and small.

The thing had raised Tammy up off her feet and she was already struggling to stay conscious. She had both her hands around the creature's arm, trying to lift herself out of its grip. The thing was hanging her alive. It had five arms and stood on two legs like an inverted centaur. A long, fat tail whipped wetly across the kitchen floor leaving smears of excrement. It was only when one of the thing's free arms extended towards Tammy's belly that Kevin finally moved. The arm ended in a pair of secateurs.

He swung the hammer down onto the arm holding Tammy and felt something break inside it. Tammy fell to the ground and staggered back against the wall. The limb that held her came away from the landfill creature, spilling stinking brown blood onto the tiles. Still the hand gripped her but now she could fight to tear it off. The landfill creature turned all its attention towards Kevin, reaching out with its remaining four arms. Scissors, pliers, meat cleaver and secateurs.

Kevin smashed the hammer sideways against the secateur arm but it was more resilient. The creature moved towards him, dragging its heavy tail. It didn't really have a head, just an opening above what passed for its torso. Kevin could hear the shearing of blades coming from inside it. It walked on mostly human legs that appeared to have been cut into dozens of pieces and stitched back together with twine and green garden wire. He struck at it again, this time breaking the pliers hand so that it hung uselessly. The creature let out a moan of pain and misery.

With a grunted scream, Tamsin tore the dislocated hand and forearm from her throat and threw it across the kitchen. It fell into the sink where both of them could hear it scrabbling to escape. Edging around behind the thing, Tammy reached for the biggest implement in the wooden knife block, her Global carving knife. The blade was twelve inches long and sharp enough to cut bone. She moved into position behind the thing and lunged.

The creature screamed again, a howl of torment and frustration. It tried to turn towards Tammy but its tail slowed it down. Already she'd lunged again, this time with more confidence. But the deep thrusts seemed only to cause further leaks from the thing's body, not real damage.

'You've got to slash it, Tammy. Tear it open.'

She nodded.

Kevin swung the clawed end of his hammer across the flank of the thing, opening up skin and plastic to reveal a mess of cobbled organs and rubbish.

It was then, perhaps knowing that it would not survive, that the thing's chest split to reveal a human head with the eyes missing. Those eyes, he now realised were set inside the creature's shoulders. Despite the wet mess inside the creature they both recognised the face.

The head hissed one word,

'Sssssssinners…'

Tammy's eyes widened in recognition and then she lashed out with total fury, sweeping the blade from side to side and opening the thing up again and again. The screams of protest became weaker. Kevin tore at it with the claw hammer. The thing lost its physical integrity and began to fall apart, dropping dead parts to the tiles. It collapsed to the floor, sighed and was still.

Panting, Tammy spat on it.

'Trashy bitch.'

In the sink, the creature's still-living hand still flailed and tried to climb out. Kevin picked it up with a pair of barbecue tongs, threw it into the microwave and slammed the door.

'How do like your garbage, Tammy?'

'Cremated.'

He set it: full power, ten minutes, and hit the start button.

"Let's get out of here."

19

There was something very sick, something cowardly, about watching it all from the bedroom window. But Ray couldn't pull himself away. The scene outside was so similar to Revenant Apocalypse it wouldn't have surprised him to discover a film crew parked up the street shooting a scene for the movie version of the game.

Accepting it was not a game took bollocks he wasn't sure he possessed. If he wanted to survive and keep Delilah safe too, he knew he had to sharpen up, start taking it seriously. He had to come up with a plan. But from the safety of her bedsit, he was still removed enough to live in a bubble. Almost. The screams from the street and nearby houses were real. The creatures from the landfill were real. Their hunger was real.

But it was so tempting to roll a joint and take a step back even farther from it all. That would be the simplest, easiest thing to do. And maybe, if they stayed very quiet and locked and bolted everything, the creatures would leave them alone until the government sent in the troops.

Delilah seemed to sense his thoughts and she pulled him away from the glass.

'Let's find something to fight with.'

'We're not going out on that street, D.'

'No, but they might come in here. I want to be ready.'

He didn't want to accept it but he knew it was true. He pulled on his Converse All Stars and tied them tightly, tucking the spare lengths of lace away inside them. If he was going to run, he was going to run fast. No silly mistakes. Delilah was pulling on one of her long, flowing, velvety dresses. Her boots had three inch soles.

'D? Babe. Are you sure that's appropriate attire?'

'What are you talking about?'

'What I mean is, if we're sprinting down the high street being chased by a throng of zombie cyborg trash, you don't want to go tripping over your hem, do you? Haven't you got some jeans?'

'Denim?'

'Well… Yeah… or, like, trousers or something.'

For a moment Ray thought she was going to lose her temper. He'd never paid her anything but compliments about the way she dressed before this.

'I've got some combat trousers. But I dyed them black.'

Ray shook his head in disbelief.

'I don't give a toss what colour they are, D. What matters is can you run in them?'

'Kidding, Ray. Okay?'

She was laughing now.

'Very funny. What about those boots. Got anything… lower to the ground?'

'Will trainers do?'

'Yeah, fine.'

'I dyed them black too.'

'Delilah…'

She was already getting changed into her combats and she hadn't lied, they were mottled charcoal and black. He watched her as she dressed. She filled her trousers in exactly the right places. On top she wore a tight black roll neck jumper over a sports bra, also black. Her trainers were silver; she winked and stuck out her tongue as she Velcroed them up.

'What now?' She asked.

'Have you got a backpack? Black is fine.'

'There's one in the bottom of that wardrobe.'

'We need some kind of weapon,' said Ray, 'and spare clothes in case we get stuck outside. Warm stuff, waterproofs, that kind of thing.'

She shook her head.

'I've got nothing like that.'

He glanced out of the window.

'Judging by the look of things out there, we should be able to borrow what we need from the shops without anyone getting upset.'

'There's an outdoor equipment place just up the road.'

'Perfect.'

A thump from downstairs made both of them start.

'Jesus,' whispered Delilah with her hand on her heart.

The thump came again, louder.

'That's the front door,' she said.

'Yeah. You'd have thought they might knock before trying to break it down.'

He peered down from the bedsit window.

'I can't make out what's down there.'

Delilah chewed the inside of her lip.

'It could be someone trying to escape from them,' she said.

'I know,' said Ray. 'Here, let me open this.'

The window only opened far enough for him to stick his head through. It was enough.

He pulled back in, pale in the face.

'Fuck knows what it is but it's not a someone. It's a some-*thing*. How strong is your front door?'

'I've never needed to test it.'

'Is there another way out of here? Like a fire escape or something?'

'No. Just the main door.'

Ray was aghast.

'Isn't there a back garden?'

'Well, there's a small patch of paving and a load of weeds but no one ever seems to go out there.'

'There has to be a back door, D. It must lead out there from one of the downstairs bedsits.'

'How do you know there aren't more of them out the back?'

'I don't.'

Whatever was outside the front door got more serious about coming in. The next impact sounded as though it had damaged the door. Ray grabbed the rucksack from the cupboard and slung it, empty, across his back. They'd have to stock up later.

'Isn't there anything we could use to defend ourselves?' he asked.

She squatted down and groped under the bed for a few moments.

Another crash came from the front door.

'Forget it, D, we've got to leave right now.'

'Wait.'

With a sigh of satisfaction, she drew out a long, flat wooden box, carved with twined serpents. She flicked the two hasps and lifted the lid. Ray forgot all about the creature downstairs.

'Where the fuck did you get that?'

'Ex-boyfriend gave it to me. He was into Karate and jujitsu.'

'Is it real?'

'As far as I know.'

She handed Ray the ornate scabbard and he slipped six inches of steel into view. He was no expert but it certainly looked like a very real and very well looked after katana. Probably the kind of trophy taken by American soldiers from Japanese officers at the end of the Second World War. He kissed her.

'This'll do,' he said. 'This'll do very nicely indeed.'

The front door came off its hinges. Ray stuck the scabbard through his belt, unsheathed the katana and opened Delilah's bedsit door.

'Whatever happens, stay a long way behind me until it's clear, okay?'

'Have you ever used one of these before?'

'Yes. Kind of. Well, no, not really. But I've… it doesn't matter. Just stay back.'

He edged out of the door onto the landing. It was a tiny

house converted into four bedsits – two upstairs and two down. From the landing, the stairs led straight to the front door and the downstairs entry where the other bedsit front doors led off.

But Ray had stopped worrying about how to find and get out of the back door. Blocking the downstairs hall was something bigger than he'd expected. Much bigger. Filling the doorway from shattered lock to ripped-out hinges was a giant, black centipede raised up on its belly like a snake ready to strike. All along the exposed lower part of itself were two rows of human fingers that waved like cilia. Its face was an upside down satellite dish and set in the middle of it was a single cow's eye. The transmitter protruded above it like a carrot and stick and at its tip was the centipede's other eye. The mouth was below all of this, a twelve inch vertical slit lined with the tips of a hundred or more serrated bread knives, three rows deep. They reminded him of a shark's maw.

The thing gurgled at him, more satisfied now to have its prey in front of it. The centipede wheezed like leaking bellows as it breathed but when it moved forward it was surprisingly fast. The severed fingers had become its legs and as they flickered, it glided along as though on a cushion of air. Its front half remaining upright cobra-like, it moved forwards and up the first three steps. The unblinkable eyes stared and swivelled. The shark's-teeth knives clashed against each other.

Ray lifted the katana and chopped downwards, closing his eyes at impact, like a novice firing a handgun for the first time. When he opened them he saw he'd merely taken off the thing's protruding eye. The creature shrank back, hissing and turning its 'head' from side to side until it could see the severed eye. It backed up on its hundreds of fingers, lay down on its front and when it raised up again, the eye that had been lying blind on the stairs was gone inside the thing's gnashing mouth. Shit, thought Ray, they even recycle themselves. The creature didn't look happy to have lost a piece of itself and its remaining eye now appeared bloodshot with anger. It approached again more slowly and then lunged at Ray's feet.

He brought the katana down in the centre of the thing's concave head and spilt it open, but in trying to step back at the same time, he fell over, sitting down hard on the top step. The creature, he now realised, was the length of the whole staircase and almost as wide. It swarmed up towards him, its radar dish split almost in half but its teeth clamping shut again and again like machinery.

Ray scrabbled backwards and stood on the top step. Delilah had retreated back into her room to keep out of his way. Ray's hands were shaking. His knuckles were raw, bone white.

He took a deep breath, raised the sword up and over his right shoulder, as he'd made his character do so many times in Revenant Apocalypse, and brought it down in a diagonal arc. Whatever he cut through in the movement was enough to finish the creature. It immediately sagged and deflated and a wash of foul, brown gore spilled down the cheap stair carpet. Hundreds of fingers from God knew how many previous victims twitched and were still.

He poked the mess with the tip of the katana but it no longer stirred. He sank to the floor.

Delilah edged out behind him.

'Nice moves, Ray.'

'Thanks.'

'Where'd you learn to do that anyway?'

He glanced up at her.

'Never let it be said that computer games are a waste of time. Or that they promote antisocial behaviour.'

'That wasn't exactly a friendly thing to do, babe,' she said.

He looked up again, not amused.

Delilah grinned

'Sorry, Ray. Thanks for saving my life. You can put

down the sword now.'

Ray looked at his hands but didn't disarm.

'Actually, I can't seem to let go of the bloody thing. Can you help me?'

That was the first time Delilah had to peel Ray's fingers from the katana's haft. It was not the last.

Mason Brand walked through the estate in awe and horror.

Everywhere, versions of the shed-thing he'd found in his own garden many weeks before were crawling, slithering or walking, depending on what they'd eaten or scavenged. They made use of absolutely everything, not a scrap was wasted. Some of the creatures were as fragile as the paper that formed their skins; others were sturdy with boxes or crates forming an efficient carapace. They'd copied themselves from the living things of the world or attempted approximations of them. Some were more successful than others but at each new taking-in of living tissue, they re-forged themselves into something better, something stealthier, something faster.

Mason considered the consequences of this. Right now, it was probably possible to contain this invasion because it was a land-based advance. But how long would it be before some of the creatures caught a bird, one of the gulls from the landfill for example? Then they'd be able to go anywhere they wanted. They could let the wind spread them like seeds.

The pets of the neighbourhood, the ones that had been outside when the influx began, had not fared well. In several front gardens Mason saw dogs being assimilated a piece at a time or cats still hissing and clawing at the advancing menace. None of them would survive unless they had the sense to hide and even those, in the end, would be absorbed – their very cells re-educated.

He walked among them like a visitor to a zoo and it was only after almost an hour of watching and wandering that his situation fully dawned on him. They had no interest in him. He stopped then and observed in a different way. Did they not sense he was there? He tested the idea by getting in the path of one of the more embryonic ones, something that looked like a large black comma with a single eye. He stood in its way and when it came within a foot of him, it turned its eye upwards and then changed direction. To go around him. In case the thing was blind or it was a fluke, he placed himself in the way of a larger creature, one that had used a feline template and a box of car spares to shape itself. The thing clanked along on four shaky legs and had a tail of unravelling steel cable. When Mason stood in front of it, it paused, regarded him then turned and staggered away in the opposite direction.

That was all the proof he needed. They saw him and they left him be.

Why?

Heavens. Wasn't it obvious?

He shouted at the retreating cat creature.

'You know me, don't you? It's told you to leave me alone.'

He'd been so ready to die that morning, so ready he'd have willingly lain down in the road and let them take him apart after he'd done what he came to do. It wasn't going to be like that, he now realised.

There was something to be done and he'd perhaps wasted too much time already. From all around came the sounds of a new mayhem. The cries and calls and snuffles of thousands of landfill creatures, no two of them the same. And over these cries, the howls of animals being dismembered and disembowelled one useful piece at a time and the screams of disbelieving people suffering the same end or fighting to avoid it. Sirens chittered and screeched from several directions, though there were no rescue vehicles in view. When he looked around, he saw the smoke from fires both accidental and deliberate.

Somewhere overhead but still out of view, he heard the distant thump of rotors cutting the morning air.

Despite his diminished weight, he felt no weakness. There was a lightness and resilience in his entire frame. If he was to be in time, he had to hurry and so he ran, dodging between the slower landfill creatures, jumping over the larger ones. There was still time to atone.

11 Bluebell Way was no less besieged than any of the houses around it. Landfill creatures blundered, some crippled by their choice of manifestation, others a little more agile, across the wrecked front lawn. They climbed over each other in their eagerness to get inside the house. The front door appeared secure – it was one with no glass but the downstairs windows were vulnerable and might last only minutes depending on the strength and numbers of creatures assailing the place.

He decided the best course of action was to try and get in from the rear of the house or at least make contact from there. There was a six-foot wrought iron gate on the walkway beside the house. It separated the back from the front and didn't appear to have been breached. In fact, none of the creatures seemed to have tried to gain access that way. Of course, there was always the possibility they knew something he didn't. He wasn't about to start underestimating them. He might not have understood their intelligence but that did not mean they didn't possess it.

He walked calmly past the Volvo in the driveway, beside the garage and down the block-paved walk. He lifted the latch on the gate and walked through, shutting it behind him. As he'd hoped, the back of the house was undisturbed. He paused for a few seconds to make certain of this before approaching the back door and trying the handle. It was locked, which he took to be a good sign.

Standing back from the door he cupped his hand around his mouth to direct his voice and called quietly to the upper windows.

'Mr. Smithfield? Mrs. Smithfield? Are you up there? If anyone can hear me, come to the window.'

He waited for only a few seconds. Three faces appeared at a rear upstairs window; father, mother and daughter – the incomplete family. Aggie acted as though she didn't know him. She looked gaunt, aged and frightened. He felt a rush of shame but stayed where he was. At first the parents looked hopeful, relieved to see someone had come for them. Then the obvious got through to them: he was no policeman, no soldier. He wasn't even armed. They saw a skinny man in a suit too big for him. A gaunt man with too much hair on his face to suit the times and enough fresh cuts to make him look like he'd walked away from a traffic accident. Or a fight. But still they must have hoped, in spite of this, that he could help them. He was, if nothing else, a friend when all about were enemies.

The window opened and Mr. Smithfield leaned out.

'Who are you?'

'I'm here to get you away. You can hide here for a while, but they'll break in soon enough. If you want to be safe you should come with me.'

The man looked doubtful.

'Why aren't you helping anyone else? How do I know you're not here to rob us or worse?'

'You don't know that and I can't prove it. But what could be worse than what's happening already. Believe me, I want to help you.'

'What's your name?'

'My name is Mason Brand. I… I knew your son.'

He wasn't sure if he should have told them that. Equally, he didn't believe they'd have come with him if he hadn't mentioned it. In time he'd know if the risk was worth it.

The wife pushed her husband out of the way and leaned through the window.

'Did you say you knew Donald? How?'

'Please, Mrs. Smithfield, there isn't very much time. If you want to survive this, if you want your daughter to be safe, you must all come with me and you must come now. Otherwise I cannot guarantee that any of you will live to see another sunrise.'

Kevin had never imagined that he would end up using his sports car as some kind of battering ram but as they drove through the changed streets of Shreve he realised he had no choice. The trick was to knock the landfill creatures out of the way without letting them get under the wheels. He'd already seen the damage they could do to tyres. But the streets were crowded with the things and sometimes they were unavoidable.

He'd never taken the car to a circuit, though he'd always told himself he would. Now he was driving the equivalent of a high speed cone test through the town's streets. There were other obstacles to avoid too; wounded people he had no chance of assisting, stopped or overturned cars – some of them on fire, goods spilled from the back of half unloaded vans. The various emergency vehicles and personnel he passed were too busy attempting to stay alive to bother to try and slow him down. To them he was just another terrified driver about to wipe himself out through sheer panic.

But Kevin wasn't panicking.

He had set a goal – two goals, actually – both of which would be fulfilled by his arrival back at the college. There, inside the building and removed to the highest floor, Tamsin would be safe and he would have done his duty to her. There, too, he would be reunited with Jenny and, live or die, they would be together. That was all he cared about. It was, therefore, not a time for panic but a time for focus and determination.

He swiped the car across into the empty oncoming

lane, clipping one of the largest landfill creatures he'd seen yet. It was the size of a motorbike and seemed to incorporate motorcycle parts, but strange legs propelled it along on its two wheels instead of a motor. He hit it with the passenger side of the BMW, denting the door badly and making Tammy scream. Her window cracked but did not shatter and the creature was thrown onto its side. He straightened the car up and in the rear-view mirror saw it leaking a wash of dark fluid onto the tarmac. It was still.

The split second glance up had taken his eye off the road and he didn't even see what he hit next. He felt it pass under the wheels and chassis on his side.

Tammy screamed again.

'What was it? Did you see?'

Tammy had her hands over her mouth to stifle her sobs.

'Tammy, what did we hit?'

She shook her head, all the while staring through the windscreen; staring into some place he couldn't see, a place that likely wasn't there.

He reached over and took one of her wrists, squeezing it hard enough to bend the bones. She looked at him wide eyed.

'I need to know what went under the car, Tamsin.'

'I… I don't know what it was.'

It was becoming obvious, though.

The Z3's handling had softened and the car was pulling to the right.

'Shit,' he whispered.

He could see Shreve Tertiary College partially obscured by trees and houses and probably less than half a mile away. He no longer knew if he would make it. Though he tried to contain it, panic broke the surface and wouldn't go back down. His face prickled, irritated by a sudden heat. Beside him Tammy was rocking in the car seat like a bomb blast survivor and repeating a strange, low moan over and over through chattering teeth.

Christ, just let me hold it together a little longer.

20

With the front door hanging off and open, other landfill creatures were attracted to the scene.

Ray couldn't help wondering what sense they were using; how did they know where to come to? Was it smell or some kind of perception people didn't have, some kind of intuition?

He and Delilah knocked on the door of the downstairs bedsit – the one that had to lead into the back 'garden'.

'Quick, Ray, they're coming. Loads of them.'

'If anyone's in there, for God's sake let us in,' Ray shouted. Then he hammered. 'Here, D, you'll have to help me break it in.'

They shoulder-barged the door together and it was tougher than they'd expected. Ray jarred himself painfully and had to turn and use his other shoulder. The lock gave on the fifth attempt and they staggered into the bedsit. A skinny lad with bad acne stood holding out a steak knife in both hands. His whole body was trembling.

'Get out. This is my place. I'm hiding here. You can't come in.'

The kid saw Ray's katana and backed up a little.

'If you'd opened the door for us, you'd still have a hiding place. As it is, you've got fuck all.' Ray looked past the shaky kid's shoulder. 'That door unlocked, is it?'

'Leave it alone.'

'Didn't think so.'

Holding the katana towards the boy's face, Ray let Delilah pass behind him to open the downstairs back door.

'Don't open that,' said the kid. 'It's not safe.'

'Looks clear at the moment,' said Delilah. Ray backed towards her.

'Sorry about your door, mate,' he said. 'Needs must

and all that. If you want my advice, it's this room that's not safe. You're better off getting higher up – somewhere they can't reach. Good luck.'

In the tiny outdoor back space, Delilah had already clambered onto a rusting, disused washing machine and pulled herself up onto the wall dividing the back garden from the next property. Ray handed up the katana and followed. From there they balanced along to the rear wall. Beyond it was an alley separating them from the back gardens and houses on the other side. None of the landfill creatures appeared to have found their way into the narrow alley yet but it would become a trap if they did. Ray decided to play it safe.

'Let's stay up here for as long as we can. Don't want to be in a position we can't climb out of, do we?'

Delilah shook her head. She was already working out a way up onto the roof of a house a few properties along. From there they'd be able to assess their next move.

The kid appeared in the garden behind them. He was backing away from something and calling over his shoulder.

'Hey, where are you going?'

'Away from here,' called Ray.

'I... I want to come with you.'

'I thought you wanted to stay there.'

'I've changed my mind.'

Ray looked at Delilah.

'Can't stop him, can we?' he murmured.

'If he can't keep up, we're not waiting for him,' she said.

The kid was already up on the washing machine

'No, I suppose not. Hey, you, whatever your name is, make sure you kick that washing machine a long way from the wall after you climb up.'

'It's Jimmy.'

'I didn't ask for an introduction. Just do it.'

In the back garden, several small landfill creatures had appeared, each waving their various forms of sensory equipment around to get a lock on their prey. Jimmy kicked the washing machine but all it did was fall on its side not far from the wall.

'Fuck,' said Ray. 'Let's get moving.'

He and Delilah were agile along the wall running beside the alley. They came to the house they liked the look of and glanced back. Jimmy was wobbling along the wall like a drunk on a high wire. He'd only come a few yards. Ray looked disgusted.

'We should have said no to him.'

'Too late now.'

The house they'd reached had a stepped wall leading up to within a metre of the roof. From there they'd be able to climb to the apex for a better view. Ray was going to offer to go first but Delilah was already nearing the top of the 'steps'. She took hold of the guttering and used it to pull herself up.

'Hey, be careful, that won't take much weight.'

'Watch your mouth, Ray.'

'You know what I'm saying. Just go steady.'

She was up and waving for him to follow. He ran along the rising wall and tested the guttering. It was strong and secure. Once again, he handed her the sword. Pulling himself up was easy. Halfway between them and the bedsits, Jimmy was walking with his arms stretched out to either side for balance, staring at his feet as he heel-toed along.

'We're not waiting,' said Ray.

The tiles seemed thick and strong but the two of them crawled on all fours to spread their weight out. Ray made it to the apex first, balanced his way to a large chimney and climbed onto its ledge. Delilah stood below him, gripping the chimney hard.

'You all right?' he asked.

'Fine. What can you see?'

Ray scanned in silence for several moments.

'I think I've got a plan.'

'Go on.'

'It's a bit sketchy.'

'Any plan is a good plan right now, Ray.'

'Okay. From here we can walk to the end of the street on the rooftops. There's a high wall at the last property. It's a bit of a drop, but I think we can get onto the wall and then down to street level again. Park Street is on the left, where the outdoor shop is.'

'Let's hope they haven't closed early today.'

'Ha ha. From there we can cross the park to the river, over the bridge and then we'll be on the grounds of the College. I've been meaning to turn up for a few lectures.'

'Liar.'

'Whatever. Once we're there, we can go up to the higher levels. Lots of rooms with decent locks on them. Plenty of equipment for dealing with all this trash.'

'What about the things?'

'There's plenty of them down there but most of them seem interested in getting to the people and all the people are hiding indoors. The shops and the park look pretty clear.'

'Ray.'

'What?'

'That's actually a really good plan.'

'Thanks.'

'I have to admit, I'm kind of surprised.'

'Well, it was just a matter of...' Ray looked down and saw the grin on her face. 'You know, if we do make it to the College, I'm going to slap your arse.'

'That's all I need to keep me going, babe.'

Ray climbed down from the chimney.

Behind and below them, Jimmy wasn't even halfway along the alley wall. Following him, three large landfill creatures with the right kind of appendages for climbing were catching up. The kid still held his ridiculous, plastic-handled steak knife in his right hand as he faltered along the two-bricks-wide wall.

'This kid is really bad news, Ray.'

'I know.' He turned his back on where they'd come from. 'Let's get moving.'

They walked along the apex, skirting around each chimney with extra care. When they'd made it across two houses, Ray stopped to look back. Jimmy had managed to get as far as the stepped wall. He knew something was behind him but Ray could tell he was too scared to disrupt his balance by looking round, in case he fell. Jimmy got a hand to the guttering, put the knife in his mouth like some gangly pirate and tried to pull himself up. He seemed to lack the necessary strength to do it. The first of the landfill creatures had reached the alley end of the same wall.

'Christ,' said Ray.

'We said we'd leave him.'

'I know what we said but look at him. He's fucked. What if it was you down there, D? Or me?'

'It isn't.'

'How can you be so cold?'

She took hold of his hands.

'What about us, Ray? What if, because of the kid, you and I don't make it? Or only one of us makes it? I want a life, Ray, a future with you in it. I don't want to survive all this for nothing.'

'I want the same thing, D. Believe me. But if we can't take care of people like him, we don't deserve a future. Anyway, think of the guilt you'll feel knowing you could have helped but didn't.' Ray pushed past her. 'He's coming with us.'

She watched him balance his way back to the first roof they'd climbed. Jimmy was still trying to climb onto the guttering. The way he was doing it would surely bring the whole structure down. Instead of using it to assist a jump, he was letting it support his whole body weight while he tried to get one leg up. It wasn't working. The landfill creatures had reached the first of the steps in the wall. Ray was descending the roof towards Jimmy.

Delilah watched, refusing to move.

'Shit,' she said.

And then she was hurrying back to them.

Mason watched the family come out of the back door like animals testing the air of a new dawn. Mr. Smithfield led the way followed by his wife and then Aggie. This was no longer the world they recognised, certainly not the world they wanted it to be.

From every dwelling in the Meadowlands estate came the screams of people fighting off an army of nightmares. More helicopters circled in the sky, still uncoordinated. Mason saw an air ambulance hesitating to land, a couple of circling TV choppers, a police surveillance helicopter and the arrival of something that looked more military – something big enough to contain troops perhaps. He didn't believe any of the aircraft or their crews could do much good. He doubted anyone really understood what they were faced with.

He'd instructed Mr. Smithfield to bring his car keys. All they had to do was get inside the Volvo and they'd be safe. For a while.

'Follow me,' he said to the Smithfields, 'And stay as close as you can. We'll have to move quickly, so don't get separated.'

'Where are we going?' asked Mr. Smithfield.

'I'm not sure yet. Do you have much fuel?'

'I filled it up yesterday.'

'Good.'

Mason walked to the gate and opened it. The others hesitated.

'Please, you have to stay right with me. Close enough to touch me or you won't be safe.'

Richard and Pamela Smithfield exchanged glances then, wondering at the idea of touching this man. Was he some kind of deviant here to kidnap them? Mason saw the look but he didn't let it bother him. Nor did he wait. He opened the gate and walked quickly towards the car. Immediately the Smithfields appeared at the front of the house, all the living garbage on their front lawn and on the two neighbouring properties swarmed towards them.

Mr. Smithfield looked around in incomprehension.

'Please hurry,' said Mason.

Mr. Smithfield pressed the key fob and the doors unlocked. Aggie and his wife jumped in and closed their doors but he stood a moment longer watching the creatures approach with a look of horrified curiosity. Mason opened the passenger door and got in. Creatures converged on the car from all sides.

'Mr. Smithfield, get in the car. NOW.'

Richard's reverie broke and he walked around to the driver's side. In front of the door was a creature with six desk-lamp legs and the teeth of a dog in its hinged head. It snapped at his leg and he jerked away as if realising for the time that he was in danger. Animated refuse approached from every direction. The dog-thing was not put off and it advanced, causing Mr, Smithfield to retreat towards the front of the car. Looking behind him, he realised just how many creatures were now coming his way.

In the car Aggie screamed,

'Dad! Hurry up!'

His wife's hand went to the door handle but Mason spun in his seat and pulled her away.

'You help him, then,' Pamela yelled. 'For God's sake, do something.'

Not knowing what exactly he would do if one of the creatures got hold of Mr. Smithfield, Mason stepped out of the car again, careful to shut the door behind him immediately. The creatures nearest to him hesitated. He put himself between Mr. Smithfield and the ones approaching from the front of the house. They stopped moving.

In front of Mr. Smithfield, the six legged thing was advancing fast. Mason touched his arm.

'Let me get in front of you. I'll block it.'

The creature didn't wait for that. It lunged, snapping its canine jaws. Mr. Smithfield jerked his leg out of the way reflexively, stumbling back into Mason. A strange laugh, like a popping bubble escaped his mouth.

'Bloody thing tried to bite me.'

With the laugh came realisation. Mason saw a new tension tighten Mr. Smithfield's frame. The next thing he saw was Mr. Smithfield's right foot arcing up under the dog-headed creature's front section. It broke open on impact and the thing flew back to land among the dozens more behind it. Mr. Smithfield launched himself around the front of the Volvo and snatched the door open, turning the engine over before Mason was properly back in his seat.

'We have to go away,' said Richard Smithfield, more to his steering wheel than to his family. 'Far, far away from here.'

Mason looked at him and then at his wife and daughter. They were not special. They were just people. Living things from the old world succumbing to the dead things of the new. He wondered why he'd bothered to come back for them when they couldn't think properly, couldn't see what was really going on here. Didn't they even begin to understand what all this meant? What it was leading to? Aggie, at least, should have known better but she didn't care any more than her family. All she'd done was sever contact with him.

'I don't think that's going to work, Mr. Smithfield. What we really need to do is find somewhere nearby where we can be safe for a while. A place where we can wait.'

'Wait? What the hell are you talking about, "wait"? Wait for what?'

'To be certain about their motives. To see if we can... communicate, construct... *relationships* with them.'

'We don't talk to shit – whether it walks or crawls. Someone should be down here blowing these freaks into fart-clouds.' As though he'd summoned his own angels into view, two hovering blots appeared over the houses of another street on the estate. 'See those? They're helicopter gunships. That's what's going to save us. That's what's going to turn this around.'

Aggie giggled at her father's language and then shut up when she saw he wasn't being funny. Something crawled up onto the bonnet of the car and both she and her mother screamed. Mr. Smithfield slipped the Volvo into reverse and pounded the accelerator. Everyone's heads snapped forwards as the car leapt back. The smell of rot and excrement was heavy in the small space – it came from Mr. Smithfield's fouled right shoe. No one was prepared to roll down the window to let the smell out, however. The thing on the bonnet, something black with light bulb eyes, slid back onto the driveway where its eyes shattered. Mason heard it scream but he didn't think anyone else did. Perhaps he'd only felt it. Perhaps he'd only imagined it.

'You know, Mr. Smithfield,' he said as the head of the family reversed the car around in a tight curve and thrust the gear lever into drive, 'That's the kind of attitude we really need to dispense with if any of us are going to survive this.'

The car screamed out of Bluebell Way, dodging obstacles all the way. Behind them came the whine of high-speed chain-gunfire and the whump of a gas tank exploding. Mason strained around in his seat in time to see a black smoke cloud, with fire bursting inside it, roil skyward. He'd been a fool to come here, he realised. What was he doing delaying his final moment this way? And for these people who thought – or failed to think – in just the same way everyone else did? There was no point to it.

Mr. Smithfield had turned his car onto the main road into Shreve, but he was driving away from town. Mason turned to him.

'Stop the car.'

'What? No. No way.'

'Stop and let me out. Then you can continue with your family wherever you want to go.'

'You said you were here to help us. You're not going anywhere until you get us to safety.'

Mason took a deep breath, pushed his lips out as if deciding something.

'How do you know you're safe with me?'

He felt the atmosphere in the car shift and swell.

'How do you know you can trust me? Aren't you curious why those things out there never came near me? Don't you think it's strange?'

Mason looked into the back of the car and his eyes met Aggie's for a few brief moments. He knew she didn't intend to keep her promise. Her mother must have seen the look passing between them but, for the moment, she ignored it. Perhaps later she'd question her daughter about it. Discover that this was not the first time they'd ever met.

Already the car had slowed to below the speed limit. Richard

Smithfield looked at his gaunt passenger.

'What are you talking about?'

'I don't think you really want me in your car, Mr. Smithfield. Not with your family.'

The car slammed to a halt.

'You'd better explain.'

'I know where your son is.'

Mrs. Smithfield stifled a strange whimper in the back of the car. In it, Mason heard the twined hope and despair of a mother wishing her child safe, of a mother not knowing.

'Donald's… alive?'

'That's very difficult to say, Mrs. Smithfield.'

Mr. Smithfield's voice was flat and direct, barely contained.

'Well, you'd better find a way of saying it, or it's going to be very difficult to say whether *you're* alive or not.'

'I didn't kill him but I might as well have,' said Mason, more to himself than to the boy's family. 'It's my fault he's where he is now.'

Up ahead, swarming over the hedges were more landfill creatures, larger ones that had been feeding longer and on more varied prey. They moved in jerks and stumbles or humped along like sea animals trapped on land. But they were faster, stronger than the others. They moved with more certainty. There were enough to block the road. Mason glanced behind. More were waiting in the direction they'd come from. Mr. Smithfield followed Mason's eyes.

'Shit.'

'Let me out, Mr. Smithfield. I've got you and your family this far. Let me out and I promise I'll tell you where Donald is.'

'Richard, let him out, for heaven's sake. Those things are everywhere. They're coming!'

'Christ.'

The locks flipped open and Mason jumped out before the man changed his mind. He slammed the door and the window slid down. Creatures converged on the car in front and behind. The road was half clogged by them already.

'Where's our son, you maniac?'

Mason leaned down, caught each of their gazes for a moment.

'I gave him to the fecalith so that all this could begin. I gave him for the new world, for this world to have a chance.'

Mrs. Smithfield's hands were over her mouth. Aggie's mouth was a black hole of shock. Mr. Smithfield, Mason could tell, was weighing up whether there was time to leap out of the car and beat him to death before the landfill army blocked the Volvo's escape route. There wasn't.

'We're going to get through this and when we do, I'll be coming back for you, Mason Brand. Remember that.'

The window slipped shut as the car sped away. The space in the road was closing fast. Mr. Smithfield drove into the oncoming traffic lane to get past the creatures, running over limbs and pseudopodia and tearing open fragile bodies as he went. But the car made it through and Mason listened to its engine fading up the road for a long time.

Long enough that when he returned from the reverie to the moment, he found himself surrounded by the life forms born of the landfill.

21

The car was drivable but directing it demanded full concentration. One lapse and the BMW's responsive steering would swing the car off course. The tyre flapped around and occasional sparks came from the steel rim. Kevin knew the wheel would be heating up with the friction and pretty soon the sparks would be flying as though from an angle grinder. Then they were at risk of catching fire, of exploding.

'Come *on*, just a little farther.'

He dropped his window and leaned out to see the damage. The car swiped around and he brought it back on track. They were down to fifteen miles an hour. The tyre came off altogether and was left behind in the road. A stray spark caught his cheek and stuck there, burning.

'Fuck.'

He brushed it off. The car wobbled badly in response.

'Okay, okay. Concentrate.'

Down to ten miles and hour. In his rear-view mirror he caught sight of something coming down the road behind them. He couldn't make it out clearly because the mirror was vibrating too hard.

'Hold the mirror steady.'

She didn't respond.

'Tammy!'

She put a hand to the mirror and the image in it settled down. He wished he hadn't seen it.

Behind them taking up the whole road was a *flood* of landfill creatures, mostly in shiny black bin liner skins. It looked like some kind of mutant army hunting them down. The noise from the damaged wheel worsened, got louder.

Eight miles an hour. He stopped the car.

'Get out.'

She didn't move.

He jumped out of the driver's side, crossed to hers and ripped the door open.

'They're coming. Hundreds of them. If you don't get out and run, they'll have you.'

Still she rocked, not wanting to hear, not wanting to accept any of it.

'Tammy, for fuck's sake, I'm going to leave you here if you don't get out of the car right now and come with me.'

When she didn't move he took hold of her hair and dragged her from the seat. He pointed her in the direction they'd come from.

'See that? Quick, aren't they? You want to stay here, fine. I'm leaving.'

He turned and ran toward the college main gate. When he turned back she still hadn't moved. He ran back to her and took her hand.

'Tamsin, I know it's over with us but we're still married. I don't want to see you die out here. They *will* kill you, you know. And they'll eat you. And then you'll be one of them. Is that what you want? Are you committing suicide?'

She looked into his eyes.

'I'm sorry, Kevin. I've screwed everything up. Nothing ever made me happy, not even you.'

'Make it up to me. Run with me. Will you do that?'

He pulled her and she came a few steps.

'I can't. I killed our baby.'

The words didn't fit the situation. He didn't understand.

'You did what?'

'I was pregnant. It was our baby, Kevin. I killed it. I went to the hospital and they cut it out of me like it was cancer. I could never be a mother. The only thing I ever cared about was myself.'

The strength went out of Kevin as he understood what she was telling him and realised it was true. He remembered now all the nights she'd woken up sweating with a scream forming in her throat, how she'd cut the scream short as she reached consciousness. It had been so deep in the night he'd never really remembered it too clearly in the mornings but now he recalled, now that it mattered. Sometimes Tammy had mumbled through her nightmares. *Poor little baby*, she'd said that many times, hadn't she? And once: *why can't you just let it die?*

Oh, Christ, not this. Not now.

This was not the time to be sorting out the past. If they didn't shift, there wouldn't be a future. All this – was it more of her lies? there was no way to tell – it had to wait until they were both safe. He had to make her move.

'Tamsin, listen to me. Whatever happened, we can talk about it later. Right now we have to run.'

Still she stood there like a drugged lunatic.

'Tammy, please. Come on, you're a competitive girl. Fight one more battle for supremacy with me. Race me to the front of the college. Think of the satisfaction you'll feel if you win. Then we can talk.'

She smiled through messed-up mascara and shrugged like it was a bet for a pound. Behind her the army of landfill creatures were coming up fast, some of them could run now, not well but well enough to cover ground efficiently.

Suddenly regaining herself, she broke first, tearing away like the cheat she always was. He didn't hesitate. Soon he was beside her, about to pass.

Unable to bear the idea that she might lose, she made it a sprint.

He rose to the challenge.

Some of the things behind them broke rank, running faster than the rest. Kevin, looking over his shoulder, saw them, humanoid cripples they were, but somehow powered by hunger and determination and ignorance of pain. They lumbered on their makeshift, cobbled-together legs.

And they gained ground.

Kevin could hear every kind of sound when their limbs impacted the pavement – cracks, slaps, knocks, judders, thumps. The fastest ones were only twenty yards behind them now. He gave it everything and powered past her knowing she'd have no choice but to give everything she had to the chase. He looked back again. She was only five paces behind him. It was a good two-hundred metres to the first of the front steps of the College. Another twenty bounds from there to reach the safety of the doors at the top of them.

He wanted to call to her, to scream encouragement, but he didn't have the spare breath. As he glanced back, he let her see his eyes and hoped his expression was enough. And then he pounded the pavement, pounded it like never before. His lungs were raw and sore and aching and a sharp pain dug upwards from under his ribs on the left side. He cursed every butt he'd ever tugged on but still he ran. Despite his lack of fitness, he was faster than Tammy. Maybe a simple competition was no longer enough to goad her. Perhaps he was more frightened than she was, had more reason to live. Jenny was waiting for him just a few more steps away; a few more seconds and he'd be holding her in his arms again and saving Tammy too.

He angled in from the main gate, leaning over to make the corner like a racing driver. He found new strength he didn't know he possessed, broke through into a new reserve of power. He gave it everything he had; heart and soul and pure animal instinct.

He was going to make it. He knew it.

He reached the bottom of the steps for the hardest part, the final upward dash. He took the steps three at a time. At the top he saw the faces watching through the steel-framed glass doors. They were urging him silently on, waiting to unlock the doors and let the pair of them through before slamming and locking them again straight away. Then he heard a scream and the slap of hands on concrete. With it the muffled click of something breaking. He could hear in her voice she wanted to make it now, he knew she wanted to survive. He looked back and Tammy was down. She'd tripped on the first step and was flat out on her front, already trying to lift herself up.

He reached the door as she lifted her face to him and he saw that she'd smacked her mouth on the corner of one of the steps. The impact had snapped her front teeth off at the gum line. Even with death as close as it was he could see in her eyes the disgust with her sudden ugliness. Her lips were lined red and glossy, but smudged. As she pulled herself upright he saw her stop and wince as the pain in her knees flared. She'd taken the rest of the force of the fall across both patellae as they smashed into the edge of a lower step.

There was time for Kevin to look forward again and see the many faces beyond the glass and the look of dismissal in every pair of eyes – she's history now – they were all thinking. But no, he could still go back for her. There was still time.

He turned away from the doors – doors opening to let him pass into safety and back to Jenny – and started back down the steps.

It was impossible.

The landfill army had arrived and there weren't hundreds, but thousands of them. And now that they were this close he could see how big they were. Some of them were twice the size of people, more like cows. They came on legs of timber, legs of steel. They scrabbled along like millipedes on the claws of a hundred hedgehogs. They ran on two legs, galloped on four. They waved their arms and tool-hands like winning ticket holders. They were here for the flesh that would allow them to add to themselves from the crud of Shreve, the crud of the world.

They had Tammy in their hooks and pincers before he could take another step.

As she disappeared among them he saw the nearest ones inspect her with eyes of flesh, eyes of glass, eyes of plastic. And then their cutters appeared, made from hedge trimmers and hacksaws, the tiny blades from inside food processors. They mobbed her for her limbs and organs, took them while she still breathed. Her softened manicured hands were snatched from her in a single shear, her eyes were sucked out, the tongue clipped out from deep in her throat and he found himself wondering,

Why? What the fuck do they need that for?

She wasn't enough for them. They tumbled up the steps towards him. Instead of moving he was simply thinking, considering. Was there any point in running and hiding any longer? Wouldn't it be easier if he just let them take him now?

Hands grabbed him and yanked him back through the doors before he could finish the train of thought, before the landfill creatures could finish it for him. The locks were flicked shut and the crowd of faces retreated from the door with his now safe among them. He collapsed to the floor, panting, all the strength haemorrhaging from him.

'Kev. Oh, Kev.' Jenny held his head in her hands, cradled his face into her lap as she leaned over him. 'I thought you weren't coming back.'

'What just happened out there, Jen?'

'I'm so sorry.'

'Just tell me it didn't happen.'

She held him tight.

'I can't do that, Kev. This is real. All of it.'

'But… Tammy… I mean, she was right there with me. She was right behind me and then… Christ, what have I done?'

'You did everything you could. You risked yourself. You risked *us*, Kev. There was nothing more you could have given.'

'I did it, Jen. I got her here. All the way here. But she... she just wouldn't try. It was like she didn't really want to make it.'

'Maybe she didn't. Don't think about it now, love.'

'What else is there to think about?'

'Staying alive.'

'Yeah, but for what? What's going to be left? They take everything.'

'We're not going to give up, Kev. We're not.'

Ray reached Jimmy just as the guttering gave way.

The kid threw up his hands as he fell backwards and Ray caught hold of one of them. Jimmy steadied himself with the other hand as one foot landed back on the top step of the wall and the other slipped off the side. Jimmy grabbed the steak knife out of his mouth as though it would save his life.

'Listen to me, Jimmy, and do exactly what I say. I'm going to haul you up here but you have to help me. On the count of three, you jump and pull yourself up with your free hand. I'll pull at the same time. Nothing to it. Talk to me, Jimmy.'

The kid just nodded, wide eyed. He could hear the things right behind him, scraping and scratching as they came.

'One... two—'

'No! It's got me. It's got my LEG.'

'Shit.'

Ray let go and looked over the edge of the roof. The first creature did have the kid's calf in its grip – a claw made of rusted barbecue tongs. There couldn't have been much strength in it.

'Hold on to the roof, Jimmy.'

Ray unsheathed the katana and aimed. He severed the thing's 'arm' with one sure stroke. It released a pathetic shriek and recoiled, backing into the one behind it. There was a struggle and both landfill creatures fell off the wall into the bushes below. The remaining one moved forward eagerly to take their place. Ray sheathed the katana, feeling fairly impressed with himself, and reached out to the kid again.

'Okay, here we go again, Jimmy. No hesitation this time. One, two, *three.*'

Jimmy weighed nothing and he popped onto the roof like Peter Pan.

'Go up to the apex. *Carefully*, Jimmy.'

Ray waited, sword drawn again, for the last creature to reach the top step of the wall. It extended concertinaed arms to grip the roof tiles and Ray slashed them off. The thing screamed but from underneath its body, two more arms reached up. These were larger – human arms with curtain hook fingers on one side and an edging spade blade on the other. Ray stood back this time and allowed the creature to get a purchase with its hooks. Seeing a pair of arms which probably belonged to someone in this very street, he couldn't bring himself to damage them. The landfill creature was fast and once its body was on the roof it launched itself at Ray. The loss of two arms had done nothing to deter it. Ray let it come forward and merely held the katana in front of himself. The thing gored itself on the blade in its eagerness to have him and then, finally, something more important damaged within, it stopped. Ray drew the blade out of it and the dead thing slid back to the edge of the roof before falling into the garden below.

At the apex, Jimmy was looking down at his feet. Delilah had an arm around him. Ray shot her a look that said, 'you've changed your tune' and she gave him a barely perceptible shrug in return. When he reached them the kid said,

'Th… thanks, mister.'

'I'm not old enough to be a mister. My name's Ray. This is Delilah. Now you can come with us to the college but you're going to have to pull your weight, understand?'

The kid nodded.

'I'll do my best.'

'Let's hope that's good enough.'

Ray led the way the end of the terrace of houses. He'd hoped for the last wall in the row to be usable as a way down to the street level but he'd completely misjudged its height. It was a challenging drop from the roof to the top of the wall and a dangerous one from there to the ground. He peered over the gable end of the last house, following the guttering. There was a black downpipe, not plastic but cast iron. It was bracketed to the bricks and looked secure. Even if it wasn't, it was their best and safest escape. The problem was it led straight down to the street. Ray had hoped to get into the garden and make a run for it from there when they were all ready. As it was, they'd be arriving one at a time at street level in plain view of every creature nearby. He scanned the distance between the bottom of the down pipe and the row of shops they planned to loot on the way to the college. It was fairly clear at the moment. If they were fast they could dodge most of the landfill creatures in their path – none of them looked particularly large or agile. Between the shops and the expanse of parkland leading to the college there were far less creatures visible.

He turned back to Delilah and Jimmy.

'It's this pipe or it's nothing. I'll go first and keep things clear at street level. Come down one at a time or the pipe may not hold. Jimmy, you follow me, I'll need your help at the bottom.' He kissed Delilah hard and fast. 'I'll see you down there.'

It wasn't a graceful descent. Between each bracket the pipe had no hand holds. It was a matter of stopping himself sliding so fast it became a fall. About two thirds of the way down, before he was ready to jump, Ray lost his grip. He fell and landed awkwardly, jarring his ankle before landing on his arse in the road. He jumped up quickly testing the injury. He'd twisted it badly enough to make him swear, not badly enough to stop him walking. A sweat broke on his face just thinking about what would happen if he couldn't run. As soon as he hit the ground, creatures turned and made their way in his direction. He drew the katana, testing his ankle again and again. Running was going to be a problem.

At the top of the pipe, Jimmy struggled just to get his legs over the edge of the roof. The kid was obviously frightened of heights. Ray didn't care.

'Get your arse in gear, Jimmy.'

A ragged semicircle of monstrous garbage creatures had already formed before Jimmy was a quarter of the way down. Ray turned to face the interlopers. *What am I waiting for?* He went out to them, choosing the largest and most dangerous looking ones first and wielding his Japanese blade with as little force as possible. It was a lot heavier than he'd imagined it would be. There were dozens of them and he needed to conserve his strength. From time to time he glanced back to assess Jimmy's 'progress'. It was like a watching a slug cross a garden path.

'Come on, Jimmy! You're making it worse for all of us. Just fucking slide down.'

The creatures he'd killed formed a protective crust around them. The ones still approaching had to crawl over it, bringing them nearer to his sword. Even so, keeping the gaps plugged was like playing Tetris on level nine. Every time he moved around the perimeter his ankle expanded with pain.

Finally he heard Jimmy hit the pavement behind him. Delilah was already on her way down.

'Come here,' said Ray. 'When you see one of these bastards get near the edge of this ring, slash 'em. Got it?'

The kid nodded, knuckles white around the handle of his steak knife.

'What are you waiting for? There's one right there.' Jimmy looked at the small creature scaling the growing hump of its now inanimate brethren. It mewled like a starving kitten. He didn't move. The thing reached the top of the mound and made faster progress down their side of it. It hoisted itself along on the thrashing tails of dogs and cats.

'Jimmy, do it.'

'I... I've never killed anything before.'

'Even if you waste a thousand of them you still won't have killed anything. They're not living like you and me.'

'I know but...'

Delilah arrived behind them having slid down the pipe like a fireman.

'Forget it, Jimmy,' said Ray. 'Time to go.'

Ray found the least busy part of the ring of trash, took a run up and leapt over. On landing he fell to one knee. Delilah was right behind him.

'What's the matter, babe?'

'I'm okay. Just twisted my ankle a bit.'

Jimmy still hadn't joined them. Creatures had breached the wall of rubbish and were closing in on him. He looked at Ray and Delilah with desperate eyes. It was obvious that in the greatest part of his mind, he didn't believe in himself. Or perhaps he didn't believe he was worthy of surviving. Whatever it was, the instinct that was driving Ray and Delilah had not surfaced in him. Jimmy was thinking instead of acting. Ray beckoned him frantically.

'Jump them, Jimmy. For fuck's sake. Do it now or they're going to dismantle you for spares.'

The idea must have affected the kid. He took a run up and leapt the trash wall like a hurdler. Then he stopped to look back, barely able to take in that he'd come this far.

'Right,' said Ray. 'Let's see if we can get into that outdoor shop.'

When Mr. Smithfield saw the wall of garbage strung across the road he knew there was only one course of action.

'Belt up and hold on.'

Aggie and his wife braced their arms against the front seats. Pamela cried out:

'Oh God, Richard.'

'I know.'

It was the first time he'd ever put the accelerator to the floor. The Volvo responded with enthusiasm, pushing him back into the seat. He resisted, leaned forwards, kept his eyes open. If there was a weak point in the swathe of living trash up ahead, he couldn't see it. It was a straight section of road beyond; plenty of time to correct and slow down after the impact. If they made it through. He looked at the speedo. Climbing towards ninety already. Was that fast enough?

They hit the rubbish, tore through it. Rumbles, snaps and louder impacts vibrated up through the foot wells. The Volvo shimmied on the uneven surfaces, slithered on unnameable substances but stayed straight. Richard Smithfield, elbows locked, jaw vicelike, prayed. They cleared the roadblock and the car settled down onto smooth tarmac. White-faced and rigid in the back seats, Aggie and her mother cried hesitant tears of relief.

Richard was laughing in tiny, machinegun bursts.

'Hu hu hu hu… hu hu… hu hu hu.'

The road curved and he realised he was doing a ton. He touched the brakes as gently as he could. The bend sharpened.

'Darling, look ou—'

Something popped and the car sank on the front passenger side. Richard hissed through gritted teeth.

'Shit.'

Not knowing what to do, he stepped harder on the brakes. The car began its spin, no longer following the road.

Full brake. Hand brake.

Three interwoven trails of black rubber and something like a curl of stripped black hide.

Whirligig G-force.

The world smearing to green all around.

For all of them an awareness of the car moving beyond its proper environment.

Flying briefly, peacefully.

Tearing and scratching as the Volvo erased a section of hedge.

Blackout.

22

They set off but Ray couldn't run. Jimmy and Delilah tried to put their arms around him and help him along.

'I'm fine. I can walk fast. I just can't run yet. I need a couple of minutes off the pitch and then I'll be fine. Come on, we've got to keep moving.'

They reached the front of the outdoor shop quickly and safely. Someone had half closed the shutters but hadn't finished the job. Ray expected the main door to be locked but it wasn't. There was no need to smash the display window. They all just ducked under the shutter, pushed on the door and walked in. Ray locked them in for safety.

It was gloomy inside but there was enough light to see by. It seemed safer not to use the electricity and draw attention to themselves. Ray went to the rucksack display.

'Why don't we ditch your old backpack and get some nice new ones, D?'

'Good idea.'

'Pink? Light blue?'

She didn't answer.

'Black it is, then.'

Ray started filling their backpacks with anything he thought might come in handy.

'What are you doing?' asked Jimmy.

'Stocking up. Being prepared.'

'You're stealing,' said the kid.

Ray stopped and turned to Jimmy.

'Are you serious?'

'Well, it's not right, is it?'

'Let me explain something to you, Jimmy. Law and order have succumbed to the vicissitudes of survival. Primal urges are to be encouraged.'

'Come again?'

'We're trying to stay alive. Nothing else matters now.'

'I think the owner of this shop might take a different view.'

'That's my point, Jimmy, we're not thinking that way any more. I'd have thought the owner of this shop is probably dead by now. Either that or trying to escape. I don't think he'll miss a few items.'

'I'm not going to be drawn into criminal activities.'

Ray and Delilah exchanged a glance.

'What?' said Jimmy.

'If you don't stop living by the rules, you're going to stop living. At least find something better than that stupid bloody steak knife.'

Jimmy saw the penknife display – all the items locked behind glass – and had a close look. He put the steak knife down and, for the first time since he'd escaped from his bedsit, Ray saw the kid smile.

'You might want something a bit... bigger... than a Swiss army knife,' said Ray. 'You know, so you can stay out of reach.'

Jimmy looked disappointed and wandered away towards the darker part of the shop.

'Alright. Don't listen to me, just take whatever you think you can use.'

Aggie comes round to the screech of a disk cutter chewing through steel panelling. She smells the scorched rubber, engine oil and petrol.

There's been an accident.

Yes.

They were running away but they'd made it. They were free.

Images queue up in the wrong order.

The firemen are cutting someone out of the car. Her father or...

Please, God, no. Not Mum. Let them be alright. Let them be alive.

She can't understand why she suddenly cares about them. They are the most precious things in the world to her. She's weeping, realising what a stupid, deluded bitch she's been. She doesn't want this. She doesn't need them to be hurt for her to admit to herself she loves them. Through the rising haze of her own pain, she resolves to be a better, more loving daughter.

Oh, God, please don't let them be dead. Please, please, no.

Wait, Aggie. Think. Don't be stupid. They cut people out because they're still alive.

Yes. Yes. They're alive. They're both alive.

She tries to call out but there's no breath in her. Feels like someone's forced a lead football right through her guts. Can't breathe. The world shrinks again.

That's when she notices she's not in the car any more. On her back. In the grass. Indifferent sky far above. Vision contracting as she suffocates.

Suddenly something releases inside and she draws in a huge breath.

It hurts very much but the sky expands again.

She is not dying.

'Mum?'

It's a whisper.

'Mum? Dad?'

The steel disc ceases to whine. Metal is wrenched apart. The firemen are setting her parents free from the wreckage. The paramedics will help them.

She turns her head towards the sounds. Just a glimpse of them will be enough until the paramedics come to attend to her. A vision to keep her going through the pain. Strength transmitted by the sight of her begetters.

She sees no emergency service personnel. Only two monsters, each half the size of the car. One towers over her father. The other over her mother. She can't tell if her parents are alive. Neither of them is moving but they appear to be uninjured by the impact. Her instinct is to scream. She overrides it.

Tools and instruments open from the aberrant bodies of the creatures. Facsimiles of hands – too many hands – arrange the adults with finicky precision. On their backs, to attention, like sleeping guardsmen. Faster than Aggie's eyes can follow, blades split her parents' clothes open and mechanical fingers sweep them away. She is embarrassed to see them this way. Then embarrassed for them. Now nauseous with anticipation of what may follow. This would be the time either to save them or run away. She tests her body's ability to move. Hands and ankles move but she winces; everything works, everything hurts. Worst of all is the pain in her chest and solar plexus. Something there is adrift, grinding against itself. She uses her arms to push herself up and the pain makes her vomit into her own lap. She keeps the spasms as quiet as she can, squeegees away mucus from her chin with her fingers and wipes them in the grass. The monsters don't seem to have noticed her. They're busy about their work.

She has to make her assessment and act.

The creature thieving from her mother has some kind of reel inside it. This wheel ratchets and clicks several times a second. It's spooling something into itself. A slippery rope of pale pasta, dripping blood and fluid, an impossible rainbow of blue and pink. Her mother's abdomen is emptying fast. Aggie's mother is conscious now, violated and indignant. Entering wide-eyed shock but not yet death. The reeling stops with a tug that lifts Pamela Smithfield partially off the ground. Secateurs snip and she drops again, her stomach flatter than a supermodel's.

The creature operating on her father is holding up his penis and testicles – three wrinkly nubs of skin. The 'hand' holding them disappears downwards towards the creature's middle and Aggie loses sight of it. The emasculation has roused her father from unconsciousness. He screams now, not a howl exactly. Something hoarse and torn from deep within him. Aggie doesn't recognise his voice in the sound. Richard Smithfield keeps screaming as though that alone will be enough to set him free. The creature doesn't seem to hear. Maybe it can't hear, she thinks. Systematically, it dismembers her father, like a kid pulling apart a model aeroplane, prising open the plastic panels, overcoming the glue and snap-jointing. And all the time her father screams his unrecognisable protest.

Aggie has one option left.

Behind her, is a small coppice of recently planted pines. It's nearer than the road. The road equals suicide.

She rolls onto her hands and knees and in her chest, something separates. This time she can't prevent the scream. Neither does she have much breath for it. A yelp instead. She can't crawl, not grating her insides this way with every movement. So she stands up and the pain eases just a little. The creatures have seen her but they aren't following. Not yet. She falls towards the coppice, each footstep merely preventing her from going down on her knees again.

She makes it to the trees. They reach a foot or two above her head. She risks a look back. The two scrap monsters are still committing surgical larceny on the bodies of her parents. But they've seen her through swimming goggle eyes, through lead crystal tumbler eyes. She knows she has to make the distance while they're still busy.

She pushes through the rows of pines, trying to protect her chest from the branches. A couple of dozen paces bring her to the other side of the trees. She staggers into the open. She's in a field. On the far side of it there's a five-barred gate. Her choice is made. Every step sends lightning through her sternum. Breathing is getting harder.

Straps tighten around her chest. But she's moving regardless, putting one foot in front of the other, making headway.

Near the gate, the earth is churned by huge tyre tracks, now dried into deep ruts. Twice she stumbles. Twice she stops herself from hitting the deck. She knows that if she goes down, she may not get up again. The gate is held closed with orange baling twine, easy to undo. But hauling the gate open prises something open in her chest and her vision mists over for a few seconds.

She hears snapping from across the field and looks back. As her gaze clears she sees the body-thieves smash out of the coppice. She does not understand what they are. How they move, what they are doing; none of it makes sense. She doesn't try to shut the gate with the twine.

She's on a farm track. One way will lead to the farm she assumes, the other back to the road. She hopes she's picked the right direction.

The farm track curves one way and another. It meanders through the fields. Aggie realises now that she may not make it. She may become another living organ donor for these creatures that have erupted like a plague from the landfill. She's doing what she can – not running but walking fast – and that's all she's capable of. She doesn't even know if she's going in the right direction. It's all up to someone else now. She's given it her best shot.

The farm track is made of pounded stone. First, she hears the rending of the timber in the gate – sounds like the creatures didn't bother to open it. Then she hears crazy footsteps on the stone still some way behind her. It sounds like a crowd chasing her in every kind of shoe – clogs, hobnail boots, flip-flops and brothel-creepers. Despite believing she's trying harder then ever, Aggie realises that she is no longer walking fast. She has nothing left to give to her escape. Now she is just walking.

Now she is plodding.

Up ahead is the road. The main road her father was driving on. She can make it that far before they catch her, she thinks. Her mind tells her it doesn't really matter whether they catch her here or out on the road. Her instinct tells her it is better to flee, to stay alive as long as possible. Suddenly, there's a little more power in her steps, a small reserve of magical energy to keep her moving. She walks faster, almost jogs, ignores the pain because nothing matters now except escape. There will be pain no matter what happens.

She reaches the road and turns onto it away from Shreve. The road is flat and hard and easier on the legs. She breaks into an agonised trot, almost believing there's a chance now. Almost seeing herself in some kind of future. Any kind. She forces the thoughts away.

Up ahead there's a road sign. Distance to a couple of nearby villages, distance to the motorway. Beyond that is a brown sign with the name of the neighbouring county in white. She's almost out of Shreve.

She can't look back at the monsters because it would waste energy and slow her down. Anyway, she can hear them, clattering faster than before now, abusing the tarmac with their stolen, mutant limbs. She passes the road sign running with everything she has left. She passes the county border and keeps moving.

The pain in her chest is unbearable now, breathing is becoming impossible. Her steps slow from a run to a trot and from there to a walk and the Earth itself seems to suck the very life from her.

She stops, utterly spent.

She turns to face her pursuers.

There on the border of the county, twenty yards away, they've halted. They're not moving at all. Not breathing or panting though they should be. They watch her through their crude eyes for a long time.

Then they turn away, back to Shreve.

Delilah found a rack of ice axes and picked a matching pair which she tucked into her belt. Ray handed her a full backpack and she slipped it on. He pulled his own on and then looked around.

'Where's Jimmy?'

'He was over there a second ago.'

'Jimmy? You there? We're leaving.'

Some shuffling came from the back of the shop.

'He must be in the stock room,' said Delilah.

Ray walked after him and into the almost dark back room. He had to switch on a torch to see properly. Boxes were stacked to well above head height but a path led through them. Beyond his line of sight, Ray could hear movement. Something about the sound made him draw his katana. It emerged with a whisper. With the torch in his left hand the sword was a lot heavier and felt far less useful. If he wanted to see what was in there, though, he had no choice but to use both items.

As he neared the first right-angle bend in the corridor of stock boxes, he heard the sounds from beyond more clearly. If the lights hadn't have been off, if he hadn't learned in the last few hours that nothing was how it seemed any more, he'd have sworn there was someone working back there. Not trying to keep quiet at all but bashing and clattering around. Someone constructing something.

Ray relaxed a little. It was the kid, weird as ever. He'd found a box with something useful in it and he was putting it together.

'Hey, Jimmy, when we call you, you've got to answer. Don't just fucking ignore us. We're meant to be sticking together. Trying to stay alive. Jimmy. Jimmy?'

Ray looked back at Delilah.

'We should never have brought him with us, you know.'

'I know.'

Ray rounded the first corner and shone the torch. Nothing there but more stacked boxes. The noise was coming from further back. Maybe Jimmy wasn't in here, after all. Maybe someone had left a machine running back here in their haste to get away. He could see light up ahead. There must have been a small window letting a little glimmer in from an alley or car park behind the shop. A little further with the torch and then he'd be able to see. He took the last few steps, aware of Delilah right behind him, and turned the final corner in the maze of boxes.

It wasn't someone constructing something.

It was something deconstructing someone.

Jimmy was dead and they'd never even heard him scream.

Maybe that was because the thing that killed him had one limb stuffed into Jimmy's mouth. His jaws were stretched so wide that his cheeks had ripped open from the corners of his mouth to his back teeth. The limb was pulsing as it searched around inside Jimmy's body like a kid rummaging for the prize in a bran tub. Kev could see the movement inside Jimmy shirt as the limb ferreted for what it needed. Then there was a contraction along the whole limb and a slurping sound. The creature's limb was some kind of industrial vacuum cleaner attachment or the pipe from a large water pump. Something slipped along inside this hollow limb making it bulge. Ray thought of anacondas eating wild pigs.

The other limbs were busy cutting Jimmy's body into useful pieces and attaching them to itself. Then Ray realised it wasn't one landfill creature he was looking at but three. They were working together melding flesh and waste with the tools they had amongst them. Bones were attached to steel frames, plastic and skin were clamped or stapled together, veins and tubing were welded with a festering ichor that blurred the distinction between flesh and inanimate material.

The creatures made Jimmy fall apart. They made him disappear.

Then, right there in the torchlight, the three of them made themselves one. In an act of reverse fission, the three became a huge junkyard amoeba. The newly-fused thing rose up, delighting in its new frame and extra mobility; humanoid in shape but with extra appendages no man would ever wish for. The fat, flexible hose that had been thrust inside Jimmy stretched towards Ray like an exploratory trunk. He backed away and the creature advanced. It was fast, more agile than any of the others they'd seen.

Ray heard Delilah run back to the shop but he didn't dare turn away. He walked backwards, torch shining right at the creature, reflecting on a film of fresh blood and oily effluent. He kept his katana stretched towards it, though his right hand was now aching from holding the sword unassisted for so long. His back came to rest against a wall of boxes and he adjusted. One more corner to negotiate and he'd be within reach of the stock room door. It was tempting to make a slash or stab at the thing but he didn't trust himself to make a decent job of it with only one hand. On top of that, the creature moved with a fluidity and grace that scared him. He had a terrible feeling that it could overpower him the moment it decided to lunge.

He backed around the final corner and this last corridor of boxes was light again. Still he didn't turn the torch off, just shone it into the compasses the thing was using for eyes. The needles inside them spun and flashed, reflecting the beam. Delilah's hand reassured him as he backed to the doorway. He stopped. Surprised, the creature stopped too.

Then Ray dived through the door and let Delilah slam it shut.

Before it closed and she could lock or block it, the creature slipped a couple of limbs between the door and the frame, pushing it open.

'Shit, Ray.'

'I know.'

Ray launched himself back at the door but both their shoulders were doing little to deter the creature. It was forcing its way out.

'We've got to run, D.'

She nodded.

'Go!' he shouted.

She made straight for the front door of the shop. Ray kept his shoulder wedged against the stock room door but he was slowly being pushed backwards. Delilah was fumbling to open the lock and still hadn't succeeded when Ray decided to give up and run for it. He pulled down every rack of goods that was loose as he made for the door. Behind him, outdoor products scattered across the floor along with their toppled display units. He turned and threw the torch at the creature, amazed when it ducked to avoid the impact. He reached Delilah, pushed her out of the way and flicked the lock in a single turn. He hauled the door open. She darted out.

He followed her and together they dragged down the steel shutters. Bizarre limbs appeared between the shutters and the pavement. Ray and Delilah looked at each other.

'Run,' he said. 'And don't look back. I'll be right behind you.'

She kissed him and sprinted away.

Things reached for his ankles and he let go of the shutters. Already other creatures in the street had seen him and were coming his way. A few yards away and making good speed, Delilah was drawing attention of her own. Ray limped after her, through the park gates and across the well-kept lawns. Leaves had fallen since the last raking, so the grass was a tapestry of ochre and chestnut over green. The trees were almost naked and ready for their long months of sleep. Ray wanted to see the spring more than anything else he'd ever wished for. He paid his screaming, leaden leg muscles no mind, fought against the threatening pain in his ankle and, still holding the flashing katana in his right hand, he gained on Delilah.

They moved as a huge mass with a space at their centre, a space like the eye of a storm, and in that space, walked Mason Brand, untouched and unharmed. They took him to the landfill, a place he'd seen from a distance every day, a place he'd touched with his bare skin on so many nights.

The stench from the army of creatures around him was so strong he didn't notice the smell of the landfill when they reached it. What he noticed was how the level of rubbish in every part of the site was now sunken far below the lips of the vast pits dug to enclose it. The whole site, acres and acres of it, in canyons hundreds of feet deep, had been stirred up. The areas already buried under compacted topsoil had become active, the earth becoming mixed in with the crushed waste below. Huge manmade trenches extended away in many directions from the main pit of what had once been one of the deepest and broadest coal mines in the country. The army of creatures encouraged him to the very edge of the largest trash-filled chasm, parted and retreated preventing him from backing away.

Mason scanned the surface of the rubbish in every direction. Standing this close to it in full daylight, it was hard to imagine where so much waste came from. How much was brought here each day, he didn't know. How many sites there were like this around the country, he didn't know. How long it would take for the rubbish to degrade and disintegrate, he didn't know. Nor did he know what kind of damage the decomposition would do to the land and life around the site. He'd spent years wondering about it and now, here he was, standing at the mouth of the place and still without answers. What he did know, what he still believed, was that the Earth was still transforming all the garbage as best it could and that here was one of the places where that transformative power was strongest.

Below him the surface of the rubbish billowed and swelled; the waves on an ocean of decomposing filth. Something broke through.

Rising up from the sea of detritus, rising as though levitated, came the fecalith, the thing that had begun its life on the night of the storm, the thing that had survived because Mason Brand had taken it in and nurtured it. It was huge now. It stood at least four storeys high, its giant feet floating on the trash beneath it. Mason remembered the pathetic, mewling embryo he'd found in his garden and wondered what had drawn it there. Was it merely coincidence that it had found in Mason the only possible way to grow safely? He would have liked to believe that – if it was true he could still turn his back on all this, take no responsibility for it – but he knew it wasn't true. This was some kind of natural pre-destiny that could never have been avoided. The farmer had seen all of this, Mason was sure about that. That was why he'd forced an education in the ways of nature upon him. And on every page of the A4 pads Mason had filled to clear his head of the calling, was the intelligence behind the creation of the fecalith and its legions of living garbage. There was no point in trying to deny it now; if he was honest with himself, it was the foretelling of these very events that he had been trying to ignore ever since the calling among those Welsh oaks first began.

The fecalith was a monstrous humanoid tower. It was fashioned of steel and timber and plastic and glass and circuitry and was welded together with the flesh of a thousand living creatures. It had begun life as a human foetus, removed from its mother's body and discarded here in a new and acidic amniotic fluid. Since leaving Mason's shed, it had hidden here in the landfill, growing, thinking and plotting. Staying safe until the correct moment arrived. Now, Mason was certain, the fecalith would make its presence known to all.

A hand reached down to him, a giant hand of vile reclaimed machinery and gore. It closed around Mason's chest and lifted him away from the ground until he was staring into one of its eyes. The eye was an old television screen. It studied him, turning him this way and that like a toy. Still, Mason was not frightened. He and the fecalith shared the same blood.

Its inspection complete, the hand dropped to the fecalith's chest and there a rusted panel the size of a door slid open. The smell from inside was so rotten, Mason choked. The hand pressed him into darkness and there, inside the fecalith's torso, he heard the beating of its giant, borrowed heart. The door slid closed behind him. Wires and tubes reached out towards Mason in the resounding blackness. Copper and rubber arteries pierced his head and neck. Animal veins and capillaries melted through his skin and attached themselves to his own. The plasma of poisonous excrement and homogenised bloods which flowed through the fecalith's vessels began to flow in his. And now, finally, Mason hoped and believed he would die.

Instead, the fecalith showed him something.

And Mason perceived it with every part of himself.

23

Shreve Tertiary College was one of the few places to escape the kind of destruction wreaked upon the rest of town by the fecalith's legions and the troops called in to quell them. The two campus maintenance men, trapped there on the first day of the attacks, re-wired the canteen television to run off a car battery. The teachers, students and other residents who had taken refuge on the campus therefore had two versions of what had happened to their town.

On the one hand, the trapped survivors had their own personal experiences and the things they could still see from the windows of the main building's upper floors.

On the other, was the fiction broadcast by the news teams of every terrestrial and satellite channel. The lies were so unanimously broadcast, it was almost possible to believe them, even for the people who'd experienced otherwise – the news stories were far more feasible than the truth, after all.

What would have caused awkwardness in any other situation brought Kevin, Jenny, Ray and Delilah together as allies, at least to a degree. They respected each other for making it this far alive. And they were incensed by the fabrications on the news.

'Look at this bullshit,' said Ray as the four of them sat together in the front row of plastic chairs.

In the television version of reality, the 'incident' was pitched as a disease outbreak with massive loss of human life. There was no mention of the monsters that roamed the streets. The only footage, repeated again and again, was of people running, people trying to hide. Editing made some groups of frantic survivors look like they were chasing the others: the diseased attacking the uninfected. Quarantine was the ideal solution. It was demanded by surrounding councils, terrified the outbreak would destroy their communities next, and the government was only too happy to comply.

Kevin sat there shaking his head.

'Can they really get away with this?' he asked.

'You can tell the newsreaders believe it,' said Ray. 'Why shouldn't everyone else? There's no one out there to tell them any different. No one that's seen what we've seen.'

Jenny was crying, hot angry tears.

'No one would listen even if there was.'

Ray knew why she was so upset. They'd had to lie about her toe because no one would ever have believed the truth – and now the same thing was happening on a national scale. Kev put his arm around Jenny to comfort her and Ray, for the first time since they'd broken up, didn't care. He was happy for Jenny and he was happy for himself. They were all still alive; that was what counted.

'We'll always know what happened here,' said Delilah. 'We should promise each other right now that we'll keep the truth alive. Government cover-ups have a habit of resurfacing. One day we might get a chance to share this.'

'I'm in,' said Ray.

'Me too,' said Kevin.

Jenny wiped the tears away from her cheeks and the corners of her eyes and nodded eagerly.

'Absolutely. I promise.'

The helicopter gunships were successful in their way; every landfill creature they fired at was immediately neutralised, becoming inanimate trash once more. Paper and plastic and all manner of rotting animal tissue littered the streets. The gunships left the suburbs worm-eaten with chain-gunfire, houses half torn down by missile strikes. They killed the landfill creatures and they killed the people hiding from them.

They could not, however, find and destroy all of the fecalith's forces. And, no matter how many they gunned down, more of them returned to take their place. As soon as it was clear that this kind of tactic wasn't going to settle the issue, the army arrived on the ground in force. They gathered what intelligence they could.

It soon became obvious that the problem began and ended with the town's waste disposal area. The quarantining of the county made it easy for the army to set up a fully functioning mobile headquarters not far from the centre of the incident, The Shreve Landfill. Not fully understanding what was causing the creatures to spawn wasn't seen as a problem by the top brass.

And all the while, military intelligence, backed up by dozens of its own scientists, epidemiologists and game theorists, came up with their own carefully planned solution.

Olive drab tankers arrived in convoy at the landfill and emptied their liquid loads into the pits of rubbish. Infantrymen in breathing apparatus lined the edges of the quarry. Live ammunition was not issued. Anything rising out of the pits was slashed open with bayonets and pushed back into the landfill. For days the trucks came until the haze of petrol vapour shimmered over the expanse of the vast rubbish pit like a mirage.

All army personnel on the ground then retreated to a safe distance. A lone gunship rose into the sky from a mile away and fired a single missile into the centre of the trash. In a searing, gargantuan hiss, air was sucked towards the ensuing fireball as flames boiled upwards three hundred metres high. The burning fuel and waste vomited pure blackness even higher on the still, cold air. The smoke mushroomed upwards, leaning westward when it hit the air currents higher up. From a hundred miles away, people saw Shreve erect its own leaning tombstone against a chilled sky.

In the town, creatures and people alike watched the flames consume the trash that had been dumped in their landfill. Twenty years of the filthiest, least degradable rubbish from all over the country burned. The fields and hedges and trees around the landfill were scorched by the heat. For three days the site was unapproachable by any living thing.

Meanwhile, armoured units supported by ground troops mopped up the remaining landfill creatures street by street and house by house. Much of Shreve also burned at their will. The troops were efficient and indiscriminate. Human bodies lay alongside the bodies of the landfill creatures in every street. Only the larger concentrations of survivors were safe from stray bullets and twitchy trigger fingers.

On the third day, the streets, now silent and safe, the fire dwindling to a glow from below the edges of the landfill canyon, the army advanced to assess the outcome of their action.

Ray was drawn to the landfill. He persuaded the others to go with him.

Sneaking out of the college and away from the skeleton crew of troops 'protecting' them wasn't difficult at all. The four of them slipped out via the covered glass corridor to the science block and from there it was yards to the perimeter hedge. Keeping low, they stayed in cover out to the woods, past the secret place that Delilah had shown him and onward to the edge of the tree line.

From their vantage point they looked down over the smouldering landfill.

No longer was it mounded with trash and well-packed soil. Now there was nothing but blackened gouges in the earth where the trash had been incinerated in white heat.

The trenches and pits were almost as deep as the mine had been when it was abandoned. The surrounding land looked scarred and wasted, as though nothing would ever grow there again. It was the charred stump of an amputated limb, the socket of a burnt-out eye. Overhead, the smoke column still rose up but it was a ghost now, riddled and twisted by the slightest breeze. The smell of blackening was still in the air, the very soil itself smelled scorched. Everything was silent but for the diesel engines of the tanks and trucks and the shouts of soldiers watching each others' backs.

'Fuck,' said Ray. 'It's just… gone.'

'Too right,' said Kevin. 'Good riddance to bad rubbish.'

They all ignored him.

Delilah looked pale, sick.

'It's not right,' she said. 'What they've done. It can't be the answer. Just burn everything? Children would do that. Stupid little boys.'

'Come on, Delilah,' said Jenny. 'The whole landfill's been obliterated. They did the right thing. What other solution could there be? Those things were… feral. They'd have hunted us all down in the end.'

'What makes you think a big bonfire is the end to this?' asked Delilah. 'Do you think they'll never come back now? Maybe there are seeds of them scattered in the bottom of every one of those pits just waiting for something to set them growing again. Maybe they'll be stronger next time. Smarter.'

'They weren't smart,' said Kevin. 'They were hungry. It's different.'

'They were smart enough to set up road blocks,' said Ray.

Kevin wouldn't be persuaded.

'Every carnivorous animal can hunt. It doesn't make them intelligent.'

'Intelligent enough to hunt is way too intelligent for trash, as far as I'm concerned.'

Kevin shrugged.

'Let's not argue about it, Ray. It's over now. What does it matter?'

'It matters,' said Delilah, 'because there's some meaning behind all this, some reason for it.'

'No,' said Kevin. 'No way. Look who's cleared the mess up. I reckon the army are responsible for all of this. Some military experiment, some war machine that got out of control. Maybe it wasn't out of control at all. Maybe they meant for this to happen as a kind of live test.'

Delilah looked disgusted.

'That's the most cynical suggestion of all.'

'It's sick,' said Jenny. 'But it's certainly possible. I don't know why I hadn't thought of it before. No one's going to believe what happened here even if someone starts telling the truth. The government and military will spin it as some kind of mini plague that they've had great success in containing. They'll look like saviours and anyone speaking out against them will look like fools.'

Ray pointed down into the centre of the largest pit.

'We are fools. All of us.'

Something was moving in the blackened depths. Tanks and men were backing away from the edge of the fire crater.

An incinerated colossus rose from the ash. Ray, the only one of them to have seen the fecalith before, recognised it in spite of the conflagration it had survived. It was larger than he remembered, though damaged and fused in a way that made it look more human. All its constituent parts had run together making its blackened form elongated and sinuous. Glass and plastic, steel and rubber, concrete and wood, organs and skin. Cauterised more closely than ever by fire. It did not appear wounded. The fecalith looked strong.

The four of them watched as it reached into a cavity in its own chest and drew something out, something pink and ragged that dripped dark fluid into the ash several metres below. The fecalith was holding out a kind of doll in front of it as though it were a talisman to ward off the military and their weapons of war. It proffered this charm to the retreating troops.

On the scorched air they heard a man's voice shouting out from the pit. The fecalith, speaking through its mannequin mouthpiece, his voice tiny and human, agonised and imploring.

'What's it saying?' asked Kevin.

Ray shook his head.

'I can't quite hear it. Looks like it's reasoning with them, though.'

The pink doll was, in turn, holding out its hands to the soldiers in gestures of pleading and placation. He looked as though he was trying to explain something. He reminded Ray of speakers he'd seen on the news in places of deep human conflict. He was passionate, inspired, cautionary.

Suddenly the pink doll's body went limp. A second or two later, they heard the triple burst of machine gun fire. More followed from many men kneeling or lying on the ground. The doll's body jerked and reddened. Pieces dropped away from it into the pit. The fecalith drew the doll back, placed it once more inside its chest. The gunfire continued, intensified. The fecalith didn't seem to know what to do. It stepped back and away, its lower legs still obscured by the pit in which it stood. Like the mannequin, it held out its blackened hands to the soldiers to make them stop.

The tank's gun recoiled, rocking the whole vehicle and sending up a billow of dust from all around it. There was an explosive flash at the fecalith's shoulder, spinning the giant a quarter turn to its left and pushing him backwards. The sound of the blast reached the four onlookers, followed by a push in the air. Kevin lost his footing and sat on the ground.

'Jesus Christ.'

Smoke erupted around the fecalith's head after the impact, obscuring it.

The gunfire ceased. The giant swayed.

'No,' said Delilah. 'No, no, no. This is all wrong, Ray. Can't they see that? They can't just blow him away like this.'

Kevin shook his head as if he'd heard her wrong.

'Him?'

'It's alive,' she said.

'It's not a fucking person, Delilah. It's a freak of nature. And it's a killer too.'

Jenny felt the same way.

'They have to destroy it. It's the only one left. It's probably the one that controlled all the others.'

'We should definitely move into some cover,' said Ray. 'If the army realises they're being observed I doubt they'd think twice about wasting us.'

Another flash burst on the fecalith's hip. The noise reached them as they watched it stagger away half bent over. The damage to its shoulder was obvious now that the smoke of the first impact had cleared; black splinters protruded from a rend beside its neck. Its left arm hung, apparently useless.

The four of them backed into the trees to watch from safety.

The fecalith shared everything with Mason, just as Mason had shared everything with it.

It was the basic needs that came through most obviously and most strongly. Things Mason could have imagined: the terrible hunger the fecalith felt, a drive too strong to resist. The pain of its existence and its inability to express that pain. Every time it grew or added to itself, its wounds were raw. Physical development was like a series of operations without anaesthesia. New limbs and organs were agony to install and the places where flesh and trash met never completely healed. The fecalith walked perpetually in a filthy grey cloud of agony. It had done so ever since it was conceived by the wrath of the storm. But pain and hunger were things Mason could understand easily. They were human characteristics, human sensations.

What was not human, or what seemed no longer to be, was the sense of wonder that made the fecalith's pain bearable. It was enchanted by its very existence, lived with a permanent sense of the miraculous, like some agonised saint witnessing the hand of God in everything. Each tiny moment of consciousness was a rapture and a joy at the living fact of itself.

If only people felt the same way, thought Mason, what a different world it would be.

In the chest of the fecalith, Mason changed. The filth that flowed in its veins now flowed in his through the many tubular and canular connections between them. The fecalith's chest had become a kind of womb in which Mason grew in knowledge. The fecalith fed him of its own strange plasma, nurtured him. Kept him alive. Every union with the fecalith was painful, each penetration of wire or silicone or steel or glass an abhorrence. Mason was deeply fulfilled, though, for he had become one with the new life, the new nature and that was more than he could ever have hoped for.

The consciousness of Donald Smithfield was gone, as were the consciousnesses of the dozens of animals he'd fed the fecalith in his shed. They were simply dead; everything physical that remained of them was in use by the fecalith. But their spirits – it had let those go. Donald Smithfield was dead but he was free. This and the knowledge the fecalith shared with him assuaged Mason's sense of guilt. The boy had died for something great.

The fecalith showed him what it was. It showed him the planet's history. Mason found himself unable to be sceptical about what he saw, it made such simple sense. The fecalith displayed for him the many ages in the world's growth, the coming and going of many species that had survived mere thousands or hundreds of millions of years. Many of the species had become too successful and the Earth, in its own time, had destroyed them to save itself. The Earth was a huge living organism, within and upon which many tinier organisms lived out their tiny lives. Like the cells of the skin or the bacteria in the gut, these tiny lives were meant to exist in harmony with the whole 'body' of the Earth. When a group of cells became too successful or too prolific, disturbing the delicate balance of the whole organism, the organism cleansed itself. In this way, many creatures had come and gone since life on the planet began. Most amazing of all to Mason was the uncountable times that humans had existed, flourished, become destructive and been wiped almost totally away. Each time humanity had survived the Earth's self-cleansing process, it had changed, become better in some way, learned some lesson about harmonious survival.

The world was about to self-cleanse again, the fecalith showed him. Its birth in the depths of the landfill was only an early sign of the change. Mason had been right all along, the fecalith was a new order of life. It came from the dead things humans threw away. Human trash had accumulated to a globally toxic level. Now the Earth was working hard to get rid of the toxicity and its cause. She'd sent a new species to facilitate the operation. The new species could not be destroyed or stopped by humans but that didn't matter. There was new hope – as there always was and always had been – because the Earth would not destroy humankind totally. It would merely bring it to the edge of extinction where, as a species, humanity would learn a valuable new lesson and then rebuild itself better than before. The whole organism of the world would benefit from the cleansing. There was a bright future ahead.

Mason was happy in the darkness of the fecalith's heart, learning and grasping the secrets of new realities, seeing new hope for the world and being at the very centre of it.

Then the fire had come.

The fecalith knew it was coming when the tankers began to fill its ocean of rubbish with fuel. But he didn't pass this on to Mason – there would be no point in filling the man with fear. Mason, who had been like a father to him, was now like his child. When the flames came, it did everything it could to protect him.

Mason felt the physical shift all around him when the fire began with a huge explosion. But the noise was so muffled he didn't know what it was. Not until the temperature began to climb inside his cool heart-womb. Not until he began to cook. When the heat melted off Mason's hair and his screams were too much for the fecalith to bear, the fecalith extended fleshy tubing into Mason's mouth and nose and cut him off from the air. The fecalith oxygenated Mason in other ways, with fluids instead of air; it pumped the coolest of its liquids into Mason to keep him alive as best it could. Meanwhile, the fecalith could not help but be burned and therefore changed by the fire. It knew, though it could experience and endure endless pain, that it could not die. Not ever. And so it had faith in the world that made it. Faith that it would survive. Faith that the world would become a better place.

Mason's consciousness became an awareness of nothing but burning. Burning and not dying, though he begged and begged for its cool, black release. In that fire of three days they were both re-forged.

Facing the soldiers as the fecalith's mouthpiece, Mason had felt no fear. Instead an evangelical frenzy took him as he tried to convey to the men, the men who had not and could not live through fire, what the future held for them if only they would lay down their weapons and listen. If only they would take heed and change.

He didn't believe it when they opened fire. The bullets hurt as badly as the flames. He held out his hands to stop them but they took no notice. It was then, when so many machine gun volleys hit him that his very limbs began to drop away, that Mason began to die. It was both a terrible shock and a glad relief for his life to be over.

Withdrawn once more inside the fecalith's chest, he felt all the interfaces being withdrawn, the makeshift tubules and veins receding, his awareness ebbing.

'You said we could not die.'

'You are not we,' replied the fecalith.

An explosion sent Mason sliding around in his own blood inside the chamber of the fecalith's chest. He sensed the creature's terrible pain increasing. Suddenly it seemed that he might have been wrong about everything, that the fecalith was insane or, at worst, a liar.

'They're killing you, aren't they?'

'We cannot die.'

Mason grunted, a laugh of sorts.

'You're delusional.'

'No, Mason Brand. You can die. You *will* die. But we will live on. This fire is simply a beginning.'

Another shell, nearer to Mason this time. The black world shook and reeled. Light came in from somewhere. The fecalith's body was breached.

24

The four of them watched the army blow the fecalith to pieces. More tanks rolled to the edge of the landfill pit. They fired at will, sending shell after shell into the already charred hulk. It came apart. One side of its head disappeared in a single impact. Its right arm fell away at the elbow. No longer could it hold up its hands in supplication. It stood, resolute and fearless, one television-screen eye watching it all.

The soldiers on the ground fired until their muzzles were hot and their magazines empty. Then they reloaded and started again. They aimed at every part of it; limbs and thorax, head and neck, even its sexless groin. But it was the tanks that did the real damage, each shell breaking the fecalith open, tearing it down. Finally, they broke one of its legs and the four onlookers watched it topple into the ash.

The tanks and troops retreated swiftly from the landfill, pulling back towards the main road. Seconds later, whining thunder swelled in the distance and three jets approached the site. Each loosed two missiles that left smoking trails as they hissed into the pit and ignited. White light burst upwards followed by a crackling roar. They felt the heat even in the trees. Whatever was in the missile burned with an almost purple whiteness, flashing and giving off a much lighter-coloured smoke.

They watched for most of the morning as the flames died down to nothing. When it was cool enough, convoys of huge trucks began to arrive, tipping and leaving mounds of earth and hardcore at the edge of the largest pit. Green bulldozers arrived to push the earth over the remains. Hour after hour the trucks brought in a mountain of soil for the earth movers to push into the smoking void.

They didn't stop until that section of the pit was filled level. By then it was cold and dusk was approaching.

'We'd better go,' said Ray.

He took them to his place because it was the closest. Around the streets of Shreve the army presence was far less obvious. Nevertheless, they checked around every corner and stuck to the quietest routes.

Inside his flat, away from the chaos of the streets, Ray handed everyone a can of cider. No one raised their drink for a toast. Ray watched Kevin sit with his arm around Jenny's shoulders, no longer even surprised by his lack of reaction. It didn't matter that she was sitting there with another man. Ray was glad to be a survivor. He was in love with Delilah. Now that they'd made it through the worst of this nightmare they could have a life together. They'd fought for it. They'd made it this far. They'd earned it.

'Don't know about you lot,' he said, 'but I'm walloped. I'm going to crash. You two alright with the sofa? There's plenty of extra cushions and stuff.'

Kevin nodded.

'We'll be fine.'

In bed, Ray held Delilah tight. She'd been very quiet all day.

'Are you okay, D?'

It was such a long time before she replied he thought she'd fallen asleep.

'I'm afraid.'

'Afraid?' he asked, half-asleep himself. 'You haven't been afraid of any of this. What's changed?'

'It's the way they dealt with it. Burning him. Burying him. Doesn't seem any different to what we would have done before. It doesn't seem any smarter.'

Ray was having trouble keeping his eyes open.

'I'll have to talk to you about this in the morning. I'm too tired to make sense of any of it.'

She squeezed his hand.

'You're right. Let's forget about it until tomorrow.'

The army left as quickly as it had come.

The clean up operation in Shreve was carried out by local services and thousands of volunteers. Truckloads of waste, now mingled with human and animal flesh, were ferried from the town to the landfill site where they too were burned in petrol and then buried. Thick black smoke rose and drifted wherever the wind took it. In the aftermath of such tragedy and destruction, complaints from neighbouring communities and villages about the stench and fumes were ignored.

Even though Shreve was now regarded as a 'plague' town, most of the survivors stayed, imbued with a sense of pride at their staunchness and finding ever more beauty and simple wonder in a town that had woken up from a nightmare. Their town. Shreve.

It was quiet in the streets. Many people had died. And it was quiet in the surrounding countryside where so much of the wildlife had been taken and 'used'.

Ray and Delilah agreed they'd see Kevin and Jenny for drinks, maybe dinner, very soon. It seemed right, after all they'd been through, that they should remain friends. But the days after the fecalith was shot and burned gathered as quickly as autumn leaves and the four of them didn't make contact.

Ray was philosophical.

Perhaps we all need time to heal quietly. Perhaps we'll come out of ourselves when we feel brighter inside.

Aggie Smithfield woke up in warm, clean sheets in a hot room.

Tubes in each nostril blew a steady but fine stream of pure oxygen into her. Each time she breathed out, her nose hissed as two jets of air collided. In her left hand was a syringe driver that she could squeeze to alleviate the pain in her chest. In her right arm a saline drip kept her from dehydrating.

The nurses were kind to her, their faces full of concern. The doctor, a young, dark man with far too much beard, spoke to her softly. Inspired her to feel better with his intense, confident eyes.

She did not know what day it was.

She could remember running away from something but she didn't know what it was. The doctor told her she'd had a terrible shock and serious injury and that she wasn't ready to remember. One day, soon, when she was stronger, her mind would let her recall what had happened. In the meantime, he said, she was to lie still, relax and let him and his team take care of her.

The pain in her chest – due to her cracked sternum, broken ribs and punctured left lung – was very bad at times. She used her syringe driver a lot. Depended on it for sleep. But the morphine had its dangers; it was in her sleep that the monsters came. Nameless, shapeless things that dragged themselves along after her with endless determination.

Screaming hurt the most. She screamed often, always on waking.

After so long without contact, the text from Jenny came as a surprise.

Ray and Delilah were drinking in the pub but both of them felt off colour. The lethargy and heaviness of their limbs had come on overnight. They had stomach cramps and couldn't face food. Ray suspected the previous night's

Chinese takeaway. He awaited the diarrhoea and vomiting without enthusiasm. As there was nothing better to do, alcohol had seemed the only solution. They were both drinking whisky with ginger wine to ease their stomachs when Ray's phone had bleeped.

'Who's it from?' Asked Delilah.

'Jenny. Asking us if we feel all right. She says they're both laid up. They must have ordered from the same place last night.'

'Text her back. Ask her what the symptoms are.'

As Ray keyed his phone, Delilah looked around the pub. It was quiet. None of the people there looked particularly happy. In fact, several looked quite pale. Maybe it was the light. Doug, the landlord, always a cheerful sort in his laconic way, was sweating in the gleam of the bright bar lights. She was about to shout over to ask him what he'd been drinking the night before when he leaned down and vomited into the bottle trolley behind the counter.

'Shit,' she whispered, and then: 'Ray?'

He looked up from his phone.

'What?'

'The landlord just chucked up. Look around. Everyone's ill.'

Ray stopped texting and glanced around.

'Nah... they're probably just...'

'Just what?'

He studied the other patrons more carefully.

'Fuck,' said Ray. 'This is not good. Drink up and let's take a look outside.'

Beyond the pub car park the streets were deserted. Ray shrugged. More to himself than her he said:

'That doesn't prove anything. It's been like this for weeks.'

He walked quickly towards the main road. Already he could see there was little or no traffic on it. Then they heard an ambulance siren. Then two.

'Christ, D. What's happening?'

'It's starting again.'

'No. This is something different. It's—'

A gut spasm cut him short and, utterly unable to control himself, he vomited onto the pavement. The stream of puke was dark, almost black. The puddle it made was oily. Not a bean sprout or water chestnut to be seen. Not the ghost of a spring roll. He looked at it, trying hard not to think about what it might mean. His body was shaking.

'I'm freezing, D. I need to get inside.'

Walking back to her bedsit, Delilah was sick too – so suddenly there was no way to prevent it. All she could do was turn her head away from the pavement and retch over a small brick wall into someone's front garden. Ray couldn't stop himself from checking out what she'd produced. It was the same stuff. He remembered the smell from somewhere but he said nothing.

'Maybe there's an outbreak of stomach flu. E-coli or something.'

He didn't believe it, though, and he knew she wouldn't either. At her place they took turns in the shared bathroom. Then, as they weakened, they allowed themselves the use of bowls next to the bed. By the time the black puke overflowed, they were too frail to get up and empty their bowels. The vomit seeped into the carpet.

Ray watched it from the corner of his eye.

Each time he fell asleep and woke up again the puddle had changed. Grey threads appeared in it like rootlets or tendrils. They gripped the bowl and wormed into the threads of the dirty carpet. They spread like veins. Soon they pulsed and Ray felt the rhythm inside himself.

He turned to look at Delilah.

Her beautifully pale skin was turning black, the black of rubbish sacks. Her hair, silky as crow feathers, was whitening, the same colour as the vein-like threads expanding from his sick-bowl. To find happiness, to survive the landfill war and then to lose it all like this… He wasn't too sick to cry. The tears that seeped from his eyes were viscous, dripped too slowly too be natural. It only made him weep more. He didn't want to know what he was becoming, didn't even want to assess himself in the mirror. She was silent beside him. Very still. The effort of lifting his arm to reach out to her was great. Like he was wearing lead armour. His hand was coal black shot with grey, dendritic capillaries. What flowed inside those veins now? The chalky veins had grown from his fingertips, protruding like shoots. His hand was shaggy with hair-like extensions.

He rested this strange hand on her chest. He wanted her to know while he still meant it, while it was still him talking. Her chest rose and fell intermittently. Her heartbeat seemed distant through his fingertips.

'Love. You. D.'

Kevin and Jenny sat in her tiny white Mini with a length of green garden hose drooping in through the window. All the other windows were tightly rolled up. Kevin had used half a roll of duct tape to seal the hose inside the exhaust pipe. He didn't want there to be any mistakes. No brain-damaged comebacks.

They reclined the seats and held hands but there was nothing comfortable about breathing engine smoke. They lay there coughing and crying. Kevin was dizzy and nauseous but he didn't know if that was the fumes or the disease. They'd had so much to look forward to, had already put so many bad things behind them.

When the sickness had first hit them, Jenny was iron-hearted in a way he'd never anticipated.

'Whatever made those things rise up, it's in us now. I'm

not having it. I've survived once and there's no way I'm going to give in to them now. We have to kill ourselves before whatever's inside us takes over.'

He'd argued with her for the whole day and all the while they both got sicker. He couldn't believe they'd bickered away their final hours together. Nothing beautiful there to remember. No, for good memories he had to go back further. Back to when being with Jenny was adultery. For some reason, that was when he'd been happiest. Not knowing her, only knowing something was developing between them. Something stronger than he could deny. Something bigger than both of them. Too suddenly, too quickly, their happiness was ending.

'How do you know?' he'd asked her. 'How can you be certain this is anything to do with what happened.'

'Oh, come on, Kev. Don't be so fucking ignorant. How many diseases have you heard of that turn your skin and vomit black? That turns your veins grey? That continues to live even when it's outside your body? This is all *connected*.'

'But how in God's name did it happen?'

'Delilah was right. She's not just some stupid Goth chick. She was tuned in. Burning the landfill and the fecalith was the wrong thing to do. What if all it did was release what was inside those things into the atmosphere? What if it turned the smoke into a cloud of germs or spores? We're turning into human trash, Kev. Can't you smell it?'

He could. They'd both begun to reek of shit and decomposition the moment they'd begun to feel queasy. They'd made it to the toilet to be sick but soon the toilet was overgrowing its bowl with heaps of grey threads that strained outwards across the whole bathroom, crept under the door.

It was only when Jenny's now grey hair began to move by itself and her screamed pleas became those of the insane that he did what she asked. He'd rather they fell asleep together in the car than watch her slit her throat with a carving knife as she'd threatened to do. That would leave him there to die alone, too frightened to finish himself off.

So now they held hands. And the car filled with smoke. Kevin was afraid to die and he hung on. More than once he lost consciousness and came back with a start, the interior of the Mini whirling around him. He tried to take his hand away from Jenny's to steady himself but they had grown into each other somehow, the veins twining them, plaiting their arms together.

He'd stopped coughing by then. The inside of the Mini was like the inside of a cloud. Not so frightening as it had been at the start. He allowed his eyes to close.

25

The gaps between visits from the nurses became longer. Their faces when they did come no longer had the look of compassion and empathy they'd had before. The nurses looked preoccupied. They were thinking about something else.

One day the doctor didn't come. The doctor with his sparkling eyes, his face a mystery behind his beard. Aggie thought she was falling in love with him but didn't know how to tell. When he didn't come she panicked a little. The pain in her chest had receded but she still pressed on her driver for hits of morphine, more out of habit than of necessity. When the doctor didn't come, she put herself to sleep. Later that day, when the nurses didn't come, she knocked herself out again. Her dreams were of vivid, patterned silence as vast as space, terrifyingly quiet, terrifyingly huge. She awoke sweating and needing to pee.

It was night. The hospital was noiseless but for the hiss of her breathing against the oxygen flow. She was wide eyed, more awake than she'd been since she'd found herself in the hospital. Certain things were very clear in her mind. Her mother and father were dead. That was why they hadn't visited her. There was something wrong in the hospital, otherwise there would have been nurses to pass her a bedpan.

Tomorrow, she would have to get up and she was fairly certain she'd be doing it by herself. She listened to the hush of the hospital and clung to it. Somehow, silence was safe. The urge to urinate came and went in waves. She decided she could probably hold it until morning – another incentive for her to get up when it was light. She pressed the syringe driver control to help her sleep but nothing happened. Carefully, she reached a hand to the side of the bed where the cylinder containing the morphine lay. She picked it up and inspected it in the dim glow from her nightlight.

The morphine was all gone.

The urge to pee had become part of her pain at some point in the night.

Now, as the light rose across the high dependency unit, she could no longer ignore it. She looked up behind her head to the stand from which the saline hung. The clear bag which had held it was also empty. She peeled the micropore dressing from the back of her right hand and removed the needle that had supplied her with the fluid. She did the same on her left hand, slipping out the morphine needle. The hissing in her nose had ceased; even the oxygen had run out.

The back of her bed was already partially raised. Instead of trying to push herself upright, she used the electronic controller to raise the back of the bed and bring her into a sitting position. It hurt but not as much as she had expected. Once sitting, she dropped the safety bar away from the bedside, braced her hands under herself and swung her legs to the edge.

A bolt of pain tore through her chest and she almost pissed herself right there on the sheets. She waited, surprised how quickly the pain receded. She pushed her legs over the side and waited to recover from the next onslaught of chest pain. Finally, she edged her feet to the floor and stood up. Her legs were very shaky. She wasn't sure she would be able to stand unaided. As her bare soles touched the cold flooring, a huge draining sensation sank through her body. The room faded to white and receded, her ears whined. She collapsed.

Pain brought her around and she had the impression that it could only have been a few seconds of blackout she'd suffered. Her chest, having been something approaching comfortable for many days as she lay in bed, now raked her with hot claws. As bad as it was, she knew it wouldn't stop her from getting up.

Using the plastic chair by her bed, she hauled herself upright again. Again the room spun but this time she held it together until the spell passed. She looked around for something to help her walk. Not far away there was a Zimmer frame. For the moment she didn't care how that would look to anyone coming in. She had to find out what was going on. Sliding along the wall she reached the walking frame and from there she crossed, a shuffle at a time, to the window.

She stood there a long time trying to understand what she saw.

The dreams she'd suffered under the influence of the morphine were not just nightmares from her imagination. What she saw outside reminded her of the things she'd tried not to remember through all the time she'd been stuck in the hospital.

Down in the hospital car park and in the streets and parks beyond, nameless things shambled once more. Only this time she could recognise what the things had been. Each of them looked like black scarecrows. Their heads sprouted white roots instead of hair and these roots hung down like the tresses of a witch, tangled and matted. The hands and feet were the same but smaller, nothing more than shaggy outgrowths of grey and white stalks that might once have been veins. It was obvious that the things had once been people. Their shiny, black bodies thronged the streets like crowds of partygoers all wearing the same costume.

But their movements weren't random or confused. They seemed to be searching for something. They looked lost and forlorn.

Aggie was afraid, remembering what the other creatures had done, what *they'd* been searching for. As she watched, it became clear she probably need not be afraid of these new creatures. They were foraging for leavings. And they were hungry.

Very, very hungry.

A group of six or seven had found the large dumpsters at the back of the hospital. All of these waste containers were now overturned. The scarecrow witches lay among the mess holding refuse sacks to their black faces and tearing large bites out of them. They chewed down everything: glass jars and tin cans. Paper towels, tissues and food wrappings. They ate leftovers from the kitchens. Nothing was passed over, not even the plastic bags.

One of them had discovered the medical waste dumpster. It was eating a gangrenous lower leg, having no difficulty biting clean through the bones. As Aggie watched, it opened its mouth unnaturally wide and chomped off all the toes and half of the foot. Others soon arrived. They tucked into the bags as though they were giant haggises. Crunched through boxes of disposable scalpel blades and used hypodermics. Their faces, a tangle of white veins over unctuous black skin, bore one simple expression: voraciousness.

On the pavement on the opposite side of the car park, one of the scarecrow witches stopped and looked down at the concrete it was walking on. A dog had fouled the pavement, leaving a crusted-over pile of sausage-like excreta. The creature dropped on to all fours, dipped its shaggy grey head down and sucked up the turd in one enthusiastic bite. Having found something so good on the floor, the thing crawled away into the shrubbery to see what else it could find at ground level.

Aggie remembered she had to pee then.

She struggled across the chilly linoleum to a unisex toilet. Inside she used the frame to help her sit down. She peed for a long time but the relief she felt was overshadowed by what she'd seen of the world outside. She stood, more easily this time, turned and flushed away her waste. Where would it end up? she wondered. In the belly of one of those things down there? Things that had once been people?

She began to think very hard about how to keep everything clean around her. She was fairly sure the creatures weren't interested in what was living – that much she'd worked out from watching them. All she knew was they were ravenous. With no one left to stop them, they'd eat every last scrap of garbage in the world.

She stayed in the high dependency unit for a few more days eating the food left in the nurses' station and then, on the ground floor, she found the staff canteen and devoured what was still edible from the refrigerators. The electricity was off. She'd always been too warm in the hospital but now the cold was penetrating every room.

The hospital was deserted. As her strength returned she searched every room from roof to basement. No one was left. When she was well enough, she risked crossing from her unit to another building. The scarecrow witches still roamed the grounds, some on their hands and knees, others sniffing the air as they searched for refuse. They ignored her as she passed.

Every building in the hospital was empty.

As soon as she was able to walk without feeling faint she stole some clothes from a locker in a staff changing room. They were men's clothes – jeans, tee-shirt, jumper and jacket, all too large – but she didn't care. She needed to be war m. The shoes were never going to fit and she ended up having to use a pair of slippers from one of the wards. The slippers were pink and fluffy. She wept when she thought of her mother and the agony in her chest returned twofold. There were painkillers in the nurses' trolley and she took a bottle of Cocodamol with her to help with the pain. It was when she was still that the ache in her broken chest was at its worst. Once she was on the streets and walking, it eased.

She wasn't as strong as she'd thought. It took her two days to walk to the Meadowlands estate. She had to spend the night in an abandoned house. Even though the scarecrow witches didn't even seem to see her, she still locked all the doors. The following evening she arrived at her own house, deserted now and the back door still wide open. She found the key she was looking for in a box under her bed, changed into some of her own clothes and walked to Mason Brand's house.

The garden had gone to seed, the overgrowth beginning to die back now the cold weather had come. In the bottom corner of the garden where they'd knelt together in the moonlight there was still a patch of bare earth. At the centre of it grew a plant, some kind of weed she didn't recognise. It had flowered and where the flowers had been were small knobbly pods. The pods had split and their seeds lay on the ground. She picked a pod and shook the dry seeds into her pocket before heading up the garden to Mason's back door and unlocking it with his key. In the cupboard of an upstairs bedroom, she found a small pine chest.

It was time to take responsibility, to grow up and keep the promise she'd made him. She would learn the Earth's ways. She would pass them on.

Day by day, winter put the world to sleep.

It chilled the sap of the trees, chasing it deep into their hearts. It sent the animals to their burrows to wait for warmer days. It forced the human survivors to go to ground in their own way; finding safe places, places to be warm and quiet. Places where they could think about survival and the future, if there was to be one. Places to remember all they'd possessed – and all they'd lost because of it.

They hid from the new breed of creatures, born of the fecalith's spirit and of the ashes of its children. They hid from the winter's long season and they hid from the Earth as she cleansed herself.

They hid and they waited.

Also by Joseph D'Lacey

Meat
Blood Fugue
Splinters: Short Fiction
Black Feathers
The Book of The Crowman
The Veil: Testaments 1 and 2
Clown Wars: Blood and Aspic
(with Jeremy Drysdale)

Find these titles on Amazon

Visit Joseph's website for more information
https://josephdlacey.wordpress.com